CROOKED

Dietrich Kalteis

CROOKED

A Crime Novel

Published by ECW Press
665 Gerrard Street East
Toronto, Ontario, Canada M4M 1Y2
416-694-3348 / info@ecwpress.com

Cover design: Ian Sullivan

LIBRARY AND ARCHIVES CANADA CATALOGUING
IN PUBLICATION

Title: Crooked : a crime novel / Dietrich Kalteis.

Names: Kalteis, Dietrich, 1954- author.

Identifiers: Canadiana (print) 20240404181 |
Canadiana (ebook) 20240404238

ISBN 978-1-77041-707-6 (softcover)
ISBN 978-1-77852-260-4 (ePub)
ISBN 978-1-77852-263-5 (PDF)

Subjects: LCGFT: Thrillers (Fiction) | LCGFT:
Detective and mystery fiction. | LCGFT:
Historical fiction.

Classification: LCC PS8621.A474 C76 2024 |
DDC C813/.6—dc23

This book is funded in part by the Government of Canada. *Ce livre est financé en partie par le gouvernement
du Canada.* We acknowledge the support of the Canada Council for the Arts. *Nous remercions le Conseil
des arts du Canada de son soutien.* We would like to acknowledge the funding support of the Ontario Arts
Council (OAC) and the Government of Ontario for their support. We also acknowledge the support of the
Government of Ontario through the Ontario Book Publishing Tax Credit, and through Ontario Creates.

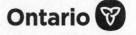

PRINTED AND BOUND IN CANADA

PRINTING: MARQUIS   5 4 3 2 1

This book is printed on Sustana EnviroBook™, a recycled
paper, and other controlled sources that are certified by the
Forest Stewardship Council®.

ECW Press is a proudly independent, Canadian-owned
book publisher. Find out how we make our books better
at ecwpress.com/about-our-books

To Andie
always

... Torremolinos, Spain
August 14, 1979

"I forget half the names I went by. These days it's just Karpowitz, the one I started with."

Lifting his glass, the old man smiled into the honey-gold of the rebujito. Sipping and looking from the husband, then to the wife — Graham and Edna Lovett — a couple of well-to-dos, guessing from the accents, hailing from midtown New York. Middle-age tourists that spoke English. Edna with the dyed blonde bob under a wide-brimmed hat, a tight body in a Catalan outfit she likely picked up in town, paying tourist prices. Graham with a Nikon and telephoto on a strap around his neck, sitting on a wallet fat with traveler's checks. Their kind looking him up more and more since the days when he first moved here, thinking the world would forget about him and what he'd done.

A quiet fishing village back then, the bars opening at five for the trawler crews, before the Costa del Sol sprang to life with its cabañas, sun beds and parasols littering the coastline, bars like Harry's and the Fat Black Pussycat, British pop music playing at El Mañana, discos like Cleopatra's and

Papagayo's, five-star digs like the Cervantes and Castillo de Santa Clara, and an endless string of chiringuitos with their straw roofs.

When the oil crisis kicked tourism in the hind, some of the local haunts fell aside, and it was lean times for a while, but those times began to pass when the con men started coming from the UK, quick to pick up on the treaty lapse between England and Spain, getting away from gray English skies and Her Majesty's Prisons, coming for some of that *buena vida*, bringing their money, laying it down and staying free. His kind of people. And not long after that the package holidays started appealing to middle-income families and their pocket-books, bringing on the new *edad de oro*.

Now he was asking the good-looking wife, "So, where'd you say, Edna?" This typical American woman clinging to forty while closing in on fifty, tanned skin under the billowing print top, legs oiled and crossed under a short skirt. Made the old man think of painting autumn leaves green, the way the mujeres americanas liked to cling to their youth. A contrast to the Spanish women still stunned by Franco's death, just starting to gain some rights, stepping out of those old gender roles.

His eyes strayed to the V of the crossed legs, a dangling sandal showing her painted toes, a few spider veins above the arch, but the leg had a nice shape. Looking at her eyes, he could see she read his mind, a smile creasing the corners of her mouth. And he tried to recall the last time he felt the old stirring. Who knows, a decade younger and maybe he would've made a fool of himself, slid his room key to her, suggesting she ditch the ball-and-chain and his dumb camera, and skip all the tourist questions. And he'd show her how to vacation. Wondering if he could still pitch a tent — but at seventy-two, the warranty on his old bones had expired long ago. Who was he fooling?

"Manhattan." Graham answered for her, leaning back in his chair, the Nikon bumping the armrest. "And if I remember right, you hailed out of Topeka, is that right?" Showing his perfect teeth, along with what he had read.

"Was born in Montreal," the old man said, taking the mint leaf from his glass, laying it down and sipping the drink, loving the taste, waiting politely as Graham tried to signal the elusive waiter, calling out, "Hey, señor! Por favor." Snapping his fingers.

"You're not in Mexico," the old man said. "Here they go by *camarero*, and try 'perdone.' And no snapping. You do, and they just let you sit, taking offense to it." The old man mimicked snapping his fingers, his arthritis ebbing this past week. He'd been in a light mood, the sleeping pills and painkillers getting him through most nights, helping him feel less like a relic in these changing times of test-tube babies, landing on Mars, and music he couldn't begin to understand, one broad singing about "Hot Stuff," another screeching about "Bad Girls," then a guy who sounds like an emphysema case asking, "Do you think I'm sexy?" Plain awful, nothing like Glenn Miller or Kate Smith, or Jeanette doing "Porque Te Vas," the local stations playing that one to death. He just hoped the medication wouldn't disagree too much with the drinks.

Willing to talk about his past — those long-ago times when he topped Hoover's most-wanted list — to anyone willing to cover the cost of a few rounds.

"Vous devez parler français . . . uh . . . si vous venez de Montréal?" Edna asked, smiling equally white teeth at him.

"Never learned it." He shook his head. "Moved to Topeka when I was two. My folks spoke Lithuanian back then, mixed with some English. No French, *nada*."

"So, you were schooled there, Topeka?" Graham asked.

Turning to the husband, he said, "Matter of fact, grade school's where I came up with my first gang." Waiting for

9

Graham's smile, not usually caring for this soft-hand type with the manicured nails, the Swiss explorer's watch on the man's wrist, the gold class ring on his finger, the thousand-buck camera around his neck, but as long as the man was buying . . .

"Grade school, God, I didn't even smoke till I was fourteen, and I thought that was badass." Graham clapped his hands together, guffawing.

The waiter glanced over, nodded as Graham ordered by holding up three fingers, giving the big smile.

"Oh, you did not." This from Edna, play-kicking a foot at her husband under the table.

"You have no idea, my dear." Graham enacting the bad boy, smiling and shaking his head, saying to the old man, "So, all that's true then, what I read about you?"

"Not sure what you read, Graham." The old man smiled, saying, "Not much truth in the papers back then — pretty much the same as now."

"That's the truth alright, but, being public enemy number one . . . must have been a trip, uh? Just walking in a bank and saying, 'Stick 'em up . . .'" Graham pointing a finger gun, making it sound like they were talking about a hit record, or some kind of real-life achievement.

"Well, I'm just a pensioner these days, Graham." The old man tried not to, but he coughed into his fist. "But I guess I was in short pants and already heading my way for the number one spot on Hoover's shit-list." Looking at Edna, saying, "Pardon my French, dear."

Getting a smile back.

Running his hand through his thinning hair, eyes glancing to the sun, and going on, "Only ever four of us on that list, at the time anyway."

"You, Dillinger, Nelson, and Floyd. Like the Beatles." Graham Lovett said, shaking his head at the thought, showing what he knew.

"Wrote about it too," the old man said, smiling back.

"You wrote a book?" Her eyes went wide.

"Two of them. First one came out in '71, and did pretty well, making its advance in a month, the publisher sending me on tour, lined up some TV and radio, talking it up. Had a mountain of time for plotting and rewriting the next one, calling it *On the Rock*, revisiting my twenty-six years of Alcatraz." Throwing in, "It'll be out soon."

"Funny, all those things you did, you seem so . . ." Edna said.

"Old?"

"No, I mean nice, you're nice." She touched a hand on top of his, patting it, her diamond flashing in the afternoon light, slow in taking it back.

"Well, thank you, my dear. I'm what they call reformed." God, her hand felt warm, giving him a charge.

"Now tell me this if I'm not out of line, but why'd they call you Creepy?" Graham asked.

"Graham!" Edna acting astonished.

"Well, it's true, what I read."

"No problem," the old man said, smiling and patting her hand back. They were all friends now.

"Well, I just don't see it," she said, smiling again.

Winking at her, the old man said, "Nobody called me that, unless behind my back. It's something the papers dreamed up on account of my smile. See? Kind of crooked. Anyway, to friends I was always Ray, and to that Quaker shit-bird Hoover — there I go again with the French — I was public enemy *número uno*. Anyway, all that was about a hundred years ago."

"Read somewhere you met Dillinger. That true?" Graham said, sounding like a kid.

"Everybody asks that. My age, I could've met Crazy Horse too." He grimaced, couldn't believe Dillinger was still getting the attention, admitting he never got the chance.

"I saw that film with what's his name? Warren Oates! And *Bloody Mama*, the one with Shelley Winters, about how old Ma was the brains. She must've been something, huh?" This from Graham.

"The poor soul couldn't plan a picnic, bless her big heart. Well, maybe she wasn't a nun either, but nothing like in that movie."

"Who'd play you, in the film, I mean?"

"Who knows, just don't go believing all you see on the screen, okay?" The old man sipped from his glass, guessing if they turned his book into a film, it ought to be James Caan playing him, but they'd likely cast Ernest Borgnine, giving the Dillinger part to good-looking Warren Oates, Ben Johnson playing Melvin Purvis. Surprised how fast he was feeling the drink, the warmth starting in his feet, and moving up his veined legs. Betting any minute, Graham would act like he remembered the Nikon was hanging from its strap, and he'd want a snapshot, set the timer gadget, come around the table and throw an arm around both of them, get a few for the family album, something he could talk about the rest of his life.

"How about the Barrows?"

"You asking about the movie or real life?"

"Real life. I bet you met them." Graham looking hopeful.

"Ran into Clyde one time, think Bonnie had a banged-up leg then, remember her being sickly, didn't look too good, all their running. Never talked to her much, but Clyde, he was alright. Neither of them anything like in that movie. Hollywood's just about spinning stories and filling seats."

"I read how Hoover did the mopping and stopping, nailing Dillinger, Machine Gun Kelly, Baby Face, and all the rest. No offense, it's just how they put it," Graham said.

"Was mostly local cops doing the mopping." The old man shook his head, saying, "Like I said, you can't believe all you read or what's on TV."

"PBS, I think — Hoover flying in to make the big arrest when they got you, put the cuffs on you himself. There any truth to it?"

"Small part of it. How the man flew in on account they had me under surveillance, the chief hiding across the street, waiting till his men surrounded the car I just got in, me and Freddie Hunter." He smiled at Edna, then looked back to Graham. "Had a dozen or more guns on me, none of them noticing Freddie starting to step away, moving down the sidewalk. Nearly got away too, with all the G-men aiming at me."

"Oh my," she said.

"One telling me to keep my hands on the wheel, the other telling me to get out, step out on the running board, another wanting me to lie on the ground, a guy in back yelling, 'Don't move.'" The old man laughed, reliving it, back at that place in time, saying, "Was Hoover peeking from behind a fender, came out and yelled, 'Get that one too.'" The old man shaking his head and grinning about it. "Had a newshound with him to stage the shot, making it look like the big chief flew in from Washington to make the arrest, show his boys how it's done, get his face in the papers. Came all the way from the capital on the taxpayers' dime, you believe it?"

Graham shook his head, grinning like a kid and draining his drink, asked if he was ready for another, looking around, wondering what happened to the waiter.

"Guess it can't hurt." The old man hoped that was true, knowing he'd need to pee like a racehorse in a half hour, be standing at a urinal for five minutes praying for drips.

Graham was making hand signs at the passing waiter, back to calling him señor, calling, "Por favor." Then trying, "Hey, jefe!"

The old man went on, "Half those feds were green as salad and scared too, accountants and lawyers standing behind a couple of mean Texas Rangers — the same ones who gunned down Bonnie and Clyde, Hoover bringing them in like pinch hitters. One pointing a Tommy gun at the windshield, the other a sawed-off. Looking at me like they were begging me to try it."

"How awful," Edna said.

"And nobody bothering to bring bracelets . . . handcuffs." The old man laughed. "Guess they weren't planning on me getting out of that car alive. So, I just sat behind the wheel and smiled, disappointing the whole bunch, none daring to shoot on account of Hoover's newsman standing like a witness, his flashbulb at the ready. Ended up tying my hands with a necktie. Best thing about it, I outlived that son of a bitch." Apologizing to Edna again for the French.

"Speaking of photos . . ." Graham said, holding up the Nikon, looking hopeful.

"Sure." The old man smiled, slid close and put an arm around Edna's shoulder, the woman leaning into him, the warm hand patting his thigh, Graham picking his shutter speed and f-stop, twisting the little dials, pressing the timer button, and hurrying behind them, putting an arm around them both, going, "Say cheese."

"Don't know how you managed all that time in prison," she said as Graham put the camera in its case, going back to his seat. Edna not in a hurry to pull away, reaching and sipping from her glass, leaving a trace of lipstick on the glass, saying, "All the things you had to give up, would have driven me batty — no creature comforts."

"Had twenty-five years of it," the old man said, easing back in his chair, glancing at her legs again, saying, "Some comforts I missed — lot of pent-up energy."

"Must've been awful." She caught him looking down, her foot touching his under the table.

Clearing his throat, saying, "Well, you'll have to read the book and find out all about it, my dear."

"I'd love a signed copy." She recrossed her legs.

"Well, write down your address, and I'll get my publicist to send you one." The old man slid his coaster her way, patting a pocket for a pen and paper, thinking he ought to start bringing one with him, getting asked for his autograph all the time.

The waiter came around and set down three more glasses, and took the empties away, telling the old man he'd bring a bolígrafo.

Thanking him in Spanish, the old man said, "Guess being sent to the Rock beat going in the ground, it's how I felt at the time. Thinking there'd be plenty chance to escape later, get a chance to meet my son, and look up my girl after she got out."

"You mean bust out like Dillinger?" Graham said.

The old man sighed. "He was good at busting out of places, I'll give him that. But nobody got off the Rock, except maybe Frank Morris and the brothers. Only ones sure about that are the sharks."

"Well, those fellows sure left their mark," Graham said. "And you sure left yours, that's for sure."

"Think what any of us left is more of a stain." Looking at Edna under the big hat, he said, "You sure you want to hear more, dear? Maybe ask me about places worth seeing." Knowing neither of them could help themselves.

Smiling as she nodded, saying she loved hearing it, Graham grinning like a fool.

The old man knowing he'd be drinking rebujito for the rest of the afternoon, hoping his liver could keep the pace.

. . . Tulsa, Oklahoma
April 19, 1931

Walking past the crossbuck, Alvin Karpis followed the railway line, curly dock and grass tufts sprouting between the rusting rails. Going the way the kid manning the pump told him, the Magnolia station about a mile behind him now, he felt the morning heat rising. Stepping between the ties, going another quarter mile before stopping to shake a stone from his shoe, thinking what the kid at the pump warned him about: a bunch of freebooters working the area, robbing passengers at gunpoint after their tour bus slipped off the shoulder, taking the driver for the fare money and relieving passengers of their rings, wallets and watches. The same gang that hijacked a cab driver two days back, binding the man to a willow outside of town, robbing his pockets and stealing his taxi. Alvin thinking these were his kind of people.

Catching sight of the rusting tin roof over the shrub-land, a sway-back shack coming into view as he walked, its red paint faded brown, boards loose and showing rot, sitting fifty yards off the tracks. The sound of cicadas. Rings of bald tires, an axel going to rust, tin cans used for target practice pocked with holes, set along the gravel rise by the rails, scrap wood piled for a bonfire, an old table on the hardpan yard, nothing any freebooter would want.

A squat woman of middle years stood in bib overalls with her dark hair pinned up, atop a crate, up on her toes, fixing the screen in the porch door, tacking in the corners, turning when she heard the scrape of his shoes.

"I help you with that, ma'am?" he said, stopping halfway across the yard, putting on the friendly.

Shielding her eyes with her hand, she took stock of him, saying, "Why, I look like I can't do it?" The other hand holding the tack hammer, resting it on her hip. Taking him in.

"Looks like you're doing just fine, ma'am."

"And by your own look, I'm guessing you're here for my boy." She stepped from the crate.

"Fred talked of you so much, I guess I feel we already met." He looked hopeful, waiting on a response that wasn't coming, throwing in, "Best fried chicken south of heaven, the way he liked to tell it."

She softened at that, nodded and said, "Could lead that boy around by a drumstick, and that's the God's truth." Then she frowned, saying more like a statement than a question, "You were up in Lansing with him. You wrote the letters for him."

"Yes, ma'am, I helped him some." Saying it like it weighed on him. "I ain't proud of it — I mean the being there, not the writing — but I got early release, same as Fred, out on good behavior. Set us free a couple of days apart, and I figured I'd hitch down and look him up."

"Call getting let loose being set free — making it sound like you were in for choir singing. A jailbird coming all this way to get my boy in fresh misery."

"I can't sing for beans, ma'am. You want, I can give you a show right now." Pretending to clear his throat.

"'Cause that boy don't need help with misfortune."

"I'm taking the high road, ma'am, turning the page, coming to Jesus, and that's the gospel." If he had a hat, he would have tugged it off and held it to his chest. Alvin dialed down the Okie a bit, trying to show he was her kind, not wanting to overdo it. "Something me and Fred talked over, the two of us looking out for each other on the inside. Figured being of the same mind, we'd help each other on that straight street."

"Uh huh." Her look said no sale.

Daring a step closer, he wondered if he should extend his hand to a woman in these parts, or offer to take the tack hammer and fix her screen again, seeing she was doing it wrong, tacking it on the outside instead of from the inside, saying, "They call me Ray."

"Well, that may be, Ray, but my boy ain't here." She studied him another moment, lightened up, saying, "Well, seeing you're here, how about you call me Kate."

"Kate. Okay, Kate." He smiled, getting somewhere. "You got an idea where I can find him?"

"I ain't sure yet." Taking him in a moment longer, then she sighed, saying, "May as well come inside. Got the look like you could use a cup." Nudging the crate aside with her foot, she pulled back the unfixed door.

"How about your screen?"

"It'll keep." Muttering something about the weather, and not having any rain in a dog's age as she turned.

Feeling the dry in his throat, he guessed a cup meant coffee, following her inside the dirt-floor place, bottle flies buzzing around.

Past the stove, a slack-faced man with graying hair lay back in a stuffed chair, seesawing snores coming from a mouth cranked open dentistry-wide, same bib overalls as Kate's, his with the straps hanging down, a near-empty jar on the floor within reach. The old man's head tipped back on a neck that looked like it wilted. Snorting himself awake, he blinked and wiped something from an eye, swiping the hand on his overalls, shaking the cobwebs and blinking a couple times, saying, "Who you got there, Donnie? Another of your brood?"

"Friend of Fred's." Going about pouring water in a blackened pot, she busied herself with making coffee.

Stepping close, Alvin extended a hand to him, saying. "I'm Ray, sir, glad to meet you."

The old man straightened, showing hands that looked like he'd been wrestling with the stovepipe, his palms blackened.

"Don't mind Arthur. He's in a mood," Kate said, asking the old man if he wanted coffee.

Shaking his head, Arthur Dunlop sent his fingers searching for the jar, lifting it from the floor, narrowing his eyes like he wondered how it got half-drained, taking a taste, saying, "Peach." Not offering it.

Taking the water pail, Kate poured some in a pot, setting it on the stove, saying, "Birthed four boys, the oldest one, Herman, he's passed now." Not looking from the stove.

"Shot by cops in Kansas, supposedly finished himself off," Arthur said.

"Fred told me about that, and I'm sure sorry for your loss, ma'am. Must be an awful thing, losing a boy."

"Nearly four years now, and I can tell you, it's a pain that don't avert."

"I bet so, ma'am."

"Second one's Lloyd," Arthur scoffed. "Up in Leavenworth for robbing a mail truck, didn't learn from the older one. Got it in mind thieving was easy money. Then we got Fred and Doc, one a burglar, the other a car thief. A fine brood, and not an honest day's work between the lot, all of 'em dumb as stumps."

Not showing it, Alvin was building a dislike for the man.

"Well, Fred's out now," she said like she was hopeful, ignoring Arthur. "And Doc's up in Oklahoma. Maybe in a year, he keeps his head down, he gets a chance at parole. Who knows, maybe he goes and finds that street you're talking about." She nodded, then crossed herself, saying, "Didn't have no girls."

"A fine brood, yup," Arthur said, shaking his head and sipping from the jar. "Her old man walks from thirty years of wedlock, just up and leaves her to live in this hole. Guess if I had offspring like that, I'd likely pack and go, or at least give myself a good gelding."

"Hope you take it black, son, the coffee?" She said it like Arthur wasn't there.

"Best way I know, ma'am."

"Except when you tip in some peach," Arthur said, lips tightening to a smile with nothing friendly about it, lifting over horse teeth.

"Call me Kate now," she said to Alvin. "Same as everybody, except Arthur, he calls me Donnie."

"Kate it is." Alvin brightened, turning his back to Arthur.

"You know Amos 'n' Andy?" she said, turning on the Philco Tombstone set on the table, taking down tin cups, blowing into them, then pouring from the pot.

"Guess I heard of them."

"Well, they got the Kingfish, a geezer always planning to skip the work and pull a fast one, like life's gonna get easy."

"Holy mackerel," Arthur parroted the actor, catching a glance from Kate.

"Point is, it never works out the way the Kingfish thinks," she said, handing Alvin a steaming tin. Then she was sighing again, saying, "Fred's up at Joplin, seeing this gal he used to go with, finding out if she got hitched and had a kid while he was gone." Her face clouded, like she figured that could lead to another kind of trouble. Looking pained, she said, "I can send a wire, maybe get word to him."

"If it's not too much trouble, Kate. I'd appreciate it, and I'm happy to pay for the wire."

"Don't worry about that, just don't go getting my boy in deeper."

. . . *Tulsa, Oklahoma*
June 10, 1931

"Your ma's good people, made me feel right at home,"
Alvin said in a low voice over his shoulder, climbing
out the smashed-out window, putting a foot on the ground and
stepping from the darkened midtown house, glancing around.
Getting his mind off the skinny take: a watch, a couple of
rings, one with what might turn out to be a diamond, along
with a handful of silver coins.

"Yeah, she's a pearl alright," Fred Barker said, climbing out
behind him. The swag jangling around in Fred's jacket pocket.

They were heading back to the car, hoping to fence the
lot for ten bucks — the pawnbroker working late in his shop,
the one who lined them up with these places, assuring them
the family was on a Miami holiday, the man of the house
in the banking trade, rich and keeping a safe stuffed like a
holiday bird, a Colt single-action with a ten-inch barrel in
there, one supposed to belong to Wyatt Earp himself, worth
two hundred dollars easy.

Busting holes in the plaster, upstairs and down, they were
in there a half hour, but didn't find the safe. Alvin thinking

the break-in would get pinned on the gang the kid at the Magnolia station had talked about.

Fred was disappointed not finding the safe or the Colt, careful not snagging his only pair of dungarees on the busted window, shards sticking up like teeth. "And from the sound, she sure took a shine to you."

"Well, good to hear." Never got that growing up, his off-the-boat parents fighting half the time, Jonas and Ona Karpavičius pouring blame on each other for how he turned out, calling him a lousy hood, hanging in the shadows of Toledo, a town rocked hard by the crash, causing a rise in the number of felons and pimps and homeless, followed by the dry times that spawned the bootleggers. Alvin selling dirty pictures by the time he turned ten, earning enough for a pack of Wings and a quart of Buckeye, and sharing it with his street corner pals.

"Not so keen on Arthur though," Alvin said, keeping his voice low.

"That mean old drunk don't care for a soul, and not a one likes him back," Fred said. "No idea why Ma keeps him around, a bum like that. Well, now I'm back, I got a mind to put him in a boxcar." Ducking along the cedar hedge, Fred looked out to the street, the light of the street lamp casting on the sidewalk ahead. "Gonna get her out of that dirt shack and in some place decent too."

"Better up our game," Alvin said, thinking of the skinny take, sticking to the shadows, looking ahead to Fred's wreck of a Model T sitting on the next corner. Ninth or tenth place they hit this week, and what they hawked barely covered the ethyl.

"By upping the game, you mean walking in a bank or filling station? And by walking in, I guess you mean sticking them up?"

"Know it ups the risk, but you can't beat the pay." Alvin tried to sound convincing.

"Man, you got it all figured." Fred smiled over his shoulder, like he was happy to hear him say it.

"'Course if we get nailed, and some judge bangs his gavel," Alvin said casual, "then we're looking at one-to-three for unarmed, five-to-seven if we go in heavy."

"Nothing comes easy. The trick's not getting caught, then," Fred said, growing up in times of no honest work; farming men finding the land dead and useless, heading for California or joining the soup lines. Able-bodied fellows in lines or on street corners. The lucky ones worked some grind, sweating for as much as a buck a day — not enough for a man with a family or any true ambition. Fred telling him, if nothing else, he had plenty of that ambition. "Pawnbroker can get us a couple of bean shooters, I mean if we're serious," he said, fishing in a pocket for his car key, taking a last look over his shoulder.

Alvin saying he was, and the pair walked like it was their home town, both in dark jackets and caps, looking like they were coming off a late shift, working construction at the Union Depot, or at the new Philcade Building springing up downtown. Passing under a street lamp.

"Hold it!"

And they froze.

A stumpy cop stepped from some buttonbush, the shield on his cap catching light off the lamp, his pistol aimed at Alvin's middle. Telling them, "Get 'em up."

"What's going on?" Fred said, looking around for a chance to run.

A second cop stepped off a darkened porch across the street, crossing and thumping a nightstick against his palm like he wished Fred would try it.

"Something wrong, officer?" Alvin said to the cop coming from the bushes, his hands held out to the side, making fear look like surprise, his mind searching for a way out.

Stumpy stepped close, holstering his revolver, not answering, but saying to his partner, "This one look like a runner, Pete?" Then to Alvin, "You a runner, boy?" Cranking his shoulder, he threw a heavy punch.

Doubling in pain, Alvin sputtered like he might throw up, gasping in air.

"Not gonna run, now," the cop said.

"How about you, son?" the second cop asked Fred. Prodding him with the stick. "You wanna dash?"

"Feel like I'm gonna remember you." Fred stared him in the eyes.

"Well, then let's get you singing, and how about you make it something catchy?" The cop swung and thumped the nightstick across the back of his knees, beaming as Fred buckled, not making a sound. The cop swung the stick across his shoulders, sending Fred into a ball, arms covering up as more blows reigned down.

Stumpy swung a shoe into Alvin's gut, grabbed him by the hair and yanked him to sitting, saying, "You even think of soiling my leathers with the contents of your guts boy, I'm gonna double the hurt, you get me?" Hanging onto the fistful of hair, he tugged him to his feet and roughly patted him down with his free hand.

The second cop rolled Fred over with his shoe, laid his stick across his neck and frisked his pockets, feeling the plunder in his jacket, smiling and saying, "Well, well . . ."

The stumpy cop grinned, reaching for his handcuffs, spinning Alvin around, saying, "Let's get you mugs under glass."

... *Tulsa, Oklahoma*
June 13, 1931

Watching the horizon for squall lines and dusters, Alvin turned his collar up to the wind, shrinking into the worn jacket, the weeds taller since he walked the same rail line two months back, passing a one-time wheat field, a barn beat worse than he'd been, some boards missing and its roof caved in on one end. Going past the same filling station, taking his time and slowing when the shack came into view, Alvin working on how to put it to Kate since the jailer said he was free to go.

Released two days back, spending the first night in a Union Pacific flatcar, then hitching a ride, and staying at a camp with a *Welcome to Hooverville* sign stuck in front, the hash slinger fixing him a tin of wheat pudding, another of chicory to help wash down the supper. Conjuring a story, finding a way to tell her: Fred being charged with the smash-and-grab, enough to send him back to the state pen. Fred taking the heat for both of them, swearing Alvin had nothing to do with it, just an old pal he ran into. The cops having no choice but to let him go.

Retracing his steps to this place, Alvin figured he owed Fred that much. Aiming to tell Kate a version of the truth, maybe stay and help her around the house on account old Arthur Dunlop didn't look much good for anything.

Now, there she stood taking laundry from the line, folding it into a basket by her feet, dropping the pegs into her apron pocket, the rain starting to patter down, looking around like she sensed his approach. Alvin waved a timid hand, a couple of yard birds clucking and scattering as he crossed the dirt plot.

"See you fixed the screen." He stopped and bounced the toe of a shoe off one of the bald tires.

"Had trouble finding that straight street, looks like."

"It eluded me some." He forced his eyes to meet hers. Shrinking into the thin jacket, as much from the rain as from her look, not liking what he had to tell her. Helping her take down a sheet, the two of them folding it.

Furrows crossed her forehead, and she looked up the rail line like she was making sure he was on his own. "He alive at least?"

"Yes, ma'am."

"Jail?"

And he gave a nod.

When he didn't say more, she took the basket, turned and pushed the screen open, saying, "Come on, then."

Walking past the yard birds, one pecking in the rain, the rest retreating to their coop, Alvin stepped inside.

Arthur was deflated in the same chair, looking stinko, putting rheumy eyes on him, slurring, "Might'a guessed it. Take one no-good and put him with another, bird-brained and pig-ignorant, and what do you get? Well, what'd you get into now, boy?"

Alvin wasn't a big man, five nine and a hundred and thirty pounds, smaller than Arthur, but he sure wanted to spring on the old man and tear him up.

"Button it, Arthur," Kate said. "You're in the way of my conversation."

"You birthed four no-goods, Donnie. Why not face it? Can hang it on old George for the bad blood, then running off on you. But you're being blind to it."

"We don't talk about that man." She snapped at him.

"You look at it clear, Donnie, this one's cut from the same cloth, another no-good. Can tell just by looking."

Alvin put his eyes on the dirt floor, the anger making his face hot. Hearing the rain drumming on the tin roof, a few drops finding a way through and dripping down to the dirt floor. First time it had rained in a long time.

Setting the pot on the stove, she said, "Expect you'll stay for supper. Give you time to think of something to say." Looking at Alvin a moment more, she busied herself about the kitchen.

Sipping from his cup, he stepped close so only she could hear, saying, "They picked us up, looking for some local fellas going around robbing busses and such. Maybe you heard about this gang — anyway, soon as they found out we'd been inside, well, they just made up their minds. Stuck us in a cell and laid on their questions. Finally ended up letting me go, but they held Fred over, so I got no idea —"

Raising a hand to cut off his words, glancing to the leaking ceiling, she muttered something like a prayer, didn't hear the screen door open on account of the drumming rain, saying to the ceiling, "Lord, don't let them send him back up."

"The hell they will." Fred stood at the door, a dumb grin on his face, then coming past the screen door, shaking off the drops. Holding his arms out wide, saying, "I'm free as a bird, Ma."

Kate was on him in a rush, throwing her arms around him, saying, "You must'a read my mind, boy. Was just getting set to roast up a bird."

"Well, you get no quarrel from me, Ma. Had nothing but hobo hash and hardtack for two days straight." Fred winked at Alvin.

"Well, look who dropped in." Arthur steadied the grimy jar on his lap, looking sour at Kate with her arm around Fred in the kitchen, holding him tight.

Ignoring the old man, Fred clapped Alvin on the shoulder, saying, "Got out same as you, little brother. The coppers seeing their slip-up. Was hoping I'd catch up to you."

Alvin bobbed his head, grinning like a fool, knowing they had Fred cold: the watch, rings and coins in his pocket. And here he was, talking like coppers meant well and sharks were good fellows.

"Well, glory be," Kate said, setting aside her own horse sense, saying to Arthur, "If you're seeing straight, old-timer, get the hatchet and go fetch me a fat one."

Arthur complained it was raining, Kate staring at him until he pushed himself up out of the chair, stumble-stepping past them for the door.

A supper for folks in clover: fried chicken, prairie turnips she dug up the day before, corn meant for the neighbor's grunter, gravy and biscuits alongside the scrawny bird. Kate fixing supper on her pot stove, doing it with no electricity, the only running water dripping down from the tin ceiling.

Leading Alvin out for some after-supper air, Fred lifted a pack of Chesterfields from a pocket, two left in it, offering him one. They stepped around the puddles and crossed the yard. The soaked earth giving off a smell like it was coming back to life.

"Didn't exactly let me go." Fred struck a match, holding it out.

"I figured that." Alvin straightened the smoke, leaned in and caught the light of the match, dragging it to life.

"Jailer got careless with his keys, so I gave myself some of that early release."

"Some might call that a jail break." Alvin said, puffing and feeling content.

"Didn't hang around to chat about it."

"You know they'll come looking."

"I know it." Fred led the way to the vacant lot along the track, stepping to the bag-of-bones of a tree, out of sight of the gravel road, reaching up to its crook and pulling down a wrapped burlap, a pair of old Colt .38 Army Specials inside. Saying the pawnbroker gave him a deep discount on account Fred didn't rat him out, what with all the stolen swag he had in his hawk shop.

"Looks like we're heading to the future," Alvin said.

"Getting out of here, and taking Ma with us."

"She know it?"

"Was hoping you'd help me tell her, you fitting in the way you are."

"Me?"

"Sure. From the look, you're practically family."

... *Pocahontas, Arkansas*
November 8, 1931

The only bank sat a half block from the police station, too close for Alvin's liking. The Hardee store was on the main drag, close to the two-lane out of town.

"You say general store, and I say bank, like we been talking about." Fred smiled through his irritation. The pair driving around this two-bit town, parking in different spots for better than two hours, running low on ethyl, drinking bottles of Buckeye, deciding on a place to rob, mustering their courage, the pistols under the bench seat. Alvin was set on hitting the General Hardee before it closed, the place busy with customers earlier in the afternoon, figuring its tills would be rich, Fred wanting to stick to the bank, though he had to admit it only saw a few customers on the day. The two of them staking out this one-time home to the Army of Northern Arkansas, seeing enough rifles in gun racks, locals riding around in pickups, looking well-armed, Alvin hoping these handguns would be enough. Recalling a story he heard about the Daltons hitting two banks at the same time, this place called Coffeyville, five hours west of there, two of the four brothers and other gang members gunned down by irate townsfolk.

Passing by Palace Drugs for the third time around, its sign boasting a refrigerated soda fountain, this town looking like it still celebrated the time the state seceded from the union, the one-time likely spot for an invasion from the north. Looked like they were still armed and waiting for it. Down the block were Emma's Pies and Every Crete's Barber Shop, then they were rolling past the Court Square and Lewallens Hotel and the Rendezvous Cafe again, some places starting to lock up for the night.

"Don't matter how many go in and out, bank's where the money's at the end of the day," Fred said, then he sighed, knowing it would have to keep till the next day, admitting he didn't care for the police station being in easy sight. "Okay, how about we flip a coin and leave it to Lady Luck?"

"May be the best way," Alvin said, glancing out the window, not happy with the prospect of sleeping in the car, waiting for the next business day.

"First I got to answer the call. This stuff's like shit through a tin horn," Fred looked at the bottle, passing the same Sinclair station and pulling off Bettis Street, looking for a suitable tree. A couple of empties rolling on the floor of the Model T. Driving partway down the block, the exhaust backfiring as he pulled to the curbside, saying, "Make yourself useful and fish out a coin, will ya?" Getting out, Fred set his bottle on the roof, left the door hanging open and walked around back, unbuttoning his pants.

Coming back to the driver's side, he spotted a man in silhouette across the street, standing under an elm, looking at him.

"What the heck you looking at?" Fred said, taking him for a pervert, or worse, another cop about to roust him.

"Been watching you drive up and down, eyeing joints and acting fishy." The man stepped off the curb, a night marshal with a notepad, jotting down the license plate. "And your wreck's disturbing the peace. Me, I'm wondering what you two are up to."

"That night watchman cap come with a whistle?" Fred took in the uniform, the man not wearing a sidearm, saying to him, "Figure it makes you a lawman?" Taking a step into the road, not appreciating any kind of lawman after the way they were roughed up in Tulsa.

"Night marshal, not a watchman, and if you want, I can take you in, let the sheriff explain the difference." The man straightened and held his ground, a head taller than Fred, with maybe twenty pounds on him.

Turning like he reconsidered, Fred stepped to his open door and reached under his seat.

Alvin started to object, but Fred held up a hand, "You got that coin?"

Alvin holding it in his palm.

"I got heads." Fred waited, Alvin wrapping his hand around it, flipping it in the air, opening his hand, showing it.

And Fred had the Colt and was walking back into the street, saying, "How am I acting now?" Holding it loose at his side, letting the night marshal see it, and asking the man's name.

The man looked at it like he was deciding if it was real.

"Asked what's your name?" Fred said.

"How about I do the asking?" The watchman was clinging to his authority, his voice faltering, saying, "First thing, put that back where you got it."

Fred thumbed the hammer back and pointed it at him. "And suppose I don't?"

"Well, if you got to know, I'm Manley, Manley Jackson. And you're making a big slip up, pal."

Fred kept his aim, standing like a duelist, saying, "Well, Manley Jackson, seeing I got this, and you're aiming a finger, how about you hop in, and let's go see your sheriff, see what he says about you messing with federal agents working a case."

"Federal agents?"

"That's right — the Bureau of Investigation — this look like a toy to you?" Still aiming at the man.

"Well, suppose you put it down, and let me see the badge that goes with it?"

"And I just told you to get in."

Manley didn't move, putting up both palms, trying to diffuse things, saying, "If you people would get us word —"

"You think the bureau's got to tell a night watchman its business?"

"Night marshal. And just so we'd know, me and the sheriff — keep us all from crossing our wires."

"Ain't telling you again." Fred wagged the Army Special.

"Well, in case you're full of it, and not who you say, I wrote your plate." Manley tapped his notebook and tucked it in his top pocket, then went to the driver's door, got past the seat and got in the back, looking at Alvin over the seat, saying, "How about you, you got a badge?"

"Manley thinks he's got us." Fred said to Alvin as he got in, relaxing now, telling Manley to button it, and he drove off, the bottle sliding off the roof and shattering on the road behind them.

"You go on, write that up if you want," Fred said over his shoulder.

"Hey, the station's that way."

Alvin reached his pistol from under the seat and turned to the back. "What did my partner just say about talking?"

Fred drove back along Bettis, heading out of town.

... *West Plains, Missouri*
December 13, 1931

"I look fat in this?" Fred asked the third man, Bill Weaver, thumbing the lapels of the new suit, part of the clothing they heisted from McCallon's Clothing Store. That got the blond-haired Bill grinning.

He'd been telling jokes since he joined what Alvin and Fred dubbed their gang, there when they hit the People's Bank of Mountain View, an easy score, Fred and Alvin pulling their Army Colts on employees arriving to open for business. Armed with a hammer, Bill forced the assistant manager to open the safe, telling the man if he had to, he'd belt him across the skull.

An easy getaway, their first daylight robbery. Fred saying they ought to flip another coin, decide if it was going to be the Barker-Karpis Gang or the other way around. Rolling south to a wooded area, Fred removed the license plate, and the three of them put their backs into it and tipped the ailing Model T off a ridge, putting it out of its misery. Then, walking to town, Bill wired up a green DeSoto 8, parked along the side of a well-to-do house that looked like nobody was home.

Bill checked the mounted spare and found it was flat, as Fred stuck on the plate, and Alvin drove from there, Bill Weaver telling his jokes from the backseat.

Two days since then, and Bill was patting his slicked-back hair, turning to get the mechanic's attention inside the garage, trying to snap his fingers, but couldn't on account of the slip of the pomade, grinning and calling, "Hey, buddy?"

Wearing the new glen plaid suit, Alvin considered it a good fit, but thinking it was a little loud for walking in banks. The straw boater and Oxford shoes were a nice touch, trying the hat at a tilt, the stiff leather pinching his toes, guessing it would take a couple of days for the hide to relax. Walking to the front, flicking a finger at a fly squashed against the headlight, he raised a shoe to the bumper, thinking somebody ought to take his picture and stick it on the cover of *Photoplay*.

"Get you to fix a tire?" Bill asked the mechanic coming to the door, the tall Black man wiping his hands on a rag.

"Sure thing." Looking over the DeSoto, the mechanic said, "You got a beaut there, mister. Worked on one last week, a rock steady ride."

"Good to know." Thanking him, Bill led him to the back, the mechanic taking off the cover, rolling the flat into the garage. Bill chewing gum, his herringbone cap at an angle, standing at the garage doors in pleated pants, crisp shirt and cuffs, hooking his thumbs inside the suspenders like he was playing Gary Cooper.

Looking past the Davidson Motor Company sign, up East Main, the post office across the way, Alvin thought Bill had done alright. Except for telling dumb jokes all the time, the new man had been cool when they walked in the bank and was the same way when they looted McCallon's. Alvin cutting two of the bars from a back window the same night, breaking the glass and climbing in. Fred crawling in after him, the two of them passing armloads of clothing out the window, and Bill filling the DeSoto's trunk, floor well and backseat to the windows.

Fred had made a present to his ma, walking into the farmhouse he rented for her, carrying an armload, setting it on the kitchen table, saying he got her a whole wardrobe, hoping he got the sizes right. Sure wasn't going to return anything to McCallon's.

It surprised Alvin, Kate not asking where any of it came from, or how they got enough money to rent the place. Just showing delight on her face, she'd lifted a blouse from the pile, picked a skirt to go with it, then kicked off her old slippers and tried on a pair of shoes, started taking everything that looked like it might fit to her room, trying things on. Saying something about hoping she had enough hangers.

Getting out of the passenger seat now, Fred came to the front, looking like he was living the milk-and-honey life through these hard times, the tan suit and flat cap, a chain looped from the watch pocket. "Next bank, they'll be calling an all-points on a gang of movie stars, calling us the dude bandits."

Smiling, Alvin figured it was dumb wearing the clothes they just stole not ten miles from this spot, but it did feel good.

The owner of the garage was Davidson, coming to the office door and asking if they needed gas or oil.

"Just the tire," Fred said.

Davidson pointed to a sign in the window: *All repairs strictly cash*.

Reaching for his roll, Alvin asked what he owed, was told fifty cents, peeled off a bill, stepped over and handed it to him, saying, "Don't worry about the change, and, uh, there a place open for breakfast?"

Unimpressed, Davidson pointed toward Darlie's, a cafe two blocks up on East Main, taking the dollar and going inside to the cash register.

"Not a friendly man," Alvin said to Fred, returning to the front of the DeSoto, bothered by the way Davidson had looked them over.

"How about we rob the till, teach him to smile once in a while?"

Alvin's stomach had been roiling since last night's bourbon, the three of them celebrating and talking about heists in the times to come. "Breakfast first."

Fred looked at the clear sky, like weather had something to do with it. They had passed the West Plains Bank on their cruise down what passed for the main drag, a prosperous enough looking place, given the tough times. At least there weren't gun racks in the back of every pickup. "Good day for a little banking."

Alvin grinned, thinking they could use more loot after paying three months in advance on the house Fred rented just outside of town on a dozen acres, a two-story place of modern convenience, even had indoor plumbing. Getting them out of that dirt-floor shack like he said he would. Glancing toward the garage door, looking at the new man, Fred said, "How you figure Bill measures up?" Just released from McAlester, where Fred's brother Doc was doing his stretch. Bill traveling the three hundred fifty miles, looking Fred up on Doc's say-so.

"Bit of a dude maybe," Alvin said.

And the two of them were grinning, Fred saying the man couldn't tell a joke to save his life.

Alvin looked back up East Main, then over at Davidson through the station's window, the man on the phone glancing their way again. Alvin getting an uneasy feeling, looking into the garage, Bill telling the mechanic a joke, talking like he was W.C. Fields.

"How we doing there, Bill?" Alvin called to him, getting waved off.

He nudged Fred, watching a tan car roll down the drag, coming their way and pulling up in front of the post office. The man getting out was tall and wore a sheriff's uniform, not looking over, just walking easy into the post office. Fred looked to Bill in the garage, the man getting to the punchline. He called, "Hey, Bill, time to go." Getting waved off like he was spoiling the man's act.

A black Ford pulled up behind the sheriff's, a gray-haired man getting out and walking across to the garage, going past them and into the office, talking to Davidson, both looking their way.

"Think we'll get breakfast someplace else," Alvin said, the bad feeling growing.

"Bill, let's go," Fred called again.

Alvin glanced past the office, the same man coming out, not giving them a look, crossing the street and going up the post office steps.

Fred kept his eyes across the street, stepping to the passenger side, Alvin going around front and getting behind the wheel.

The gray-haired man came out first, the sheriff following him, going down the post office steps and going to his car, getting something from the backseat well, tucking it up under his coat, waiting on a passing car and crossing the street, not making eye contact until he was halfway across, then calling, "You men, I want a word." One hand going under the coat.

Fred leaned into the car and told Alvin, "Get her started." Reaching under the passenger seat, he came up smiling, held the Army Special across the roof as the sheriff stopped and drew, Alvin dropping across the seat as Fred fired.

The sheriff rocked back, looked down at the hole in his vest, then tried to raise his pistol, Fred shooting him again, hitting him square, the man dropping back in the middle of the street, his arms outstretched, the pistol knocked from his hand. The gray-haired man ran back into the post office.

Somewhere a woman screamed. Davidson was yelling, coming from his door with a rifle, trying to work the bolt.

Slapping the shifter in gear, Alvin was thinking, "We're in it now." And roared out of there. Fred barely getting in and slamming his door.

Rushing from the garage, pistol in hand, Bill Weaver was yelling after them, seeing Davidson with a rifle, trying to load it. Calling them sons of bitches, Bill Weaver ran past the bleeding sheriff and went flat out, zigging and zagging, trying to make a hard target, his feet pounding on the pavement, hearing a rifle shot behind him. He half-turned and returned a wild shot. People coming out of doors, getting a look at what was going on. No way Bill was going to catch the DeSoto, he veered right on the next side street, his cap blowing off, pumping his arms and running for all he was worth, no idea which direction to take, just cursing and running from town.

... West Plains, Missouri
December 13, 1931

"Don't like it any more'n you, Ma." Fred waved an arm, standing in the front room of the farmhouse, feeling bad they had to move, not wanting to explain why. "Just how it's got to be."

Kate was miserable, taking the new clothes off hangers, out of drawers, and tossing them on the bed.

Getting water from the jug in the kitchen, Alvin was regretting the rent Fred paid up front, and now having to run.

"The hell kind of jackpot you in now, boy?" Arthur said, coming from the bedroom in back, frowning at him. Getting no answer, he went on, "Just a bunch of no-goods, like I been saying."

"The ones who pay the rent." Alvin set the jug on the table and got in the old man's way, catching the booze breath, Arthur wearing one of the sweaters they took from McCallon's.

"You got something to say to me, boy?" Arthur rising to his full height, putting on a show.

"One thing I didn't say, old man . . ." Catching hold of the sleeve, Alvin said, "Didn't say help yourself."

"Found it lying around, same as you." Arthur tugged his arm free, narrowing his glassy eyes.

"Take it off."

"You're stretching it." Arthur pushed him into the table.

And Alvin was on him, swinging his fist, clutching a mittful of sweater and tugging it up, spinning the old man, shoving him into the table, the water jug sloshing, a chair tipping. Then he was yanking with both hands, pulling it over his head, driving a right into his gut.

Reeling back, unbalanced, Arthur couldn't see on account of the sweater, but he swung back, not much behind it.

Letting go, Alvin buried another fist in the exposed belly, the old man letting out a whoosh of air, buckling and bending to his knees. Alvin tossed the sweater on the table, it landing in the spilled water.

Kate came to the kitchen, wondering about the racket, making a face at Arthur, picking up the wet sweater and tossing it at him, saying, "Get dressed, and go find your comb." Only glanced at Alvin and went back to the bedroom, unhappy about having to pack.

"Take all you can carry, Ma," Fred said, passing her in the hall, coming into the kitchen, looking at the two men, realized something happened between them, shaking his head.

Stepping to the porch, Alvin was back to thinking it was hare-brained, driving into town, wearing what they just stole from McCallon's, a robbery like that causing a stir around a two-bit town like West Plains. Now, the killing of Howell County's lawman meant they'd be coming with a posse. He fished his pack of Chesterfields from a top pocket, put one in his mouth, patted his pants pocket and took out his Italian lighter, part of the plunder back in Tulsa, Alvin not remembering which house he stole it from.

Fred had done it cold, shot the lawman, not showing regret. Not like Alvin could see a way around it. Wasn't like that with the night marshal, Fred getting him out of the car, pointing the pistol at him. Did it like he was getting payback for the beating they took at the hands of the two Tulsa cops. Alvin wanting to tie the night marshal up and leave him in the stand of woods. Fred saying he'd get loose and go run to the sheriff, give a description and they'd be on an all-points, go from night marshal to deputy, and the two of them would end back in the slam. If they were going to be in it, they couldn't go half-baked, leaving eyewitnesses behind. Saying again he wasn't going back inside, and like that, he looked at the night marshal and shot him, watching him fall backwards, then he walked back to the car, asking if Alvin wanted him to drive.

Alvin stood on the porch, hearing footfalls inside, everybody going around the farmhouse and grabbing what they could. He left the dress and feathered hat he meant to send to Dot. The wife he hadn't seen since getting sent up — Dot showing up in court two years back after he got arrested for a stolen car, a bunch of stolen clocks in the trunk. Dot asking to approach the bench, having a word with the judge, swearing to him she'd make an honest man of Alvin, saving him from being sent to the reformatory that time. And he married her the next day, and they made it six months before he lit out and ended being sent up on another robbery charge, landing in the state pen where he met Fred. Now, he pictured her alone in that place on Brady Street in Chicago, wondering if she knew he'd been released, or if he was even alive. And if she ever got that dog she used to talk about, a spaniel to keep her company while he was making his way in the traveling jewelry business, what they told her folks. And how long before the law put it together and went banging on her door, maybe showing up with a warrant and tearing holes in her walls, looking for more stolen loot that wasn't there?

Pulled from his thoughts, he dragged on the cigarette, seeing a lone figure coming along the dirt road, alarmed at first, thinking it was a cop, then recognizing Bill Weaver in the dude outfit, sweat circles under his arms. The man looked like he was boiling over — sure was coming fast.

"You forget something, Ray?" Walking stiff-legged with his fists clenched, dust rising around his feet as he came across the yard.

"Next time I tell you, maybe you forget the punchline and come like you're called." Alvin got himself set, second fistfight in ten minutes. Taking one more puff, he thought of the pistol he left under the DeSoto's front seat, tossing the cigarette down and grinding it under his shoe. Given Bill's size, he figured to hit him as soon as his foot took the first step, catch him off balance.

"Mistaking me for your mutt." Bill tossed off the jacket, throwing it down, getting as far as the steps when Fred showed at the door behind Alvin, leaning on the frame and looking on, giving a lazy look, saying, "Something on your mind, Bill?"

"You two left me holding my pecker."

"Well, you and your pecker got two minutes to pack, then you get left behind — twice." Fred looked at him, his words easy. Stepping next to Alvin, the pistol tucked in his belt, saying, "And you keep running that mouth, Bill, I promise to mess up your good shirt."

Bill Weaver looked from one to the other, shaking his head, stepped up and angled between them, going to get his pack.

"Between him and Arthur, I'm getting a sore head," Fred said, asking if Alvin had a smoke.

"You got an idea where to?" Alvin said, taking out the

bent pack, fishing for the Italian lighter, surprised how easy Fred was, shot two men and not regretting a thing, looked ready to shoot one more.

"I heard of a guy inside, Deafy Farmer, you know him?" Fred put the cigarette in his mouth, waited for the light, saying, "Well, he lives someplace south of Joplin, been known to help folks with law trouble."

"Doing it out of the goodness of his heart?" Alvin scratched behind his neck, flicking the lighter, the flint sparking.

"I doubt it." Fred inhaled, blew a cloud of smoke.

... *St. Paul, Minnesota*
April 26, 1932

The rented duplex was on Robert Street, Kate loving the kitchen: the floor a checkerboard of linoleum, a GE icebox and range, and an ironing board in the wall. Deafy setting it up, the man not able to speak, using hand signs and penciling notes, letting them know they'd be safe in this place. Folks in the sister city over the river calling this place Lowertown, where cops were paid to look the other way. Fred helping to get Kate settled, hanging her clothes back on hangers, trying to convince her she could do better than Arthur, but letting the old man tag along on her say-so. Kate telling Fred it was for better or worse, the two of them as good as hitched, something he better get used to.

Shooting the sheriff made the front page of every paper in the Midwest, the man's name had been Roy Kelly, a dedicated lawman and a good family man, loved by one and all. The manhunt forcing them to shelve banks for a while. Bill Weaver made peace with Alvin and Fred, but called it quits and headed back to Chicago, reconnecting with his former outfit, the Forty-Two Gang out in Little Hell.

After moving in, Fred checked out the Green Lantern on Wabasha, Deafy writing a note, letting him know it ought to be the first stop for trouble boys on the run, a good place to bump into their own kind. This place with its long bar and booths along the wall, an upright piano in the far corner. First time Fred and Alvin walked in, they were surprised the joint had some class, not the dingy dive they expected.

The bartender set them up with a round, telling them Piano Red showed up some afternoons to plunk his heart out. The joint was run by Harry "Dutch" Sawyer, a friendly sort in spite of rumors that he planted a bomb under his former boss's Paige coupe. Dapper Danny Hogan was killed in the blast, leaving Dutch to inherit the saloon and other operations once run by his former boss, along with the man's woman.

They sat in a booth, and Dutch introduced them to Kid Cann, Bernard Phillips, along with Clyde Barrow. Alvin buying the boys a round. And next time they came in, they were shaking hands with Harvey "the Dean" Bailey and Frank "Jelly" Nash, not much these two didn't know between them about hitting banks. Worst thing about the place, Arthur Dunlop followed them in, then making it his regular spot, likely out of spite, sitting on his own at the end of the bar by the door, likely coercing pocket money from Kate, the money Fred handed her for groceries every week.

Turned out the Dean liked to tell how he made it: the mint robbery in Denver, the Lincoln National in Nebraska. Jelly Nash pointing out that one was the biggest heist in the history of sticking up banks — more than Butch Cassidy, Henry Starr, or the James boys ever took, close to what George Leslie robbed from the Manhattan Saving back in '78 — bagging over two-point-seven million on one robbery — the reason the Dean counted himself as mostly retired these days. Jelly Nash crowing how his pal had more to his name than Henry

Ford. The Dean coming in the Lantern to rub elbows and keep in the game, talking with old chums and making new ones, always buying rounds for the house.

After dropping in that first week, Dutch had them glad-handing with police chief Big Tom Brown, recently promoted from detective — a good man to know, and a good town to call home, whiskey bars instead of prison bars, with brothels like Nina Clifford's on South Washington. Nina taking a shine and getting to know Alvin, finding out he hailed from the Great White North same as she did, the two of them spending evenings together, talking about a Canada he barely remembered.

Joining Alvin and Fred at the booth one night, Big Tom bought a round, explaining the layover plan, something Deafy had mentioned — how local law turned the other way so long as they did their banking fifty miles or more from the city limits, and as long as Big Tom got a slice. Rapping his knuckles on the table like he was emphasizing that point, Big Tom slapped back his drink, told them five hundred would show good intention, something like an initiation fee, and he left them to talk it over.

Coming in the next day, Alvin waited for him, bought a round and handed Big Tom an envelope of good intention. Big Tom smiled, felt the envelope's thickness between thumb and forefinger, tucking it away, saying they were going to get along just fine.

Feeling eyes on him, Alvin turned and caught Arthur watching from his perch by the door, the old man seeing him hand the lawman the envelope, then dropping his gaze back to his glass. The next day Big Tom came back, advising Alvin the duplex on Robert Street was heading for a raid, some citizen tipping off the state troopers, telling Alvin and Fred they better get out of that place, giving him the address of a

49

guy with a house to rent over in South St. Paul, a secluded rancher by the river.

Fred tried to explain to Kate she had to pack the wardrobe again, take down the pictures she just hung up. And they were on the move again, Kate complaining every step of the way. Big Tom sending a couple of off-duty recruits with some brawn and a truck.

Once they re-settled, Big Tom and Jelly Nash dropped by the new place, bringing flowers for Kate, playing the gentlemen, claiming she was all the boys talked about. The top cop acting like he was courting, something Arthur didn't like seeing, storming out of the house in a drunken rage. After Kate fixed them a lunch of pork sandwiches and lemonade, she made tea, Big Tom giving her a hand she didn't need. Jelly stood with Alvin and Fred on the back porch, letting them in on a good score, the Citizens State Bank in Redwood Falls, wanting them in on it, along with Bill Weaver who just showed up in town, things not working out for him in Chicago. Jelly asking if they were okay with Bill. Fred shrugged, saying, "As long as he don't start with the jokes."

And they pulled it off, an easy score, going in and drawing pistols, two of them cleaning out the drawers while the others took care of the safe, getting out in under ten minutes without a shot fired, making their getaway back to St. Paul. The next week, Jelly had them hitting another branch in Wahpeton, North Dakota. Bill Weaver walking in, shouting for attention, saying, "If you bankers can count, then how come you got four windows and only two tellers?" Not getting any smiles, he drew his pistol, announcing this was a stick-up. In and out, and easy as pie. Big Tom getting his envelope.

Dutch Sawyer came from behind his bar a couple days after Wahpeton, coming to their table, giving them a tip on a fat bank in Minneapolis, the Third Northwestern National doing a brisk trade, not falling victim to the bank runs and panics happening across the country.

Bill Weaver joked, "Bank's got a better chance of getting forced into closure than of getting robbed."

Thinking it might be too close to home, Alvin waited around and ran it past Big Tom.

"Like I told you," Big Tom said, "My job's keeping the citizens of St. Paul safe, the Twin's not my domain."

His domain.

Big Tom smiled, saying, "But since you brought it up, a taste is always nice."

Jelly Nash was in, and the four of them sat in the back of the Lantern, Harvey the Dean stepping over, buying a round. Saying he liked the way they did their business — smart — humbly suggesting they get some Thompson guns. And asking if they could use an extra man.

Alvin looked around the table, then back to the Dean, saying, "Thought you were out of it, Dean?"

"Watching you fellas gives me the itch." He was smiling, taking a seat at the table, Dutch bringing a tray of drinks. Alvin catching Arthur coming from the can in back, looking over, then settling on his stool at the bar.

Two days later, they had the Thompsons, four of them, brand new and in their cases. They sat in Dutch's room in back looking at plans of the Third Northwestern, a three-sided building with tall glass windows and two entrances. Harvey showing how two men could go in the Central Avenue entrance, another two coming through the Hennepin Avenue doors. One more outside with a Tommy gun. Jelly wanting to use two cars, with drivers waiting outside, making it a seven-man job. All of them agreeing. Then they went, found a secluded spot out past Swede Hollow, and practiced with the Tommy guns, each man emptying a drum, getting the hang of it.

That night, Alvin and Fred sat at the bar with Jelly Nash, Big Tom coming in, rapping his knuckles the way he liked to do, leaning in and saying one of his plainclothes boys got an anonymous tip: Fred and Alvin seen hanging out in this place, identified as two wanted fugitives. "The caller said he was notifying the bureau, telling my sarge at the desk the local law's been looking the other way. Imagine saying a thing like that on the horn — and to the feds of all people." Rapping the table hard, Big Tom said, "Sure like to meet that caller." Wondering if it was the same one who tipped the state cops about the duplex Fred and Alvin rented on Robert Street.

Alvin glanced down the bar, Arthur in his usual spot, slumped forward and nursing a drink. Jelly suggesting they mothball the job and see if any feds came nosing around. Nobody liking the sound of postponing it, but all agreeing it made sense.

When it was just the two of them, Alvin looked at Fred. "I got an idea about the caller."

Fred did too, looking down the bar at Arthur, the old man sinking a free drink the Dean had paid for. Downing his own shot, Fred got up, lit a smoke and went to Dutch behind the bar, coming back with a bottle of Old Overholt. Nodding to Alvin, he went and put a friendly hand on Arthur's shoulder, saying, "Come on, Arthur, let's give you a ride home."

"Who says I'm going home?"

"I just did. You need me to repeat it?" Fred smiled, clapping his shoulder again.

Alvin hooked his other arm, lifting him off the chair, the man wearing that same sweater from the McCallon's job, and they walked him out the door.

"Never gave me a lift before." Arthur looked back at his unfinished drink, not sure about going with them.

"Well, it's high time, then, you being Ma's paramour and all." Fred patted the old man's back, wondering aloud what Ma had on for supper, betting on chicken. "A plump one, not like them yardbirds. You remember them, Arthur, running and scratching all over the place?"

"Had bird the other day, didn't we?"

"Making today another perfect day for it. With spuds the way she does, and gravy and biscuits, *mmm mmm*. Makes my mouth water." Getting to the hot DeSoto, Fred got in and started it up, Alvin helping Arthur in back, then getting in the passenger side.

Driving away from the Lantern, Fred took them across the river, halfway out of St. Paul before Arthur noticed they were heading north, away from the house. "Hey, what is this?"

"The day's not done, Arthur. Think it's high time the three of us got in some fishing. Hell, we're like family."

"Except I don't fish."

"Oh, you're gonna love it, I promise you. And I got a primo spot in mind — Yellow Lake, you know it?"

"Just told you I don't fish." Looking from one to the other, Arthur wasn't liking it, looking more fearful. Staring out the window like he was deciding if they were moving too fast for him to jump out. "How about poles and bait, you got any of that?"

"Man just told me he don't fish," Fred said to Alvin, then looking across the seat, saying, "Stop fretting about poles and worms, Arthur. We got all we need in the trunk. You sit back and take it easy, let me worry about the worms, how about it? I tell you, I'm seeing fish in your future. You're gonna love it, man." Fred reached to the floor and passed the bottle to Alvin, asking him to do the honors. Telling Arthur the makers of Old Overholt got through prohibition times by calling their juice medicinal.

Fred stood by the shore of the small Wisconsin lake, took a look around, the sun dropping to the horizon line, the air warm with a nice breeze for the time of year. He let Arthur tip the last swig, easy waves lapping around his shoes, the man's pant cuffs wicking it up.

"Why'd you do it, Arthur?" Fred said.

"Knew it bothered you, me living with your ma. But, if you're that bent about it . . ." Arthur was looking at the pistol in Fred's hand, the same Army Colt he used on Sheriff Kelly.

"Yeah, being a miserable drunk and treating her poor, on top of being a sponger. Would've run you off for that. This's about you being a rat."

Arthur twisted his face, like he didn't get it.

"You rang the cops and pointed right to us," Fred said.

The old man snorted. "Think I'd stitch you up, my own gal's boy — one who's paying the bills? Think I'm crazy?" Wobbling from the booze, Arthur shook his head, then looked down, noticing he was standing to his ankles in water, taking a drunken step toward them.

"Maybe it was the twelve-hundred-buck reward," Fred said.

"Wasn't like that."

"Tell me how it was?" Fred looked to the sky, saying, "No getting around it, old-timer. I just want to hear you say it."

"Drive me out here, trying to cow me. You want it so bad, I'll pack up and go. How about that — and you never see me again?" Arthur raised his hands like he was reasoning, saying, "In spite of denying your ma my deep affection."

Fred glanced at Alvin, saying, "You think he gets it?"

Alvin shrugged like it didn't matter and drew his pistol, raising his arm along with Fred.

Arthur turned to the water like he might plunge in, then looked back, his hands up in front of him, having nowhere to go. "You can't just —"

They fired, knocking Arthur back, falling with a splash, the shot rolling across the lake.

Looking down at him — Arthur's mouth open to the water, a look like he was surprised, his blood mixing with the waves lapping in.

"I ain't going back inside," is all Fred said, turning for the car.

They left Arthur like that, his mouth open with the water washing in, and they stopped at a bridge over a murky river some miles off, threw the pistols in, and drove the four hours home. Fred said something how they ought to take the Tommy guns out to a field someplace and get in more practice, neither of them saying much else.

Coming in the door, Fred went and pecked his ma's cheek, apologizing for being late and holding up supper.

"The hell you boys been? You know I got supper on the stove."

"Got stuck helping Dutch move some boxes, had a shipment come in. Cracked open a couple. Then of all the luck, we had a blow-out on the way back," Fred said, showing hands that weren't dirty. "And you think we had a spare in the trunk?" Saying something else about trading in the DeSoto, getting a Ford with a big V8.

"That's common sense, ain't it, having a spare?"

"Maybe so, Ma, and you think I'd know it."

"You seen Arthur?"

"Seen him this morning, think it was . . ." Fred said, looking surprised, then over to Alvin.

"Was at the Lantern, wasn't he?" Alvin said, scratching his head like he was trying to remember. "Not sure if he was getting top heavy, but I guess he'll be along."

"Well, never mind him. Sure smells good, Ma," Fred said, putting his nose to the kitchen. "Don't smell like chicken, but let me guess . . ." Sniffing and leaning to the stove, lifting the pot lid to the stew, going, "*Mmm mmm mmm*. Love the way you do it with the carrots and potatoes. And don't tell me you made biscuits."

"There's gravy, ain't there?" Kate said, frowning like she knew she was being played.

Over bowls of mutton, she eyed them, gathering her hunches, but keeping them to herself, knowing peach pie wouldn't pry the truth out of these two.

Fred fixed his attention on his bowl, asking Alvin to pass the biscuits.

"Only one left," Alvin said.

"Yeah, why I asked you to pass it."

Kate reached it and set it next to her own bowl, saying, "You boys just can't be straight with me, not one time, always leaving me in the pitch."

"This about Arthur?" Fred said, watching her butter the biscuit.

"For my own good, is that what you wanna tell me." Taking half the biscuit in a bite.

"Don't know what else to say, Ma." Fred hunched his shoulders, saying, "If we're still talking about Arthur, then I go along with Ray — your man's likely stumblebum down someplace, if you want the truth, and he'll likely find his way home anytime now, same as always." Looking to Alvin.

Alvin nodded.

"I dish up stew, and I get the wild goose." Taking the corner of her apron, she tossed the rest of the biscuit on her plate, wiped her mouth, then rose from the table. "Leave you two to clean up, something you're good at." Then said she was going to work on a puzzle.

When the dishes were stacked, Fred went on the porch for a smoke, and Alvin went and tapped on her door, saying, "Tell the truth, Kate, we stay clear of Arthur any chance we get, think you know that."

"I know he's no-account, but he's what I got." She looked up from the wooden puzzle, halfway through a scene of a cowboy shoeing a horse.

"You're selling yourself short, Kate, a woman like you."

"A woman like me, yeah, just look at me."

"Well, you wanted the truth, and there it is."

"You boys shut me out, treat me like I'm here for the cooking and cleaning. Guess I'm okay with it, 'cause I don't want to know what you do, but then you go and treat me like I'm a dope."

"Never ever thought of you that way, Kate. Tell you what, you want to be part of it . . ."

She looked at him, saying, "What, cooking and cleaning not enough?"

"You want to hear me, or not?"

"Take part of what?"

"Help us do some banking." He brightened, an idea building.

"One time, I was a fair shot, but I can't run in these Florsheims." Putting her hands on her hips, Kate shook her head at him, curious about what he was thinking.

"How about you get decked out, walk in and see the manager, tell him you're moving to town, and you got, let's say, fifty grand to stick in his bank, enough to make most of them slaver."

"Can't tell if you're funning me." Kate studying him, smiling at the thought. "Be like playing a part."

"Like taking center stage, treading the boards. You ask me, I think you'd be a natural — and the bank's your stage."

"Get all dressed up?"

"Sure."

"But not with a gun?"

"No need for it."

"And you think fifty grand's enough?"

"How much you thinking?"

"Why not a quarter million?"

"Put on your finery, and put it to good use. I think you could sell a quarter million, maybe more."

"Drive up in the DeSoto, you as my chauffeur."

"Well, I didn't say that."

"Fred's got the Clark likeness, so it's got to be you. Don't need a uniform, you just come around and open my door. I stroll in, swing my mink, tell the man I got a sky-high sum and want to make sure it'll be safe."

"I think you got it." Alvin nodded, seeing her get into the role, saying, "How about he asks where the money's from?" Alvin not recalling a mink in the McCallon robbery.

"Then I say I don't kiss and tell. Bat my eyes while I'm counting how many guards and where they're posted, look for an alarm, and where they got the vault."

"You sure you never done it before?" Alvin was all smiles.

"Fred in on this?"

"He will be."

Kate smiled too, sitting straight, putting on the role, calling him a dear boy, then said, "So, when do I get my mink?"

. . . *Concordia, Kansas*
July 25, 1932

S even months since the killing of Sheriff Roy Kelly in West Plains, and the law hadn't come close, and nobody was asking after Arthur W. Dunlop anymore, if they ever did. Kate accepted that he ran off, another good-for-nothing like her first hubby, George. That man taking off after their eldest, Herman, was laid to rest.

Jelly Nash targeted one more Kansas bank, the Cloud County promising to be ripe with payroll and savings, the gang shelving the Third Northwestern in Minneapolis for the time, worried about a rat, fearing the feds got tipped and were lying for them to try it.

Treading the boards, Kate went in playing the rich investor, Mrs. Bea Raitt, scoping the Cloud County, plying her charms on bank vice-president Chick Peck. The July heat not allowing for draping the new mink, Kate donning a string of pearls and a zebra print frock with ruffles, the latest from Paris, a pique hat with a bow, kid leather shoes, and a matching clutch bag, all courtesy of the McCallon's haul. Alvin in a suit and cap, mustache and glasses, cast as her chauffeur, opening the rear car door. Kate winking at him and walking up the bank steps in her props.

Rolling out of town over the Robert Street Bridge the night before the job, Fred ditched the DeSoto they had used for too long, driving back in a dark Hudson Major, one of the Greater Eight models, plenty of room and engine power, parking the stolen ride along the alley side of the Lantern. Joining Alvin, Earl Christman and Jess Doyle, they dealt cards and wise-cracked about Alvin being Ma's driver. Jelly Nash joined them in the back room. Going over every aspect, they ordered a last round and called it a night.

Next morning, Fred offered Alvin the keys to the Hudson, in case he wanted to stay in role, playing the chauffeur, the rest of them all smiles. Alvin flipping him the bird, sliding in on the passenger side, cupping an empty carton in his hands.

"Hell you got there, Ray?" Jess Doyle asked.

Alvin opened the lid, balled socks and underwear inside.

Jess Doyle saying maybe he'd lost his marbles — they were robbing a bank, not a Chinese laundry — the rest of them laughing.

"Just wait and see," is all Alvin said.

Fred put on the miles, driving the eight and a half hours, stopping once to let them water the horses, the gang taking adjoining rooms at the Bigsby, an out-of-the-way motel outside of Jamestown. Sending out for sandwiches and beer, they kept to the rooms, Earl Christman, Jess Doyle and Jelly Nash playing blackjack, blowing about past heists and how they evaded the heat, Earl explaining the game of Spades, dealing a few hands, all of them going easy on the booze, just a few beers and calling another early night.

Rolling along Main as Concordia came awake the next morning, the start of another work week. A minute apart, the four of them walked into the Cloud County Bank, Jess

Doyle standing next to the entry with a Tommy gun under his draped jacket, playing sentry and smiling at a pretty brunette customer walking out.

Should have been an in-and-out robbery, nobody knowing about the vault's time-lock, not something vice-president Chick Peck divulged to Kate.

Grabbing the sleeve of one of the tellers, Fred told her, "You do what I say, sister, and you'll be home for supper; you don't, then Chick here's gonna be mopping up your mess." Pointing his pistol against Ida Cook's wasp waist, promising to spoil her day.

Sinking to his pinstriped knees, Chick Peck blubbered, swearing he couldn't open the vault. "Nobody can. Not God — not nobody."

Letting go of Ida, Fred pointed the pistol against the man's temple, telling Chick, "First cop I see, she gets to meet her maker, and you get to watch." Fred telling him to get up, and stop being a disgrace, told him to think of how Ida was going to see him the next day, piss on his fancy pants. "Providing you get through this one."

Bobbing his head, Chick stopped crying, getting off the floor and standing next to her.

Jess Doyle at the door, gripped his Tommy gun, saying he wished somebody would try something — wild eyes watching out the door.

Holding the carton with his laundry, Alvin told Chick, "Anybody comes in, there's a bank inspection going on, you understand? You tell them to come back. They go, and there's no harm. They don't go . . . well, then this goes off." Holding the box out to him, making Chick hold it. "Got your life in your hands, Chick." Told him to be careful not to jiggle it. And Alvin walked from him, took a sack from his pocket and went to the teller cages.

Chick Peck staring at the box.

Frank and Earl helped turn out the cash drawers, everybody waiting on the time-lock.

Chick standing statue-still, the box in his hands. Ida and one of the tellers started crying when the time-lock released with a loud clank, Chick turning his neck to the ornate ceiling, communing his thanks, his hands steady on the box.

The currency in the safe was stuffed into bank bags, and Alvin came out, took the box from Chick, setting it by the teller's window, saying loud enough for all, "Folks, here we got a bomb! A hell of one." Letting it sink in, then saying, "The sensor picks up any kind of motion, well, then, God bless you all." Crossing himself and walking past the employees and customers, telling them, "You folks have a nice day now."

Holding a bank sack, Fred went to Ida Cook like he was asking for a dance and took her by the arm. "Don't want it happening to you, doll." Walking her out the door.

Ida clutched onto his arm, saying, "Thank you, mister."

"Call me Fred." Asking her name and escorting her out to the car, guessing the cops would figure who pulled the bank job, no point lying about his name.

Jelly Nash got behind the wheel, the rest of them in back, Fred opening the passenger door, getting in and rolling down the window, telling Ida to step up on the running board. "Going for a short ride, Ida. Promise we won't go too fast, case you feel a little wind up your skirt, but, I got you." Keeping hold of her forearm.

"Thank you." Clutching his sleeve, her feet on the running board.

"You got an old man at home?"

She shook her head, couldn't let go of his sleeve to wipe at her tears.

Wiping his palm at her running eye shadow, he said, "Come on now, Ida. Told you you'll be alright."

"Well, I must be a sight."

"One for sore eyes, if you ask me," Fred said, then had Jelly slow to a stop six blocks from the bank, letting go of her arm, saying, "There you go, Ida, free as a bird. Sorry I can't ask you to supper. Maybe some other time."

Stepping off the running board, she nodded, looked after them and waved as they drove off.

"You're one slick dog." Jelly grinned at him.

"Jesus, think I been struck by an arrow."

"Better'n a bullet," Bill said, that line getting some laughs.

Nobody gave chase, the gang making off with a quarter million.

... *South St. Paul, Minnesota*
September 11, 1932

"Oh, my God, Doc!" Kate hurried to the door, her slippers slapping down the hall, this house where the three of them had been posing as speakeasy musicians. Alvin buying a used six-string, learning some chord shapes, trying to finger pick. Fred working on a harmonica, going for that Noah Lewis sound. Kate told the neighbor lady over the fence she was the singer. And she wasn't bad, the three of them practicing some June Christy and Ginger Rogers numbers. Kate singing along with the radio with the window open, and anytime she was hanging the laundry out back.

Beaming at her third-eldest, Arthur, everybody calling him Doc since he was a tad — standing on the veranda, worldly goods in the canvas bag he was issued by the state. Kate threw her arms around him, kissing his cheek, holding him tight, then at arm's length, saying, "Let me look at you, boy. Good God, you're down to the bone. What do they feed you in that place?"

"Nothing like your cooking, Ma, that's for damn sure," Doc said, smiling at her, and not letting her go. "Just the thought of fatback and black-eyed peas kept me going."

"Well, sounds like you come hungry." Kate let go of him, smoothing her apron, calling into the house for Fred.

"Well, you ain't changed a minute," Doc said to her, stepping into the hall. "Fact you look like a million."

"Million years maybe." Putting a hand to the French bob, something she was trying out.

"Hair's different and you're . . . I don't know . . ."

"Not so backwoodsy?"

"All the way uptown, I'd say."

"Guess I been getting my fashion sense. This is French."

Coming down the hall, Fred heard his brother's voice.

Kate stood aside as the brothers locked hands, both grinning ear to ear.

"How you doing, brother?" Fred stepped back, getting a look at his older brother, saying, "Can't believe I'm looking at you."

"Pays to appeal, brother."

"Wasn't shaving last time I seen you," Fred said, his eyes getting wet, giving his head a shake, then introducing Alvin, "Come here, Ray, and meet Doc." Saying Ray was one of the family now. Clapping them both on the back.

Doc offered his hand, saying, "Good to know you, Ray."

Kate bid Fred get his brother settled in the spare room, going about fixing supper, singing "Keepin' Out of Mischief Now," calling for Alvin to fetch a fat hen from the coop she kept out back, something she'd been getting him to do since Arthur ran off.

Could pull the trigger on a man, but Alvin wasn't fussy on lopping off the heads of dumb birds. But he didn't put up a stink, taking the sharpened knife and going out back and grabbing one of the hens, going to the old table, pinning the wings, holding it fast, slipping its head in the kill cone Kate had set up, slicing across the throat below the jawbone, and letting it bleed out. Plucking and gutting it, bringing it in the house.

After supper, the men stood on the back porch, Doc saying, "Heard you fellas threw in with Jelly Nash. That so?"

Surprised word got to him in the Oklahoma pen, Fred said they got to know Jelly real well, named some of the other fellas, some names Doc had heard.

"Ma got an idea what's up?" Doc asked.

"You kidding me?" Fred telling how Alvin got Kate going in the Cloud County Bank, playing the rich patron and casing the joint, sounding proud about it.

Doc asking about Arthur Dunlop, remembering the old man as a sour drunk who hung around.

"One day he just run off," Fred said, taking out his pack of cigarettes. Not saying more about it, or how they got word from Big Tom a week after they took the old man fishing. Turned out it was the landlady's kid at the duplex on Robert Street who came across a wanted poster of Fred and Alvin in back of some detective magazine, the boy's mother making the call to the state cops. Nothing to do with Arthur Dunlop. Fred offering his brother a smoke.

Taking one, Doc said it was the first store-bought he'd puffed in a long while, running it under his nose, catching the aroma, patting his middle and saying through the screen, "And a feed like that, I think I died and gone to heaven."

"You just let out the belt, son, and get used to it," Kate called, humming along to "Little White Lies" on the radio, the happiest anybody had seen her in a long while.

Looking to see she was out of earshot, Doc said, "Whatever you boys got cooking, you can count me in. I mean, if you'll have me."

"If we'll have you? Sweet Jesus, son, you hear that, Ray? Doc says if we'll have him." Fred slung an arm around him, kissing the top of his head. "Why hell, brother, you taught me what I know, and last I checked, a good man's in short supply. You throw in with us, we'd be proud as punch. Ain't that so, Ray?"

"It's so," Alvin said.

"Now, don't just stand there smoking," Fred said. "Let's go see if we got something smart you can wear, you look like a man just got his release. Take you out and get you laid, good and right." Guessing his size and going to the trunk in the back room, seeing what they had left from the McCallon's job.

... *Minneapolis, Minnesota*
December 16, 1932

G etting into the role, Kate stepped out of a black
Lincoln, winked at her driver, and told him to wait,
then walked into the Third National at the junction of 5th,
Central and Hennepin. The wealthy patron swinging her
string of pearls, asking for the manager.

Fred and Alvin joked about it on those long nights of
planning, followed by days of staking it out, sitting in the car
and counting the heads of those going in and out, checking
who worked there, the position of the lone guard, how many
cops worked day shift, the times the patrols made their rounds,
the busiest and lightest times of day.

Jelly Nash had to opt out, working another job out of
state, and Harvey the Dean got busted back in September, a
citizen recognizing him from the papers when he walked in
a bank in Kingfisher, hadn't even pulled his pistol, the note
for the teller found in his pocket when the cops nabbed him
as he stepped to the teller's window. His lawyer trying to get
it tossed out on the flimsy evidence.

On Big Tom's plug, Alvin and the Barkers brought in Verne Miller, the one-time sheriff of Beadle County getting tired of the job and walking out with the entire department budget in his pocket. Along with Bill Weaver and Jess Doyle, they added Larry "the Chopper" DeVol, a one-time prison pal of Fred's who'd been working as a triggerman for the Cornhusker mob.

A two-car job — they parked a green Chevy by Como Lake for the switch. All of them getting in the big Lincoln, three of them stepping out a block from the bank, splitting up and walking in. Alvin and Verne going in the Central Avenue doors, Fred and Doc walking through the Hennepin doors, Bill staying with the car, Jess and Larry each guarding an entrance, Tommy guns under light overcoats.

Smiling at the uniformed security man, looking ready for a nap and not up for any trouble, Alvin put a cigarette in his mouth and stepped close, asking for a light, wanting him to point out the manager, being told he wouldn't be in till noon.

"That's a shame." Alvin leaned closer and stuck his pistol against the man's belly, waiting for him to put it together, reaching the man's revolver from its holster, dropping it in his own pocket, asking, "How about the assistant? Walk me over and introduce me. I need to tell you about moving fast and thinking slow?"

"Guess not." The guard dialed down the hard look, understood the situation and kept his hands at his sides, moving slow and taking Alvin to the assistant manager.

When Alvin and the guard walked over, Fred stepped to the middle of the marble floor, held his pistol in the air, did a turn and called out, "This is a hold-up, folks." Giving them a moment, looking at each of them, judging if any would give him trouble, saying, "Now, anybody think I'm kidding?"

Drawing his pistol, Doc walked next to him, had the bank employees line up with the early-morning customers, getting them face down on the marble. "No tricks, no alarms, and do like you're told, and you'll come away with supper talk — 'less we got a hero."

Getting the guard down on the floor, Alvin pulled a sack from a pocket and kept one of the tellers on her feet, told her to empty the drawers.

Taking the assistant manager by the arm, Verne Miller asked him, "You got a name, buddy?"

"Paul, it's Paul."

"Bet you got a wife and kids, huh, Paul?"

"Sure I do."

"And you wanna see them again?"

"Yes, sir." Paul nodded.

"Then let's get that vault open, like the road to your future."

"I only done it once," Paul said.

"You see that guy, Paul, the one you met?" Verne nodded over to Alvin. "They call him Creepy. You wanna guess why?"

His hands shaking, Paul was led to the back, staring at the steel door. Verne prodded him with the pistol's muzzle. Paul mixing up the combination, couldn't get it right on the second try and spun it again, his mind going blank, saying, "Oh, Jesus," when it didn't open.

"Being hard on yourself, Paul. Take a moment and breathe deep," Verne said, putting the pistol against his ear.

"I — I can't think."

"Gonna think worse if I got to shoot." Wiggling the muzzle into his ear, saying, "Try it again — one more time. Then I get somebody else to step over you, try again."

Paul dialed it right, left, then right, pulling the safe open, sweat beading on his face, his breath coming out like he was deflating.

Verne handed him a sack, telling him, "Get to it, just the bills. No bonds. You hear —"

Machine-gun fire rattled from outside the walls, the men inside looking around.

Rushing to a window, Doc looked out, then smashed out the glass, aimed and fired into the street, yelling back, "Time to go, boys!"

Guessing a silent alarm got tripped, Alvin and Fred hurried, helping Verne empty the vault, filling the sacks, shutting the assistant manager inside, all of them moving for the exit.

Middle of the street, Larry DeVol held his Tommy gun, standing before a shot-up police car, steam hissing from its radiator, its windshield blown out, tires flattened, two officers face down in the street.

They jumped in the Lincoln, and Bill roared them out of there, bouncing sheet metal against a parked van, tearing along 5th. Fighting the wheel, driving on a flat. Bill looking to Larry.

Larry looked sheepish, saying, "Guess when I sprayed the cops." He touched the barrel of the Tommy gun, turning in the seat, looking for pursuit.

The rubber tore off at Stelling Avenue, the wheel making a grinding sound, sparks flying. Bill fighting the steering along what Alvin mapped as Bank Robber's Row, getting them to the Chevy at Como Lake.

Fred was first to jump out, switching the plates, Alvin and Doc tossing the sacks in the Chevy's trunk. All of them stopping, reaching pistols as a car drove toward them, slowing, two men inside looking at the Lincoln on its rim, one of them pointing.

Pulling his pistol, Fred put a round through the passenger window, the man behind the wheel slumping forward, the horn blaring. The passenger shoved the driver against the door, grabbing the wheel and getting them out of there. Fred took aim again, but the car was gone.

They got in the Chevy, and Bill sped along the planned route, Alvin keeping watch out the rear window.

. . . Reno, Nevada
December 25, 1932

"A daring daylight robbery," Alvin read from the *Evening Gazette*, punching the *d*'s like he was a newsreel announcer. Sitting in the lounge chair outside of the suite, the sun beating down, the thermometer climbing north of ninety, the concrete around the pool baking underfoot, the pool water sparkling like jewels, glasses of bourbon and ice sweating on the table.

Arms folded behind his head, Fred sat across from him, taking in the sun. "What else it say?"

"How we grabbed forty Gs, a hundred more in securities, and blasted our way out." Alvin hearing Kate inside, saying something to make the women laugh. "Well, they got the blasting part right."

"Me shooting that cop eating at you?" Fred looked over the sunglasses, squinting into the sunlight.

"That and wondering who taught them bankers to count? How twenty-two Gs got to be forty."

"Now, there's the true bunch of crooks." Fred gave an easy smile, saying, "A robbery goes down, the bank claims more

73

went missing, robs the insurance. Insurance jacks its rates, and the little guy pays the freight — how it works, the American way." He kept looking at him, saying, "Now, back to what's on your mind . . ."

"Leaving bodies cranks up the heat." Alvin sipped his drink, mostly ice water now, looking back at him, holding his gaze.

"They come to take us, it's us or them. It's always that way, us or them."

"Wasn't a cop you shot." Alvin ran his finger down the newspaper, scanning the page. "Oscar Erickson, twenty-nine, accompanied by Arthur Zachman, twenty-two. Driving home from selling Christmas wreaths door to door, doing it for charity. Erickson, behind the wheel, slowed to offer assistance. According to Zachman, the gang leader opened fire, striking Oscar in the head. Didn't know what hit him. Taking the wheel, Zachman rushed to University and St. Albans, a police ambulance racing the dying Erickson to Ancker Hospital downtown. The poor man never regaining consciousness, his twenty-year-old widow by his side."

Sipping his drink, Fred said, "Figured me for the gang leader, huh?"

Alvin scanned the article, "Widow says he was in high spirits that morning, happy for the new job after months of no work, a pile of unpaid medical bills from St. Joseph's Hospital for an appendicitis operation from months before. Her having to move from their house, going to live with her sister, hoping to find work herself. Her life turned upside down, heaven to hell." Folding the paper, he dropped it on the side table between them.

"Car slowed — looked like he was aiming a pistol." Fred shrugged.

"Making us public enemies." Alvin thinking how Dillinger robbed banks, the man claiming no jail could hold him, somehow getting folks loving him and hating the banks.

"Saying we got to work on our public relations?" Fred holding back the hot temper, still smiling.

"Hoover laid it on 'Ma Barker and her boys.' What he calls us."

"Now we caring what that fool thinks?"

Alvin looked at him, drawing a breath. "Saying, how about we don't shoot the next guy who gets in the way?"

"Now we're getting to it." Fred sat up, saying, "Look Ray, I pegged them for cops, two of them in a dark ride, tailing us after a radio call. Guess I was standing up front again, having to make up my mind. Looks different up front."

"Think I was hiding in back?"

"Saying it's how it looked."

Alvin picked up his glass, swirling what ice was left.

"Look, cops come for us, I got no regret how it goes," Fred said. "Like the sheriff in the street, the guy going for his gun, making his play."

"'Cept we're talking about a guy selling Christmas wreaths . . ."

"I'll say again, I pegged them for cops, the way of the light, and the way the guy was pointing."

Alvin thinking it, but not saying the night marshal Fred shot was standing with both hands raised when Fred put him down. Back in the pen, Fred kept his cool anytime an inmate got in his business, tried to reason before letting go.

"Shooting bystanders makes bad headlines, for sure I get that," Fred said.

"Kind of thing shifts public sentiment." Alvin thinking of the outlaws hiding out in St. Paul, what the papers were calling Lowertown, seeing the outlaws hiding out as more menace than folk heroes, the kind of thing that put pressure on the underhanded politicos and bureaucrats who'd crumble like a mud wall, quick to point the finger. And when that wall fell away, investigations into police corruption would lead to a sweep-up of the criminal element.

Reaching in a pocket, Fred took a wad of cash and slid it between the glasses. "Stick it in an envelope and send it via the *Trib*. Oughta be enough for the gal's unpaid bills. Give us some good relations." Picking up his glass, he frowned at the melted ice, saying, "Now, if there's nothing else, I got drinking to do." Turning to the open French doors, hearing the women inside, Fred called, "Hey, you women! We got an emergency out here."

"Who voted me the secretary?" Alvin looked at the money, not letting the parlay go.

"You know I don't write so good." Fred looked at him, eyes going dark, saying, "Look Ray, maybe you ought to go sit with the women."

Alvin forgetting the brothers never went to school, Kate teaching them what they needed to know. Tucking the bills away, he eased back on the lounge chair, done talking about it, setting his straw boater over his eyes, letting the heat soak in.

Dolores came to the open door in her swimsuit, saying to Alvin, "What're you hollering about?"

"Ray wants to play dress-up," Fred said. "You got something he can try on, a nice dress — yellow, I think — some shoes to go with it?"

"Want to walk in a bank in my clothes, Ray darling?" Dolores got in Alvin's sun, looking down at him.

"And look like your ugly sister," Alvin said, shielding his eyes, looking up at her.

Waving a hand, she dismissed them and walked to the pool, saying she was going for a dip, asking if Alvin was coming.

Watching her from under the boater, Alvin tipped it back over his eyes, the sun and the booze taking its toll, thinking of Dot as he drifted, his wife since they got hitched in '31. Dropping her home in a swiped car after their first date, calling on her again and taking her along to a jazz party with some pals. He'd been good and drunk when he dropped her off, getting her home, then driving across town, falling asleep and crashing through a United Cigar Store window. Not hurt, he climbed out among busted glass and found the register empty, grabbing whatever he could, filling the backseat with cartons of cigarettes, boxes of cigars and shoe trees, looting the place, not remembering if it was a Ford or Dodge that time, its radiator dripping and hissing, both tires flat from the busted storefront glass. The chassis high-centered on a brick wall.

A patrol answered the silent alarm, and the two cops arrested him with his pockets filled with packs of cigarettes, a humidor under his arm. Asked the one cop if he had a light, explaining he had a nasty habit.

Alvin got to the wrong side of the street before the age of ten, hanging with folks his parents didn't favor, the two of them arguing all the time, blaming each other for the way he turned out. His mother sobbing and his old man turning his back and wishing Alvin was never born, not saying much to him since the copper brought him to the door for selling dirty pictures and running errands for hookers. Alvin still in short pants, estranged from his folks, when he was sent to the pen at Lansing, where he met Fred.

After getting his release, he thought of going to Chicago and looking up his wife, Dot, saying something like, "Hey girl, you remember me?" Instead he went to look up Fred, that time he met Kate, living in the dirt-floor shack by the tracks. All before Fred shot Sheriff Roy Kelly, and before

Dolores Delaney and Paula Harmon walked into the Green Lantern one night, two seventeen-year-olds drawn to the dark end of town, wearing sweaters that showed their budding shapes, plenty of leg below the skirts, both with curled hair and pencil-thin eyebrows, long lashes and lipstick, coming in to meet some bad boys.

"Well now, if you want bad boys . . ." Fred told them they came to the right spot, sliding over and making room in the booth, Paula sitting next to him, Dolores next to Alvin. Fred asking what was their pleasure, motioning to Dutch for a round of drinks. Smiling at Alvin, Dolores said her name, Alvin asking if it was true, about them coming down here to meet some bad boys.

"Why, you know some?" Dolores looked him over.

"Well now, depends on how bad you want?"

"Medium bad, I guess, not real mean, I mean cold-hearted, but they got to be interesting."

"And cute," Paula threw in.

"Well, you see anybody in here fitting the bill?" Fred asked, feigning a look around the place, saying, "Looks like a quiet night, just Dutch behind the bar, and he's spoken for, so I guess you're stuck talking to us, that or the old bum at the bar."

"By bad, how bad you mean?" Dolores said, smiling and playing along.

"Well, we rob banks, so I guess we pass muster." Alvin smiled from one to the other. "But let me ask, what do you girls do?"

"Me? Well, I hawk ladies' things at Frank Murphy's, downtown at 5th, everything from dainties to hats. Maybe I shouldn't tell you that, in case you come by to rob the place."

"That give you a thrill?"

"I don't thrill so easy." Raising her brow, Dolores looked at him, meaningful and smiling, and he was liking her straight off.

"So, let's say I walk in, say stick 'em up . . ." Alvin said. "Tell you to show me the cash box."

"That your best line, stick 'em up?"

"Never thought of it as a line, but maybe I'd come up with something better."

"Like what?"

"Well, what fun is it, if I tell you now?"

"Well, I wouldn't know what you'd expect me to stick up, but I guess you can try." Dolores shrugged, taking his glass and sipping from it, saying it was real nice.

Fred said to Paula, "How about you, you work there too?'

"Me, no."

"So, what do you do?"

"Mostly, I get lonely."

"But not at some place of employ?"

"Me, I'm a widow, stare out of windows."

"Well, I'm sorry for your loss, I mean . . ." Fred said, looking around, seeing where Dutch was, wanting to order more drinks.

"Yeah, losing Charlie was awful, but he left me snug. It's no secret. Sorry if it's not what you want to hear. Guess I come off hard-hearted."

"Just hard to see you as the widow type."

"You don't believe it?"

"Well, you're young for it, but I believe about your husband being departed and all . . ." Fred said, then trying to show a soft side. "How did it happen, he get sick all of a sudden? If it ain't too painful . . ."

"He got shot."

Fred looked at her, not sure if she was pulling his leg.

"You ever hear of Charlie Harmon? If you're bad as you say, maybe you know of him?"

"The Charlie Harmon worked with Dillinger?" Fred said, looking poleaxed.

"That's him. Poor Charlie — got shot running from some Wisconsin bank."

"Well, we never met, but, I'm real sorry for your loss," Fred said. "Leaving you on your own."

"Yeah, that's the worst for me, being on my own, but Charlie didn't leave me flat."

Catching Dutch's eye, Fred waved him over.

When Dutch went for their drinks, Alvin asked Dolores, "So, how are things at the Frank Murphy? Busy?" Trying to lift the mood.

"Boring."

"Boring, huh?"

"As heck."

Alvin thinking of more to say, Dolores saying, "But, my sis, Jean, went with this guy, Tommy, think he ran with Dillinger too." Shrugged like it was no big deal. "How the two of us met." Dolores wagged a finger at Paula.

"Maybe I heard of this Dillinger, and maybe he heard of us."

"How'd he hear of you?"

"Well, depends, can he read?" Alvin said.

"Oh, I bet he can. He's real smart."

"And cute as a button," Paul threw in.

Since that night he stopped pining for Dot, but still thinking he ought to call, promising to look her up, see that she was alright. Figuring his name showed up in the papers enough times, guessing Dot knew what he was up to, and put together why he hadn't come to see her.

"You up for a round, son?" Fred said now, pulling Alvin from his thoughts, leaning forward, his shirt sticking to his back, taking his glass and tossing the melted ice at a planter of ornamental grass.

"Guess I'm going dry."

Coming out the French doors, Kate sat in one of the lounge chairs, the girls inside, laughing and getting their make-up and hair just right, Paula getting in her swimsuit. Kate saying she was thinking they'd head for the Carolina Pines for supper, saying they had an all-you-can eat for sixty-five cents.

"That sounds fine, Ma, whatever you want," Fred said, then called into the open door, louder this time, "Said we got a couple men here in need of cooling off." Fred winked at Alvin, knowing how this would go.

"You're swatting the hive, my boy," Kate said.

Fred grinned.

"You need cooling off, baby?" Paula came to the door, looking hopeful, a seltzer bottle in hand, waited till Kate moved to the next chair, letting her get out of the way.

Dolores came behind Paula, shaking another seltzer bottle, eager and saying, "How about you, Ray darling, you want a cold one?"

"It was him that asked," Alvin said.

Sitting in wet and fizzing clothes, Alvin and Fred dripped soda. Fred grinned and said to Paula, "You keep acting up, girl, I'm gonna peel you naked, make you swim around bare-assed. How about that?"

"Like to see you try," Paula said, shutting and locking the door when he started to get up.

Fred banged on the glass, wanting that drink, Paula not letting him in till he promised to behave.

"You're the one doing the spraying and yelling, acting like a kid. Sure to get us kicked out of here."

Kate said she was going for a walk, getting up and looking less than impressed by their pranks, walking past the pool.

Watching her go, Alvin spotted George Nelson and his wife passing Kate at the deep end, saying their hellos and coming around the pool, guests they had been introduced to by William Graham last night, the manager flashing a veneer of respectability, known to offer shelter to anyone on the shady side of the law, getting his staff to put on a Mexican fiesta night that couldn't be beat: pozole followed by cañitas, tamales, pico de gallo, churros, a three-piece mariachi band playing, tequila and beer flowing.

George Nelson had come over with a plate of food in hand last night, said he picked up on their Midwest accents, found out who they were, telling them he hailed from the Windy City himself, said his true name was Lester Gillis, waiting for them to acknowledge it, like they ought to know who he was, adding, "What kind of bank robber goes around with a handle like Lester, more like a bank teller, am I right?" Taking a bite of pork, he said, "Back in school, kids turned it into a girl's name, but that only happened one time." Picking up a slice of papaya and biting into it.

Alvin figured George Nelson liked gassing to impress the women, drinking more of what the bartender called Mexican Firing Squad than he could handle, making a fool of himself, his eyes resting all the time on seventeen-year-old Dolores, moving on to Paula, up and down, then back to Dolores. All the while tipping his plate of food, chunks of meat and cheese falling off, his eyes glassy and his fingers greasy.

George telling Alvin the real reason he changed his handle was on account he was a one-time driver for what he called the boss of the dagos back in the Big Apple, got mixed up in some things there and ended up hitting a Chi-town bank with the Touhys before having to go on the dodge, bringing his wife, Helen, and their kid along.

"You confessing to something, George?" Fred had said, smiling.

"Saying it takes one to know one." George telling them he knew the look, admitted he'd seen their mugshots around, then setting his plate down before all of it spilled off, he told how he started out stealing tires before running shine, back before he was driving the dagos. Looking at them, saying if they had something going, maybe he was up for the work — said it like he was doing them a favor.

Alvin said, "Think you got us wrong, George." Telling him they were a couple of traveling lightbulb salesmen, on vacation with their wives, along with Fred's mother.

"Yeah, and I'm a Baptist preacher." George grinned.

"What makes you think so, Father?" Alvin said.

"Like I said, it's the look. A guy in the life sees another guy in it, there's no mistaking it. Just wondering if you got something going, is all. You don't want to say, that's fine, suit yourself."

"Guess we got to work on the look," Alvin said to Fred.

Now George was coming back — sober — and introducing them to his wife, Helen, shy-looking with dark-hair and a pretty face, about Dolores's age, a little taller, but without the curves.

"Sell any lightbulbs since last night?" George sat, drawing his chair close, blocking Alvin's sun as he did it. Didn't offer Helen a chair.

"Told you, maybe you don't remember, we don't mix work with pleasure," Alvin said, getting up and dragging a lounge over for Helen, offering her a seat.

"But, you been wondering about what I said, though?" George looked at him, his hand shielding his eyes.

"Except you didn't say all that much," Alvin said, sitting back down, looking at George.

"But, you're still wondering about it?"

Fred came out the doors with two drinks in hand, saying, "Hey, opportunity's come knocking again. George, right?"

"Yeah, that's right." George introduced Fred to Helen, saying, "Mistook you for a couple of guys interested in making a score, but if I got it wrong, I'll leave you to your lightbulbs."

"Have a drink, George." Fred slid him Alvin's glass, passing his over to Helen, calling inside for Paula to mix a couple more. Saying to George, "So, what counts as a score, son?"

"Ten grand sound good to you?" George said.

"Sounds like a start."

"I mean you got to set the bar, am I right?"

"You're still kinda dancing around, George," Alvin said.

"You want it plain? Okay, I'm talking about robbing a bank, right down here, the Riverside branch, you want particulars. Understand they got a safe stuffed like a holiday bird. How's that?" George had a sip, looking from man to man. "I mean, it's where the money is, the bank, am I right?"

"About the only place to find any these days," Helen said, like she was part of it.

George looked at her and frowned.

Dolores and Paula stepped through the doors, Dolores in yellow latex, Paula in a red silk-wool number, setting down more glasses. George introduced Helen to them, had to ask for their names again, forgetting them from last night. Paula sat on the side of Fred's lounger, George giving up his chair for Dolores, looking around for another chair, not finding one, so he just stood on one leg, his drink in hand.

Alvin watched him, thinking this sunburned guy could be talking shit, playing peacock for the ladies, a guy about his own age, a chubby face, a mouth drawn on in pencil, but there was something cold in the man's eyes.

Finishing the drink, George set the glass down, put a hand to the burn on his neck, saying, "My skin's wrong for this kind of sun." He motioned to Helen, saying, "Thanks for the dog soup. Maybe we'll catch you tonight, think they got some dance planned." Nodding to the ladies, helping Helen up, and they left.

"Think we offended him?" Fred said.·

"Think the man's full of feathers?" Dolores said.

"Could be." Alvin leaned back and tipped his boater back over his eyes, holding up his empty glass, saying to Dolores, "Honey, while you're up . . ."

"You want it with the seltzer?"

He kept jingling the glass, and she sighed, getting off the lounge, taking it from him, and Fred's too, going back inside, calling them a couple of fuddy-duddies.

"George got you thinking?" Fred said.

"Man said we got to set the bar higher."

"Sounds kind of low, I mean ten grand, come on. How long'd that last?" Fred smiled and ran his hand up and down Paula's back.

"Well, he's just starting out." Grinning from under the hat, Alvin got the feeling he hadn't seen the last of George Nelson.

... *Fairbury, Nebraska*
April 4, 1933

G len Johnson pressed the flesh with a man of ample proportions, putting on the friendly, saying, "Good to meet you, sheriff. And let me thank you again for seeing me."

"Well, good of you to come, Mr. Johnson," Sheriff Ackman said.

"Call me Glen, by all means." Following the good grip, Glen passed his card from the Federal Laboratories, Law Officers' Supply House, the logo in gold leaf, looking like an official badge. Saying in a low voice, like he was admitting to something, his dream had been to join law enforcement if it hadn't been for the trick knee, an old gridiron trauma. Throwing in he was doing his bit working for the company, getting high-grade firepower into the right hands, those of the brave men who served in blue. Making the appointment, following a lead that the department was looking to boost its firepower, Sheriff Emil sounding keen on the horn, though giving Glen the usual fair warning he was likely to run head-on into grief from town council about frittering away funds, reminding him of it now. "Tell you these office stiffs got short hands and deep pockets."

"My pleasure, and no pressure. Happy to talk Thompson guns all day long, Sheriff."

"Emil." Tucking the card in a pocket, the sheriff's eyes dropped to the two maslin cases Glen reached for, each two feet long. "No violin case?" He grinned.

"Wouldn't fit, maybe a trombone case. What I got here's the special police case, ones I'm hoping to be leaving with you," Glen said, watching the sheriff turn his neck to the footfalls of a lanky officer coming down the hall.

"Oh, this here's Deputy Wes Davidson, my strong right hand, and a true whiz at math," Emil said. "Asked him to sit in."

"Well, now . . ." Setting down one of the cases, Glen shook hands with this rawboned farm boy in uniform, looked like he just graduated high school, a face once ravaged by acne, the scars leaving an old battlefield. The two of them exchanging good-to-meet-yous and how-are-yous. Glen being told to call him Wes.

"Fore we get to it, what say to coffee, Glen?" Emil clasped his padded hands together.

"An eye opener'd sure hit the spot, Emil," Glen said, being agreeable.

"I'll see to it." Wes said it like a man who knew his place, making a military about-turn, striding back down the tiled hall.

"That young fellow's gonna make a fine lawman," Emil said.

"Can see he's got the right mentor," Glen said.

"Oh, and see about a sweet tray, will you, Wes," Emil called after him.

"Will do, sheriff." Wes waved a hand, turning into a door down the hall.

"We're down here." Emil led Glen the other way, toward the rear of the courthouse.

"This place sure is something," Glen said, looking along the marble corridor, the oak detail and beamed ceiling, portraits of statesmen along both walls, looked like they were staring down with discernment, like they were watching out for the city coffers, seeing funds didn't get frittered away.

"Yeah, the home of some fine townsfolk over the years, that's for sure. You can set up in here, Glen." Pushing open an ornate glass door to a darkened boardroom, Emil held it and let him enter first, feeling along the wall for the light switch.

"Appreciate it," Glen said, stepping in and setting the cases next to the long board table, taking in the view from the window, looking out onto 5th. A *Vote Today* banner spanned over the street, townsfolk bustling between moving cars, a stone and pillared bank on the opposite corner. "Sure is a busy place — voting today, huh?"

"Yes sir. Local election's got folks flapping, all anybody's talking about — who's it gonna be, Buckley or Grimes? You think it'd be about going dry or wet, but around here the hot topic's letting the Bonham open on Sundays; that's our theater." Emil shook his head. "You ask me, it'll be a landslide for Buckley, the man knowing to lean to the wet and leaving the Bonham as she is, setting Sundays aside for church, the way the good Lord meant it. But, I tell you we got townsfolk here, can't get enough of Wallace Beery the rest of the week."

"Now, that man's sure something," Glen agreed.

"Well, Wallace is Wallace, but Jesus still rules on Sundays, least round here."

"Of course he does. Lots of other places too."

"You seen *The Champ*? Well now, do yourself a favor 'cause it's a heck of a moving picture. And if you know the name, how about that Lupe Vélez? I seen her in *Hot Pepper*, and man oh man. That gal's one sure spitfire and a talent to boot, and I'd say more'n that, except . . ." Showing his wedding band and grinning. Sobering his look, Emil said, "You staying at the Mary-Etta?"

"Just like you told me on the blower. And sure looking forward to that supper of prime rib, all you can pack away the way I understand it."

"Walsh and Kerr put out a good spread, though two bucks a night's a touch steep, but, if you come hungry enough, you can make a bargain of it. And if you're looking for something to do while supper settles, think they're running *Hot Pepper* at the Bonham."

"Well, thanks for the pointer, Emil. Think that's exactly what I'll do. Prime rib and a good picture." Glen nodded, no idea about local affairs, and he didn't know Wallace Beery from Jackie Cooper, or Lupe Vélez from Greta Garbo. Just happy to find some common ground, saying, "And, way I understand it, we're a few short miles from where Wild Bill made his bones."

"Oh, where's my head." Emil palming his forehead, saying, "Sure don't want to pass that up."

Something Glen had looked up before he drove down here, hoping for a good ice-breaker, reading up about the Hickok legend: the sometimes lawman, sometimes outlaw, mostly legend.

"More'n seventy years back, yes sir," Emil said. "Went down just west of here, place called Rock Creek Station. Wild Bill getting on the wrong side of old man McCanles. Working as a stockman and barely shaving back then. And old man McCanles being a reputed son of a gun, drinker, card player and general nuisance. Anyway, legend goes the old man kept joking at the local watering hole where Bill tended bar, going on how the young fella had the look of a girl, told the boys at the rail to watch out when they bent to dust a boot, calling him Duck Bill on account of the younger man's nose, had a size to it. But, going along and being good-natured, Bill just shrugged it off. And likely on account of his youth, Bill went and took a flyer at McCanles's old lady, on the theory a man with a big honker had other parts that fit the bill, pardon the pun. And he went around making no secret of it, the tryst, I mean, showing he gave no cause for the boys at the rail to worry about bending and dusting a boot. Wasn't long till McCanles got wind young Bill was shooting twixt wind and water, some saying he came with six riders, but in truth he rode in with two thugs he hired and called Bill out."

Glen smiled, the sheriff getting into it.

"McCanles tells him he better lay the broom down and go strap on an iron, that is if he wanted a chance to show he wasn't just a stack of taradiddles. Told one of his boys to swing around back, keeping watch in case the kid went in and ran out that way.

"Wild Bill says to him, 'You got me all wrong, old man. I ain't running from you.'

"McCanles tells him then here's his chance, boy, go and strap on a pistol.

"'Be one less son of a bitch when I do.'

"McCanles grins at him and says he'll be right there waiting.

"When Bill comes back strapped, the old man points out, 'Seeing there's three of us . . .' and asks what he wants put on his marker. Tells one of his boys to take a pencil and write it down. Young Bill says he can count as good as he shoots, then tells McCanles to worry about his own marker. Asks if he wants his last minute to tell his man what to write down. And like that, McCanles pulls, and Wild Bill goes like lightning and clears all three saddles." Sheriff Emil jerked up a finger gun, going, *"Pow, pow, pow."* Telling it like he was proud, saying, "Past that day nobody called Wild Bill 'Duck Bill' ever again. No sir, a legend born from then on, till he met his own misfortune, shot in the back by the coward Jack McCall. But, that's a story for another day."

"Must've been something, those times," Glen said. "And I bet Wild Bill could've used one of these." Slapping one of the maslin cases, Glen was ready to get down to business, lifting it and setting it on the table.

"Not that man, not if there's an ounce of truth in what's been handed down," Sheriff Emil said, watching Glen slide back the bolts, opening it and revealing a shining Thompson gun on navy velveteen lining.

"Well, maybe not that man, no, but these days the lawless seem better armed than the law, wouldn't you say, Emil?"

"That's the God's truth." Shaking his head about it.

Glen lifted the weapon from the case, holding it up, saying he was sad about a few of these getting in the wrong hands, attained by illegal means, his company only selling through lawful channels. Holding it up, saying, "This here's the 21AC. What we call the anti-bandit gun." Glen swung its barrel above the window, letting the sheriff take it in. "Comes with the police model hard case, clip, and C-type drum. Safest thing to shoot in the street."

"The criminal model come in a crook case?"

Glen smiled at the joke, not the first time he heard it, guessing from the look this lawman was halfway sold. Taking his time and going over the operating modes, showing the selective fire setting from semi to auto, explaining how the bolt gets held rearward by the sear when cocked. "You just pull the trigger, and the bolt's released, travels forward — see — chambers, and she fires till you ease the trigger, or till you're out of .45-cal ammo. And no chance of cook-off with this baby, no sir." Glen offered it to Emil.

"Heard it called a Chicago Organ Grinder." Emil grinned, taking it and running a hand along its smooth wood stock.

"Yeah, I heard that one. And the Chicago Typewriter, and the Chopper."

"They call it that?" The sheriff grinned.

"Sure. And the Annihilator, and in the service they call it the Trench Broom . . ." Glen Johnson smiled, sensing the sale. "Got lots of names for her. You come up with some of your own, I'd sure like to hear'em." Giving him time to look it over, then saying, "She takes a twenty-to-thirty-round magazine. You see here, feeds ammo into the chamber at six to seven hundred and twenty-five rounds a minute."

The sheriff giving a low whistle. "My, that's sure something."

Glen saying, "Let's see Dillinger come to your town, huh, sheriff?"

Catching himself, Emil got to business, asking, "How much you say?"

Deputy Wes came in with a tray: carafe, cups, creamer, sugar bowl and a dish of butter cookies. Setting it down, saying the cookies were fresh-baked, then, "That's it, huh?" Kid-at-Christmas eyes on the weapon.

The sheriff pawed a cookie, and Glen bent for the second case, setting it next to its twin on the boardroom table, unlatching it, saying, "This one's the 21A, one the company calls the Persuader."

"That's a good handle too," the sheriff said, his mouth full of crumbs.

"Works on a belt-feed system," Glen said. "Delivers better'n fifty rounds at the same firing rate." Repeating the specs for the deputy, flipping up the leaf sight.

Taking another cookie, holding it in his teeth, the sheriff passed the 21AC to the deputy, taking the 21A. Told Glen to help himself.

"Looks homemade," Glen said, eyeing the cookies.

"Yeah, Butterworth's up the street, best bakery in the county. You go on, get fixed up," the deputy said, taking the weapon from him and hefting it, looking it over. "Whew, she's lighter than she looks, huh?"

"But, like a force in your hand," Glen said, biting into a cookie and pouring coffee, asking, "Anybody else?"

"How much you say?" Emil asked again, waving off the coffee.

"The AC goes for two twenty-five, and comes with the Cutts Compensator." Clearing his throat, Glen explained it had a muzzle brake and recoil control. "Company usually tacks on an extra twenty-five for the option, but today — let's call it two hundred even for the 21A, of course, assuming you'll take both these babies off my hands . . . and order a couple more." Pouring coffee in his cup.

"Two hundred, huh?" Emil gave another low whistle.

Letting the figures sink in, Glen added milk from the creamer, saying, "Both come with the case, cleaning rod and a box magazine. And for a mere five extra, I'll let you have the fifty-round drum, or an extra three for the twenty-round."

Emil trying to do the math in his head.

"Size of your department? How about I put you down for these plus the rest on back order? Have them in two months." Glen pressed the sale, guessing that's the kind of stretch the department was good for, adding, "At that, I'm authorized to toss in the spare drums. A sixty-dollar savings right there." Glen getting set to give his General John T. Thompson speech: the true-blue American inventor, holding the founder right up there with Edison, Franklin and Bell, or in this case, an American great like Wild Bill. Taking the 21A from the deputy, Glen field-stripped it, did it in no time after the hours of practice, making it look like child's play, demonstrating the ease of breaking it down, detaching the stock and sliding off the lower receiver — something the company made its sales team practice a dozen times every week like a field drill after the office meeting. Pointing out the internal parts as he did so, Glen explained how to clean and oil it.

"Piece of cake, but still a real chunk of money," Emil said, sighing and taking another cookie, ready to play hardball, looking at the deputy for backup. "What do you say, Wes?"

"Sounds like a bunch alright, sheriff." The younger man overfilled a cup with coffee, the saucer catching the overflow.

"The price of keeping the voters safe, wouldn't you say, Emil?" Glen said, smiling and showing how to feed cartridges into the drum, sliding in live rounds, saying, "Now, if you gents have the time and a spot in mind, how about we go set up some tins, and take these babies for a little spin? That is, if you got enough tin cans around." He kept feeding rounds.

Emil grinned, and Glen knew he had a sale, stopped loading the drum, taking his cup and saucer, fingers pinching the tiny handle, washing the cookie down.

A sound like a pistol shot from outside, and the three looked at each other, Glen coughing up coffee, the sheriff smiling, chalking it up to a truck backfiring.

Then another shot, followed by a woman's scream — then all hell broke loose. Auto fire and shattering glass, the sounds coming from somewhere outside.

Fuddled a moment, Sheriff Emil considered it part of Glen's pitch, the scream and rip of fire changing his mind, snapping him out of it.

A clerk rushed down the hall, stopping at the door, panting and blurting, "The bank's getting robbed!" Then he turned and was gone.

"The hell with the tin cans, son." Emil snatched the assembled Tommy gun, reaching in Glen's case for a drum, trying to set it on the way he'd been shown, shoving it at Glen, saying, "Fast as you've ever done it, son."

Glen snapped the drum in place, trying to tell him it was unloaded as the sheriff went charging out the way the clerk had gone.

Lightning fast, Glen reassembled the 21A, setting and aligning the trip, sear and lever in the frame, inserting the pivot plate, setting the safety on FIRE, positioning the rocker.

Deputy Wes reached for it.

"Didn't clear you on it, son." Glen twisted it away from him, setting in a loaded box magazine, taking the last cookie in his teeth and hurrying out after the sheriff.

"Hey, hold on — you're a citizen, Mr. Johnson," the deputy called, nothing to do but hurry after him. "And those weapons are the property of —"

"Not till I see a check." Glen ran down the marble hall, charging down the rear staircase, the sheriff ahead of him, moving fast for a big man.

... *Fairbury, Nebraska*
April 4, 1933

C hecking his watch ahead of nine a.m., Alvin looked up at the election banner spanned across the main drag, reminding citizens to vote, thinking they would have more on their minds before this day was done.

Wheeling the Chevy, Fred passed the stately stone courthouse, looked over at him, saying, "Hope they don't forget to vote."

Ahead of them, Jess Doyle parked the hot Buick out front of the First National. Pulling in behind, Fred turned to Earl Christman and Volney Davis in back, a man new to the gang. Earl clipped the stick magazine on the Tommy gun, Volney with the sawed-off and double-aught buckshot, both nodding they were set.

Doc, Jelly Nash and the other new man Eddie Green got out of the Buick, Doc and Jelly going straight inside. Eddie stood in front of the doors across from the courthouse, Earl Christman outside the other, both holding Tommy guns low under jackets. Jess staying behind the wheel of the Buick, kept it running and ready, his eyes on the cars, his .45 next to him on the seat.

Inside, Doc and Jelly stepped in front of the teller cages, Doc raising his pistol, letting the tellers know he was making a sizable withdrawal.

A woman dropped in a faint like she'd been shot. Alvin and Volney rounded the employees and early-morning customers, forcing them face down on the marble at the side wall. Doc got the reeling woman to her feet, helping her to lie down next to the others.

Alvin watched Jelly go behind the cages, went to work emptying the teller drawers, then he followed Fred.

Leading the assistant manager by the elbow, Fred stuck his revolver into the man's ribs, advising, "You be quick opening the vault, and maybe you make it."

The man bit his lip and shook his head, saying, "I'm not entrusted, mister. Only the manager knows the numbers. And he's not here."

Fred looked at Alvin, shook his head, reading the man's name on the tag, Frank Nelson, saying, "You a married man, Frank?"

"Yes sir, I am, but I —"

"Well, you keep lying to me, Frank, and I bet they'll throw you a dandy service, you leaving a widow and differing stains on this fine floor. Now, I'll start the count." Fred racked the pistol, giving him a deadpan look. "One . . . two . . ."

Alvin doing nothing to stop him, watching a stain spread across the man's trousers, Frank Nelson fumbling the combination, turning the dial right, left, then right again, pulling on the thick door, slumping when it opened with a clank.

Grabbing him and straightening the man, Fred pushed him in ahead, taking a sack from a pocket, and telling him,

"Fill it, and no more of your horse shit, you understand me, Frank?"

Frank nodded, doing like he was told.

Alvin looking around, seeing nothing got left behind, hearing a pistol shot, then another, followed by a burst of auto fire out in the street.

Yanking Frank Nelson by his tie, Fred made him carry the sack, shoving him toward the exit, saying, "Got one more job for you, Frank."

Alvin following them, seeing Jelly Nash holding his pistol on the ones on the floor, Fred pushing Frank Nelson for the exit.

Alvin and Volney got on either side of the door. All of them going out behind the hostage, guns and sacks in hand, Volney guarding their retreat. People yelling and running in the street, cars honking, jammed along 5th.

Jess Doyle was up on the Buick's running board, his pistol aimed across the roof. Eddie Green and Earl Christman stood in the street, like traffic cops with Tommy guns, the traffic stopped in both directions.

The two of them seeing the three men rushing down the courthouse steps, running at them across the open lawn, the sheriff and another man wielding Tommy guns. The sheriff yelling and dry firing an empty weapon. Coming at a dead run, the deputy fired his pistol, the one in the suit letting go a burst from his Thompson.

Alvin ducked down as Earl Christman grunted and stumbled, folding over, his weapon clattering to the pavement. Jess Doyle firing from the Buick's running board.

Eddie Green returned a spray of fire, hitting the deputy, sending him stumbling for cover, the next burst aimed at the man in the suit, the Tommy gun dropping from the man's hands as he fell.

Getting behind the Chevy, Alvin looked up and took a

shot, the sheriff tossing away the empty Tommy gun, heaving himself behind a stopped car. The driver inside, on the floor, yelling for him to get away from the car. Rising behind the fender, the sheriff unholstered his sidearm, used the hood for leverage and chanced a shot in Alvin's direction, then ducked and moved, using the next car for cover, trying to get better vantage, firing again from behind the panel of a Dodge van, now aiming at the men crouched by the bank, hitting the stone wall above them, then taking out a window. Jess Doyle fired from the Buick, keeping him pinned down.

Looking at his wounded partner, Eddie tillered Earl Christman toward Fred's Chevy, Earl clutching his side, his hands red, blood dripping onto his pants, his shoes leaving bloody tracks.

Covering them from the bank entrance, Doc fired at the sheriff behind the van, putting rounds into the van's side panel, flattening a tire, shooting out its windshield, a delivery man inside on the floor yelling for help. Doc reaching in a pocket, slapping in his extra clip.

Uniforms came on the run along E Street, four of them, sending fire from a new direction. Alvin seeing the cops were cutting off their escape, running past the election sign. Calling to Fred, he darted back into the bank, grabbing the first cashier from the floor, steering her out the door, saying, "What's your name, doll?"

Her mouth trembled, the woman saying she was Olive.

"Thanks for the dance, Olive. Just follow my lead." Clamping a hold on her arm, he looked up and down the street, saying, "You do like I tell you, and you'll live. You get that?" Yelling to the cops, "I got a hostage here!"

More pistol fire, and glass smashing behind them, shards raining down. Olive forced herself to move, tears running down her cheeks.

Holding Frank Nelson in front of him, Fred caught movement to his left, the bank's security guard crawling from behind one of the cages, the man going for his holstered sidearm. Twisting Frank Nelson in front of him, Fred yelled to Alvin, and he fired through the glass door, sending the guard diving back behind the counter. Keeping his fist on Frank's necktie, Fred gave Alvin time to get his hostage to the car, the security guard rising from behind the cage, trying for another shot. And Fred shot him through the broken glass. The security man spun and dropped to the floor. Fred tugging Frank Nelson, turning him for the Chevy, keeping him on his toes and off balance. The cops coming from E Street fired in spite of the hostages.

They roughed the two hostages, Alvin getting in and forcing Olive up on the running board of the Chevy. Fred moving around the front, shoving Frank Nelson ahead of him, the man struck in his shoulder, Fred keeping him from falling. Getting behind the wheel, he forced the bleeding man on the running board, yelling out he had a hostage.

The gang piled in the cars, lead zipping around them, horns blaring and people ducking in the crowded street. Cops shouting for them to give it up.

Bucking the Buick between cars stopped in either direction, Jess Doyle plowed up the center line, banging on his horn, waving his pistol for the cars to get out of the way, firing into a truck's radiator. The driver twisting his wheels, mashing into the car next to him, making room. More cars tried to angle out of the way, Jess plowing down the center like he was making a new lane, scraping the fender of an ice truck, the young driver turning into the car next to him, making space.

Easing Earl Christman across the backseat of the Chevy, Eddie climbed in after him, blood streaked across the seat. Setting on another fifty-round drum, he turned on the seat and kicked out the rear window as Fred drove, following the Buick's path, his left hand holding Frank the banker by the shirtfront. Eddie fired a burst into the packed street, the squad of cops coming behind them returned fire, didn't matter about the hostages on the running boards. The election sign falling onto the cars in the street.

Olive screamed, struck in her hip, falling from the passenger side running board, crawling and dragging herself to the sidewalk. Fred keeping hold of Frank Nelson, steering with his free hand. Frank Nelson was hit again above the elbow, pleading to be released. Fred let go without looking at him fall. Putting both hands on the wheel, he stayed on the Buick's tail, losing a headlight against the ice truck's wood panel, the Buick ahead scraping metal, its side mirror knocked off, Jess forcing his way between abandoned cars, his tires spinning and smoking, shoving them apart.

Leaning out the passenger side, Alvin fired across the roof at the sheriff, the man moving along with them, using cars for cover, firing back.

Ahead, Jess was forced to slow out front of a medical building, waving his pistol, getting a driver to pull out of the way. The man throwing up his arms, having no place to go.

Jess put one through his windshield, aimed at him, his eyes wild, sweat on his face, desperate to get out of there, yelling, "That your last word?"

The man cranked his wheel and bucked his car into the one next to his, shoving his foot on the pedal, using the horsepower, twisting metal, screeching rubber.

Doc and Jelly Nash jumped out, grabbing two women huddled by a wall, knocking away grocery sacks and forcing them on the running boards on either side of the Buick, Doc telling the one he grabbed, "Think of the story you got for the supper table." Jelly yelling back at the cops, they had hostages.

Jess Doyle squeezed past a Dodge fresh off a sales lot, scraping its paint, twisting its fender. Doc yanking his hostage against the door, kept her from being crushed against the Dodge.

Banging past the Dodge, Jess bulldozed his way out — no way he was going to be taken.

"I got you." Doc held the woman and kept her from falling. Sheet metal crumpling as Jess rammed a Madame X, peeling its bumper half off, getting clear of the Cadillac, the road clear enough for him to drive out of town, one wheel wobbling, steam and a clunking sound coming from under the hood, the front bumper twisted like a steer's horn, the Chevy right on his tail.

Firing a last shot at the running sheriff, sending him diving for cover, Alvin leaned over the rear seat, looking at Earl Christman, the man curled up and moaning, his shirt soaked with blood.

Reaching boxes of roofing nails from the floor, Eddie Green shook them out the shot-out rear window.

Alvin telling Earl, "We're getting you to a sawbones." Having no idea where to find one, firing another round out the window, the sheriff running between the path of cars, pistol in his hand, trying to get a clear shot. Eddie Green holding the Tommy gun out the window, the sheriff dropping behind a car as Eddie fired. Fred driving them out of there.

A mile out of town, hearing no sound of pursuit, Jess stopped the ailing Buick, thanked the hostages and told them to count their lucky stars. Then Jess drove on, fluid dripping from underneath the Buick, the battered Chevy following, leaving the two women in a cloud of dust and fumes.

Fred flashed his lights and signaled the Buick a few miles farther, his engine on its last gasp, his oil gauge red-lining, pulling to the shoulder near someplace called Odell. The

Buick was a wreck, the Chevy not much better, but still able to drive. Alvin and Eddie checked on Earl as Jess Doyle and Jelly Nash went looking for another car.

Taking the whiskey flask from the glove compartment, Alvin drank and passed it to Eddie. Eddie taking a gulp, stripping off his own shirt and soaking a patch, packing it against Earl's wound. Earl twisting and grimacing at the sting. Alvin getting the syringe of morphine they carried in the glove box, leaning over the seat, telling Eddie to make a fist. Finding a vein, he shoved the needle in, looking in Earl's eyes, seeing the pain ease, a dreamy look in the man's eyes.

"Get Abby my share," is all Earl said.

"Get it to her yourself, you'll be fine," Eddie Green said, looking at the others, having his doubts.

Alvin saying, "We'll get him to Verne Miller's." Praying Verne knew a doctor working off the books. Not saying the man lived south of Kansas City, about two hundred miles away, not sure Earl had that long.

Seemed like forever, Jess and Jelly returning with a Ford, stolen from a nearby ranch building, Doc getting in with them. Fred pushing the Chevy, following the Ford, keeping it at about seventy, looking at Alvin, taking a pull from the flask and passing it across the seat to Eddie, saying, "How much you think we got?"

"Think I was counting?" It registered his hands were shaking, Alvin glancing back at Earl, blood streaked across his chest and stomach.

"A hell of a score, that's for sure," Fred said, passing him the flask. "Could be we topped Dillinger this week, maybe Floyd too." Keeping his eyes on the road, his foot hard on the pedal.

Alvin turned to him, his partner talking like he was keeping score.

Fred pushed it, driving behind the Ford as fast as he could get the Chevy to go, the engine grinding, not sounding right. Earl Christman drifting in and out of consciousness.

. . . *St. Paul, Minnesota*
April 6, 1933

The sacks were stacked behind the cellar's boiler, Alvin figuring his share of the cash and bonds at over a hundred and fifty grand, tallying it to what he had stashed in a few places, bank accounts under different aliases he used, some in stocks he kept in deposit boxes, bought into a business, owning shares in an apartment block, a management company running it, considering himself a rich man, with more than enough to last his days.

It was time to minimize the risks, time to consider making easy money without the chance of getting killed before he could spend it — remembering the Lindbergh kidnapping the year before. Whoever grabbed the kid got away with fifty grand without a shot fired, but those guys were dumb. Leaving a dead infant made them the most hated pariahs on the planet, law enforcement never going to stop the hunt till they were put down. The kind of people Alvin would kill himself. Right now, he needed a couple of easy scores, then he'd disappear for good and fade from the lawman's memory.

If you pull a kidnap, grab somebody deserving it — not a kid, and somebody worth more than fifty grand, a lot more. Alvin thinking about who deserved it, going back to his bootlegging days, the distillers and brewers who got rich selling it out the back door, dealing with runners and speakeasies, quick to turn their backs on old friends after the repeal of prohibition, going back to running things by the book.

He came up with a couple of names, guys who deserved to be pinched and squeezed, then he was thinking again back to the time he got hitched to Dot. Dorothy Ellen Slayman just seventeen in the fall of '31, the girl he met at her aunt's massage parlor, the girl working after school, greeting the rich men and introducing them to the ladies. Alvin thinking of some of those rich men, politicians and lawyers, all of them worth a bundle. He remembered coming in the door of her aunt's place that first time, and she asked what he was after. Looking in her dark eyes, Alvin saying he liked what he saw. Dot smiling, telling him she wasn't on the menu. "Well, that's good then. So, when I say let's go to a picture show, bet you can get time off."

She admitted she could, but didn't care to waste it with the type that came in here. Promising she wouldn't be wasting it, he asked if she'd seen *The Big House*, not taking no for an answer, and asking when she got off, coming back with flowers and escorting her to the Odeon, buying candy sticks and sodas, acting the gent, not even trying to hold her hand when he walked her back. Dot allowing a kiss at the back stoop of the massage parlor, putting a hand on his chest and pushing him back, saying, "Told you, I'm not one of the girls." With that she gave him a smile and went in the door, turning the lock, leaving him standing, not getting a chance to ask her out again.

Alvin was back the next afternoon, a fistful of daisies in hand, inviting her to go for a drive. Telling her he borrowed a car for the occasion, explaining there was a nice spot where they could catch the sunset by the lake. She told him she didn't get off till late, sighing when he gave her a hangdog look, and she went and talked to her aunt, came back with her jacket and got in his car, Alvin driving to the spot, the two of them talking and watching the sun go down, drinking beer for the first time in her life, and liking it. And liking him too. All of it going well till the ride home, the two of them getting pulled over in the hot Dodge. The cop coming up behind them, whooping the siren and flashing the cherry light. Alvin trying to explain that he just borrowed the car, only did it without asking. The cop had him open the trunk, Alvin popping it, looking at a box of mantel clocks, said he'd never seen them before. Dot coming to his appearance before the judge, vouching for his character, telling the judge she believed Alvin borrowed the car, that he had no idea it was stolen, or anything about the clocks in the trunk. Telling the judge her young man just wanted to impress her on their date, asking if the judge remembered his own salad days, declaring this was the man she intended to marry, promising she would set him straight, asking the judge to tie the knot right then, showing she was serious. But, the judge wasn't buying it, Dot asking if she could approach the bench, have a word in private. When she stepped back, the judge told the court he reconsidered, this being an upstanding young woman, one that showed the correct measure of moxie, the kind needed to steer this young man straight, better than any house of corrections could. And it was his belief she could turn the accused around, then explained to her this was criminal court, looking from Alvin, then back to her, pointing his gavel toward the clerk's office, sighing as he looked down at him, the kind of hood he'd seen a hundred times, asking him, "Do you intend to marry this girl, son?"

"Well, if you ain't locking me up, judge . . . then yes sir, I do."

The judge handed down what he called "leniency," a year of probation, and dismissed the case. Dot thanking him for guiding her fiancé down the aisle of the straight and narrow, taking Alvin by the arm and leading him from the courtroom. Alvin trying to figure how she just spared him from the reformatory, asking what she whispered to the old goat. Dot saying, "All I said was I recognized him from my auntie's, only he wasn't wearing no robe then."

Both of them going to a back room at her aunt's place, getting high on Eli Lilly extract, a cannabis potion that promised to work wonders as an antispasmodic, a sure poison if you exceeded the one drop, at least that's what she told him. With a sly look, she said it was her way of living on the edge, revealing another side to herself.

Alvin read the label, saying, "Eighty percent alcohol, well, that ain't too bad." Taking a good swig and passing her the bottle, putting a Charlie Poole platter on her aunt's Victrola, the two of them dancing to the North Carolina Ramblers, then to Louis Armstrong and his Hot Five. Dot hooking his arm the next day, and dancing him up the city hall steps. The two of them grinning through the ceremony.

Renting them a place in Chicago, Alvin believed he could settle down and go straight, maybe not that day, but likely the next, the newlyweds having a chance at a regular life. One day drifting into the next, drinking plenty of the Eli Lilly extract, taking her out most nights until his money went below the waterline, seeing his income was no match for his intended lifestyle.

Getting cleaned up and into pressed clothes, he went to find work, just wasn't much out there since the big crash. And when he did find day work, mostly stocking or loading, he came home dirty and tired with little to show. Dot becoming frustrated, calling what they had was holy monotony, having to go back to greeting customers at her aunt's parlor just to help make their rent.

Smiling at her that morning when he said he was going on the road, promising to be back by Christmas with his pockets full, setting out on his own, breaking in and robbing places with a fierceness. Getting arrested and thrown into prison. Nearly two years since that day, Alvin was seeing the outlaw life wasn't a good match-up for the married one, sorry for letting her down, and what he put her through.

Since the killing of Sheriff Kelly in West Plains, he couldn't risk going to see her at all, suspecting the cops likely made him and had her place staked out, expecting him to show up, dire and lovesick. But since meeting Dolores Delaney, and having his head turned around once more, Alvin put off thoughts of going to see Dot at all, feeling bad about it, writing her a couple of times, telling her it was too dangerous, sending along some money to help her out, never leaving a return address. Wondering how she felt about him now, promising to go see her some day and explain things, tell her he was sorry for making a mess of their married life, maybe send her the dollar to file for divorce if she wanted, and that would be that.

Pulling himself from his thoughts, he tugged the stopper from the bottle he took from the Green Lantern, and he went to the front room and poured three shots in a line, sliding one Fred's way, the Tommy gun with the drum magazine propped against a cushion at his back. Passing the other glass to Eddie Green. Eddie keeping watch on the street out front of the low-rent place. Fred liking the apartment on account it had a back lane, networking with other lanes, the Chevy facing out and ready for a fast getaway.

They were quiet most of the day, waiting for Doc and the others to show up so they could make the split. When they did talk, it was of Earl Christman, and when they drank, they toasted the man, saying what a stand-up fellow he was. None of them expecting him to make it, gut shot the way he was. Alvin making the call to Verne in Kansas City that night and hearing Earl had passed that afternoon, Doc and Verne wrapping him in a sheet and burying him past some piney woods out back of Verne's property.

Alvin broke the silence now — maybe it wasn't the time to talk business, but he needed to get their minds off Earl, saying, "Dutch gave me a tip when I got the bottle . . . on the Fed Reserve, and I been thinking on it."

"What happened to kidnapping?" Fred said.

"Still working on that. Meantime there's this."

Fred and Eddie looked at him, both happy to put their attention on something other than Earl.

Alvin explained how the cash was transferred to banks by hand trucks. Just a courier, sometimes two, along with an armed guard or two. All they had to do was catch them napping.

Fred sipped from his glass, considering it. "Fed Reserve, huh?"

"We're pretty hot 'round here," Eddie said, lifting his glass, looking like he was set to jump, his eyes flashing to the window.

"The Fed Reserve's in Chicago," Alvin said.

"Hate that place and all them buildings, and the mob with their thumb in everything but the soup lines. Think I'll take my cut and lay low," Eddie said, looking at Fred. "If your brother ever shows."

"He'll show." Fred gave him a look, tired of Eddie's nerves, the man coming apart, sitting in back of the car, watching Earl Christman bleed.

Alvin stood and raised his glass, saying, "Well, here's to Earl, a fine fellow. O Lord, grant him eternal rest and let perpetual light shine on him. May his soul join the souls of all the faithful departed, through the mercy of God, rest in peace. Amen." With that, he slapped back his drink, and sank into the chair.

Fred and Eddie looked at him.

"Where'd you learn that?" Fred said.

"Been to church a time or two. Some of it stuck."

"Scares me thinking what goes on in that cabbage of yours." Fred refilled the glasses, wanting to hear more about the Fed Reserve.

"Trick's to waylay the guards. Dutch says there's usually two, armed to the teeth, so we need to get the drop."

"I guess it beats robbing a bank, with silent alarms, time-locks and cops jumping out of every place," Fred said.

Reaching his glass, Alvin was thinking kidnapping topped it all, still deciding on a fat pawn to bag.

... St. Paul, Minnesota
June 15, 1933

"A fraid you're gonna miss lunch with Mother," Doc said it matter of fact, stepping in front of the man and blocking his path, eyes behind dark glasses, wearing a navy suit from the McCallon job two years back.

Putting a hand on the man's chest, stopping William Hamm from going up the hill to his mansion, the gent smelling swell, decked in a homburg and a nicer suit than Doc had on. Came down the back stairs from his office, the head honcho wending his way to lunch with the matriarch, like he did every day.

"I beg your pardon?" Hamm's brows tried to knit, confusion in his eyes, yet he shook the outstretched hand.

"You're going to be begging for more than that, Willy. I promise you." Doc kept it friendly. "Okay if I call you Willy?" He smiled and clamped the hand tight, taking the man's elbow with his free hand, leading him from the side of Hamm's Brewery, away from the stone and arched windows, the name carved into the granite above the main entrance, a sign in the front window declaring *From the Land of Sky Blue Waters*.

"Do I know you, sir?" William Hamm tried to pull his hand back, but Doc was strong, and kept him wheeling and off balance.

"You're Willy Hamm, the prince of St. Paul," Charlie Fitzgerald said, coming from the shadows of trash cans behind the metal staircase, the same dark sunglasses and a low cap over his face. Charlie out to prove himself with the gang, had his hand out like he wanted to shake.

"Would someone kindly tell me —"

"I'll tell you this, Willy, that's one fine beer you put out," Charlie said, clapping him on the back, giving a light push. "Bet you sell it by the barrels."

"Thank you, yes, I suppose so."

Charlie had size, younger, but about the same height as Hamm, acting like he was glad to make the man's acquaintance, steering him by his other elbow, helping Doc lead him to the street.

"You do like we say, Willy, and we won't even rumple your suit," Doc said.

A dark Hudson rolled along Greenbrier, coming off Minnehaha, its brakes squeaking to a stop, Alvin behind the wheel, a pair of dark glasses and a cap pulled low.

"What do you men want?"

"What everybody wants, Willy, money, and a heck of a lot of it." Doc smiled good-natured, opening the rear door.

"You tried the bank?" William Hamm attempted to jerk his arm free, starting to get the meaning now, looked like he was making up his mind to put up a fight. Doc socked him in the kidney, easing him down.

"More times than you know, Willy," Alvin said, turning from behind the wheel as Charlie opened the door, watching them push Hamm inside. Alvin looking around to make sure nobody was watching.

William Hamm looked at the driver, like it dawned on him who it was in spite of the cap and glasses, the most wanted face from the papers. "You're that Dillinger!"

Doc and Charlie shoved him in back, both grinning.

Alvin frowned and turned, straightening behind the wheel.

"Watch your head, Willy," Charlie said, tossing the man's homburg to the floor, shoving him, forcing the man to step on his own hat.

Climbing in after him, Doc slipped a white hood over William Hamm's head. Charlie had a look around, convinced himself they hadn't been seen, and got in front, grinning to Alvin. "Piece of cake, huh, Jackrabbit?"

Putting the stick in gear, Alvin tossed off the cap and sunglasses, not liking the beer man, and starting to not like John Dillinger, the crook always showy, vaulting over bank counters, and letting little old ladies keep their savings, always playing the folk hero. The papers running his smiling mug, not mentioning he shot anybody who got in his way. Driving along Minnehaha, Alvin watched his speed, not drawing attention.

Hearing the man's heavy breathing under the cloth hood, Doc told Hamm to take it easy, had him get down on the floor. "No need to wet yourself, Willy, it's just routine."

"What the hell kind of routine?" Hamm tried to tug up the knees of his trousers, an awkward position on the floor between the seats, crushing his hat more.

"Folks see you, they'll get the wrong idea." Retrieving the bruised hat, Doc tapped it back into shape, trying it on, thinking it wasn't a bad fit. Saying to Charlie, "What do you think?"

"Looks better on him." Charlie said, then went back to looking out his window, making sure there was no pursuit.

"May I ask where you're taking me?" Hamm said.

"We got a nice spot, don't you worry. Ain't the Drake, mind you, but nothing's crawling round at night," Doc said.

"I'm being kidnapped?"

"There you go," Doc said, clapping Hamm on the back. "All you need to know for now, Willy. You're doing alright."

"No, I'm not alright. I need my pills, helps with my breathing."

"Well, you may as well ease up, just go like this." Doc drew a loud breath and let it out in a slow gush, saying, "Just see this as going for a ride, your chauffeur in front." Doc patted his back again, grinning at Alvin.

They drove thirty miles with Hamm hooded and kneeling on the floor, the man asking a couple more times where he was being taken, and what they wanted, not getting much of an answer. Finally saying he was going to be sick.

"Wouldn't recommend it, with the hood on and all," Doc said, rubbing the man's back.

With the St. Croix River in sight, Alvin pulled onto a side road, near the Wisconsin border, rolling over the clotted ground, tires spinning and slinging muck under the rockers, drawing opposite a parked Chevy Confederate, Fred waiting behind its wheel, flicking a cigarette out the window, two others they hired for the job: George Ziegler next to him, and Bryan "Red" Bolton in back. Ziegler, a one-time button man for Capone, came to work with the gang, saying he liked what he heard. Rumor was he and Bolton were in on the Valentine's Day hit of the North Side Gang back in '29, making them no strangers to Tommy guns.

Putting on Hamm's hat and his own dark glasses, Doc tugged off Hamm's hood — the man's eyes fluttering and adjusting to the light. Doc letting him catch some air and stretch his legs, leading him around in a circle, told him not to make eye contact with any of the boys.

Rolling down the window, Fred watched his brother walk the hostage around, saying to Alvin, "Man give you any trouble?"

"Man's a gelding, a true blue-blood gent."

George Ziegler got out, put on his cap and glasses and went to the Hudson as Doc got Hamm back inside.

Ziegler leaned in and said, "Got some papers need signing, Willy."

"Make it a habit not to sign anything without my attorney —"

"This look like that kind of situation?" Ziegler said.

Glancing at the typed notes demanding a hundred grand, Hamm raised his brows, saying, "I'm not worth that."

"Well, you best hope you're wrong." Ziegler frowned and handed him a pen, pointing where to sign.

"I'm not —"

Ziegler stabbed at the papers, saying, "Here . . . and here." Waiting till Hamm was done, Ziegler blowing at the ink, checking the signatures.

Doc saying, "You got a nice hand there, Willy."

"Thank you."

Ziegler taking a blank paper from the bottom of the stack, saying, "Now, write like I tell you, word for word. Ready . . . Dear Father — do it! If you're reading this, then I'm dead." Telling him a second time, holding up his hand like he'd slap him, waiting as Hamm wrote. The man crying. Checking it, Ziegler told him to sign this one too, then said, "Last thing, and the most important thing you got to get right, Willy . . . who you want for a contact man?"

"Why are you asking me?" Hamm having trouble with his breathing again.

"On account it's your funeral," Doc said, grabbing him hard by the arm, his sleeve catching on the man's wristwatch.

Hamm shook his head and tried to think, saying, "Billy Dunn, my vice-president of sales."

"Why not your mother?" Doc said, looking at the timepiece.

"She'll want to call the police."

"A good choice then," Ziegler said, checking the papers.

Doc grabbed the hood off the seat, Hamm holding his breath like he might drown. Doc putting the hood over his head as Ziegler headed back to the Chevy.

"Tell me about the watch, Willy," Doc said, looking at Alvin and shrugging, like he couldn't help himself.

"It was a gift from Mother." His shoulders sagging, Hamm sighing. "Guess it's yours now. That what you're saying?" Fumbling and unstrapping it, holding it up to Doc.

"I got a mother too, and she gives me things. Cooks like you can't believe," Doc said, got the hooded man back on the floor, then strapped on the watch, put it to his ear, then went on admiring it, saying, "Here's to mothers."

... *Bensenville, Illinois*
June 15, 1933

The vacant two-story sat two blocks off the main drag, the grounds unkempt, grass and weeds sprouting along its gravel drive. George Ziegler knowing the woman who inherited it, keeping it until someone wanted the land under it. Switching off the headlights, Alvin pulled the Hudson to the garage in back, weary after five hours behind the wheel. William Hamm was feeling worse, hooded and on aching knees on the rear floor, wheezing for air, the man not saying anything since signing the papers, like he was resigned to fate. Letting him out one more time to water the horses south of Chippewa Falls, allowing him to stretch his legs after they gassed up outside of Madison. The man looking like he aged a decade since they took him.

Backing the Chevy up behind the Hudson, Fred switched off the lights, a stand of apple trees blocking them from sight of the neighboring places. Doc pulled open the wood doors, Alvin rolling the Hudson into the garage, leaving Fred's car outside. Fred picked an apple off a tree, checked around as Alvin and Doc got Hamm up the sagging back stairs to the room with a boarded window. A bunk and a wobbly table passing for furniture, old copies of the *Saturday Post* on the floor.

Putting on the hat and glasses, Alvin led him in and tugged off Hamm's hood. "Here we are. How about a beer, Willy? We got Hamm's."

Shaking his head, Hamm said he was feeling ill, sagging onto the bunk, kept from looking up at Alvin.

"Well, you change your mind, you rap on the door, but not too loud, you understand?"

Hamm nodded.

"No calling out, no trouble, and we'll try it without the hood, but if you get cute . . ."

Hamm nodded again, saying he wasn't feeling cute.

"And you turn your head anytime we come in. You understand me?"

"Yes."

"Now, I'm going to fix some supper. You'll feel better if you eat, missing lunch with your ma. How you like your eggs?"

Hamm shook his head, saying, "Can't face an egg."

"Place don't come with room service. It's beans, or eggs, or both. And nothing else till breakfast. And then, the only thing's different is toast."

"An egg's fine then."

"Scrambled?"

He bobbed his head.

"Alright then." Closing the door, Alvin locked it from outside and went down the stairs.

Setting tin plates on the table, he worked a wooden spoon through the yolks and whites, tossing in a pinch of salt. The water in the pot of beans started its boil. Slicing up a tomato, adding a wedge to each of the plates, then slicing from a loaf of bread, serving it up, saying the clean-up belonged to Charlie.

"Why me?" Charlie said.

Alvin turned to him, saying, "'Cause you got picked."

"It come with an apron?" Charlie said.

Doc laughed, saying he had a French maid outfit on order.

Charlie saying he didn't figure he had the legs for it, but, yeah he'd do the damn clean-up.

Taking a beer from the icebox, Alvin scraped off the label with his thumbnail, not wanting Hamm to see a competitor's brand. Uncapping it, he set it on the tray, took it up the stairs. Hamm stared at the plate, but not up at the man. Alvin telling him he was doing fine.

Backing the Chevy from the driveway, Alvin drove through town, past ramshackle storefronts, through the city's core, past the First State Bank, looked like a couple of ten-year-olds could rob the place, pegged it for unguarded and having a safe that cracked like an egg. Bumping over railway ties and parking in front of the Talbot Hotel. Taking a room upstairs, he signed in as Raymond Hadley, went to the bar, checking his watch, picking up the courtesy phone in the lobby at five on the nose, the operator putting him through.

"Mr. Dunn, you know who this is?" Alvin altering his voice, going for gravelly, a touch of the Deep South.

"You best not have harmed —"

"Shut up, Dunn."

"Now, you see here. You just made the biggest —"

Hanging up, Alvin went for another bottle of Atlas at the bar, then went back to the phone box, asked to be put through to Big Tom Brown in St. Paul. Told Big Tom they had the package, then hung up, and asked the operator to put him through to Dunn for a second try.

"You set to be mum?"

"Just tell me Mr. Hamm's alright," Dunn said.

"Not if you keep yapping," Alvin said. "Now, I could tell you anything, couldn't I?"

Silence on the line.

"Same way you could tell me you didn't call in the feds, a thing not in your man's best interests." Knowing Dunn had called, Big Tom confirming it.

"Well, I can assure you —"

"Can't hear you, Dunn — all the clicks on the line. But from the way you're talking, you want your man back a piece at a time."

"I want him safe. We all do, and I'm speaking for his family."

"Next time I call, I hear a click on the line, just a one, and your man goes in a trash can, and I bury the chunks. And you get to tell his mother."

"Look, please —"

"Get the assholes off the line, Dunn. Better understand they're not on your side. And next time I call, I hear any clicks . . ."

"Yes, yes, I —"

"Meantime, get one hundred grand in clean bills — fives, tens, and twenties, nothing bigger. You with me?"

"I'll have to speak to the family, get their okay. And it'll take time, raise that kind of money, maybe a week —"

"You got till I call again."

"Now, just a —"

Alvin hung up the receiver, nodded when the woman at the front desk wished him a good evening, calling him Mr. Hadley. Returning to the bar, he had a couple more Atlas, limiting the drinking to beer, then he went to the room and slept a few hours. Going through the empty lobby just past two, he called the cabbie ahead of calling Hamm's man again. Dunn picking up right away, saying, "Yes?"

"Step outside, Dunn, and have two bucks handy."

"Why would I —"

Alvin hung up, going back upstairs, getting in bed about the same time the taxi delivered the second typed note signed by Hamm:

Billy,

Do what they tell you, and have the ransom ready by 5 PM on Friday. If you don't, you will never see me again, and you'll have to explain that to Mother.

Yours,
William

Checking out of the Talbot the next morning, Raymond Hadley gave Dunn and the Hamm family time to sweat, returning on Saturday morning, enough time for them to demand the feds take off their taps, and for Big Tom to get his cops to quit hiding in the bushes.

Sitting at the lobby phone, Alvin said, "We still playing three's a crowd?" Knowing from Big Tom that old man Hamm ordered the feds to take off the taps.

"They're out of it," Dunn said. "You have my word."

"How about the money?"

"I have it."

"All of it?"

"Every cent."

"Drive to L.J. Sullwold's, and check the mailbox out front."

"I don't know where that is?"

"Ought to get to know your people, Dunn. Come down from your ivory tower once in a while. She's one of yours, works at your brewery. First name's Lynn." Giving him the address, Alvin hung up and left the hotel about the time Dunn found the second note in the bookkeeper's mailbox, signed by Hamm, directing him to a stolen Ford parked a block from the Sullwold house, its doors and trunk lid taken off. Instructions telling him to get on Highway 61 and head toward Duluth, driving no more than twenty miles an hour. Alvin grinning, thinking about the cold air rushing past the missing doors Doc removed — a nice touch.

Somewhere on the route a Hudson would pull behind the freezing Dunn, follow a few miles till Doc felt sure they were alone. Dunn was to keep his eyes trained on the road, waiting till the car behind flashed its lights three times, then he was to slow to the shoulder and toss the case out the open passenger side, the man saying goodbye to a hundred grand of the family's fortune, and drive on to Zenith City. The note telling him to register at the Duluth Hotel and wait in the room for Hamm to be dropped off.

——

"Good news, Willy, you're heading home," Doc told him, got the hooded man down the stairs, into the car, and onto the rear floor well of the car one more time. "You're heading home." The early morning damp and cold.

"Oh, God. Thank you." The man was sobbing, his breath coming in a wheeze.

A job that took four days, and nobody getting shot, the ransom paid on the same day of the Kansas City Massacre. The *Star* alleging Pretty Boy Floyd, Vernon Miller and an unidentified man attempted to bust Frank "Jelly" Nash from custody, the man arrested after stepping from a corner store in Hot Springs, Arkansas, a few days earlier. The police chief escorting his prisoner back to Kansas City by train. Floyd and company getting word, and armed with Tommy guns, they waited on the Missouri Pacific to arrive, ambushing four lawmen turning Jelly over to fed agents, the gang opening fire as the lawmen put their prisoner in back of the feds' car. The mess ended up with the police chief, two FBI men and Frank "Jelly" Nash shot to death by his own rescuers. An eyewitness identified Floyd, claimed he'd been wounded in the attack, but getting away along with the others.

It bothered Alvin, losing Jelly Nash that way, and knowing the Justice Department was sure to crank up the heat on account of the dead lawmen, Hoover fighting his war on crime, that man craving his headlines. Wondering about the third man, getting a feeling it was George Nelson, the punk who hung around the pool that time in Reno, the papers dubbing him Baby Face after a string of armed robberies, the man making his own legend.

Wearing the same hat and glasses, Doc helped Hamm in back of the Hudson, telling him, "Gonna be home in time for supper, Willy. No more eggs and beans."

"They paid you?"

"Your loved ones stepped up, and you oughta sit down with a couple cold ones tonight, thank your stars, and put it behind you," Doc said. "Want to tell you, we'd all be proud to drink with you, Willy — you're upright in my book — but, you can see how it is."

"Yes, sure."

Swinging the suitcase with the money into the trunk, Fred got in the passenger side, Doc sat in back, next to Hamm, hooded and kneeling on the floor. Alvin driving Highway 1 until he spotted the sign for Wyoming, Minnesota. Pulling to the gravel shoulder.

"Well, Willy, you been a gent and a good sport," Doc said, swinging open the door. "And you make one fine beer."

"Thank you."

Helping him out, Doc listened to the man sniffling and breathing hard under the hood, saying, "Leave it on till you can't hear no more car. Then you go and have yourself a good life. And Willy? You best go see a doctor about that breathing thing, for Christ's sake."

"Will you come back?"

"This is it, Willy." Doc clapped him on the back like he was seeing off a relative, this brewer who they knew about from the days of bootlegging, his family doing what they had to do to see the company through tough times. Doc slipped something in Hamm's pocket, wishing him well, then got back in the car. And they drove off, leaving him standing by the roadside, the hood over his head.

When he dared to tug it off, William Hamm looked around at the empty highway and fields, and he sat on the roadside, getting his breath under control, the kidnappers disappearing in the road dust with a hundred grand of his money. He put his hand in the pocket and found his wristwatch, looking at the Cartier, strapping it on his wrist. It was just past ten in the morning, and he was weeping like a child.

... *St. Paul, Minnesota*
June 26, 1933

Doc stomped a shoe like he wanted to put it through the floorboards. "Like hell we will!"

Dutch Sawyer looked over from behind the bar.

"You think Nitti's negotiating?" George Ziegler said, slapping the table, bringing them word the crime boss wanted half the ransom.

"Fifty thousand? The man's a mook." Doc glared at Ziegler. "And you come here talking like it's a natural thing."

"I'm delivering a message," Ziegler said, staring back.

"Capone gets sent up, and the next greaseball's playing boss."

"He calls it rent, then it's rent," Ziegler said, knowing better than to cause a scene in here, trying to keep it under control, looking over at Dutch.

"Don't give a shit what he calls it," Doc said. "And how come you didn't set him straight?"

"The hell you saying?" Ziegler said.

"Fifty ain't rent, it's a shakedown. He told me something like that, I'd'a told him to fuck his mama."

"Sounds like you figure I got a part in it." Ziegler looked at the others, getting a read.

"I find out you do . . ." Doc leaned forward, wagging a finger.

Putting a hand on his brother's arm, wanting him to ease up, Fred said to Ziegler, "It's extortion, any way you cut it, is what Doc's saying, what we're all saying."

Alvin sat quiet, signaling to Dutch for another round.

"What I wanna know, how Nitti found out?" Doc said, not letting up, eyes drilling into Ziegler.

Ziegler stood, saying to him, "How about you and me —"

Alvin slammed a fist on the table, stopped Ziegler, saying, "Wondering myself how he got wind." Nobody knew they held Hamm in the abandoned house in Bensenville, west of Mud City, what Nitti figured as mob turf.

"Tell him from me he ain't getting a fucking cent," Doc said, stabbing the air with his finger. "He don't like it, he can come tell me."

"You think I like a bite coming out of my end — way I see it, I got no choice, none of us do. This is Frank fucking Nitti." Ziegler looked to Alvin like he was hoping for reason, not getting any, then looking resigned, sitting back down and glancing around the table, saying, "Look, I'm the guy bringing the word, that's it, but . . ." Looking at Doc, he said, "He keeps looking at me like that . . ."

Coming to the table, Dutch set drinks from a tray, glanced at them without a word, going back behind his bar.

Ziegler saying to Alvin, "That what you want me going back with . . ." Starting to get up again.

"I'll go see him," Alvin said.

The brothers looked at him like he was crazy, Alvin saying there was no way around Frank Nitti, the Enforcer, the front man for the real acting boss, Paul the Waiter, at least while Capone was on ice. The thing of it, Nitti was crazy, and had a crew of crazies. Killers like Greasy Thumb, Charlie Fischetti, Willy White and maybe a dozen more. Alvin and the Barkers were in no position to take them on, the Chicago outfit just a bigger bunch of crooks. Alvin knew it, Fred knew it, Doc knew it too. They could throw in with the Touhys, an outfit having a long-standing feud with the Chicago mob, going back to the days of prohibition, back to when the mob killed Roger Touhy's brother. But where was the money in that?

"I'll go with you, two of us talk him down, slide him say . . . ten Gs," Fred said, drumming fingers on the table, causing little rings in the drinks, adding, "Got to tell you though, the thought makes me sick."

"Talk Frank Nitti down, well, be my guest." Ziegler shook his head. "But I can't stand by."

"How about you stand by while I push him off the Trade Building," Doc said, glaring at Ziegler.

"You want to pay ten, make threats, then I got nothing to do with it." Ziegler tossed back his drink, and started to get up again.

"We're paying the fifty," Alvin said, and that stopped him.

Doc sputtered some of his drink. "How many you had, Ray?" Doc backhanded Alvin's glass off the table.

Dutch looked over from behind the bar.

Fred put a hand on Doc's shoulder, saying, "He's saying we got no choice."

"Fuck that." Doc sat back against the seat, fuming.

Bringing over another tray, Dutch set down the glasses, saying, "The next drink spills, I bring the mop."

"Sorry, Dutch," Alvin said, still looking at Ziegler, then saying, "You tell him I'm coming. Can you do that?"

Slapping back his drink, Ziegler got up, saying, "Yeah, I can do that." And he headed for the door.

"We run the risks, and the greaser sticks his fat hand out," Doc said, watching Ziegler leave. "Think Nitti ought to swan dive off that tower they got. Maybe Ziegler with him." Then looking at Alvin.

"Something happens to Nitti, means we take on Chicago," Alvin said. "Got like a hundred soldiers."

"We do a job and give up half . . ." Doc said. "Guys in the joint'll be saying we gone schoolgirl. I say, we go middle of the night, and the greaser has a slip-and-fall. Who's to know — the fucking end of it."

Alvin shook his head, appreciating the balls if not the brains, saying, "We give him what he wants."

"Fifty Gs, Ray." Doc winced like he was passing stones, his eyes round and wild.

"Maybe I got a way to take off the sting," Alvin said, taking his glass, swirling the whiskey around, a plan coming together.

"Well, I'd sure like to hear it," Fred said, patting his brother's back.

"Pay it, and we make another grab." Alvin shrugged. "Only this time we double it."

"We grab Hamm again, tell his momma we want more?" Doc said.

"Thinking somebody else."

"Who's worth double?"

"It ain't retail, Doc. It's what we say," Alvin said. "The ones on the other end of the line just got to believe it."

Then Fred grinned, clapping Doc on the back, saying, "He's saying in the end, we're up fifty instead of down."

Alvin sat back and nodded.

"Only next time, we stash the guy far from Frank fucking Nitti," Doc said, still not liking the idea of giving up half the ransom.

"We're gonna use the same place, and we're doing it with Nitti's blessing," Alvin said. "The fifty Gs gives us a pass."

"And he's gonna go with it?" Fred said.

Alvin shrugged, saying, "That's what I'm going to find out."

"He don't like it, then we push him off the building," Doc said, adding he wanted to leave Ziegler out of the next heist.

Alvin was back to wondering who was worth more than a hundred grand. Thinking to the article in the morning *Star*, saying, "The fed in charge of the Hamm case, guy named Purvis, thinks he's got an ironclad case, a cabbie eyewitness pinning it on Roger Touhy." Thinking it gave them some time.

"Taking us off the hook," Fred said, nodding, starting to like the idea.

Alvin nodded, saying, "And we get a safe house with Nitti's blessing."

. . . east of Michigan City, Indiana
August 16, 1933

A two-story with stucco walls and a red-tile roof, perched on a rise above the southern shore of Lake Michigan, paper birch and jack pines rising past the white dunes. Renting this place through Dutch Sawyer from a mob-connected politician. It was the right move, getting out of St. Paul and lying low, Alvin waiting on the Hamm money to be cleaned.

Dolores fell in love with the place, all the modern conveniences, even had a telephone and a Steinway piano in the front room. The first time she sat at the upright, she got to work on "Chopsticks," a number she remembered from lessons she took as a schoolgirl. Plunking keys and leaving rings from her drinks on the polished black surface. Alvin promising to get her some sheet music, maybe get another flattop and learn to play along with her, planning to take her to the Lantern on a night when Piano Red showed up. Ask the man to give her some tips. Alvin knowing she had no ear for it.

Franklin D. had set J. Edgar loose on his war on crime, Alvin seeing the safe-haven days of St. Paul were speeding to an end. Big Tom Brown and the rest of the warped and shady in their suits and neckties would be jumping from the flames of Lowertown, saving their asses and giving up the outlaws hiding out in hopes of lessening their own sentences.

Making it worse, the Kellys blew into town like an ill wind, George "Machine Gun" and Kathryn gassing at the Lantern about the kidnapping of Charles Urschel, their gang bagging two hundred grand, dropping the man off in Oklahoma City and leaving a trail straight to St. Paul. Kathryn walking in, a diamond on every wagging finger, a sable stole round her shoulders, middle of the summer. George parking a new cream Hudson out front, had it armor-plated and added bulletproof glass. Ordering drinks for the house, asking around about laundering the ransom dough. Showing off and drawing a lot of heat.

"I'm gonna dip a toe, Ray, you coming?" Dolores cut into his thoughts, giving up on "Chopsticks," going to the bedroom and changing from her shorts and top, coming out wrapped in the new yellow swimsuit he bought her, one like Loretta Young wore in some magazine picture, flaunting her young curves.

"I'll be along, Lolli." Betting Ed Bentz was on the beach in his folding chair, talking to George Nelson, the guy hiding out after the botched springing of Jelly Nash, turning up without the missus this time.

An old pro, Ed Bentz had run with the Kellys, quitting before they hijacked Urschel, a dumb move in Ed's opinion. Treating George "Baby Face" like his protege, teaching the young hood the finer points of robbing banks and slipping away. Nelson wanting to pull together a new outfit, and showing an interest in bumping gums with Dolores on the side, always eyeing her in her swimwear, shoveling the same crap he did that time in Reno, how he was making a name for himself, telling her how he started out by driving for some

New York mob boss, but not saying which mob, just a guy trying to play around while the wife was back in the room.

"Watch out for the ass kisser," Alvin called as she went out the door, knowing Nelson was ticked since Alvin turned him down.

Dolores called back, "Why Ray, I do believe you're a little green-eyed." Following it with, "Abyssinia."

Going to the ice chest for a beer, he went and sat in the armchair, looking out the window, wondering if she'd like it if he went and punched George Nelson in the nose. Dolores admitting he was kind of cute. Alvin wondering what the hood would think about her recent miscarriage. Getting his own wife, Dot, on the blower a week back, the woman sending a chill through the line, moaning how he never showed up, forgetting her birthday two years straight, doing none of what a husband was supposed to do, didn't matter he was running from the law, using that as an excuse.

"Well, I'm calling now," he told her. "And taking a risk doing it."

"A big mistake, getting hitched to you." Reminding him she got him sprung for the clocks he had in the trunk that time, then saying she wanted a divorce.

"Well, that's fine, and why I called, part of it anyway."

Then she flew off the handle, Alvin not understanding it, putting up no fight, saying he was going along with what she wanted, surprised she was crying. "Come on, Dot. I can't just stroll in city hall, file for one kind of freedom, get another kind taken away. I'm a wanted man for Christ's sake."

"Not around here, you're not. Not anymore." Dot telling him to stop talking to her like she was a dimwit, saying, "Just tell me you don't got another woman. Go on and try it."

"That what you wanna hear?"

And she hung up the line.

Looking at the empty bottle of beer he didn't remember drinking, he threw it, the bottle smashing against the wall behind the Steinway, suds sliding down, making a hissing sound.

"Fuck 'Chopsticks.'" Getting out of the armchair, taking the last Hamm's from the icebox, he slipped on his sandals and started for the beach, thinking he ought to call Fred at the St. Paul house, ask him to check the medicine kit, a code for planning a heist, Alvin always careful about their lines being tapped. He wanted to set up a quick stick-up, make some cash to tide them over while the kidnap money was being cleaned, give him time to work on the next kidnapping, come up with a fish that would land them a bigger score, and come away with more than the Kellys scored.

... *South St. Paul, Minnesota*
August 30, 1933

D rizzling rain turned the morning cold, letting up before nine. Checking his watch, he felt the tingle in his blood, same way before every job. What he called the kick. This time they were breaking Big Tom's rule and pulling one on home turf, Alvin and the Barkers done with playing by the rules in St. Paul, knowing it was all coming apart. Stepping around the rear of the building, the rain washing the back alley reek of hobo piss, graffiti brushed on the post office bricks, not where most folks could see it, but still it was there:

John Dillinger slept here

A goddamn folk hero, the man drawing attention like a movie star — Dillinger walking into a bank in Daleville a month back and posing as a rep from a company selling alarm systems, another time acting like a filmmaker scouting a location to film a heist scene. Had to give him credit, the man had style and was flashing the lawman the middle finger, still just a bit too showy for Alvin's tastes.

Finishing the walk-around, Alvin checked the exits for any kind of security he missed when he cased the place days before, circling around front and standing on the stone steps like he was waiting on a lift, looking up and down the shop-lined street, some old guy with a cart making a delivery up the block, unpacking bushels and baskets of vegetables. The armored bank car pulled up out front on time, the driver inside giving him the once-over, making up his mind about him.

Moving off, acting disinterested, Alvin stood by the post box, checking his watch like his ride was late, looking out at Concord Exchange, spotting Doc in the overalls across the street, the Colt .38 with the special loads that could pierce armor, wrapped in his work jacket, looking like he was waiting for a lift the other way, heading to some blue-collar job. Five more minutes and the messengers and guard would come from the rail station, carrying two bags of payroll down the alley to the bank car, thirty-three Gs heading for the employees of Swift and Company, shipped via the Great Western railcar loaded at the Federal Reserve Bank in Minneapolis, another tip from Dutch Sawyer at the Lantern. Alvin wondering if the messengers would spot the graffiti.

Morning sun showed through rolling clouds, shadows fading between the buildings, light glinting off the black sedan's bumper idling up the block, Charlie Fitzgerald behind the wheel. Feeling the weight of the .45 in his pocket, Alvin shifted so it couldn't be seen by the driver in the armored car.

Glancing across at Doc, he heard voices echoing from the alley, the uniformed guard emerging first, looking and nodding at the driver of the bank car, then he looked Alvin over, a hand at the open holster on his hip. The messengers, with Stock Yards National Bank patches on navy shirts, were young, both talking about the Cubs' chances against the Dodgers in today's game. Alvin looked away from them, seeing Charlie start to roll the black Buick onto the street a block up. Glancing back at the messengers, smiling, he said, "Not that you asked, but the Cubs got no chance at all." Alvin acting good-natured, his hands loose at his sides.

"Who're you, Hal Totten?" the blond messenger said, the kid no more than eighteen, smiling back, saying, "No offense."

"None taken." Alvin slipped a hand in his top pocket, getting a pack of smokes, sticking one in his mouth.

The siren they rigged in the Buick bleeped, and the driver and the guard both turned like Alvin figured they would, the guard unsnapping his holster.

Pulling his own .45, Alvin dragged on the smoke, the guard catching his movement, seeing Alvin's pistol aimed at him, Alvin saying to the messengers, "If you're gonna bet, fellas, don't go more 'n a buck, okay?" Thinking he was starting to sound like Dillinger, hamming for attention. Telling the guard to toss it away.

Crossing the street, Doc reached in the coat, aiming the Colt at the driver, saying, "Got special loads, cut through sheet metal like butter. And I'm dying to try them out, but let me ask, you want to get out or die?"

The guard on the street had his hand on the grip, just had to draw, Alvin squaring his barrel, borrowing Verne Miller's line, asking, "You got kids, Mack?" Calm about it, taking his pack from his top pocket left-handed, flipping another smoke up and lipping it, never taking his eyes from the guard, letting him decide. "Two fingers, and drop it down."

The guard eased it out, the pistol clattering on the walk, the driver opening his door and stepping out, setting his sidearm on the pavement like Doc told him, then raising his hands.

"Not getting away with it, pal, you got to know that," the guard told Alvin.

"Another bet you'd lose."

Exhaust coughed and fumes trailed from the Buick's tail-pipe, Alvin guessing it idled too long waiting on the couriers, the men sitting inside, along with the weight of the steel plates they welded into the doors and behind the rear seat, an attempt to make the sedan bulletproof, an idea they got from George Nelson.

Charlie Fitzgerald stayed behind the wheel, Fred getting out of the passenger side, Bryan Bolton and new man Fred Goetz climbing from the back, all holding pistols and checking the office windows and along the street.

Pocketing his .45, Alvin reached for a bag, taking it from the blond kid, Doc taking the other one, tossing them in the back of the Buick.

Would have been clean if the squad car hadn't come around the corner, the cop drawn by the siren's bleep. Fred Goetz stepped into the street, emptying his clip into the car, shattering the windshield, moving to the driver's side and yanking the door. The dying officer spilling out, his pistol clattering down, the man shot in the throat, another hole where an eye had been. Looking inside, Fred Goetz reached behind the seat, coming out with a Thompson gun, grinning like it was Christmas.

The guard saw a chance and bent for his pistol, catching Alvin distracted, the messengers throwing themselves down like they were diving for home plate, scrambling to get to the armored car.

Doc caught the movement, firing and winging the guard, hitting him in the leg, knocking him down. Alvin kicked away the man's pistol, pointing his own in the man's face, saying, "What'd I tell you?" Backing to the Buick, keeping his pistol on the guard.

Doc kicked the driver's pistol under the armored car, then he got in back of the Buick, Bolton sliding in next to him.

Still in the street, Fred Goetz blasted the Thompson, spraying the wall of the post office, shattering windows, then getting in back on the driver's side, the car already rolling, weighed down by the armored plates.

Charlie Fitzgerald had caught one in the shoulder, saying it was Goetz who tagged him, the cop and the guards never getting off a shot. Cursing Goetz, he drove them out of there, his sleeve wet with blood.

Switching on the siren, Fred cleared motorists, Bryan Bolton emptying boxes of roofing nails out the rear window.

. . . east of Michigan City, Indiana
September 1, 1933

Dividing the take, Goetz and the Barkers headed for St. Paul. Alvin and Bryan Bolton driving Charlie to a medic in Calumet City, getting him patched up off the books. The man unconscious on the backseat for most of the drive, groaning through the morphine fog. Bolton stayed with him, along with Charlie's share, Alvin driving the last hour to the Indiana beach house, opening the door, saying, "Well, ain't you a sight for sore eyes."

"You been to hell?" Dolores said, sitting sideways in the armchair, her bare feet over the arm.

"That how I look?"

"Pretty much."

Alvin banged the case through the door, his take from the robbery inside, his laundry in the shoulder bag. Setting both down, he looked at her. "You painted your toes, and you're wearing pants."

"That how you want to start?" She looked at him, knowing not to ask where in hell he'd been.

"They mine?"

"The toes?"

"The pants."

"You even know who Katharine Hepburn is?"

"They hers?"

"You got no idea about . . . oh, God, nothing. You got no idea, Ray." She shook her head, tried to look miffed, but couldn't hide the smile.

"Well, I guess I better check and see what the modern felon's gal's wearing these days." Going and kissing her, saying, "They got a magazine for it, or maybe I'll call up old Dillinger, ask for his tailor."

"That who you been with?"

Looking at her in her pants, pink toenails, her hair pulled back. Could see she'd been drinking, but still looking good. "Told you I was on business."

"The kind we don't talk about."

"Right."

Dolores rolled her eyes, looked at the suitcase, curious about it, but not asking.

Alvin looked around the place, dirty dishes stacked like the Tower of Pisa on the table, clothes on the back of a chair, an empty wine bottle on the piano bench, the place untidy, saying, "How you coming with 'Chopsticks'?"

"Meant to work on it, then stepped on some glass." Lifting the bottom of her foot, showing a cut. "Some dope busted a beer bottle, didn't bother cleaning it up."

Alvin kicked off his shoes and headed for the kitchen, saying, "Speaking of a drink, there any beer left?" Opening the icebox, uncapping a bottle and tipping it.

"Waiting for you to bring your guitar. Wanted to play with me, remember?"

"Don't need a guitar for that."

"You little pig."

"Well, doll, you get 'Chopsticks' down, then I'll get it, give us a place to start."

"Talking like you're Lonnie Johnson."

He looked at her, no idea who that was.

"Got to be off my rocker, believe half the bull you shovel." She smiled, not upset, just playing like she did when she was bored, saying she bet he couldn't play a note. Taking a cigarette from the pack on the table, striking a match, shaking it out and tossing in at the ashtray, a near-finished drink in front of her.

"Stick around, find out," Alvin drank down the beer, taking a smoke from her pack and lighting it, twisting his face. "The fuck is this?" Looking at the offending cigarette.

"Spuds. Menthol, something new. Kinda fun, huh?"

"Fucking hell." He stubbed it out, the overfilled ashtray spilling butts and ash on the table. He took her drink and tasted it, wanting to drown the menthol taste.

"Fix me one of those, will you?" He was bushed, needing a shower after taking over the driving from Charlie Fitzgerald, getting the wounded man to Calumet City, stopping once to poke him with the syringe of the morphine they kept in the car for anytime somebody took a bullet. Couldn't believe Fred Goetz winged Charlie Fitzgerald, going crazy with the cop's Tommy gun, shooting up the post office.

Not arguing, she got up, fixing him a drink. Dolores waited till he got out of the shower, stood at the bathroom door with it in one hand, a towel in the other, saying, "Want me to dry your back?"

Taking the drink from her, he stood naked, dripping and sipping the drink, setting it next to the sink. Pulling her close, he kissed her, getting her wet.

"So, how come we never talk about it?" She pushed him back, turned him by the shoulders, dried his back and slung the towel on the doorknob.

"About what I do?"

"Yeah, like who am I gonna tell?"

"You don't know, then you can't testify — not that you would. Plus, it'd just bore the hell out of you."

"You worried about me getting bored, leaving me on my own, with cute and randy Georgie just up the road?"

"Randy Georgie's got a wife."

"You got one too, the one you ditched. Remember?"

"Hard to forget with you reminding me."

"And you don't want me acting like another one? What'd you say, a boat anchor?"

"Something like that." Downing the rest of the drink, saying she was his fun girl, and knew her way around a martini.

"Think you're a jerk, Ray." But she wasn't angry, just playing with him. "Don't want me knowing how much you got in the case, the one you take to the bathroom, like you don't trust me." Glancing at it on the floor behind him.

"Pretty smart for a girl." He put a finger to her lip.

"I'm more than that, just waiting for you to figure it out," she said, taking his hand and placing it on her belly, looking in his eyes. "Fact, I'm more than just me." Letting him work it out.

He looked at her, then looked at the empty glass. "Late again?" Handing it to her.

"That the best you got — late again?" She rolled her eyes, saying, "This's where you say we'll call him Ray if it's a boy."

He got a flash of George Nelson hanging around while he was gone on business, always had his eyes on her, then he was thinking about Joseph Moran, the back-room quack in Chicago, working for the Teamsters, taking care of the underworld off the books, gunshot wounds and stitches, a pin artist for this sort of thing.

"Penny for your thoughts," she said, frowning. "No, never mind. The look says it."

"How'd it happen?" Taking the towel from the doorknob and drying off.

"Well, not from spooning. What, I got to draw you a picture, huh?" Making a motion with her hands, taking her index finger and poking it into her curled fist. Grinning.

"I mean we're careful, right?"

"Maybe one of your boys is on the swim team — guess he got past the old dyke."

When he didn't say anything, she leaned against him, "I'm your floozy of fun, the old catcher's mitt. That it?" Taking the towel from him and tossing it on the floor.

"You're not so old." Patting her behind.

"You talk about leaving the ball and chain, what's her name . . . and the two of us making a life . . . well, here's the life."

"Two's not three, and that's for someday, later down the road, when we get settled someplace, then we'll talk about a kid." Not something he ever thought about. "I ever commit to it, it'll be with you. That's a guarantee."

"Gee, swell." She looked in his eyes, searching for the truth in that.

Setting the glass on the sink, he slipped his fingers in her pants pockets, drawing her close, saying, "Floozy of fun, huh?"

She shrugged and leaned into him, feeling him naked against her, reaching down and undoing the buttons of her pants and letting them drop to the floor.

... *Chicago, Illinois*
September 22, 1933

The cream-colored Hudson idled off the main street, Alvin borrowing this one from George Kelly Barnes back in St. Paul. Kelly owing Alvin a favor for lining him up with the Teamsters, who laundered some of his ransom cash through a strike fund. The two of them sitting at the Green Lantern with Kelly's wife, Kathryn, Alvin offering him two hundred bucks for use of the car for the day, admitting Kelly had the best getaway wheels in town on account of the armor plates, bulletproof glass on the driver's side, loving the smoke machine he rigged in the trunk, the only thing that man ever got right, aside from marrying Kathryn. Alvin keeping that part to himself, calling him Machine Gun, playing to the man's vanity. Gangsters loving the handles the daily papers hung on them. Everyone but Alvin, the rags still calling him "Old Creepy."

"So, what do you say, Machine Gun?" Looking into the man's round face, looked like he forgot to shave this morning.

"As long as you bring her back washed." Kelly grinned.

"How about an extra hundred for every bullet hole." Kathryn said, not falling for the soft soap, her own life of crime starting back in the bootlegging days, working with her mother, running shine.

Alvin not sure if she was kidding, smiling at her.

"And tell me you want it for an out-of-towner." Kathryn not wanting to get in dutch with Big Tom Brown, all of St. Paul's gangland still abiding by his rule — not shitting where you eat.

"Not even close." Not saying the job was in Chicago, guessing she'd charge him mileage.

Clearing his mind now, sitting on the passenger seat, Alvin pulled the hat brim down, saying, "Let's go."

Bryan Bolton lifted the kerchief over his nose, driving the Hudson along Jackson, past Clark, the Ford coupe following behind, George Ziegler driving the Barkers, Fred on the passenger side, ready with the sawed-off pump, Doc in back with the Tommy gun.

The messenger pushed the cart, balancing five heavy sacks, the Federal Reserve man walking alongside, both packing sidearms, talking to each other, the two guards with rifles flanking them, watching as the cars approached. Seeing Bolton's masked face in the Hudson, both guards started to swing up the rifle barrels.

"Wouldn't do it," Alvin called out the window, his pistol pointing at them as he stepped out.

Fred and Doc were out of the Ford, drawing beads. Both guards thinking better of it, laying their rifles on the sidewalk. The messengers raising their hands.

"Guess we got an understanding." Alvin slipped his pistol in his jacket pocket.

Gathering their rifles and sidearms, Doc tossed them onto the rear floor of the Ford. Alvin emptying the cart, tossing the bank sacks onto the backseat of the Hudson, not enough room in the trunk with Kelly's smoke machine in there.

Alvin and Bolton got back in the Hudson, the Barkers and Ziegler climbed in the Ford, both cars speeding west, past LaSalle and crossing the river, leaving the guards running in search of a telephone.

Bryan Bolton saying, "Easiest money we made, less you tell me I got to give up half to Nitti again." Peeling off his hood, still hating that he parted with half his share of the ransom money.

"Like I told you, that was one-time rent." Alvin had gone to see Nitti, hat in hand, and haggled a pass for anything else they pulled in mob territory, not handing him the cash until they had a deal. Three of Nitti's goons stood in the room, ready to kill Alvin until Nitti grunted. And Alvin looked at Willy White, asked him to give him a hand, told him the fifty grand was out in his trunk.

Bolton was grinning, saying, "They ought to call you 'Old Brass Balls.'"

Alvin smiled, becoming a legend for the way he walked in unarmed, making a deal with Frank Nitti, Capone's enforcer.

"Well, he changes his mind and wants another piece, he can take it out of Ziegler's end, on account Ziegler won't be needing it after." Bolton glanced in the rearview at Ziegler driving the Ford, like most of the others he felt it was Ziegler who whispered to Nitti about the Hamm kidnapping, letting the gangster know they were holding the beer man hostage in mob turf — Ziegler playing up to the boss and kissing ass.

"You really walk in and tell Nitti like that?" Bolton cranked the wheel at Jackson and roared up Halsted.

"Had to be done," Alvin said, shrugging.

Bolton was happy he got to keep his share, late seeing the two flatfoot cops on the near corner, and missing the dark

Model A speeding through the intersection at Adams, the Ford sideswiping their passenger side, throwing Alvin into Bolton, sending the Hudson skidding and hopping the sidewalk, slamming against a lamp post, the lamp top crashing onto their roof and folding it like a tin can. Alvin holding his bleeding head, staring out the smashed windshield as the Model A lost control, crossed the lane, and hopped the opposite sidewalk, its front end mashing a brick storefront, busting through the plate glass, the driver sagging over the wheel, the horn blaring.

One cop started for the Hudson, the other running to the Model A.

Pulling short behind the Hudson, middle of the street, Doc jumped from the back of the Ford, Fred and Ziegler getting out of the front, all drawing weapons at the sight of the cops, figuring they had something to do with the crash. Fred firing the sawed gun, winging the cop heading for the Hudson. Doc gave a burst of auto fire, the other cop stumbling and dropping below the fender of the wrecked Model A, not ready for a traffic crash turning into a gun battle. Pulling his sidearm, the cop got off a wild shot.

Firing out the window of the Hudson, Bryan Bolton hit the wounded cop behind the car, giving him no chance to clear his sidearm. The cop slumping in the street.

Having to kick open the crushed-in door, Alvin got out and pulled the sacks from the backseat, getting them out of the crumpled Hudson, his head bleeding. Bolton crawling out behind him.

Doc and Ziegler kept the wounded cop pinned behind the Model A. Cradling the scattergun, Fred helped Alvin and Bolton carry the sacks, tossing them in back of the coupe, the cop by the Model A returning fire, Ziegler jumping behind the wheel, the rest of them piling into the Ford, Doc firing another burst, keeping the cop pinned down. Alvin throwing open the rear door, Doc jumping into the moving car, the cop limping from the Model A, walking into the street to his fallen partner, firing a last round after them.

"They got the car, they'll know it's us." Doc said, meaning the Hudson, wanting to go back and finish the cops.

"Car belongs to George Kelly," Alvin said, wiping blood from his forehead, looking from Fred to Doc.

Doc grinned, saying, "Mr. Machine Gun's gonna have some explaining to do."

The rest of them laughing.

. . . Chicago, Illinois
October 3, 1933

"Just got that picture hung right." Kate stood there, her hands balled on her hips.

Telling her they had to pull stakes again, Fred promised to make it right.

Alvin came in, guessing what he walked into, Kate shaking her head and walking from the room. "Want me to talk to her?"

"Think you best leave it alone," Fred said, then telling him Ziegler left word at the Lantern. "Says he wants to see you, this joint called the HiHo out in Cicero."

Alvin not liking the sound of it, asking what else he said.

"Just called Dutch, said it's important." Fred looked at him, saying, "What do you figure?"

Alvin shrugged, like the rest of them, he had thoughts that Ziegler whispered to Nitti about the payroll heist, and the Enforcer was thinking about more rent.

"HiHo's a few doors from Capone's old hangout, the Hawthorne."

"Yeah, the best place for waffles." What Capone used to say, the real boss serving eleven in the Atlanta Pen, likely getting waffles anytime he wanted, living like a king on the inside. The Chicago mob posing Nitti as boss since getting his release, after serving time for misfiling his taxes, the puppet boss nothing but a savage. Everybody, but the FBI, knew it was Paul the Waiter, Joe Batters, Greasy Thumb Guzik, and Murray the Camel who sat in the ivory tower and shared the real power. Word was those guys were getting tired of jobs being pulled by independents, the politicians and papers blaming the mob, forcing the law to dial up the heat.

"Me and Doc'll come keep you company," Fred said.

Alvin appreciated it, but if it was a set-up, it meant they all walked into what was waiting.

Now, pulling his car up out front of the HiHo, he was wondering if he made the right choice, knowing the Barkers wouldn't back down from anybody — parking out front and stepping to the entrance, a sign claiming: *Open all hours, serving any kind of liquor with no kind of secrets*. Another sign declared Friday was amateur night. The right place for a guy like Ziegler, an amateur with plenty of secrets.

Stepping inside the glass door, Alvin let his eyes adjust, spotting Ziegler at the bar, the man in a fedora and long coat, a dozen other customers, but nobody else looking familiar. Nodding, Alvin walked over, telling Ziegler he was grabbing a booth.

"Here's good," Ziegler said, patting the stool next to him.

Alvin went to the far booth, sitting by the window, his back to the wall.

George followed, his beer in hand.

Alvin turned and looked at the wall of fight photos: one signed by Jackie Fields, after his tenth-round decision against Lou Brouillard. An action shot of Max Schmeling after taking a low blow from Jack Sharkey. A ringside shot of Kid Chocolate retaining his featherweight crown over Fidel

LaBarba in New York, the man with his arm raised by the ref. The smiling mugs of Lou Scozza, Battling Battalino and Gorilla Jones. One of Barney Ross standing outside the Marigold Gardens.

"Shook hands after the Rosenbloom bout, the one after he knocked out the Cinderella Man. Don't know if you follow it," Alvin said, pointing to the one of Scozza.

"You kidding, that man bought my house." Ziegler sat facing him. "Getting the idea you don't trust me?"

"I'm here, right?"

"A careful man, that it?" Ziegler folded his hands on the table.

"An old habit."

"You want a drink, milk maybe?"

Alvin grinned.

Signaling the waiter, Ziegler held up two fingers, saying to Alvin, "House shot's Templeton Rye, what Big Al drinks."

"Think he's getting it now?"

"That, and anything else he wants. Inside, outside, don't think it matters," Ziegler said. "Talk is they're gonna transfer him to the Rock. Might be different there."

"Guess Templeton'll do. And if we're done talking the fights and what Big Al's drinking, how about we get to it."

"All business, huh?"

"Why you called me, right?"

"There's a guy wants to see you, got a couple of questions." Ziegler shrugged.

"This guy got a phone?"

"Likes the personal touch."

"How about a name?"

"You know Willy White?"

The waiter came and set two glasses off a tray.

"Maybe we met. But, since you're pals, call him up, tell him I'm here." Alvin lifted his drink, saying, "Mud in your eye."

"Wants to see you downtown; you know the Motion Picture Operators' Union? Can take you to him. Cheers."

"Willy's got the questions, how about he comes and asks? Or better yet, you ask, then go tell him."

"You think I'm a third ear, huh? Maybe setting you up? Come on, Ray."

"What's he want?"

"Wants to know if you got something going with Touhy."

"Touhy? You know better." Alvin thinking it had something to do with the kidnapping of Jake "the Barber" Factor, word was it had been faked, Roger Touhy having a hand in it.

"It's what I told him, except Willy wants to hear it from you." Ziegler shook his head, said the feud with Touhy was a shame, a misunderstanding going out of shape. Sipping his drink, saying, "And he wants to ask about that Nelson kid you got hanging around."

"He's not with us. Think you know that too." Alvin remembered George Nelson bragging how he worked with the Touhys one time, guessing word leaked to Nitti's people. "Hangs out near the beach house I rented — like I said, nothing to do with me."

"Nitti's got a beef, don't like the mouth on Nelson. You ask me, the kid's staring at a Viking funeral he keeps it up, heading for the lake of stinking waters. And not a guy you want to be hanging around — you get my drift."

"Yeah, thanks, but, like I said, the guy's got nothing to do with me. Same goes for Touhy." The papers had hung the Hamm kidnapping on Roger Touhy, the feds staging a manhunt, suspecting Touhy was hanging around Chicago, putting more heat on the mob over the Factor kidnapping.

"Well, I were you, Ray, I'd see Willy and clear it up."

"There's nothing to clear." Alvin downed his drink, reaching in his pocket, tossing a couple of bills down, saying, "You pass it on, and we're all good."

"I got this." Ziegler shoved the money back across the table, thinking a moment, then saying, "Whatever you think's between me and Nitti, you got it wrong." Offering his hand across the table. "Hope you believe it."

Taking the money back, Alvin eyed him a moment, then shook his hand.

"Anything else comes down the pike, you got my number," Ziegler said, looking him in the eye. "And I mean it."

"Yeah, something comes up, I'll be in touch."

"So, we're alright?"

"Yeah, we're alright." Alvin nodded and walked for the door, looking at the men along the bar, then up and down the street, a grocer setting a crate down out front of his market, putting tomatoes and eggplants on display. Going to his car, Alvin looked at his shaking hand holding the key, drawing a breath before sticking it in the ignition and turning it, happy to be driving out of there.

. . . east of Michigan City, Indiana
October 3, 1933

Walking in, Alvin headed for the icebox, Dolores stretched across the sofa, long legs crossed, wearing the same pants, the cuffs rolled up, looking out at the dark clouds rolling over the lake. Telling her, "Go pack a bag."

"Well, hello yourself."

Turning, he stopped and forced a smile, saying, "Got a lot on my mind."

"Smooth, like a regular Ronald Colman."

"The guy from *Bulldog Drummond*?" He went over, leaning down and kissing her. "Go on, get packed."

Not making a move, she put a hand around his neck, pulling him close, smelling of drink and cigarettes, saying, "I been thinking . . ."

He took her hand, pulling away, saying, "Hold the thought." And heading for the kitchen.

"Not gonna let your ghoul pull the rabbit, not this time."

Now he was frowning, looking back, saying, "You get knocked up, you take care of it, thought we had an understanding." Something they had talked about, thinking they were of the same mind.

"You had an understanding." Making a face, she flung a cushion at him.

"Ain't exactly the daddy kind." He caught it and set it on the table by the dirty dishes.

"Not everything's about you, Ray." She turned back to the window, fighting away tears.

"Okay, you want it, so have it." He went into the kitchen.

"Meaning I'm on my own." Picking up the ashtray, she sent it smashing against the kitchen wall, ashes and glass shards flying.

He stepped to the doorway, sweeping aside a wet mess with his shoe, careful of the broken glass, saying, "Have it, and I'll help you out."

"Not with your quack with a coat hanger." Dolores thinking of the long-ago abortion she had at the hands of Joseph Moran, chalking it up to being a dumb kid back then, before she met Alvin.

"You're young, you hear a ticking, I get that. Me, I hear a different ticking — like a bomb. Look, go on and have it, a natural thing, I get that."

"Can see why Dorothy wants a divorce."

"That was a mistake, never should've told you."

"Telling me's not the mistake, Ray. But you know what? You ought to give lessons, being a wet blanket. Starting to see why they call you Creepy."

"Why you got to start? I just walked in here."

"That quack of yours gives me the shivers, told you about that time. Something goes wrong, something inside, then what? Easy for you, you go find another bimbo."

"If I wanted one, a kid, it'd be with you. And I don't want

no other bimbo. Come on, Lolli. We got something good. Why twist it out of shape?"

"I got to be blind." Talking to herself now.

"Like I said, maybe someday."

"You know what to do with your someday, Ray."

"A few drinks, and you don't see things the right way. Always got to start."

"Had this dream . . ." She turned to him. "The kid, our kid, woke you up, crying, and you stuck it in a basket and floated it down the Chicago River."

"Nothing floats in there. Look, go get packed. I'll make some coffee, and we'll talk a while." Alvin turned to the kitchen, wanting that beer.

"What's more important than bringing in a new life?"

"Hanging on to my old one," he said. "You got no idea what I'm dealing with."

She stood, looking at him. "This about George?"

"George?" That stopped him.

"Baby Face."

"What about him?"

"I don't know, sometimes I think you're jealous."

"Of that guy?"

"Like he wouldn't give me a look?"

"Looks all the time. Trying to get under my skin, but touching's crossing the line, and he knows it." He didn't like the way she was grinning, guessing she liked making him green.

"I told you, we're just chummy, Georgie and me."

"Told you to go and pack."

"That's it, button it, or here comes the coat hook." Dolores putting a finger in her mouth like a fish hook, her other hand across her belly, her eyes wet now.

Done with talking, he went to the icebox, stepping on the pedal, opening the fridge door, only two beers inside. Taking one, he looked for the opener, finding it behind a stack of dishes, saying, "You ought to slow it down, or your kid's gonna be a lush."

"George dropped by . . . had a couple."

Going back to the door, he looked at her, taking a pull from the bottle.

"Oh, my God. What? Now, I'm old Loose Legs Lolli."

"You're talking all by yourself."

"You think I'd let him . . . oh, think what you want." She got up and went to the adjoining bedroom, called him Creepy again, gathering her things, slinging sweaters and blouses at the bed, saying, "It okay if I ask where in hell I'm going?"

"Gonna stay with Fred and Doc, have a visit with Paula and Kate." Alvin saying, "A good time like we had in Reno."

Wiping at tears, she said, "We coming back here, my piano? Let me guess, maybe sometime." Looking at the Steinway, saying, "All that time practicing?"

"I'll get you one, soon as we settle someplace."

"How about a mouth harp. Can keep it in my pocket and blow on it any time I want." Dolores looking around like she wanted something else to throw.

He swept his shoe at the glass and ash, pushing it aside.

Wiping at her cheeks, sniffling, she said, "How long's this nice visit?"

"Not too long."

"Well, summer's done and gone anyway." Wheeling, she went to the bedroom, getting her case and her big straw bag, shoving everything inside, nothing neat about the way she did it.

Standing at the doorway, watching her, drinking the beer, he said, "Keep worrying, you're gonna get wrinkles."

He tried to kiss her, but Dolores turned her head as he put her in back of the cab, muttering, "What was I thinking?"

Handing over a couple of bills, telling the cabbie to take her to the Michigan City Flying Field no matter what she said, telling her there'd be a ticket waiting. Watching the cab pull down the gravel drive leading from the place, he got his beer and walked to the village store, made a call, arranged the ticket, then made another call, waiting for the operator to make the connection, saying, "Hey, Fred." Asking after Kate and Doc, telling him the short strokes of the meeting with Ziegler, then saying, "You pick something up for me?"

"Sure, what you need?"

"Lolli."

"Picking her up?"

"If you don't mind."

"And taking her where?"

"Hang onto her a while."

"You two on the outs?"

"Not that I know."

"Well . . . guess Paula'll love it, and Ma too. The girl any good at jigsaws?"

"Give her a drink, she'll do whatever you want."

Back at the summer house, he took the last Hamm from the icebox, stepping past the pieces of ashtray, looking around the disheveled place, thinking about taking Dolores back to Reno, asking Fred to bring Paula and Kate. Stay until things cooled down with Nitti and the mob.

Getting his linen jacket, one he still had from the McCallon's job, thinking it was two years since they hit that place, getting to be time to upgrade the wardrobe. Walking up the beach to the cottage Ed Bentz was renting, seeing the gray roof past the pines, then George Nelson sitting on the front steps, an empty bottle next to him, the man looking sullen, like he had a weight on his shoulders. Walking past the picket fence. His sandals slapping up beach sand.

"What's up, Creep?" George looked up.

"Looks like rain, huh?" Alvin glanced at the sky, ignoring the insult.

"Come to tell me the weather?"

"Come to tell you about another kind of hard rain coming your way." He wasn't doing this for George, but for Ed, guessing whatever was coming, Ed Bentz would get caught in it. He tipped up the beer bottle, waiting for George to slide aside.

"Telling me what to do?" George not making a move.

"More like giving you a tip." Alvin talking to this guy who liked to act first and think about it later, the guy in on getting Jelly Nash killed, trying to set him free.

"You talk a lot of shit, you know it, Creep?" George forced a smile, nothing friendly in his eyes. "This about your twist, the one you knocked up? Let me guess, you think it was me?"

"If I thought that, we wouldn't be talking." Alvin not showing his surprise, this guy knowing she was pregnant.

"Maybe I played a little, tickling her with words, you know, but hey, I ain't interested in giving the old heave-ho. You got no worries, pal. Already got a ball and chain of my own." Egging Alvin on, he kept smiling. "You remember my Helen. Now, that's some kind of woman, you got no idea."

"Figured you forgot you had a wife, a kid too."

"Look, Creep, what I'm saying, you got nothing to sweat about." Gesturing with his hand like he was brushing him off.

A passing moment, Alvin wanting to clock this son of a bitch with the beer bottle, a good roundhouse ought to knock out half his front teeth. Taking a breath, he screwed on a smile, saying, "Tell you what, Baby, you have yourself a nice day." Alvin turned to go, wasting his time, sticking his neck out for a guy like this.

Ed Bentz creaked open the screen door, saying, "I get you another of those, Ray? Looks like you're walking off without so much as hello."

Looking at the empty in his hand, Alvin nodded and turned. "Sure, one for the road, Ed. Why not?"

Ed looked down at George on the step, frowning and said, "Sounds like the man's trying to tell you something, kid." Opening the screen door with a squeak, holding it for Alvin. Motioning with his hand for George to slide over.

"I wish you people'd just talk plain," George said, shaking his head and moving aside.

"Hard to tell a man a thing when he's busy running his mouth," Ed said. "Man comes here after taking a ride to the big town, telling you something's coming. And you think he's talking about the weather."

George Nelson looked confused.

"Telling you Nitti's the hard rain."

"Like I said, plain talk'd be nice. Thank you."

"Well, you chew on it a while, kid," Ed said to him, holding the screen for Alvin.

Walking past him into the house, Alvin wondered how the old bank robber knew about the meet with Ziegler, and the trouble with Nitti.

"Don't mind him. Kid's got a way of poking a stick at the hive, wonders why he gets stung," Ed said, letting the screen shut.

"He saying Nitti's coming at me?" George called from the steps.

"You sit there and figure it out," Ed called, shaking his head and going to the icebox.

... *St. Paul, Minnesota*
December 15, 1933

O n his second bourbon in the rear booth of the Lantern, waiting for George Ziegler to show, the man wanting another face to face. Alvin making it on his turf this time, keeping an eye to the door, wanting to be sure he came alone. Feeling better knowing Dutch Sawyer had the twelve-gauge loaded with buckshot under the bar. Thinking of Dolores losing the baby, not having to argue about taking her to Joseph Moran again.

"Cold as a witch's tit." Ziegler came in, stomping snow off his shoes, nodding to Dutch on the business side of the bar, rubbing his hands and nodding at a couple of yeggs on barstools, the floor slick and wet from patrons coming and going, bringing in the slush.

"How's it in Chi-town?" Dutch asked.

"A foot of the white stuff dumped in off the lake, with more on the way. Ask me, you got it easy."

Alvin nodded for a round of drinks, and Dutch came over with three shots and bottles of Schmidt's Select, setting down the tray, and sliding in next to Alvin. Dutch often weighing in, helping to connect the dots. Picking up a glass, saying, "Salud."

"Want to cut you in," Ziegler said, looking at Alvin. If he was bothered with Dutch joining them, he didn't show it. "Got wind of this egg man Dennis Clooney, you hear of him?"

Alvin shook his head, but Dutch knew the name, saying, "Pimp in Chicago, runs half the skirt in town. That Clooney?"

"Yeah. Hear the man's wife's got like three hundred Gs in a safe deposit box. This from her housekeeper, a guy I know's keeping time with her."

"Meaning she's got it in a bank?" Alvin said.

"The First National."

"This going where I think it's going?" Dutch said, putting up a hand, stopping Ziegler. "Way I hear it, you and this pimp have the same pals, the ones you don't wanna upset." Downing his shot, saying, "You ought to know that, George."

"He knows some guys, I know some guys, maybe the same guys," Ziegler said, flailing a hand at the air. "One guy serves drinks, the next guy's a pimp." Then to Alvin, taking a breath and easing up, "Look, you cut me in, so I'm returning the favor. Top of that, you know your way around banks."

"Say it any way you want, but if this guy's connected to Nitti . . ." Dutch said, holding up his palms.

"I asked around, the guy's nothing to worry about," Ziegler said, looking from one to the other.

"Count me out, but thanks," Alvin said.

"You worked out the rent thing with Nitti, and you got a pass. Trust me, this egg man's nothing to him."

"Like I said . . ." Alvin took a drink.

"You piss off that fed Hoover just by breathing, same as all of us . . . yet, here we are." Ziegler shrugged like it didn't matter, saying, "Heard me say the broad's got three hundred in her safe box, right?"

"I heard that, yeah," Alvin said.

"Three hundred Gs in safe deposit's got me wondering, what else they got under the mattress."

"Lots of guys you can get," Alvin said.

"Yeah, lots of guys." Ziegler shrugged, knocking back the shot.

Shaking his head, Dutch got up and said the drinks were on the house, then went to tend to the men on the barstools, all of them looking thirsty.

"A bartender with his nose in everybody's business," Ziegler said when he was gone.

Alvin staying quiet, working on the beer.

"Look Ray, we go in masked, like we did with Hamm, and we snatch this pimp's wife, force her to open her box, money, you know what I'm saying. And being the guy's a pimp, what's he gonna do? Can't run to the cops. You ask me, this trumps the Hamm set-up."

"Doesn't feel right."

"Doesn't feel right." Seeing he wasn't getting anywhere, Ziegler tipped back his beer, then saying, "You know your trouble, Ray? You only play if it's your game." Draining the bottle. "What you don't see, I know what I'm doing, fact, I been doing it longer than you. You want to sit here like you're the prince of Lowertown, go ahead."

"I told you no, now I got to explain it."

"Nitti doesn't even see you, man." Getting his temper under wraps, Ziegler sat quiet, drinking, then said, "While I set it up, find the right guys, you got something else . . ."

"I do, I'll let you know." Alvin watched him drain his glass, suds sliding down when he set it down, Ziegler got up without another word and went out the door.

Coming from the storage room in back, Dutch stopped by the table again, seeing Ziegler leave, saying, "Didn't take it so good?"

"Doesn't like hearing no."

Ziegler was back the next week. Alvin at the bar with Kid Cann, a Romanian guy Alvin knew from the bootlegging days, had ties to the Chicago outfit and the Genoveses in New York, Alvin saying, "Hey George, you know the Kid?"

"Yeah, we met," Ziegler said, shaking Kid's hand, asking how he was doing, the two recalling that New Year's when every con and escapee seemed to drop in, before Alvin and Fred ever stepped in the place. Throwing names around like the Evergreen bandits, Gus Winkler, Crane-Neck Nugent, Fred Burke, Johnny Moore, Big Homer Wilson, Tommy Banks and Tommy Gannon.

"Gals from Aunt Gracie's and Beth Walsh's houses were on hand, working the party," Ziegler said. "A hell of a way to ring in the New Year."

Downing his drink, Kid clapped Ziegler's shoulder, said it was good to see him, but he had to beat it, shaking hands, leaving the two men to talk. Alvin signaling Dutch's man behind the bar.

"That thing we talked about . . ." Ziegler said, putting up his hand. "I know, you ain't interested. Thing is, I nosed around, talked to some guys, and next thing, I get a call, Nitti wants to see me. Fucking town's like the wall's got ears. So I go to the HiHo, middle of the day, but Nitti's not there, just Willy White and another guy at the bar — you ever see the eyes on that guy? Guy with him is this Clooney, the one I'm planning to rob. I put out my hand, like I don't know him from Adam, and the pimp just gives me the stink eye, won't shake. White says his pal got wind somebody's set to snatch his old lady, wants to know what I know. So, I put up my hands, make like it's the first I heard."

"Guess you talked to the wrong people," Alvin said.

"Pimp doesn't say a word, just keeps looking at me like he's not buying it. And Willy tells me to look into it. I say, 'Why me?' And this Clooney says, 'It'd be like a personal favor.' I say, 'No offense, man, but do I know you?' And White says he knows me, and more important, I know him. Wants me to take care of it."

Alvin shook his head, the Chicago mob wanting Ziegler to go look for himself.

"You believe something like that?" Ziegler said. "So, I say, by 'take care of it' . . . he wants some names? And White tells me again to take care of it, and nods to the door, like I'm dismissed. Got to tell you, I never been so happy getting out of a place in my life, don't mind telling you."

"So, they want you whacking yourself?" Alvin was grinning.

"Joke if you want. What I did, I went and looked around a couple days, talked to a few more guys, then went back to White, told him I got nothing, was just talk on the street. White looks at me with those fucking eyes, and says he figures it's you."

Alvin lost the grin.

"Knows we worked on a couple of scores, wants me to get next to you and take care of it."

"You son of a bitch."

"Told him your name never even came up on the street."

Dutch's bartender came and set down fresh drinks, then went in back.

"You ask me, it's on account of making a stink about paying Nitti rent. But, you lay low, it'll blow over, maybe stay out of

Chi-town a while. But look, meantime, I got to eat." Ziegler slapped back the drink.

"And I got to keep breathing." Alvin lifted his glass, wanted to hit him with it.

"Look, I told White there's no way it's you, on account you and me talk, the two of us working some business. Maybe I'll tell him again."

"That's you doing me a favor?"

"Didn't expect you'd see it." Ziegler frowned, glancing to see where the bartender was, saying, "Look, speaking of business, and I know I asked, but if you're working on something . . ." Trying not to sound desperate.

"Thinking of taking my girl someplace warm. Been giving me grief about snow and ice and no sun, going pasty she calls it." Dolores still feeling bad for losing the baby, Alvin telling her not being born was doing any kid of his a favor. Told her again, maybe someday when things settled down. Baffled about what he'd do with a kid — teach it to hustle and shoot, not be a cookie pusher or chump to a con like this. Looking at Ziegler, saying, "Look, George, I get back, maybe we'll talk."

Remembering that line about keeping your enemies close, guessing if he worked with Ziegler again, then Willy White would get wind, might buy that he never planned to kidnap some pimp's wife.

... *Daytona, Florida*
December 31, 1933

A lvin looked past Fred and Doc and out the window.
"Was a Stroh's man," Doc said. "Old Julius the only
guy playing it straight, making ice cream in dry times."

A twin-prop taxied down the coquina runway, the city
fathers sticking their airport in the heart of town, the constant
buzz of engines, the airport sign painted on a surfboard. This
place of land-speed records and its Ocean Pier Casino, a
never-ending stretch of golden sand against blue Atlantic,
and women in bathing suits as far as the eye could see.

The suites were first-class, and Florida had him feeling
easy. No Frank Nitti or Willy White, and no lawmen hunting
him under the royal palms. Signing the Morgan's register as
George Heller, Dolores calling herself his missus, telling him
she was trying it out, taking his fake name. Not bringing up
talk of losing the baby again, starting to put it behind her.
Making love to him every night.

Out for dinner and cocktails with Fred and Paula, Doc
and his new girl Ellen, along with Kate. The maître d' introducing the party to Ransom Olds and his wife Ursula in

the lounge, Alvin telling Ransom the first car he ever stole was an Olds, a touring model with a six, banging out forty ponies, nothing like a flathead Ford was putting out, but still a decent car in its day. Ransom laughed, thanking him for the compliment, not believing a word of it, thinking it was the booze talking.

The group having a high time, Alvin downing enough cognac, smoking reefer for the first time, getting up to dance, Dolores trying to teach him the Lindy Hop, giving up on account of his two left feet, moved on to the foxtrot, giving up on that too, saying he was mashing her toes, suspecting he was doing it on purpose, so he wouldn't have to dance. Alvin denied it, getting Kate out of her chair, and waltzing her around the tables, never stepped on her once.

They called it a night at two in the morning, and he took her to the room, then went to find a lobby phone. Past midnight in Chicago, he tried calling Dot, betting the feds had a bug on her phone. Not getting an answer, he hung up, wondering if she went back to live with her aunt, or maybe she was seeing somebody new, not sure how he felt about that. Before they left Florida, he'd try again, tell Dot he was heading to Mexico, hoping to send any eavesdropping feds on a false trail, ask if she needed more money to get by, and see about that divorce.

Next day on the patio outside the suites, he was thinking he might ask Lolli to marry him. As smart as bait back when he met Dot, blinded by her seventeen-year-old body, even thinking he was in love when she got him off of robbery and car theft charges. Felt like the real deal when she walked to the judge's bench, setting down a box of stolen loot, promising she'd lead Alvin down the aisle, keep him on the straight and narrow, the judge looking at her and saying he just bet she could.

No recollection of the clocks he swiped that time, just small-time smash-and-grabs back in his salad days of crime, the dumbness of youth. Released with his personal effects, he took Dot around the corner of the courthouse, making a show of getting down on a knee. Guessing it was a kick for her, going with a bad boy, getting hitched after she got him sprung, likely believing she could change him, now regretting it and feeling only suckers fell in love.

"Hey, Ray, you with us?" It was Doc, pulling him from his thoughts.

He smiled at the brothers, all sitting in patio chairs, hearing Lolli talking in the kitchen, helping Kate and Paula fix a fish supper for their bad men.

"Forget Stroh's," Doc was saying to Fred. "I'm talking Hamm's or Schmidt's, the guys we're in business with." Twisting his neck to the kitchen, making sure the women were out of earshot, calling, "Hey, Ma, sure I can't give you a hand?"

"You help by keeping out of my kitchen."

Doc grinned, hearing the giggling from the inside, saying he bet Ma was on the folding chair in the lanai with a jigsaw, sorting the pieces. Dolores and Paula doing the work, scaling and cleaning the redfish they caught off the pier that morning, peeling spuds and cutting onions, baking a desperation pie or those whoopie cakes Paula liked to bake. Kate calling it an all-the-trimmings feast on account it was New Year's. Truth of it, she stayed out of earshot in the back, not wanting to hear what her boys were mixed up in.

"You sure, Ma?" Doc called back, grinning at Fred and Alvin.

"I got my help."

Back when they were at the St. Paul house, Alvin sat with Kate on nights when the bourbon wouldn't help him sleep, sorting puzzle pieces, the two of them talking, Alvin finding she was better company than his own folks, and as smart as a whip.

The *Star* had run a piece calling it the Ma Barker Gang, the law offering a reward for her and any of her boys. Alvin feeling Fred and Doc ought to get her a place of her own, not wanting her mixed up in their mess, a chance of being charged with accessory or whatever else the prosecutors could dream up. Bringing it up again now.

"This family sticks together," Fred said with an edge. "Look, Ray, your folks were glad to get chuck of you. No offense, that's on them, not you, but Barkers ain't like that — we stick."

"Just don't want her caught in our mess, all I'm saying."

"Going to arrest her for what, doing puzzles?" Doc said. "Goddamn press ought to mind their own fuckin' business." Doc's eyes saying Alvin ought to do the same.

Seeing it was pointless, Alvin swung the talk back to the kidnap plan, Fred on board, and Doc having second thoughts.

"Why not hit a bank in some new state? A place they don't know us. Forty-eight of them, you know, oughta keep us going a while," Doc said. "We hit one, and it's in and out, and no waiting around. Not much for playing nursemaid to the spoiled and rich."

"Bremer's top dog at the Commercial." Alvin looked at Doc. "It's like robbing and kidnapping all in one. And another butter man like Hamm, and we hardly need a gun. Meaning nobody needs the morphine." Alvin feeling the times changing, the wheels coming off in St. Paul. Dillinger, Kelly and Nelson running around like madmen, bringing heat and lawmen like locusts on the old safe haven. Just a matter of time till they brought it all down.

"I'm with Ray," Fred said. "We grab this Bremer, but how about we hold out for more, say like half a million?"

"Come on, who's worth that?" Doc said.

"This ain't retail, brother," Fred said. "And who's to say what a man's worth."

"Family won't pay it, then they stall and call in the feds," Alvin said. "We go for two hundred, same as the Kellys did. We make up for the cut to Nitti like we talked about. We don't get greedy, then we're done."

"Done, what — as in calling it quits?" Doc said, looking confused.

"Been thinking of Spain, taking Lolli along."

"Well, that's real nice, but I'm in, long as the luck holds," Fred said, getting annoyed.

"Well, here's to luck then." Alvin lifted his glass, seeing it was empty, looking to Doc.

"And I ain't over the hill." Doc got out of his chair, saying, "How about it, Fred, what's your pleasure, Schmidt's or Hamm's?" Heading to the icebox, Doc bringing a couple of cases of each in the trunk, driving down here, saying what Florida brewed was piss-water.

"I'll go with Schmidt's," Fred said, looking to Alvin, saying, "A fitting way to go out, robbing the guys who screwed us." A bitterness they all felt for the brewers who turned their backs on the bootleggers who kept them afloat through prohibition, going back to being legit after repeal, the only thought was getting richer.

Alvin laid it out: Bremer's old man being the long-time brewmaster at Hamm's, going over to Schmidt's and getting hitched to Adolf Schmidt's daughter, marrying his way into it. And like the Hamms, he liked dealing under the table, selling to dives and juice joints back in dry times, the Green Lantern topping their list.

Kidnapping felt like payback. Alvin knowing taking Bremer would bring a mountain of heat — old man Bremer being tight with FDR, backing his campaign, putting up three hundred and fifty grand of his own money. Grabbing his namesake would bring Hoover and his FBI nosing around. But the family had the kind of money they were after, and this score would net him more than enough to land him in Spain. Somewhere the feds had no reach.

"Funny, when I got out, St. Paul was the safest place around," Doc said. "Always thought it would last. Back before Hogan got himself blown up, and before Dutch ran the Lantern." Talking about the O'Connor system: Guys doing their business anyplace but St. Paul, running to town and paying their dues, the law turning an eye, allowing the yeggs to walk in daylight. Nobody going to jail — taverns, cathouses, all in full swing — this town running dry, wet and safe, all at the same time.

"Used to be, you were looking for a guy you hadn't seen a while, two places you'd look . . ." Fred said.

"Prison or St. Paul." Doc nodded, turning to Alvin, saying, "You remember hearing 'bout those times, Ray?"

Alvin looked at him, trying to catch up.

"Dillinger, Kid Cann, Verne and Jelly, some of the Chicago guys, Ice Pick and them. Crooks, cocktails and a canary singing along to Piano Red. Man, must'a felt like they died and gone to heaven."

"Wish I'd seen it," Alvin said. "Just had the three rules: let Big Tom know you're in town, make a donation to his favorite charity and don't crap where that man eats."

"Been that way long before Big Tom," Fred said. "St. Paul, a place of no crime, and anytime something went down someplace else, it got headlines like *Last Seen Heading for St. Paul*."

Doc laughed and turned for the kitchen, glancing to see that the women weren't in earshot.

"Nowadays the highbinders are running scared," Fred said, frowning and shaking his head.

"Well, you give it to them, and they'll fuck it up every time," Doc said, going for more beer, saying, "Hamm's for Fred. What's your pleasure, Ray?"

"Long as it's cold . . ." Alvin said, hearing Doc step in the kitchen, telling Ma it sure smelled good, and how she was going all out. Ma telling him to get out of her kitchen.

"Think they got a pie?" Fred winked at him and called into the kitchen, "You girls make a pie?"

"Knock it off," Paula called back.

Fred grinned, then leaned forward, concerned about something he heard, saying, "What's up in Chicago, this Willy White?"

"Called him up, said I heard he was looking for me. Told me Nitti ain't happy Nelson wasn't at the beach house when they sent somebody looking. Thinks I tipped him. Told him after paying Nitti's rent, how was I gonna tip anybody."

Fred frowned, not liking the idea of being in the crosshairs.

"White tells me, the way he's going, Nelson's gonna run out of rope," Alvin said. "Tells me Nitti's looking for Verne Miller too, thinks he turned rat. Wanted to know what I know."

"About Verne?"

"Told him we don't run with rats. Then White gets back to the rent, saying he knows Nitti gave us a pass, but if it's ever up to him, it'll be different. I told him lucky it ain't up to him then. The rent got paid, and he don't like it, he can go talk to Nitti. Wanted to know if I was asking or telling. Then says to watch the shadows, things having a way of changing. Guessing Willy's got ideas of moving up the ladder."

"Say we nab this Bremer, and we take him someplace else," Fred said, not interested in the mob's pecking order.

"Big Tom ain't so big no more, with trouble watching his own back. New York, Reno, all them places — everybody feeling the heat. Think we keep him in the same place."

"Getting tough to make a living," Fred said.

"Why I'm learning Spanish." Looking at him, Alvin said, "How about coming along? We bring the girls, all the money we got. Sun like you won't believe. And they got this drink, call it rebujito, make it with lemon and serve it with mint."

"We got lemon here."

Doc came back in, beer bottles between the fingers of one hand, setting them down, sliding them across the glass table, saying, "So, when do we grab this Bremer?"

. . . St. Paul, Minnesota
January 12, 1934

The thermometer dropped and rode zero since they left Daytona, Lolli letting him know it was getting colder by the mile heading back north, the damn heater in his Hudson not keeping up with the chill. Had tailed the black Lincoln for days, Alvin switching cars a couple times, tagging behind Edward Bremer, watching him drop his daughter at the Summit School, the same time every morning — father and daughter in the car, taking the same route. Could set his watch by this guy.

Worrying about the car stalling in the cold, this place of ten thousand frozen lakes, he bought a pair of Buicks for the job, the Minneapolis dealer throwing in heavy-duty heaters, batteries and frost shields. Telling the salesman he ran a traveling sales company, selling lightbulbs, and couldn't afford lost time, handing him a fake card he had printed up.

Putting together the seven-man crew, in the face of Doc's dissent, Alvin brought in George Ziegler, on account the gunman was having more problems with the Chicago outfit. Doc bringing in prison pal Bill Weaver, spiting Alvin for letting in Ziegler. They agreed on Volney Davis, and new man Harry Campbell, a guy out of Tulsa on Dutch Sawyer's say-so. The crew met at Bill Weaver's second-floor flat on Portland, going over the plan.

The night before the job, Alvin went to dinner with the Barkers, bringing Dolores to the Commodore, the place where Kate was staying, Fred bringing Paula, Doc with Yvonne, a strip-stepper he'd been seeing since getting back to town.

Steaks, lobsters and baked potatoes, champagne and strawberry tarts, the maître d' knowing who they were, treating them like celebrities, introducing them to the couple at the corner table, Werner Wittkamp, one-time Hollywood set designer who gave the hotel's new bar its look, along with his wife, Catherine, the couple joining them for cocktails in a private suite.

Wittkamp asked, "What line are you gents in?"

"Banking mostly," Doc told him. "But we got our fingers in other pies. What we call 'versifying."

"Speculation?" Wittkamp said.

"And a little kidnapping," Doc said.

"I see." Wittkamp giving a good-natured laugh.

Going to the ballroom after dessert, they danced. Doc taking Yvonne back to her place in the West Side Flats. Alvin and Fred escorting Kate to her room, then dropping off Dolores and Paula, driving back to Bill's flat, slowing past the alley beyond his building, set to pull the Buick out front, the place called the Kensington.

"You see the guy?" Alvin said, throwing a thumb to the alley.

Fred turned, spotting the guy down the alley, peeping in a window of the building next to Bill's, his feet on a crate. The guy noticed the Buick slow, and he hopped down and walked deeper into the alley.

"The hell's that about?" Fred took his pistol from under the seat, got out and walked into the alley, circling the block. Alvin kept the Buick idling, cranking up the heater, reaching under the seat for his .45, hoping Fred didn't end up shooting a peeper.

Circling the block, Fred came back and shrugged, got back in, saying, "Some guy on the next corner, could be the same one, I don't know. Having a smoke, and making like he's waiting on somebody."

Doc pulled up and parked behind them, Alvin waved him over. Getting in back of the Buick, asking, "What's up?"

Fred filling him in, Doc taking the back stairs to Bill's place, the rest of the crew waiting there.

Alvin and Fred drove off, finding a phone box. Alvin making a call to Dutch at the Lantern, waiting while Dutch rang Big Tom, wanting to know if they were under surveillance. Waiting by the phone box, Alvin lit a smoke, rubbing his hands, stamping his feet till Dutch called back, unable to get a hold of Big Tom.

Driving back to Bill's, Fred had another look around the building, coming back, saying a squad car was parked on the same corner, the two cops looking like they were keeping eyes on the building.

Not taking risks, Fred went up the back stairs and told the crew to clear out of Bill's, taking anything they didn't want the cops to find. Ziegler having a smoke on the front steps, keeping watch while the rest went out the back, splitting up and driving off, set to meet at Fred's place across town.

Coming from the alley, Fred got in the car, and Alvin rolled back to the phone box. Fred got behind the wheel, waiting in the idling car while Alvin called the Lantern, Dutch still unable to get a hold of Big Tom. If the cops were eyeing Bill's place, they would drop the job and let the crew scatter, but they had to be sure.

Pacing the sidewalk by the phone, lighting another cigarette, holding it in a shaking hand, Alvin got back in the idling Buick, holding his hands to the heater, saying, "Let's go for another look."

Fred nodded, saying he was bringing more heat, driving off and making a stop at his apartment — the gang in his living room, downing whiskey and turning up cards, betting on blackjack. Doc kept watch at the window, his sawed double-barrel on the table.

Taking his Tommy gun from the back of the bedroom closet, Fred went back down the steps, holding the case, looking up and down the street.

Switching to Doc's Chevy, Alvin drove back to Bill's, Fred opening the case and taking the stick magazine from the Tommy, having a hard time fitting on the fifty-shot drum in the bouncing car, using the Third Hand key, depressing the magazine release, pulling the cock lever and locking the bolt back, snapping in the drum.

No sign of the patrol car now, Alvin pulled to the same curb at Bill's corner. Fred leaving the Tommy gun and getting out, having a look down the alley, coming back and shrugging, nothing there but the crate the guy stood on, his tracks in the light snow.

Heading back to Fred's, both of them eager to get indoors and let a couple of shots warm them, Alvin caught twin headlights in the rearview as he turned down a side street. The car made the same turn, staying half a block behind, keeping pace. Turning the next corner, Alvin slowed. Looking over the seat, Fred made out two figures in the car, holding the Tommy gun on his lap. The car behind making the same turn again, staying with them.

Alvin sped up between rows of parked cars, making a right at the next corner, the car keeping back, but turning again. On the next block, he slowed again, Fred making out the driver with a peaked hat, saying, "It's cops."

"I'll run them."

"They make the plate, and we're in the soup, either way. Pull up." Tossing aside the coat, Fred was out of his door before Alvin stopped, stepping to the rear of the Chevy, leveling the Tommy and ripping the night, spraying the approaching car.

The car jerked as bullets struck it, pieces flying up, the headlights gone, both men ducking down, the driver throwing it in reverse and backing into a parked car. The windows blew out, the hood popped, the sedan rocking and settling on flattened front tires, like it was going to its knees, dozens of holes in its hood and fenders, steam rising and metal crying.

"Teach you to creep us," Fred called, getting back in, his ears ringing. House lights were coming on along the residential street, faces peering from behind curtains.

Switching off the headlights, Alvin floored it through a stop sign, made a couple of turns, zigzagging city blocks, finally switching the headlights back on, nobody coming after them.

Parking the car a couple of blocks from Fred's place. The two of them walked back, smoking and waiting at the side of the building, Fred with the Tommy gun under his coat.

Spotting them from the upstairs window, Doc came down, wanting to know what's up, saying he couldn't get Big Tom on the blower, the three of them going inside, switching on the radio, along with the shortwave set they kept tuned to cop transmissions. Hearing the dispatch calls, but nothing about the shoot-up.

"Think we scrap it?" Doc said, looking at them.

Alvin wanted to wait, not wanting to let it go. Catnapping in the armchair by the window, he stayed like that the rest of the night, forcing himself to stay awake, eyes out the window, both radios on, listening to the static and squelch of the shortwave. George Ziegler curled behind him on the sofa, Doc stretched on the rug, Bill Weaver on the floor by the door, Fred in the only bed. Looking out the bay window, Alvin fed fresh cartridges into the partitions on the Tommy gun's drum, replacing the cover and winding key. Doc's sawed-down shotgun lay on the coffee table. Turning the radio knob, he went around the dial, catching some jazz and a newscast, but still nothing about the dust-up.

When dawn came, Doc went for coffee and something to eat, coming back with a tray and the *Twin City Star*'s early edition, the photo of the shot-up car above the fold. Grinning, he said, "Nice shooting, Tex. Says you blew up some airline worker's ride, Roy McCord coming off the day shift, the man still in uniform, his wife sure she'd seen some Tom peeping in her bedroom window, so Roy and a neighbor went for a look, figured it was you two. Wanted to teach you a lesson."

"Took us for peepers?" Fred said.

Doc was laughing more, biting into a Danish. "Says they followed you, wanting to get your plate when you jumped out and shot hell out of their Ford. This McCord took three rounds for his troubles, in his arm and leg, but nothing serious. By some luck he'll come away with just a limp. His buddy stayed on the floor, crying with his hands over his head when the cops showed up. The guy begging them not to shoot."

"They didn't make us?" Alvin said.

"Didn't get the plate. McCord swearing it was a Plymouth, a green one."

Fred blew air, looking relieved.

"So, the job's on?" Ziegler said, sitting up on the sofa, looking eager.

Checking his watch, still a few hours to go, Alvin said, "Looks like."

. . . St. Paul, Minnesota
January 17, 1934

The coffee and Danish were gone, George Ziegler went with Bill Weaver to his apartment. Fred crawled back to bed for another hour, and Doc stretched out on the sofa. Sitting by the window, Alvin read the paper, the top story about Dillinger and an unknown associate hitting an East Chicago bank a couple of days back. Some old lady leaving her cash on the counter, her shaking hands raised, Dillinger telling her to keep it, calling her Mother, doing it with a smile, just the bank money his gang was after. Alvin thinking Dillinger was a ham, playing the same scene, not taking some granny's money, then shooting it out with the cops anytime an alarm was tripped, using hostages as human shields, busting from the banks and getting away no matter what. Leaving one cop getting his last radio call, his partner down and wounded, striking a pedestrian as they raced out of town. Still, the papers held him up like some modern-day Robin Hood, calling him the good-natured Jackrabbit, mentioning he never used profanity, women of all ages loving his looks. His mugshot with that twisted smile showed next to the piece. Below the fold, the story of the Barrows in East Texas the day before, Bonnie and Clyde busting gang members from a prison farm, arming them and shooting it out with the guards, then making a clean getaway. No photo for that one, but the public siding with them too.

Looking out at the dawn, the glow coming over the roof-tops, Alvin didn't care about his popularity, but as far as jobs went he had a feeling they were about to top them all.

———

"So Andy says, 'What do you think if you wake some morning, put your hand in your pocket and out comes a roll of twenties?' And Amos goes, 'I wouldn't think nothing, but I'd know I had on somebody else's pants.'" Bill Weaver telling the joke, waiting for a reaction.

Behind the wheel, Alvin trying not to hear him, tailing Edward Bremer — heir to the Schmidt Brewery fortune, and president of the Commercial State Bank — keeping a safe distance since the man drove from his brick mansion on the Mississippi. The same route every morning, on his way to drop his kid at the Summit girls' school. Alvin wishing Bill Weaver would shut up, telling more of his jokes, borrowing one-liners from Groucho Marx and Stan Laurel. George Ziegler and Doc in the second Buick, parked a block up ahead. No other traffic along Goodrich when Bremer started to turn at Lexington, Ziegler pulling out and cutting in front of the Lincoln, Bremer forced to stop short, banging gloved hands on the horn, trying to crank down his window and cursing at Ziegler.

Pulling behind Bremer, Alvin pinned him in.

Getting out of the lead car, Doc hurried to Bremer's passenger side and opened the door, pulling up the kerchief.

"That man ought to learn to —" Bremer lost the steam, this man getting in his car, with his face hidden.

"And you ought to learn to read a room," Doc said, shoving a pistol at him.

"Get out!" Bremer yelled, fumbling to get out his own door, banging into the steering wheel, panicking, the gloves making it hard to grab the handle.

Sliding across the seat, Doc had hold of his arm and yanked him back. "You wanna see Betty again?"

Bremer tore his arm free and backhanded Doc, struggling to get out. And Doc was on him, smacking Bremer with the pistol.

Panicking, Bremer clawed for the handle with his left hand, shoving Doc away with his right.

Jumping from the Buick, Alvin told Bill to take the wheel, twisting his scarf around his face, slipping on the icy road, catching his balance on Bremer's fender, pulling open the driver's door and throwing the man off balance. Bremer started to tumble out. Alvin slamming the door into the man's knee, shoving him back as Doc tugged his other arm. Yelping, Bremer called for help.

Throwing a gloved fist, Alvin swung the door against Bremer's leg again, Doc clapping a hand over his mouth, stopping him from yelling, the man biting at the hand. Doc slapping the pistol against his head. Bremer making a wild grab for it, Doc turning it on him.

"Don't shoot him." Alvin twisted the man's left arm, his feet sliding on the icy road.

His head bleeding, Bremer kept up the struggle, catching the horn with his elbow. Alvin pinning and twisting the arm, Doc struck him again with the pistol butt. Bremer cowering, putting up gloved hands in surrender.

"Yell again and Betty's an orphan. You got that?" Doc held the pistol on him, panting and gritting his teeth, ready to gut-shoot him.

Taking off a glove, Bremer touched a trembling hand to his bleeding head.

"Shove over," Alvin said, watching a neighbor come from his front door, seeing what was going on. Needing to get out of there, Alvin signaled Ziegler to take off. Pushing Bremer across the seat, he tried to get it started. Ziegler and Weaver both roaring off in the Buicks.

Keeping the pistol on him, Doc handed Bremer blackened goggles and told him, "Put 'em on. Do it or you're dead!"

Bremer hesitated, then did it, not wanting to get hit again, saying, "I'm bleeding."

"Yeah, it's what happens," Doc said.

Aware of the neighbor coming down his driveway, getting a better look, Alvin tried to crank the engine, but couldn't find the starter, grabbing at Bremer's goggles, peeling them back up. "Get this fucking thing going. I mean now!"

Prodding him with the pistol, Doc told him, "Or you're gonna see some real bleeding."

Bremer pointed to the starter button, saying he just had to press it.

"Fuck Lincoln." Pressing it and turning the key, Alvin put it in gear, driving past the man halfway down his driveway, other neighbors coming out to see what was going on.

Following the Buicks, Alvin guessed the cops were on the way.

"Where you taking me?"

"Got a swell room, maid service, hot towels, the whole bit. Gonna love it." Doc telling Bremer to get the goggles on, making like he was going to strike him again, seeing the man's watch as Bremer threw up an arm to ward the blow. Taking hold of the wrist, Doc unstrapped it.

"My father gave me that." Bremer wiped a hand at his bloody mouth, giving up the fight, pulling the goggles over his eyes.

"Shows your old man's got taste." Putting the Rolex to his ear, Doc strapped it on his own wrist — not going to give this one back.

Driving east, Alvin headed them out of town, catching up to the Buicks, miles out of town when he flashed the headlights, getting Ziegler and Weaver to pull over on a back stretch of two-lane. Doc taking Bremer by an elbow, helping him out, leading him, seeing Bremer was limping over to Weaver's Buick. He forced him on the rear floor like he'd done to Hamm. Alvin got in the passenger side, the two cars driving off, leaving Bremer's Lincoln, blood smeared across its bench seat.

Thirty miles east, Ziegler pulled over at the designated picnic grounds. Weaver stopping behind him, Alvin holding typed papers across the seat, Doc pulling Bremer up onto the backseat, peeling up the goggles. The rest of them got out, stretching their legs, raising their masks enough and lighting cigarettes. Fred stepping to the ditch, watering the horses.

"Sign these," Alvin said, holding the papers and a pen across the seat.

"Never sign what I don't read." Looking worse for wear, the blood drying on his face, matted in his hair, Bremer was clinging to the mule attitude, used to being in charge, his eyes going to the men and the make of the cars.

"You got to like bleeding," Doc said, clinging to his patience, stabbing a finger at the papers.

Bremer shook off his gloves, fumbling inside his jacket, taking his own pen, then the papers from Alvin, scanning the words: *We are ready Alice*. Asking, "Alice? What's this mean?"

"Told you to sign it." Doc stabbed at the papers, his left hand clamping the back of the man's neck, Bremer signing where Doc pointed, saying, "I'm forced under duress."

"Now you're getting the picture, Eddie."

"Don't call me that."

Doc stabbed the papers, breathing the word, "Keep going."

Bremer looked at the eyes behind the mask, thought better of fighting. Scanning the typed words, shaking his head, saying, "Two hundred thousand. Guess you never met my father, or this is some joke."

"Joke like a heart attack." Alvin took the papers, blowing at the ink.

Taking the man's pen, Doc pocketed it, and held up his hand like he didn't want to hear it, saying, "I know, your father gave it to you." Yanking the goggles back over Bremer's eyes, reaching inside Bremer's coat, feeling for a wallet, taking it and going through it, taking the cash, looking at the photo of Bremer and his daughter, saying, "Cute kid." Slipping the wallet back in Bremer's pocket, patting the man on the shoulder. "You get settled in the room we got for you, Eddie, and you look at that picture, and ask yourself if you want to see her again."

"I'm carsick."

"Well, you toss up all you want, Eddie, but you do, I'm gonna sit your ass in it, mop it up with your nice suit." Doc was fed up with this guy. "And before you blow your groceries, tell me who you want as a contact man?" His hand moving to the back of the man's neck, squeezing and saying, "And think good and hard." Doc wanting to just keep squeezing.

Bremer tried to pull away from the grip, saying, "Walter, Walter Magee."

Fred, Harry and Ziegler got in the second Buick and headed for St. Paul with the signed ransom notes. Alvin, Doc and Bill Weaver waited till they drove off. Doc stayed in back with Bremer, kept him kneeling on the floor as they drove east. Bremer complaining about his injured knee. Too damn cold in the car.

. . . Bensenville, Illinois
January 18, 1934

Nitti didn't have a hand out for more rent, making Chicago the place to stash Bremer, the abandoned house where they held Hamm.

Bremer was bleating about his hurt knee from the upstairs room, Ziegler glancing up the stairs, wishing the man would shut up.

"So Hoover's targeting five gangs, this war on crime." Alvin sat reading the *Daily News*, ignoring Ziegler, the way he was looking up the stairs, saying, "They got the fugitive lovers, the good-looking escape artist —"

"That's got to be me," Doc said.

"There's the psychopath baby-face killer," Alvin said. "The misunderstood country bumpkin and the clan of hillbilly kidnappers."

"Country bumpkin . . ." Harry Campbell pointed at Doc.

"Well, I know that's a joke, Harry," Doc said. "But kidnapping hillbillies, they mean us, or the Kellys?"

"The Kellys don't make a list like that," Harry Campbell said. "Got to be us. And fugitive lovers goes to the Barrows."

"No doubt the psychopath baby's Nelson," Doc said. "And country bumpkin's got to be Floyd. You ever hear that man talk?"

"Escape artist's Dillinger," Harry said. "Except that man's not so good-looking. What do you say, Ray?" Knowing how Alvin felt about him.

"I wouldn't kiss him," Alvin said.

Doc grinned at Harry, neither saying it; of all the nicknames the papers dreamed up: Dillinger called the Jackrabbit, Nelson called Baby Face, Volney Davis dubbed as Curley, George Ziegler known as Shotgun. Along with Machine Gun Kelly, Harvey the Dean, Pretty Boy Floyd, Ice Pick Willie, Basil the Owl, Big Bob Brady, Oklahoma Jack, Slim Gray, Two-Gun Crowley, Deafy Farmer, the Baron, Billy the Killer, Terrible Ted — some rag dubbing Alvin "Old Creepy" on account of his crooked smile, more like a sneer. Nobody calling him that to his face; and anybody who knew him called him Ray, and nobody knew why they called him that.

"Family of redneck kidnappers. Think the feds finally figured who snatched Hamm," Harry said. "Was hoping they'd keep pinning it on the Touhys, this one too. Blame the Irish."

"Another beer man gets what's coming," Doc said. "Sons of bitches worked with us when it made them rich, then turned their backs, straightening their ties. Guy upstairs was one of the first calling for a crackdown on crime, playing the honest man."

The Hamms and Bremers sold barrels through speakeasies across the Midwest during the dry years, then went back to licit practices and breaking old connections.

None of it mattered to Alvin, driving to the Bensenville Hotel and Tavern in the late morning, waiting by the courtesy phone for Fred's call, finding out the ransom demand was delivered. Nothing to do now but keep a cool head and let it play out. Alvin still thinking he ought to get a book and learn some Spanish. Going to the hotel bar, he ordered a neat scotch and a club sandwich before making the next call, waiting for the operator to make the connection.

Big Tom coming on the line, his voice deep and sober, "Chief Brown."

"Got a minute, chief?"

"Hold on."

Alvin heard him shuffle and close the door, then coming back on the line. "You know you don't call here."

"Thought you fell in a hole, not picking up your ringer."

"I answer to you now?" Big Tom said.

"Want to know what you know."

"Well, start by congratulating me." Big Tom eased his tone, saying, "I just moved myself up the ladder."

"Yeah, going for mayor?"

"Put myself in charge of the kidnap squad."

"You dog." Alvin grinned, liking it, saying, "So, what you got?"

"Give me fifteen, and call the right number." Meaning the Lantern, and Big Tom hung up.

Back at the bar, Alvin flagged the bartender for one more, then made the call, had the operator put him through to Dutch Sawyer's.

Big Tom answered, saying, "So, how's our boy?"

"One cranky piece of work, upstairs staring at the wall-paper, whining about his hurt knee. Ask me, it don't look so bad, just bruised. The window's boarded so he don't know it's day or night. Complaining about that too."

"Thought of you a few nights back. A pair of crazies in a sedan went all Fourth of July with Tommy guns."

"That so?"

"Shot up some citizens' ride, two guys inside minding their own business."

"Maybe they followed too close."

"These two mutts took the gunmen for peepers."

"Well, we all make mistakes."

"Yeah, well, lucky these two pulled through. Got everybody from the commissioner on down calling me. Wanting to know what in hell I'm doing about keeping the streets safe."

"These citizens get a look?"

"No, but it stirred a pot in no need of more stirring."

"Maybe whoever did it figured you skipped town."

"Kinda thing keeps up, I may have to. Think whoever done it's forgetting the rules."

"You wanna talk about it on the blower?"

Big Tom was quiet a moment, then said, "Got called to Bremer's, the mayor insisting I show up, old Adolph demanding we stop the kidnappers hard."

"He scraping up the money?"

"Says he won't part with a dime," Big Tom said. "Ought to see this place, a stone mansion, got to be twenty rooms. Maids in uniforms and a guy who opens the door. Standing in my dress blues, and the guy asks if I got an appointment. Had to show him my tin to get in. Tell me, what's a man need with twenty rooms? I got no idea. But I tell you, old Adolph's a piece of work."

"Doesn't sound like it shook him."

"That old goat's cut from the same stone, like his house. Says he wants to negotiate, giving me and the feds a chance to lay a trap."

"He miss the blood in the Lincoln?"

"His flunky Magee took it to a car wash, got it nice and cleaned up before he called us. Didn't want the old man seeing the blood. Thought it would upset him."

"The contact man wipes the crime scene," Alvin said, looking to the ceiling.

"The old man called in the feds, this Werner Hanni, the SAC of St. Paul sitting in. You got to see this guy."

"Warned him about bringing the law," Alvin said.

"Adolph's not a guy you warn. You ask me, think you better send him a finger, ask if he sees the family resemblance — loosen him up a bit."

"From the sound, better send two, 'specially if his kid keeps acting up."

"The old man's holding fast for now, but this Magee's pacing in his office, worried for both of them, thinks young Bremer got maimed on account of the blood. Might loosen the old man after a while. That and a finger in the mail ought to do it, but just send one. Tell him you're saving the rest. The old man likes to horse trade and loves putting on a show for the press."

"Won't be any horse trade; it's two hundred grand for our troubles. And if we got to slice fingers, the price goes up ten grand a cut. Advise him he gets the money and runs the Alice ad in the *Trib*, or you fear the worst." The note instructing Adolph Bremer to run the ad when he was ready to make the drop, the words: *We are ready Alice*. Alvin not liking the idea of cutting off Bremer's fingers, but guessing it would be no different than putting a hen into that cone and making the slice.

"Telling me my job now?"

"You want your taste, right?" Alvin hearing the chief huff, not a man who liked to be pushed.

"Finger or no, give him a couple days, let him sweat. Demand he calls us and the feds off. You don't see the ad, then ring him up and let him hear you sharpen the knife. The old goat hears his boy screaming, he'll come around."

"His ticker take something like that?"

"Thing's made of granite, like I said. One more thing, don't call him direct. Hanni's bugging every phone in the place, the brewery too. Like a spider spinning webs all over. And trust me, that fed's not gonna back off just 'cause the old man tells him. Came off looking dumb on the Hamm thing, putting on a manhunt for Touhy, not considering other leads. Now he's got one of his bugs up his own ass, and already figures this is on you, calling you Ma Barker's gang."

When Alvin hung up, he felt the wet under his arms, leaving the hotel, looking at the falling snow, hearing it crunch underfoot, getting in the car and driving slow back through Bensenville.

... *Bensenville, Illinois*
January 20, 1934

They gave Adolph Bremer time to lose faith in law enforcement. The Alice ad running Thursday morning. Alvin getting word to Big Tom through Dutch Sawyer at the Lantern, waiting on his call in the same hotel lobby.

"The old man leaked it to the snoops," Big Tom said, calling from the back room of the Lantern. "Now he's got news-hawks crawling like ants. Making a statement his family's got no intent of siding with law enforcement. Doing what he can to scrape up the cash, saying he just wants his boy back."

"A change of heart," Alvin said, liking the sound of it, but wondering about a set-up.

"Demanded Hanni pull all the bugs out of his place. Oh, get this, Hanni's so busy bugging the joint, he forgets to report to his chief, a capital sin with Hoover. The chief finds out by reading about it in the *Post*, how the blood got washed off the car." Big Tom couldn't help laughing on the line, saying, "Since the press got hold of it, the feds've been plagued with crank calls, the precinct too. False leads, tips and confessions coming out of the woodwork.

"Old man Bremer gets a postcard claiming Eddie's dead and buried out by Anoka. Hanni hears it through a bug he forgot to take out, going to Bremer and demanding the postcard, threatens the old man with interfering in his investigation, forces him to give up the card, and sends it to the lab, having it dusted for prints. Meantime, he takes a squad of boys with shovels and drives to the Anoka spot, digging up the place half the night."

"Shook the old man up," Alvin said.

"Old Adolph gets on the blower to Washington and tears a strip off Hoover," Big Tom said. "Next call's to our mick mayor, wants every uniform off his property. Then leaks to the press how he figures a competitor set it up. All but said the Hamms were behind it, told me they been dying for the Bremers to sell out, forced to meet the ransom demands. Meaning Hamm gets the business cheap and adds it to his empire. Tell you, these beer boys are crooks in ties. Oh, one more thing: old Adolph's talking to the Pinkertons, in case his boy don't make it back. In that case, he's taking it to the ends of the earth. So, maybe a good thing you left the fingers attached."

Alvin liked it, the wheels were coming off, saying, "Sounds like it's time to make the next play."

"Sounds like."

━━

The lead story in the *Star* told how Dillinger and his gang had been nailed in Tucson, arrested and held over in the Pima County Jail. The escape artist was finally brought down, and giving reporters an interview from his cell. The *New York Times* calling him the modern prodigal son. Alvin shook his head, this guy gets busted, then puts on a show, his return behind bars handled like a mere setback. But it didn't get under Alvin's skin this time.

Waiting till dark, he sent Bill Weaver to chuck a bottle through the plate-glass door of the home of Harold Nippert, Adolph's personal physician. The man finding an envelope with a note amid the busted glass, instructing him to take it straight to Bremer.

Tailing him, Weaver followed the man's car to the mansion, watched him hand off the next note signed by Edward, instructing the family to put four blue National Recovery eagle stickers in Walter Magee's office window at the brewery when the ransom was ready. Eyeing the mansion overnight, Weaver waited till old man Bremer's limousine drove off at first light, tailing it to the governor's mansion, then into town an hour later where old Adolph had breakfast with a couple of his bankers. Half of a blue sticker ended up in Magee's window by noon.

Stopping at the Lantern, Bill Weaver waited on Alvin's call, saying, "The hell's that mean, half an eagle? Supposed to be four. These fuckers trying to chisel us?"

First impulse was to call Big Tom back, but any more collusion and the top cop would want more of the pie. Driving back to Bensenville, Alvin went up the stairs, putting on the bandana and dark glasses, holding a book and some paper on top.

"I'm sick of this," Bremer said from the bunk when he came in.

"That so?" Alvin set the papers aside, looked at him a moment, and he jumped at him and swung the book at his knee, striking at him over and over, waited while the man tumbled to the floor, clutching the knee, crying and moaning.

Catching his breath, Alvin said, "Nothing like a good book." One he found on a shelf downstairs, with lots of pages and plenty of heft. Saying to Bremer, "*Passage to India*, you read it?"

When the moans stopped, Alvin said, "You're gonna take a letter."

"No. I don't care what you do."

Alvin tossed the book down, saying, "You forgetting nobody can hear you bawling and yelling?" Then he moved on him, clutching the knee with his fingers, squeezing the bruised flesh as hard as he could, gritting his teeth and growling.

Bremer wailed and tried to twist free of his grip, pounding fists at him, but Alvin had leverage and didn't let go till Bremer gave up. Straightening the glasses, he picked up the battered book, looked at Bremer, saying, "Don't know why, but your old man wants you back."

"I know him better than you, and you won't get a dime."

Alvin chopped with the book, striking the knee with its spine, the book coming apart in his hands, and he waited through more howling. When Bremer had it down to a blubber, Alvin said, "How about now, Eddie, you want me to fetch another book, or you ready to write?"

Tears streaked his face, Bremer curled on the bunk, his hands holding his knee, shaking his head, saying, "I mean it, you won't get a dime. And I'm not writing anything."

Tossing the broken book aside, Alvin went out, locking the door from the outside.

Bremer was rubbing his knee, wiping his hand at his bloody mouth, when the key scraped the lock, the door opening again, a shorter man coming in, a flour sack over his head, eyeholes cut out. This was the man who had struck him with his pistol when they first took him.

He sat next to him on the cot, pulling a kitchen knife, saying. "Gonna let you pick, but I'm thinking the one with the class ring, but, like I said, you pick."

Balling his fists, Bremer held them to his chest. "I'll write what you want." Seeing paper sliding under a door.

The hooded man took a pen from his inside pocket, Bremer's own pen. Then he reached the papers, handed them over, bent for the book cover and set it in Bremer's lap, and told him to write: "Father, maybe you can wait, but I can't. You're playing with my life." Watching him scratch it on the paper, the man said, "These people are serious and know your every move. Now, the FBI may want to play hero to the press, but I'll end up the martyr. Get the money and all the bugs out, and get them to pull every lawman out — or I'm dead. Yours, Edward."

Doc had him write it a second time. Then dictated a third note: "If you're reading this, father, then I'm dead, just like I warned you. You killed me. If you want my body for proper burial, the price is the same. You wait any more, I'll just be worse for wear."

"I can't write that." Edward was sobbing, his head in his hands, tears dropping on the paper.

"Starting to take us serious?" Doc thinking the tear- and blood-stained paper was a nice touch, watching Bremer concede and write. Then taking the papers, looking them over, he walked out and locked the door behind him.

▬

A Checker cab delivered the first note to the Bremer mansion. Typed on the envelope:

We tried to play fair. From here on,
it's up to you to get word to us.

Have every cent of the $200,000.00.
Time is short.

Bill Weaver dropped the identical note to the mailroom of the *Twin City Star*, the editor-in-chief's name scrawled on it. The envelope marked *Life and Death*.

Four days since they grabbed Bremer, George Ziegler was getting antsy, drinking too much to ease his nerves, saying he was ready to call it quits, wanting to kill the heir and get out of town, sure the feds were closing in, betting they'd stay on the case.

Alvin telling Ziegler they were waiting it out. If he didn't like it he could go, giving up his share.

The next morning Edward's note appeared in the *St. Paul Daily News*. Putting on the glasses and pulling up the bandana, Alvin took the paper upstairs, put on the flour sack and unlocked the door. The man had his pants off, looking at the leg, swollen at the knee, an ugly purple-and-brown bruise running from the thigh to below the knee. Bremer swearing he needed a doctor.

Ignoring him, Alvin held the paper out.

Staring at it, Bremer shook his head, saying, "You have no idea, we just don't have the kind of money you're after."

"But the old man can get it, sell something off if he has to." Alvin feeling they were back to horse trading.

"Not in his nature, even if it was, there's not enough. Look, I'm telling you straight."

"Then how much?"

"Maybe twenty-five . . . thirty if you wait."

"I found a maul in the garage, you know what that is?" Waiting till he nodded, Alvin said, "Thinking of letting the boys take turns swinging it at your knee. Give them something to do. You get through this, you'll be walking like a duck."

"If you'd come to me at the start, told me what you had in mind . . ." Edward with his hands across the knee like he was protecting it, taking a new approach.

"Just come to your office, no appointment, and say, hey, Eddie, gonna bag you 'less you pay us up front. You being the reasonable guy you are, you'd go along. I drive off and trust you to send it in the mail."

"I'm just not worth what you're asking. No offense, mister, but you could've found that out, maybe done some homework. But, hey, but that's on — No, no! Please . . ."

Raising his shoe to kick the leg, Alvin set it back down, saying, "There's your kid, one you take to the fancy school. How about we grab her, set you loose? Maybe Grandad's got a soft spot he don't have for you?"

"Look, maybe I know somebody worth that much. Suppose I help you sketch it out, plan it to a T? And, of course, I don't want a dime, whatever you get's yours. You earned it."

"So I grab a family friend, a favorite cousin, a good neighbor, a captain of industry. How about a rich girlfriend, or why not the old man himself?" Alvin couldn't believe this guy.

"You don't understand. I've fenced bonds for people; I can tell you things of high society would curl your hair. Be like giving you million-dollar tips."

"Million dollars, huh?"

"You ever hear of Leon Gleckman?"

"King of the bootleggers, sure, who hasn't?" Alvin grinned under the hood, knowing Bremer had been in cahoots with Gleckman during prohibition, same as the Hamms had been. Gleckman having mob ties.

"Yeah, that's him. How about Sister Harriett Payne? Or the Humboldts? Or how about Bill Mahoney? Or Harry Sawyer? William Hamm, already been kidnapped, a man who knows the ropes. All of them players, and all of them loaded. All having money they don't want the feds to know about."

Alvin didn't respond, surprised to hear Dutch Sawyer's name, but getting sick of this sniveling coward, along with the fusty smell in the room — not letting Bremer bathe since they brought him here, all that sweat and wealth starting to stink. Locking the door behind him, he wondered about Bremer knowing Dutch Sawyer.

That afternoon, Fred and Ziegler drove in from St. Paul, having no further word from Big Tom, just going by what they read in the papers. The *Tribune* suggesting Bremer faked the whole thing, an attempt to save his failing banking business.

"I'm telling you we backed the wrong horse," Ziegler said. "Every move we make, old man Bremer's got feds crawling around, then saying he don't. I say we off our boy, bury him in Riverdale, and cut our losses."

"Where's the payday in that?" Harry Campbell said.

"Well, I didn't sign up for no Alcatraz. And that's what's coming our way." Getting heated, Ziegler said, "Heard Roosevelt on the radio. Goddamn president makes his address, one of his fireside chats, and calls it an attack on all we hold dear — a crime that won't go unpunished. You heard it same as me, Harry." Ziegler pointing to the offending radio on the kitchen table.

"One thing's sure, I ain't going back inside," Fred said, glancing at Alvin.

"Comes to it, he ain't seen us, we can cut him loose," Harry Campbell said.

"They'll keep coming, alive or dead, money or no money," Ziegler said. "And the fucker knows plenty, likely figured how many of us, what we sound like, maybe even caught a glimpse, likely of you." Looking at Alvin.

Bremer called from upstairs, wanting water.

Pulling his pistol, Ziegler started for the stairs. "Eddie wants water."

Harry went after him, caught him by the arm and spun him, Ziegler turning the pistol on him.

Alvin and Fred stood, Ziegler stopping by the banister, thinking better of it, tucking his pistol back in his belt, showing his hands. "Look, I'm sick of being a goddamn wet nurse with a gun, is all." And he turned and went out the side door.

"Like watching a baseball lose its stitch, the man coming undone," Harry said, looking at the others.

Alvin said he'd have a word with him, getting his own pistol from his bedroll, then going out the door after Ziegler.

. . . Bensenville, Illinois
February 3, 1934

A lvin sat by the radio, turning the set for better reception, Fred across from him, drumming his fingers on the table. Cups of coffee in front of them.

Ziegler came in and leaned by the door with his arms folded, calm now, Harry Campbell angling in past him.

The CBS affiliate in Minnesota was broadcasting, Adolph Bremer reading a statement: "I want to warn the kidnappers not to contact me or my family directly. In spite of my refusal to cooperate with the FBI, I fear our phone lines remain tapped, jeopardizing my son's life . . ."

All of them exchanging looks. Static cut the signal, Alvin tapping the top of the box, the voice coming back.

"Since you've left us no contact, I ask you to find a go-between, and I promise to deliver your money, all of what you asked. You give me back my son unharmed, and I will not cooperate in your pursuit."

"He's paying it?" Harry Campbell said, looking surprised, then beaming at them, clapping his hands.

"And nobody's coming after us." Bill Weaver walked in and turned his head to the ceiling, whispering a prayer.

Ziegler sat next to Alvin, blowing air of relief, saying he couldn't believe it.

Getting up, Fred did some soft shoe, hooking his brother's arm as he entered the crowded room, singing the Gold Diggers' hit "We're in the Money," dancing Doc around the table, banging into the stove, then into Harry, then into the table again. The radio losing its signal.

All of them grinning.

———

This is your last chance.
Make no mistake, we're watching.

Next day in St. Paul, four in the morning, Doc set the delivery instructions at the door of the Catholic priest's residence, addressed to Adolph Bremer. Banging a fist on the door, he moved past the wrapped rosebushes, keeping to the shadows, slinking back to his car up the road.

An old friend of the Bremers, the priest read it and brought it straight to the mansion, Doc following, hanging back a block, waiting till Walter Magee came from the mansion, the butler helping him load two suit boxes in back of his car. Following Magee to the spot on University Avenue, Doc watched him switch the boxes to the stolen Ford he had parked at the curb. A note with more instructions hung from the steering wheel, the ignition key in the door pocket. Doc followed Magee to Farmington, twenty miles south of St. Paul, staying well back.

The note ordered Magee to follow the nine a.m. Pacific Greyhound to Rochester, rolling past Cannon Falls, the bus pulling into the way station at Zumbrota. Following it another four miles as instructed, Magee turned the Ford past a red barn, then down a dirt road for a half mile. Doc stayed a few hundred yards behind, making sure they weren't being followed, finally flashing his headlights, closing the distance till there were fifty yards between them. Magee stopped and got out, didn't look at the car idling behind him, dropping the suit boxes in the road, then he drove off. And it was done.

Waiting till the dust settled on the road, Doc rolled up to the spot, shut off his engine and got out, a pistol in hand, listening and looking around before going to the boxes, opening each and taking a count. Figuring his share, then taking a jerry can from the trunk, shaking off his gloves, fitting on the spout and emptying the fuel into the tank, enough to make the drive back to Bensenville. Tossing the empty can past the ditch. Loading the boxes in his trunk, he set the pistol on the passenger seat, did a three-point turn, careful of the ditches on either side, and he drove back, singing what he remembered of "We're in the Money."

━━

"The cat roads are good, and it's bank season," George Nelson was smiling, clapping his hands, sitting at the table in back of the Green Lantern. Tuesday, two days on, and no cops beating down the door.

Homer Van Meter sitting next to him. "I got a good man here, and I'm looking for a couple more." Sounding like he was recruiting, Nelson looked across at Alvin and the brothers. "I thought of you boys, and I'm asking one more time."

"Told me that time in Reno, you had an aim, make ten grand and get out," Alvin said, looking at this guy acting like a pro now, felt like he was poking at Alvin with a stick.

"That time when I said it . . ." Nelson smiled, remembering it, saying, "Trouble is, you get the ten, then you want the twenty, and when you get that, well, I guess you lose count."

"Yeah, that's the game." Alvin nodded, thinking of Ziegler wanting to nab the pimp with mob connections, saying to Nelson, "But, no offense, count me out." Looking sorry but feeling good turning him down, all the money they were sitting on.

Showing nothing, Nelson said, "You made it nabbing a couple of beer men, got lucky both times. Or, this about something else, Creep?" Looking at Alvin, nothing friendly in his eyes.

"Guess you don't like hearing no, but there it is." Alvin looked at him square, not showing that it felt good saying it, looking into those cold, dumb eyes.

"You scored good the way I heard it, way everybody heard it." Nelson smirked at Van Meter next to him, then looked at the Barkers, saying, "With Harvey and John in the tank, not many yeggs left to ask." Taking out a pack of Kools, offering it around. "But don't take it wrong, you boys're always at the top of my list."

"And we appreciate it —" Alvin started.

"Yeah, you said so." Nelson put up a hand to stop him, looking at the brothers. "Talking to the boys here."

Alvin leaned back, doubting Harvey "the Dean" Bailey or Jackrabbit Dillinger would play second fiddle in a Baby Face gang, letting Fred and Doc speak for themselves.

"Had a word with this shyster, one taking the Jackrabbit's money," Nelson said. "Tells me if he can get John sprung from Crown Point, he'll throw in."

"You do it, then you got your gang," Alvin said.

Nelson threw him a glance, huffing air like he was hanging on to his patience.

"You talking about busting Dillinger loose?" Doc said, resting a forearm on the table.

"Me and Homer here," Nelson said.

"The two of you gonna bust him out?" Fred said, his look a mix of surprise and doubt.

"It's an egg of a place. Pay off a guard, slip in a piece, and the man'll do the rest. Two of us just wait out in the car."

"And he'll owe you one," Fred said.

"Some folks are grateful, yeah." Nelson looked from Fred, to Doc, eyes resting back on Alvin, saying, "Man's mouthpiece says he can slip in a gun but wants five Gs to do it. Me, I'll do it for kicks."

"That how it went with Pretty Boy?" Alvin said, sure Nelson was in on the botched rescue, sheriff's deputies turning their prisoner into fed hands.

"Think that was me, Creep?"

"Matter of fact . . ."

"You're asking if we'll throw in," Fred cut in.

Nelson frowned, looked at the brothers. "Except I got the feeling he's the mouth for you."

"Another thing you got wrong then," Fred said.

"Guess that goes for you," Nelson said to Doc, getting ready to go.

"You need a couple guys, right?" Doc said, like he was thinking about it, taking a cigarette from Nelson's pack. "How about Bill Weaver, you okay with him?"

"On your say-so, yeah, sure, Doc." Nelson reached his lighter, flicking a flame, lighting Doc's smoke.

"Pretty hot right now, with feds all over the Bremer thing," Doc said like he was thinking about it, puffing and blowing smoke, looking at the menthol cigarette like it was offending him, then stubbing it out.

"I'm talking about Dakota, near five hundred miles between." George Nelson glanced at Homer, then back to Doc. "Tell you what, think about it and get in touch." Finishing his whiskey, he grabbed his cigarettes, got up and went out without another word, Homer Van Meter looking apologetic, saying so long, then following Nelson out.

"Had to poke him with a stick?" Doc said to Alvin.

"Don't take much."

"Man's a little tense, but he's got the balls of a brass monkey," Doc said.

"Likely to get them shot off, and anybody else with him." Alvin tapped a smoke from his own pack, offering it around.

"Man ain't so dumb," Doc said, taking a smoke.

"Maybe so, but he sure likes his killing." Alvin struck a match, held it out.

"We've done it," Fred said, leaning back.

"Difference between needing to and liking it."

. . . *Chicago, Illinois*
March 18, 1934

"Son of a bitch." Alvin looked from the front page of the *Trib*, standing in the room of the Irving Hotel, laying the paper on the table. Shaking his head like he couldn't believe it.

Sitting on the edge of the bed, Fred looked at him.

"Busted out of Crown Point," Alvin said.

"Dillinger?"

Alvin nodded.

"Figure Nelson got him a gun?"

"Says he slipped the guard and disappeared. And got right back to work, hit a bank in Sioux Falls, another in Mason City. Shot their way out of both, Dillinger stacking hostages on the running boards, the paper calling it his signature move — a stunt making him the most wanted man in the country." Alvin slapped the paper, couldn't believe it.

"Signature move? Shit, we done it, Clyde and Buck done it, and the Touhys too, and Oklahoma Jack . . ." Fred said, shaking his head. "Bet he went running to St. Paul."

"Just says he vanished."

"Well, it gets the law sniffing after him, not us."

"Identified him and Van Meter, a third gunman unknown," Alvin said. "Got to be George Nelson's making friends."

"Well, to hell with them guys. We really doing this?" Fred said, having second thoughts about having his face altered by former MD Joseph Moran, and getting his fingerprints removed. Something Doc refused to do, saying it was easy for Fred and Ray, already looking like a pair of Frankensteins, but with his natural good looks, it was too much to give up. Told them while they were getting sliced like baloney, he was going to buy a new hat, get his hair colored yellow, maybe start wearing gloves like Bremer.

"And we're paying twelve hundred bucks to a horse doctor," Fred said, more sober now than when he agreed to it.

"Every paper in the country's running our mugs, the price on our heads going up like Electric Boat stock," Alvin said.

"I'm saying we ought to talk the quack down. Man's made plenty off us," Fred said. "Was joking how we paid for his boat."

"He said that?"

"Running his mouth at the Exchequer, some of Capone's crew hanging round."

Alvin not liking it, the old sawbones bragging to Scarface's old crew. "Man's mouth's getting a bit loose."

"I say we talk him down," Fred said.

"Want to dicker with a man who's got you doped, holding a scalpel?"

Fred seeing his point.

Alvin had tried, offering Moran five hundred, after he considered taking off his own prints using hydrochloric acid, then thinking better of it.

Taking offense, Moran told him, "Knowing what I know, think you'd remember this isn't St. Paul, this's my town. Way I see it, you boys are in my good hands." Giving the look back to Alvin, then smiling good-natured, clapping him on the arm, saying, "It's twelve hundred, that's my price. And one I know you can afford."

Alvin's look sobered Moran, the old sawbones saying, "Come on, Ray, you know it's just business, and the price is fair." Adding getting it up front would be nice.

"And how we know we don't come out looking like grilled cheese?" Fred said, folding his arms.

"He gets it up front, but who says he gets to keep it?"

"If he messes me up . . . so help me."

A light rap at the door, and Joseph Moran stepped in, the tang of Dutch courage following behind him, the man who had his credentials revoked for performing illegal abortions, arrested for patching gunshot wounds without reporting them, doing a stretch for it in Joliet. Working from this hotel suite since getting his release. A man known around Chi-town for his back-room operations, removing fetuses, patching holes and stitching cuts, and laundering dough through his practice. Holding a beat-up medical bag, Moran nodded to Alvin, then to Fred, saying, "Which one's got my fee?"

"Hello to you too, doc." Taking his roll from a pocket, Alvin counted off half, showed him the rest, said he'd get it after.

Recounting the half, Moran made a face, but didn't argue, making it disappear, saying, "And I told you to wear pajamas."

"Except mine are silk," Alvin said.

"You wear silk?" Fred said.

"Was a gift. Point is, I don't swipe my clothes off the neighbor's clothesline." Looking at Moran's rumpled suit, one that looked like he slept in it, then down at his scuffed shoes.

"Suit yourself," Moran said. "Blood gets on them, don't cry to me." Moran opened his bag, laying a cloth on the bed, smoothing it, and carefully setting out scalpels and instruments, syringes, a stethoscope, a jar of cotton, passing the time of day, then saying, "So who goes first?"

"How much blood we looking at, doc?" Fred said.

"Do him." Alvin nodded to Fred.

"How much?" Fred said, looking worried.

"Forget I said it. Nothing to worry about. Now, how's your threshold for pain?"

"The last man pissed me off . . ." Fred crossed himself.

"All in fun, my boy, all in fun." Moran gave a shrug and smiled, looked like he was enjoying this.

"Well, fuck your fun, let's get it over." Fred held out a hand.

Fighting second thoughts, Alvin watched the quack who took the fingerprints off a couple of Roger Touhy's boys a month back. Seemed like a good idea when he heard about it, Moran saying along with the prints, he could alter their looks with plastic surgery, just a couple of tiny slices, something he claimed he studied on. Swearing the feds, even their own mothers, wouldn't be able to identify them.

Alvin watched Moran wrap bands around the first joints of Fred's fingers, mixing a pink antiseptic in a dish and swabbing it on, numbing the digits. Pulling a flask from his bag, Moran tipped it and had a drink, saying, "Okay, here we go."

Fred reached for the flask, Moran not letting him touch it, warning about contamination. Tipping it to Fred's lips, letting him have a swallow, calling it medicinal.

"Make it a double, doc," Fred said, taking another swallow, then saying, "Okay, let's get it done." Looking away as Moran took a syringe.

"It's cocaine, going to float your fingers right off. Now, hold still." And he poked it in, injecting the tip of a finger, then did the next one.

Fred flinched with each poke.

Reaching the flask, Alvin turned to the window as Moran got in close and started whittling with the scalpel, the whiff of the antiseptic turning his stomach. Taking his pack, going out for a smoke.

"You need more light," Fred said through clamped teeth when Alvin came back in, shutting the door behind him.

"The light's fine," Moran said. "Not exactly an operating table at St. Luke's, but we're good." Taking a firm hold of Fred's hand, he put his attention on slicing the top layers of dermis, explaining he needed to cut deep enough, not wanting any unwanted layers to grow back. Whittling away for half an hour, then saying, "How are you holding up, my boy?"

"I need more." Sweat beaded on Fred's forehead, his cheeks shining. Trying to reach for the bottle.

"Nearly done the one hand." Moran took firm hold of the thumb.

Chancing a look at his butchered fingers, Fred winced and turned to Alvin. "Gimme that."

Stepping over without looking at the hand, Alvin held the flask up the way Moran had, letting Fred have a drink.

"There's a back-up one in the bag." Moran told Alvin, not looking up from his surgery. "But he won't need it, not after the morphine." Applying cotton to the finger tips of Fred's other hand.

"Thought you said cocaine," Alvin said.

"Cocaine's for the fingers, morphine's for the face."

"Not exactly feeling like a picnic here, doc," Fred said, his face pale. "Let's jump to the morphine."

"Another one telling me my business," Moran said, back to studying the hand.

Reaching in the medical bag, Alvin took a corkscrew from the table and uncorked the bottle of Old Tom, holding it to Fred's mouth.

Taking the bottle from him, Fred held in his palms, his cotton-tipped fingers fanned out, holding it between his palms, swallowing some, his Adam's apple bobbing up and down, some dribbling down his chin. Then looking to Moran, saying, "Okay, now the morphine."

When Fred was out and lying on the bed, cotton on the ends of all his fingers, bandages over half of his face, Moran looked to Alvin. "Okay, your turn." Smiling, giving his best bedside manner.

"Just the fingers, forget the face."

"You talked him into it," Moran said, glancing at Fred.

"Customer's always right, or ain't you heard." Alvin thinking the cops had their prints on file, finding them at every crime scene, but if they couldn't match them . . . or, if he was done with it and never pulled another job, what did any of this matter?

"It's twelve hundred either way. I booked you in. Now, come on and pay me, and don't be a baby. I've got plans for cocktails." Moran took a fresh syringe from his bag, glanced to the window. "And we've got failing light."

Alvin surrendered a hand, held it up and looked at it like he may never see it again, then at the scalpel on the cloth, saying, "I want the dope up front, all of it." Reaching in his pocket and paying him the rest of the money.

Positioning him on the other twin bed, Moran took his hand, put on the bands, then readied the needle. Reaching the Old Tom, taking a long pull. Putting the bottle aside, out of Alvin's reach, he said, "My degree's from Tufts. And so we're clear, this is my domain, and you don't tell me a thing in here." Moran leaned close, then grinned and got to work on the fingers.

An unbelievable pain, cocaine or no cocaine. And when the fingers were done, Alvin couldn't look at them, or up at the drunk with the scalpel, about to put him under, fixing the other syringe, drawing liquid into it from a vile, flicking his finger at the glass, losing an air bubble.

"You ought to respect what I do," Moran said, putting the needle in his vein, giving him the morphine. "If not, at least think about what I know."

Felt like he was sinking into the mattress, everything swimming, Alvin stared up at Moran's eyes, trying to keep them in focus, and he fought it, but the blackness closed around him.

... *Chicago, Illinois*
March 22, 1934

The rooms on the top floor, the boarding house on Winthrop were for recuperating, the empty bottles on the table, an ashtray stuffed with cigarette stubs, the reek of tobacco and ointment. The numbness in his right hand interrupted by the stabs of pain in the left gave Alvin trouble lifting the bottle. Bruises on his cheeks, scars lining both sides of his face, his jaw sore like he'd been kicked.

Dropping by and putting on the bedside manner, Joseph Moran said something about the change in weather, going from sunny to overcast with showers, he slowly peeled back the bandages, adding to the pain of healing, studying the inflamed skin, the ugly purple and yellow around Fred's incisions. Nodding and saying he was happy with his handiwork.

"Sure like to say the same," Fred said, giving Alvin a glance. "What're you grinning at, you look worse."

"Thanks," Alvin said, admitting he felt beat to hell.

"We let it heal, give it time, then we'll see," Moran said.

"Who's we?" Fred said.

Moran just frowned.

"Told me my mother wouldn't recognize me," Fred said.

"Like I said, give it time." Moran took a small bottle and some cotton from his bag. "Going to apply a different ointment, help with the healing." Taking Fred's chin in his palm, dabbing the soaked cotton, explaining it was antibiotic, told him to stop flinching. When he was done, he reached a mirror from his bag, holding it so Fred could have a look. Then he told Alvin to have a seat on the other bed.

"That infection, all that red?" Alvin took the mirror from Moran, looking at Fred and saying, "Why you grinning? You ain't so pretty."

"Just glad he didn't hang us on meat hooks," Fred said.

"Tell you one more time," Moran said. "It needs a couple of weeks. From there, you'll be new men." Explaining how he wanted them to lightly apply the ointment across the incisions, a dab each morning, just enough to keep the wounds from drying out. "Plenty of good food, drink if you feel pain, and keep out of the sun."

"Like we want to be seen," Fred said.

"Rub the areas like I showed you," Moran said, repeating the circular motion with his fingers.

"With these?" Alvin holding up his hands.

Moran pushed Alvin's wrists down, explaining they could massage the cuts with their palms, then he carefully smeared on petroleum jelly.

The three of them hearing footsteps coming up the stairs.

"Smells like something crawled up and died in here," Doc said, coming to the top of the stairs, going to the window and pushing it open, looking out, then at Ray and Fred, a heaviness about him.

"We look that bad?" Fred said.

"Worse, if you got to know . . ."

"There you go." Fred turned to Moran.

"Like I said, give it time." Moran feeling outnumbered.

Alvin looked at Doc, sensing something else was wrong.

Feeling it too, Moran dropped the mirror and cotton pack back in his bag, getting set to go.

Waiting for him to snap his bag shut, Doc escorted him to the landing, watching the quack go down the stairs. Back in the room, he got the bottle and set out glasses smeared with petroleum jelly, poured into them, took a glass and went back to the window, looking out to see Moran exit the front, walking across the street to his car.

"That joint in Cicero, the HiHo, where you met Ziegler . . ." Doc went and set their drinks on the table.

"Yeah, what about it?" Alvin looked at him, taking a glass with the grace of a seal.

"He gets a call from one of the Nitti's goons, this guy White says he wants to see him. Doesn't say what it's about. Drives over and walks in, Ziegler asking the bartender, the man not knowing about it. So, Ziegler waits and sinks a couple — nothing — then steps back out to his car, gets in as some Olds rolls up from behind, a guy with a twelve-gauge leans out and calls, 'Hey, rat!' And gives him both barrels."

"Jesus." Alvin forgot about the pain, tipped the glass and sunk it in a swallow.

"Killed him?" Fred reached a glass.

"Pretty much took off his head." Doc refilled the glasses.

"Ginzos are savages," Fred said, pushing his glass across the table, going to the window, seeing the dry outline where Moran's car had been parked, saying, "Could be Nitti's letting us know he ain't happy, changing his mind about the rent on the Bremer thing."

"Never mind his rent," Doc said. "Son of a bitch ain't squeezing us again. We got a deal." Looking at Alvin.

"Man's been known to change the play," Fred said, turning from the window, saying to Alvin, "What do you think, Ray?"

"Think we're done healing." Alvin looked at his fingers, the tips looking like he'd rested them against the burner of a cookstove. Not forgetting what Moran said about having them in the palm of his hand, thinking someday they'd take the quack out on the boat they paid for, and see if he swims. Pushing aside ill feelings for now, thinking it was time to tell the women to pack up again.

"I know this guy in Toledo," Doc said. "Figure we can hole up a while, less you got someplace else."

"Toledo's good." Fred shrugged and said to him, "And your turn to tell Ma."

Doc nodded at Alvin, his mouth going to a grin, saying, "You know she thinks of you like a son . . ."

"That's true," Fred said. "Fact, she told Paula you're her favorite." Smiling though it hurt to do it. "You don't get under her skin same way we do."

"On account of you helping with the jigsaws." Doc's grin going wide.

"Cowards, both of you," Alvin said.

Doc helped gather their things, packing and buckling their bags.

"Still think you ought to get her a place on her own," Alvin said.

"Back to that? I told you, Ray, Ma goes where we go," Doc said, hefting the bags. "She's no good on her own, and she's no spring chicken."

"Papers calling it her gang," Alvin said, bothered by it, going out the door, taking the stairs, saying over his shoulder, "A mother with a price on her head. That what you want?"

"For what, making jigsaws?" Doc followed after him, carrying the bags.

"Feds talk a lot of shit, and make it up as they go," Fred said, coming behind Doc.

"And if Nitti's coming for us . . ." Alvin said, turning, looking at the brothers clomping down the stairs.

"Who looks out for her when we ain't around?" Doc said.

"Nitti knows same as everybody, all she plans is breakfast," Alvin said. "He'll leave her out of it. Even savages respect the *madri*."

"Still say we throw the fuck off a building," Doc said.

"What I'm saying, it'd just be for a while." Alvin sure the FBI would eventually find the house in Bensenville, Nitti or no Nitti, and they'd go over every inch of the place, and they'd figure who nabbed Bremer. Then they'd look up relations, past and present, everybody ever tied to the gang, every family member, girlfriends, associates, dig up old prison snitches, and they'd close the gap, and they'd come for Kate too.

"Maybe he's got a point," Fred said to Doc, following them into the street.

"Yeah, I know it, just hate to do it to her . . . but for right now, I say *he's* telling her," Doc said, going for his car door, setting the bags down, looking up and down the street as he fished out his key.

... *Chicago, Illinois*
March 22, 1934

H er face lit up as he came in, Alvin handing her the puzzle box. A cowboy shoeing a horse.

"Two hundred and fifty pieces. What say to that, Kate?"

Looking at him in the dim light, her eyes searching his — did it like she was reading his thoughts — the delight fading as she shoved it back at him. "Goddamn moving again?"

"Just for a while, Kate." He frowned and set the box on the hall table.

"Them two no-goods put you up to it, soften me up with a puzzle box?" She looked at Doc coming up the steps behind him, using Alvin to flank him. "Don't you hide back there, Arthur." Calling him Arthur anytime she got steamed.

"Come on now, Kate. Not like we got a choice," Alvin said, turning on the hall light after Doc closed the door.

"My God, Ray, your face!" She stared, putting a hand to her mouth.

"Not as bad as it looks."

She came closer, lightly touching his cheek, studying the incision marks.

"Papers calling it your gang, Kate." Alvin turned to Doc standing behind him in the hall, reaching to tug him by the sleeve, flinching at the pain. Knowing now it had been a bad idea, letting her case the bank in Concordia, tying her to their business. "We're setting you up in a nice place, a view of the lake. That so, Doc?"

"The penthouse suite, they call it. Place got a pool, a front desk, somebody holding the door for you, maid service, the whole bit," Doc said, going to the front window, keeping watch.

Muttering to herself, she walked to the kitchen and went about fixing coffee.

"Remember the first time you fixed me coffee, Kate? That wood stove on a dirt floor. Got to admit, we come a long way from Tulsa."

"That's just it, boy. We go here, then there — a long way alright. And I ain't so dim, Ray. And save the pauper-to-felon muck. Sure I like my trimmings, and I know we got to move from time to time, keep in that low light. But can I just get a chance to hang a picture? Now, you gonna tell me what happened to your face? And no dodging around."

"I was in a wreck, glass cut me. Was drinking, and guess I blacked out. Hit an oak, I think. And like I said, it looks worse than it is."

"Looks worse? Looks like you crashed into a meat grinder."

"It'll heal up fine, had a quack look at it. And quit playing change-up. Now, the move's just for a bit."

"Think I'd get used to it."

"It's just the life."

"Talking about the lies."

"And I'm talking about this new place, it's sure something."

"How about you?"

"We got a place too."

He looked at her, waiting on more fuss, but she just sighed like she was resigned to it.

"It's just for a while, Kate."

"After we'll go some place nice," Doc said. "That's a promise. All of us having a time."

"I'm sick of never getting a say. I hang up my coat, and it's time to go." Going to the kitchen, she scooped beans into the grinder and cranked the handle. "Things you boys put me through. Some ways it was better with the dirt floor, old drunk Arthur in the corner . . . could depend on not depending on him. And where in hell's Fred?" she said, looking at Doc by the window. "You keep standing mute, boy, let this one do your talking, I'm gonna hang that coat on you." Turning a burner knob, setting on a pot of water, she looked from one to the other, saying, "I asked where's Fred? The one been promising me Florida for . . . oh, God, I lost count how long."

"Remember you saying there's no place like Oak Street Beach in summer," Doc said. "You remember that, Ray?"

"Yeah, you loved that picnic by the lake, and all them sailboats, so many you can't count." Alvin bringing up the one time they took her down Lake Shore Drive, found a nice spot to spread a blanket, Kate packing sandwiches, baked chicken, cherry pie and a jug of lemonade.

"Florida *pppft* . . . hot as a griddle most of the time," Doc said.

"Half this city's out of work, and the other half's muggers or mob," she said, folding her arms. "And you wanna leave me on my own."

"We aim to do right by you, Kate; I think you know that," Alvin said, tiring of her mood.

"So, that's your story, you got in a wreck?" She stepped close and looked at his bruised face again, the angry scar lines on both sides of his face. "Funniest wreck I ever seen."

"Banged the wheel and knocked out the windshield, glass cut me on both sides." Running a finger along one cheek.

"And your fingers, what the . . ." She grabbed hold of his hand, looking at the raw tips, saying, "Oh, never mind, not like you ever tell me straight." Her eyes were welling up behind the anger now. "Don't think you know how, any of you."

"We try to tell you straight, Ma," Doc said. "Don't like the moving around no more'n you."

"Say it like it's for my own good again, I'll take a shoe to you. You ask me, I don't think you boys can help yourselves. Lying's natural as spit." Vexed, looking from one to the other. "It's your kind . . . some type of lying gene. Oh, Jesus, why didn't I have no girls?" Laying a gentle hand to Alvin's cheek, still inspecting the scars on the either side of his face, taking on a look of worry. "Fred in this wreck too? Now, tell me true."

"Fred's fine. Nothing like that. He's getting your new place set," Alvin said.

"A sweet spot too, Ma," Doc said. "A guy holding the door for you, booking you a table."

"You said that, and I ain't so feeble . . ." She looked at Doc, saying, "Like I need somebody holding my door. Now, where in hell is Fred?"

"He'll be along," Alvin said.

"You just fry up some chicken, you know he'll come running," Doc said. "Smell it all the way to Toledo." Grinning and shaking his head.

"Toledo?" She pushed Alvin aside, glaring at Doc.

Doc lost the smile, seeing his mistake.

"You're going there?" She drew a breath. "And leaving me here."

"Just for a while, Kate," Alvin said.

"You boys frazzle me. My poor hands with twinges on the hinges, shaking from worry. Can hardly do my jigsaws."

"Give knitting a try, Ma?" Doc threw in. "Lot of ladies doing it."

"Knit for who? You see grandkids running round here?"

"It's the best way, Kate, being apart awhile." Alvin turned and reached the puzzle box, holding it out to her.

"The rent's squared away," Doc said. "And got a couple of boys'll look in, time to time."

"And I'll write every week or so," Alvin said. "When things die down, and the weather warms, we'll get that summer place up by Charlevoix, right on the lake, that stretch of beach you like." Alvin getting a flash of taking Joseph Moran out in his boat.

"You're good boys, I know it." She took his hand and squeezed it.

Alvin flinched.

Kate letting go, saying, "Come here." And giving Doc a hug, knowing there was no point arguing.

. . . Toledo, Ohio
April 24, 1934

"Means one wife too many," she said, getting that fire in her eyes.

"Add it to the list," Alvin said. "Come on, Lolli, you're more wife than she ever was, any day. And what's a piece of paper anyhow? Just ties you to me."

"Wife can't testify against her husband."

"But makes you an accessory."

"So now it's for my own good?"

"It's not that . . ."

"Why not keep me in a closet — till you want some?"

"Call this a closet? And I want some most anytime I look at you." He was blaming the hormones, something Kate warned him about — this teenage girl with her clock ticking, wanting to get hitched and try for another kid.

"It's your less-than-swell upbringing, Ray, and I forgive it sometimes — reason you got trouble getting close, but mostly it's a lot . . ."

He shook his head, guessing it had been a mistake, telling her what living with his folks had been like, opening up to her.

"Got shamed by your folks and turned into a hood. Then built a stone wall, with no place for feelings. Now, you think of me and a baby as anchors, slowing you down."

"Can't walk in no courthouse, filing divorce papers, go stand next to you in church and say, 'I do,' with a whole country of lawmen waiting in the pews? Maybe we get Big Tom to give you away, keep one eye on the door, throw the reception at the Lantern, have a last blast before the feds drag me away. Look, we're together. Sleep in the same bed, same as a wife. Guess I don't see no difference."

"A regular William Powell, real muckety-muck." Dolores shook her head and walked to the kitchen, done talking, going to help Paula clean up.

Watching her go, this teenager with the curves and soft skin, the shining dark hair. No lines on her face, or veins showing in her legs. Why'd she want to ruin it by having a kid? He figured she was tired of the running and hiding out, not getting to the clubs lately, or dining out, or going dancing, spending his money like it didn't matter. Not how she pictured the outlaw life.

Since the Bremer job, they moved in with Fred and Paula, living in tight quarters, all of them drinking too much, bumping elbows and starting to quarrel. Ordering groceries from the corner store, eating from tins while sitting on two hundred grand that needed laundering. Something she couldn't get her head around, not seeing the harm in spending some of it — like, who looked at serial numbers?

Wanting to keep Dolores on cloud nine, Alvin put on his hat and glasses, went to the corner phone box and called up Dot again, saying he was going along with her idea of divorce, asking her to file the papers, forward them to Dutch at the Lantern. Dot telling him she had gone back to using her maiden name, Slayman, not wanting the world to know she had been hitched to a wanted man, something that shamed her. Hanging up on him.

"What's with her?" Fred said, meaning Dolores, coming in the front room now, a drink in hand, a newspaper folded under his arm.

"On about getting hitched and knocked up."

"Could do worse, you know?"

"You gonna start?"

"The idea's to keep 'em smiling, Ray."

"Like you got an idea about it."

"Pretty much in the same boat, brother, stumbling in the dark." Fred tapped the paper on the corner of the table.

"You see me with a kid?" Alvin shook his head, faked a smile.

Fred was frowning like he had something else on his mind.

"What's up?" Alvin glanced at the folded paper.

Setting his drink down, Fred handed it to him, the way they were getting news from the outside world — pointed to a headline: *Gangster Stopped Cold.* Eddie Green had been gunned down, fed agents mistaking him for Dillinger, another one-time gang member struck off Hoover's list. The column below told how Dillinger's girl, Billie Frechette, had been nabbed in a raid two days later, that headline reading: *Dillinger Escapes Shootout in Little Bohemia.*

Alvin scanned the story.

Fred saying, "That fed Purvis puts his shoes on the wrong feet, but still, sooner or later . . ."

Alvin reading how Purvis and his squad raided this place, knowing Dillinger was inside, but didn't consider the lodge's dollar-a-plate special would have the place packed to the gills with locals.

"With all that fed surveillance?" Fred said. "Storm-trooping dummies with Tommy guns driving up as diners filed out, sucking mints and working toothpicks, heading for their cars. Purvis yells, 'Freeze,' getting folks panicking at sight of their guns, running for their cars. And some rookie fed opens up and pops one, then another fed takes a shot, sure he's seen Dillinger. When the shooting stops, they gunned three satisfied customers, filled up on the blue-plate. Sending them to their reward."

Fred telling how Dillinger and Van Meter heard the shots and went out an upstairs window in back and slipped away. "Same time, Nelson's in a cabin next door, putting it to a hooker, hears the shots and throws on his pants. Goes out barefoot, a pistol in each hand, shooting it out with Purvis and his boys.

"Man doesn't even have a shirt on," Fred said. "Plants one fed and wounds a couple more, gets in his car and hauls ass, the hooker jumping in, catching a ride. A hundred and thirty pounds of Baby Face killer, taking on the G-men." Fred shook his head.

"George Nelson's making his mark," Alvin said, handing him back the paper, thinking back to when they met him, poolside in Reno, the guy looking to get into the life, wanting to join up with them. Told them how he drove for the Black Hand, and worked with the Touhys. Alvin not doubting it anymore.

"The feds got left standing or lying in the parking lot, Purvis having to explain the turkey shoot, one of theirs cut down, a couple more winged, one dinner guest passing over, with two more rushed to hospital. A waiter giving an account of how the Jackrabbit hopped off, right out a window. Not much point looking out windows and worrying — the feds being cross-eyed and can't shoot for shit." Fred grinned, his face not hurting so much from the surgery now.

"The Jackrabbit gets lucky . . . again," Alvin said.

"Still, I guess lying low beats shooting it out," Fred said. "But I got to admit, it's got me scratching too."

"We get the money switched, we'll be good. And be around to spend it."

"On that note, Doc called. Got some of it switched, not much, but some." The older brother in Chicago, visiting Kate, and talking to their sources, most of them feeling the Bremer money was still too hot to touch.

"Who switched it?" Alvin asked.

Fred hesitated, saying, "Moran."

Alvin made a face, hated hearing it.

"Nobody else'll touch it, Ray — but the good news, the quack only took five points."

"Figures he's got us in the palm of his hand. I told you that." Alvin remembering that spin down the black hole of morphine, the drunk butcher altering their looks, leaving scars they'd carry for life. Dolores wanting to screw with the lights off these days.

"How it happened . . . Deafy got hold of Doc, tells him one of Dillinger's crew caught one, some bank job they pulled, and needed to get patched. So Doc takes him to the place on Irving." Fred meaning the hotel suite Moran used for his surgery. "Doc gets to talking to Moran, and hands him a bundle, seeing what he can do. Man gets it done, says on account we're old friends. And says he can do more, plenty more, and charging us the five."

"Feds passing circulars, and every bank in the country's watching for serial numbers." Alvin not seeing how Moran could get it done. "Could be setting us up. Collecting the reward."

"Yeah, crossed my mind, but, the girl's got a point: what good's having it if we don't spend it?"

"Can't spend it inside," Alvin said, holding up his hand, stopping Fred from saying he wasn't going back inside. "And you know Moran's soused half the time, with that loose mouth."

"You're missing it," Fred said. "Doc's getting him to trust us."

"Not giving him more money?" Alvin seeing it, but not liking it, the brothers working on something, not letting him weigh in.

"Told Doc what Moran said, how he's got us in the palm of his hand."

Sitting back, Alvin seeing there was no point arguing, brother siding with brother.

"Says we're all pals, why he's doing it for five points."

Alvin thinking of Joseph Moran as dead weight. But he didn't remind Fred there was nothing to do but sit tight, on money they couldn't touch, and read about Dillinger robbing places in the Midwest, the Barrows sticking up places in the southwest.

. . . Toledo, Ohio
May 25, 1934

F red told Alvin what he heard on the Philco. "Someplace
called Bienville Parish. On the way to pick up one of
their own, and ran into lawmen laying for them, and got shot
to bits. Texas Rangers been tracking them for months, got
tipped by the old man of the guy they were picking up, the
ambush handled like an execution. Not messing it up like
they did with Dillinger at that Bohemia place. Feds never
going to quit till we're all put down."

"Why we keep to the shadows. Let Dillinger and Nelson
play celebrities with guns, get the feds hunting them."

"Told Doc he's getting his looks changed, the Jackrabbit,
something he got from us," Fred said.

"Dillinger said that?"

"Says he wants to live in the open. Only he ain't going
to Moran."

"Wants to stay beautiful." Alvin smiled and stepped to
the hall mirror, looking at the healing scars. Running a hand
over the side of his face, remembering what Joseph Moran

said about having them in the palm of his hand, touching the edge of the scar.

"Told Doc how Moran's going around saying we paid for his boat."

"Drunk son of a bitch," Alvin said.

"Why Doc wants him doing more laundry — and bringing him here."

"Here?"

"Where the money is."

Alvin looked at him, starting to understand what Doc was up to. "Getting the man's trust."

"That's right." Fred smiled.

. . . Toledo, Ohio
July 30, 1934

"Doc's bringing Kate with Moran," Alvin said, reading the letter aloud, thinking it had been months since he'd seen her. The signature at the bottom was Joseph Moran's, penning it for Kate. Writing that he was tagging along, looking forward to seeing them and how they had healed up. Alvin folded it, looking at Fred.

"Doc tells him he wants his prints done like he did us," Fred said. "Doing it here on account Chicago's getting hot for a back-room quack with a gin habit, the man running his mouth after botching up one of Clooney's girls. Feds all over after they got Dillinger."

Dillinger had run his luck, and it ended a week ago out front of the Biograph, the Jackrabbit trusting the wrong woman and walking into a trap — every kind of lawman tired of looking bad every time he robbed a place, eluding the feds, and walking into not one, but two station houses at gunpoint and relieving the cops of their firearms, getting caught and escaping their jails like Houdini. Alvin finding it hard to believe the feds got him easy as that, the man just letting his guard down.

"Mob's past tired of the heat the independents brought to town," Fred said. "Nitti with an axe to grind, getting his boys to push us out."

"But why bring Moran here?" Alvin not liking it.

"Want him feeling easy — knowing Doc's bringing him where we got it stashed."

It was reckless, but Alvin didn't say more about it. Enough on his mind after finding out Dolores was pregnant again, taking a stand and telling him she was keeping this one. Moran taking care of it the one time long ago, Dolores feeling she came away as scarred on the inside as Alvin was on the outside, blaming the recent miscarriage on what Moran had done to her during that abortion. Alvin knowing how she'd feel about the quack coming there.

"The man got rich off us, and skimmed more," Fred said. "Scalpel in one hand, knitting needle in the other, all the time running that all-night mouth. Doc thinking the feds wired up his place. Bringing him here, the only place we can be sure about."

"Why not book him in the Edgewater — got a nice pool he can drown in."

"Don't sweat it. He won't be staying long," Fred said, getting that look, like the time he shot the night marshal.

Alvin nodded, wondering why the brothers didn't run it by him.

... *Toledo, Ohio*
August 1, 1934

"The two Docs." Alvin stepped out on the stoop, barefoot and smiling, clasping hands with Doc, then he went to the car. Doc's Buick making pinging sounds, Alvin feeling the heat off the hood, helping Kate from the passenger side, giving her the biggest hug of his life. Doc getting the luggage from the trunk. Fred coming out the door, hugging and clapping Doc on the back, then Kate.

"Looking good, Ma." Fred holding her close, like he never wanted to let go.

Joseph Moran got out of the backseat, smiling too, but looking around like something might jump from the junipers.

Fred grabbed the luggage and took it up the steps, working his way past Kate hugging Dolores and Paula, the three women crowding the stoop, all of them teary-eyed. Alvin taking the medical bag from Moran, his eyes going to the street, making sure there was no tail. Smiling at the man, ushering him into the house.

"I sure appreciate this," Moran said, rubbing his hands like he was cold in the August heat, looking from Alvin to

Fred, then to Doc, like he wasn't sure, hesitating as he stepped inside the door.

Forcing the friendly, Alvin smiled and said, "You remember Dolores." Wondering if he recalled putting her on his table, opening her legs and snuffing out a life. She had told him about the heavy bleeding and infection that followed, the quack misdiagnosing the peritonitis that followed as appendicitis, nearly claiming her life.

"Yes, yes, how are you, my dear?" Moran taking both her hands, no recognition in his rheumy eyes, saying she looked in the pink.

Dolores cringed, doing her best to say hello, smiling at the old man.

Barely in the door, Kate swept into the kitchen like she was laying claim, saying her boys were looking like beanpoles since she'd been gone.

Dolores and Paula looked at each other, Dolores untying her apron, happy handing it to Kate, taking a step away from Joseph Moran.

"You saying we can't take care of your darlings?" Paula said, winking at Dolores.

"Can learn a thing from Ma," Fred said.

"He saying I can't cook?" Paula asked Dolores, her hands on her hips, bearing herself offended.

"You do plenty right, girl, mostly what we can't talk about in front of Ma and company." Fred stepped to her, patting her backside. "But, if we're talking the kitchen, girl, Ma's got you beat any day of the week."

"Well, I been kicked in the teeth." Paula shook her head.

"Banished to doing the sweeping up," Dolores said.

"You listen up, and you'll learn a thing or two, but hey, there won't be no cooking tonight," Fred said, looking to Alvin. "Ray got us a table at Dyer's Chop House, best place in the county, and I got my mind on steak." Holding his thumb and forefinger apart two inches. "A big, juicy slab of meat."

━━

"You're riding with us," Fred said it casual, held out a hand, guiding Joseph Moran to his Chevy. "It's got the leg room . . ."

Doc and the women climbed into Alvin's Buick Special parked ahead of them.

"Nice ride without all the clucking," Fred said, winking at him.

Dolores wanted to share her good news, asking Alvin how he felt about it when they were getting dressed.

"Yeah, be the perfect time." Telling her to go ahead, and liking the diversion. Kissing her, telling her she was going to make mother of the year. Opening Fred's passenger door now, he insisted Joseph Moran take the front seat, the man looking like he was set to bolt, but getting in. Alvin shutting the door and climbing in back, making comment on the cool evening, how the temperature dropped since the heat of the day.

Cranking the engine to life, Fred rolled out and followed the Buick, flipping down his visor and taking a pack of Luckys, offering them around, saying to Moran, "How you like your steak, doc — bloody?"

"Tell the truth, I've been having trouble with a molar." Pointing to the back side of his mouth, saying, "Be happy with a soup." Holding up a hand to the cigarettes and forcing a smile, saying he quit that too.

"Dyer's got meat falls right off the bone. Pan-seared, alongside a baked potato, butter and sour cream, food a man can gum down — no need for chewing. But, you want soup, doc, well, then soup it is." Fred lipped a cigarette from the pack and struck a match off the dash, lit up and tossed it out his window.

Turning in the seat, Joseph Moran looked at Alvin and touched on old times, talking about that New Year's at the Green Lantern.

"Yeah, wish I'd been there, bet it was a hell of a thing," Alvin said.

"Thought you were there," Moran said.

"Nope, but it reminds me, doc . . ." Reaching to the floor and lifting a bag, Alvin pulled out a pint of Four Roses, saying, "I mean, if you haven't quit that too . . ." Laughing, uncapping it and handing it forward.

"Well, now . . ." Moran smiled and reached it, his hand shaking, taking a good swallow, then another before offering it to Fred. "Like an elixir."

"Just what the doctor ordered alright." Fred took a swig and passed it back across the seat.

"So, things heating in Mud City, huh?" Alvin reached and tipped it, passing it back to Moran.

"Yes, a real shame what's going on. Not what it was, that's for sure. Same as St. Paul, the way I hear it," Moran said, swallowing more.

"That thing with Dillinger, out front of the theater, it don't sit right," Fred said. "Some woman in red sets him up, the way the papers tell it."

"Yes, a true shame. I got to know the man, you know?"

"That so?" Alvin said.

"Yes, we talked about doing his prints, same as I did for you boys."

"A rat madam's what they call her," Fred said, having trouble snapping his fingers, searching for a name.

"Anna Sage, I believe," Moran said.

"That's it, Sage, Anna Sage," Fred said. "You know the bitch, doc?"

"Runs a house, the way I hear it," Moran said.

"What've you got if you don't got trust, ain't that right?" Fred glanced at Alvin, then at the old man. "I mean, that how you see it?" Fred turned and put his attention on following the Buick.

"Yes, indeed."

"Why you docs got that hypocrite's oath, right?" Fred said.

"The Hippocratic oath, yes," Moran said, nodding, taking another swig.

"Heard the Sage woman claimed feds were set to get her passport revoked, have her kicked back to some eastern shit-hole she crawled from," Fred said. "So what's she to do but give Dillinger the Judas kiss."

"That's what I read too." Taking another swallow, Moran watched Doc veer left, seeing the women talking inside the car.

Fred heading straight.

"You missed the turn." An edge to his voice now, Moran craned his neck, looking back the way Doc had gone, the rising dust masking the Buick.

"He don't know this town like I do." Fred headed straight, holding up his palm, saying, "Like the back of my hand, the part that didn't get carved up." Smiling like it was a joke.

Sucking on the bottle, Moran said, "Ought to go after him, in case he gets all turned around."

"We'll all end in the same place, doc. Worst thing happens, we miss the salad," Alvin said, holding up his own mangled fingertips.

Moran reached and took Alvin's hand, looking at his handiwork, saying, "The prints won't come back, I promise you."

"Trusting someday the feeling does."

"And speaking about trust . . ." Fred turned his head to Moran, then back on the road. "In our line, it's the only thing we got — trust. Without it, you're just a dead man walking around."

"You get no argument from me," Moran said. "Trust is utmost. Followed by confidentiality."

"That part of your oath, doc?" Fred said.

"The creed I live by." Moran drank more, the bottle half gone, realizing he wasn't passing it, offering it to Fred. "So, you boys want to get your money cleaned. I sure can help you out with that. And do it for five points."

"You go on, doc, unwind yourself, talk about old times. The business can keep."

"Old times, sure had lots of them — the old Lantern, the Exchequer, plenty of places — more'n I remember."

Alvin looked at him across the seat, saying, "You remember saying how you got us in the palm of your hand?"

Moran looked confused, saying, "Who said that?" Shrinking against the car door.

"You did, that time just ahead of the morphine."

"Must've got me wrong. That drug's a fog with a kick like a mule."

"Sounded like you can bleed us, hang us on a line any time you want. Got me thinking maybe you got a mind to collect some reward anytime you want."

"Come on, Ray, we go back. Came up on the same streets, making our way, know the same people. And I've done right by you boys — always."

"Guess I got it wrong then?" Alvin said to Fred.

"I'd say so. Now, if I said something in jest, something that affronted you, then I take it back. I apologize, one hundred percent."

"A hundred percent, well, you can't beat that," Alvin said to Fred.

"A hundred's pretty good."

"You boys know me," Moran said.

"Yeah, we do, a souse with a slack mouth," Fred said. "Letting shit spill out."

"To anybody listening in," Alvin said, agreeing.

"Come on now. I did right by you boys, every time you came knocking — took care of your girls, dressed up wounds, middle of the night, didn't matter when it was. You needed me and I was there. And now, getting your money clean."

"You do that for Dillinger?"

"Took a bullet from one of his boys. Did it on Doc's say-so."

"Man got set up right after," Fred said.

"I did a favor for Doc, is all."

"Or you drugged up his guy, found out dirt and handed it over, worked a deal with the feds," Alvin said.

"You think I . . . I had nothing to do with that. If anyone gave him up, it was that woman . . ."

"Anna Sage?"

"That's her."

"You been to her place, doc?" Alvin said.

"Her what?"

"Cathouse on North Halsted."

"Okay, maybe the one time, but come on, even the mayor knows the place. Whatever you're thinking, you got me wrong."

"Thinking the feds hooked up your blower, the way they like to do, recorded every drunk word coming from your mouth," Fred said.

"Nobody wired my phone. I have them checked every week, the whole place gets swept. I've been inside — know better than to run my mouth."

"Big Tom figures you cooked a deal with the feds, bringing heat to town," Alvin said, making it up, watching the old quack squirm.

"I wouldn't give you boys up. You know me. Big Tom knows me. God, the things I did for you, all of you — setting my career aside."

"One you flushed down the shitter."

"Look, I admit, I've had troubles with gambling, and my demons with the drink . . ." Moran trying to pass the bottle to Fred, then to Alvin, saying, "If there was loose talk like you say, it was meant in fun. If I crossed a line, then I got my regrets . . ."

"We take risks, doc, but we don't take chances," Fred said, heading them out of town, the paved road becoming gravel, then dirt, weeds and scrub yielding to dense woods on either side, a carved marker for a quarry up ahead.

Joseph Moran held the bottle to Alvin, wishing someone would take it from him, saying, "Drink with me, boys."

"To old times, doc?"

"Yes."

Alvin took it, rolled down his window and tossed it out, hearing glass shatter on the road.

... *Toledo, Ohio*
August 6, 1934

H er breasts were swelling, belly starting to show, Dolores
going through the morning sickness, pulling her head
from the toilet bowl and telling him the baby was growing
inside. Soon he could lower an ear and listen for a heartbeat,
put a hand on it and feel it kick.

And it was really happening, he was having a kid. The
night feedings, the spitting up, the wailing, the changing of
the nappies. He'd take them to Spain and get a place in the
countryside. Get her a housekeeper to help her out. He had
plenty of money stashed around the Heartland. He'd get to
enough of it, then have Fred or Doc send him more from
time to time, the only people he could trust. And he'd become
a quiet don, grow figs and olives, spend his days in the sun,
drink licor de Orujo and Andalusian wine, and push his boy
on a swing, watch him grow.

Tired of running and ducking from Toledo to Grand
Forest, to Cleveland, then back to Toledo. Remembering how
they had the real Toledo over there, smack in the middle of
the country, an ancient city going back to before the time

of the Romans. Seeing himself walking amid old ruins, on the banks of the Tagus. Like Chicago, it sounded like a place better off before the Romans showed up.

A couple of bottles and glasses on the table. Fred and Doc sat on the patio out back of the place, catching the shade of the sugar maple, a breeze blowing in the warm evening.

"Still got dough to clean," Doc said, glancing to the house, hearing the women inside. "And with Moran gone . . ."

"One thing at a time," Fred said, the Bremer case too hot going on ten months, half the money stashed in bags, buried under the house.

"Say we split it and take our chances," Doc said.

"First buck you spend's the last," Alvin said. "And for all of us."

"Come on, Ray. Volney's on board. Nobody wants to end like Dillinger or Ziegler before we get to live it up." Doc swatted at something buzzing around his ear.

"First one of us does it, and we all go down," Alvin said. "How about your ma? How's she gonna do time?"

"Best we leave her out of it," Doc said, looking like he might jump from his chair.

"Tell the ones that come kicking in the door," Alvin said, not backing up.

"We split it and go our different ways, lay low a week before we touch it. I been thinking Mexico, Fred's talking about taking Ma to Florida, and you're looking at Spain. All gone and spread out."

"We need to give it more time. Right now, one of us spends a buck, and he leaves a trail to the rest," Alvin said. "We been over it."

"Tell you what, Ray, let's get Harry, Bill, everybody weighing in, put it to a vote." Doc looked at his brother, Fred not piping in.

"Not gonna be a vote," Alvin said.

"On your say-so?"

"On account there's too much heat, like we all agreed — on account what you do leads to me."

"Sitting on a pile of dough, meantime we go on eating beans. Five of us on the same toilet."

Alvin looked to Fred, annoyed he wasn't piping in. "That time we took the girls to the pictures. Newsreel warning folks to be on the lookout, our mugs flashing on the screen, Nelson and Floyd too. Come on, Fred, you were there."

"Yeah, I saw it." Fred was looking at his shoes.

"One of these men could be sitting next to you — what it said. Have a look around, folks. You and me looking down like you're doing now, hiding next to our women."

Fred looked up, saying, "All I know for sure, I ain't —"

"Going back inside, yeah, we know it," Doc piped up. "Why we're gonna blow town, brother. All of us going a different way."

"Won't be far enough," Alvin said. Planning to sneak into Canada at Windsor, take Dolores to the land of his birth, let her have the baby in Montreal. With the help of a one-time Dillinger wingman, "Red" Hamilton, he'd get their names changed, get forged passports, and book them on a steamer to Spain. Alvin having no idea how a man with no fingerprints could go about getting a legitimate passport.

"Harry dropped word about this bank in Cleveland, ripe with payroll," Fred said. "A score that could tide us over."

Alvin shook his head, saying, "I got offered a job . . ."

"A job?" Doc said.

"Casino opening called the Harvard Club."

The brothers looked at him, the first they heard about it.

"Just gonna keep it to yourself?" Doc said.

"Telling you now. Shimmy Patton got me word, him and Artie Herbebrandt looking for a guy, wondering if I was interested."

"The Cleveland mob? What do they need, a waiter?" Doc was grinning. "Gonna bring Lolli along, get her working — what, a knocked-up cocktail waitress?"

Swallowing the anger, Alvin said, "Head of security, on account there's folks in Detroit not so happy about a casino springing up in Cleveland."

"So, you're a heavy now, taking on a rival mob. Pissing off Chicago not enough for you?"

"I keep an eye out, watch for fires starting, guys coming in with long coats. Make some money while we wait on things to cool down."

"By working for the mob?" Fred said.

"Sounds like it's every man for himself," Doc said.

"Talked to them about doing the laundry," Alvin said.

The brothers stared at him.

"Didn't bother running it by us first?" Doc said, not hiding his anger.

"Like you ran bringing Moran here?" Alvin said, looking from one to the other.

"Maybe we should've let him do it, change the money before you two went crazy." Doc wasn't letting up. "How much of it you talking?"

"All of it, and for what we paid Moran," Alvin said, making it up.

"So, you hold the door for folks, watch who goes in and out, hope Cleveland treats you better than Chicago," Doc said. "And if somebody makes you, and it leads back to us . . ."

"Gonna be wearing a tux," Alvin said, trying to lighten it up.

"So, you blow on some old broad's dice and toss out a few rubes," Doc said. "Make a living on the side, meantime the rest of us, what, sit here and eat beans?"

"You want to slip on a penguin suit, Doc, I can put in a good word," Alvin said.

"Think I'll pass," Doc said, taking a swat at another fly.

"You know I got a kid on the way, right?" Alvin regretted it as soon as he said it.

"One you didn't want." Doc got up and walked into the yard, crossing his arms, looking the other way.

Looking at his back, Alvin said to Fred, "Me and Dolores are getting a place, up by the casino."

Doc turned around, shaking his head. "Do what you want, but you ain't taking the cash."

"You know what, Doc, you hang onto to it, keep an eye on it. Guess I trust you." Alvin got up, the two of them almost eye to eye now. Then he stepped around him, looking back to Fred, saying, "They want to deal, I'll let you know." With that he went in the house, looking for Dolores, telling her to get packed, knowing how that would go.

... *Cleveland, Ohio*
August 23, 1934

Sitting by the phone box, waiting on the operator to put him through, Alvin looked along the hall of the Harvard Club, the drift of stale booze and tobacco from last night's winners and losers hung on the air. Nobody in earshot, he spoke to Fred at the Esso station, two blocks from the rented house, the call he'd been making every week, the two of them careful what they said on the line.

"You get word on Homer?" Fred said.

Alvin heard it from Shimmy, Dillinger's sidekick Homer Van Meter had been killed, on the run since the feds clipped Dillinger outside the Biograph. Rumors floated how the feds got the wrong guy, the Jackrabbit slipping past them one last time, the feds killing a lookalike out front of the theater, knowing it, but not admitting they blundered again, quick to cover it up. If it was true, it was the slickest move Dillinger pulled yet, putting an end to the feds chasing him, meaning he could drift into the shadows to live off the spoils. Homer Van Meter wasn't so lucky, gunned down in old St. Paul, by the same cops who once turned a blind eye.

"Think we got to make a move," Fred said, worried about sitting on the ransom money buried under the house.

"Except there's no move to make." Alvin telling him Shimmy was putting him off; the mobster feeling it was too hot to switch the bills, even for the Cleveland mob.

Silence on the line as Fred took it in, saying, "How's the mother-to-be?"

"Looks like she swallowed a melon. Other than that, she stopped hurling up." Alvin asking after Paula and Kate, then he hung up. Feeling the strain between them over the buried cash. Taking the stairs to Shimmy Patton's office, the casino boss wanting to see him. Rapping on the door, he stepped in, recognizing the two men sitting across from Shimmy, their hats in hand.

"Think you boys met." Shimmy smiled, an unlit La Palina in the corner of his mouth, the fat man getting up and going for the door, shutting it behind him, said he was taking a walk around the tables, putting in an appearance.

Charlie Floyd and Adam Richetti half got out of their chairs and each shook Alvin's hand. They never worked together, just crossed paths a couple of times, Alvin guessing they didn't come to talk about old times at the Lantern. Taking Shimmy's chair, he said, "So, what brings you fellas?" Guessing they were planning something.

"You get word on Homer?" Charlie said.

"Just now, but no details."

Charlie nodded, glanced down and told him, "Drove to this car dealer with Tommy Gannon. You know Tommy?"

"Think we met, yeah." Although Alvin wasn't sure where.

"Homer parks in the alley next to the place, tells Tommy to wait in the car, and in he goes. Makes a deal on a Ford, comes out and Big Tom's standing waiting for him — a friend of us all, right? Not chief anymore, and not so big, and from the sound of it, a man with a change of heart," Charlie said. "Stands there with new chief Frank Cullen and two other sons of bitches, one holding a rifle, the other a shotgun. Big Tom says they're taking him in, walking or wheeled, his choice. No chance of shooting it out, so Homer breaks for his car. And might'a made it, except old Tommy had slid behind the wheel and drove off, double-crossing Homer. According to Big Tom, Homer fired first. Nothing they could do but put him down."

"Saying Gannon made a deal with Big Tom?" Alvin said, rolling that one around.

"Like two rats shaking hands," Charlie said.

"Feds been looking into the sins of the law, and Big Tom's the cherry on the dirt pie," Adam said. "So, the man's playing real cop these days."

"Put twenty-six rounds in Homer," Charlie said, showing with his hand: "Buckshot slugs like this."

"We know where we stand, then," Alvin said, running a hand to the back of his neck.

"Sure like to run into Gannon sometime," Charlie said. "Guess a lot of us would."

"You didn't come three hundred miles to tell me that."

"More like three-fifty," Adam said. "But no, we're passing through, putting St. Paul behind, New York too. And Nitti's got the broom out in Chicago, I guess you heard."

Alvin nodded.

"Making our way, Reno maybe. Thought we'd stop in, see if you got something," Charlie said, looking at the scars like slits on either side of Alvin's face, but not asking about it.

"That, or head for the coast," Adam said. "Way Hollywood's glorifying Hoover, maybe we'll write scripts and make up fairy tales."

"I'm out of it," Alvin said, holding back that Fred was thinking about another bank, not sure who to trust anymore.

"Tossing in the chips." Adam nodded, saying, "Dillinger, the Barrows, and Van Meter gone, and the feds are saying who's next. Leaving you boys, me and Charlie here. Nothing Hoover'd rather do, catch up and scratch us off his list."

"Not a good time for hanging in any place too long," Adam said.

"Thought we'd give it a shot." Sliding his chair back, Charlie got up and offered his hand again.

When they left, Alvin sat behind the desk, opened a drawer, flipped open Shimmy's cigar box, helped himself to three, figured he'd have a smoke with Fred and Doc when his kid was born, tucking them in his top pocket, looking out the window, getting out of the chair when Shimmy came back in. Asking him, "You tell them I was here?"

"Told them shit," Shimmy said. "They just showed up, knocked on the door, asking for you." Shimmy didn't like it, pushing up a smile, doing it around the half-smoked cigar hanging from the corner of his mouth, saying, "Not so invisible, huh?" He wagged at the chair Charlie sat in.

Alvin moved around the desk and sat.

"Let's talk laundry," Shimmy said, plunking back in his chair.

"Said it's too hot."

"Yeah, I know what I said." Shimmy put up a hand, saying, "I asked around: the Owl, Leo Lips, Frankie Bones, nobody . . . even the Irish won't touch it. But, in the end, there's one guy . . ."

"Yeah?"

"You know Cash McDonald?"

"Heard the name, but never met."

"He's up in Detroit, figures he can fence some through a casino in Havana, move some through a couple of banks in Mexico, the rest through Venezuela or someplace — says there's no chance of blow back."

"How much of it?"

"All of it." Shimmy making a gesture like, what else? Opening the drawer, taking a silver lighter, puffing the stogie back to life, the paper wet where it met his mouth, saying, "Not cheap, but it gets done." Shimmy holding up his hands like what else could he do.

"What's it gonna cost me?"

"Ten."

"Grand?"

Shimmy grinned, then said, "Points."

Alvin whistled, knowing he was looking at the only game in town, finally nodding his head.

"Okay, I'll set up a meet." Shimmy leaned back in the chair, blowing smoke to the ceiling, looking back at him, saying, "And, it's time to hang up the tux. Those guys coming here, knowing where to find you, I can't have it. Next thing I got Hoover coming in the door."

"My last day playing dress-up." Alvin nodded like it made sense. A job that lasted two weeks, getting up, shaking hands with Shimmy.

. . . *Cleveland, Ohio*
August 24, 1934

"Well, maybe I'm doing it wrong." Alvin sat on the side of the bed, looking at Dolores under the covers.

Pulling the blanket to her neck, she said, "You come in and drop a bomb like that, then wanna drop your pants and play Sheik and Sheba. Acting like bad news is the new foreplay."

"Sheik and what?"

"Don't be cute."

"I get it, you don't like moving."

"Leave Cleveland? You could shoot me out of a cannon. Thing is, you don't ask, just tell me like I'm a wood head."

"Was wondering how to run with a kid."

"Meaning?"

"Thinking of running with a kid."

"So, you wanna jilt us?" She put a hand to her belly.

"Not you. Maybe find somebody . . ."

"You talking abandonment, Ray? At least call it that." Looking at him disappointed.

"I know what it is, and you knew who I was, coming in the Lantern that time, two of you looking for kicks. Now you're having a kid, expecting a swing in the yard."

"Said you were taking us to Spain."

"I know what I said." He sat on the bed, feeling the squeeze, not needing this. "How you figure it'll work, Loll? I go back to sticking up places, come home and sit to supper, ask how's your day? Say, 'Hey, what's that smell? Guess it's time to change the kid? Oh, and pass the cream corn.'"

Dolores cupped a hand to her mouth, not sure if she was going to laugh or bawl. Never seen him like this.

"What?"

"That's one thing I'd like to see, you change a kid."

"What, you think I can't?"

"A lot of things you can do, Ray, but, change a kid . . . *uh uhn*. Never going to happen."

"We're having it, you and me." And he patted the bed, wanted her to sit next to him. "Just thinking it through."

"You just told me to pack."

"Yeah, right after."

"Guess the sweet talk's over." She punched a pillow and got on her back, as comfortable as she could get.

"Maybe you get on top. Don't want to squish the kid."

"Our kid."

"Think he can see you slipping it in." She smiled.

"Now, that's a hell of a thought."

"Here comes daddy." And she was laughing, tears rolling down her cheeks.

. . . Toledo, Ohio
August 30, 1934

Doc tossed the shovel down, sinking to his knees and lifting one of the Gladstone bags from the hole, the leather water-stained. "Goddamn!"

Alvin and Fred stood looking at the muck at the base of the hole, the bags sunk in it.

Unbuckling one of the straps, Doc reached in, taking a soaked bundle of cash in his fist, shaking water from it. "Goddamn!"

Snatching another bag, Fred opened it and looked in.

"Get 'em inside." Grabbing the last one, Alvin went up the back stairs.

The three of them going to the front room — the bags dripping — shaking the cash out on the floor, Doc grabbing the wet bundles, the soaked bills smelling musty, most of them stained brown. Alvin pulling off straps and spreading bills across the floor, lining the floor of the front room. Bunching newspaper and piling kindling in the fireplace, Fred got a fire started.

Alvin telling Dolores to fire up the wood stove in the kitchen. Paula going around and pulling the window shades. Didn't matter it was already eighty degrees in the place.

"When's he getting in?" Fred said. Cash McDonald driving from Detroit, coming around the tail end of the lake for a meet-up at the casino, doing it as a favor to Shimmy Patton, the gangster reminding them Cash wanted ten points off the top, on account of the foreign bankers, the expenses and the heat. Not saying it was the only game in town. Alvin guessing Shimmy was taking a point off the top. Saying, "Be here by morning." Giving them the rest of the day to get the bills dried.

Going for the door, Doc said he was going to buy every fan in town.

"Hate the idea, this guy we don't know flying off with our money." Fred bringing it up again when they were alone: Cash McDonald getting on a flight bound for Miami, then getting on a boat to Havana, leaving them waiting and hoping he'd be back, taking a week to do it.

"Like we got a choice."

"Say we send Dutch or somebody along, keep an eye on this guy."

"Says he goes solo, or not at all."

"All the more cause . . ."

"In case somebody's got eyes on the airport — nobody connecting him to us. You think about it, it makes sense."

"Letting him take the money, that makes sense? How about he slips away?"

"You want me to ask for a receipt?"

Fred dropped a bundle, looked at him like he was set to swing.

"Well, if you got a better way, Fred, I'm all ears."

Both knowing they couldn't show their faces anyplace, the surgery not much of a disguise, taking a risk just sending the women to the corner store for a bottle of Ten High and Chesterfields. Ma Barker's gang topping the headlines lately, the wanted dodgers on every police station and post office wall. A reward of two thousand for information leading to the arrest of any one of them.

"Won't need to worry if we don't get it dry." Alvin turned and knelt, kept pulling straps from the bundles, spreading the bills and pressing them down, using the rug like a blotter.

Relaxing his fists, Fred bent down and fanned bills under the table, shoving a chair out of the way. Pulling a strap off another bundle, peeling fifties apart, saying, "We been cursed with crummy shit-luck. How's it get any worse, I'm asking you?"

"Well, how about getting shot?" Alvin thinking about Hoover crowing to the press how his storm troopers were winning the war on crime, the man talking like Teddy and his Roughriders were taking San Juan Hill, getting it down to a mop-up operation, just the Barkers, Floyd and Nelson left, promising the public the last stand was straight ahead, and the lawmen were set to hoist the flag. All his spying and taking names was paying off — making lists of known associates, questioning family and close friends — the feds keeping up their peeping and bugging — Hoover claiming it was a big, beautiful country, home of the brave, with no place for this cancer of crime to go. The man talking in headlines.

Granted a warrant, his agents searched Joseph Moran's hotel rooms, the good doctor long gone missing, the fed agents sweeping away cobwebs and searching the place, getting their hands on the books and patient lists, claiming it was loaded with gang contacts. Alvin knowing it was all lies, having already ferreted through the place for anything that could be used against them.

"Talking like we ought to count our blessings?" Fred said, flapping limp bills.

"Just got to deal with it," Alvin said, surprised he had to talk to Fred like that, the man usually a rock.

Since coming back to town, the five of them had been crammed into Fred's rented cottage, bumping into each other, lining up for the toilet. Alvin and Dolores in the basement room the size of a closet, damp with no window, Alvin bumping his head every time he stepped under the doorway. Fred and Paula in the only bedroom, Doc on the sofa by the front window, sleeping with a pistol under the covers, a Tommy gun on the buffet, a sawed-down gun loaded with buckshot in the umbrella stand. At least the brothers agreed to get Kate another place back in Chicago.

A week of that, and Alvin rented a flat three blocks from the cottage, saying Dolores needed maternity space. Nobody having outside contact with family or friends. The brothers not daring to make a call to Kate, living on her own under a new alias. Fred folding a Tallahassee pamphlet in an envelope, getting Paula to address it, his way of letting Kate know he intended to make good on that Florida trip.

Back to wondering if Dot had appealed to the courts for the divorce, Dolores bringing it up more as her belly mushroomed, calling herself his wife now, not wanting to birth a bastard child. Alvin with no idea why any woman would want to take his name from the get-go. Not good-looking, just a scarred-up outlaw on the dodge, with a shaky future. Maybe the danger was a jolt, women like Dolores liked rubbing up against it, at least for a while.

The bills would get switched, and Alvin would look to the future like he was wearing blinders. He'd take his cut, take her and slip out of the country, to Canada, then to Spain, take one thing at a time, pushing off the feeling that he was running out of time.

. . . *Cleveland, Ohio*
September 6, 1934

The rap on the door had Alvin fumbling for the 9 mm on the nightstand, doing it in the pitch. First thought was one of Shimmy's guys was bringing word: Cash McDonald getting delayed in Miami, waiting on the money coming through Havana.

Dolores shot up in bed, gasping and taking hold of his arm.

Shaking off her grip, he stepped to the door in his boxer shorts, wagging his hand, wanting her to come open it.

Hesitating, then tossing the covers back, she pulled on the housecoat, tying the sash over her belly, muttering something about not getting a chance to get the tangles from her hair.

Standing to the side, he switched off the safety, the Browning High Power raised, nodding to her.

Switching back the lock, Dolores cracked the door, sagging with relief. "Jesus, I nearly had a kitten." Backing up as Fred came in, looking behind him to the street, closing the door and looking at Alvin behind it, smiling and looking at her belly, "That's a boy, not a kitten." Then to Alvin, "Sorry to make you jump."

Setting the pistol on the table, Alvin went to the kitchen and told her, "Get my pants." And he went for a bottle and glasses.

Fred poured as Alvin climbed into his trousers and buttoned up.

"So, what can't wait till morning?" Alvin checked the time, just past two a.m.

Downing the shot, Fred lit a smoke and said, "Paula and Francine got hauled downtown tonight." Splashing more in his glass.

Felt like he'd been slapped awake, Alvin picked up his own glass.

"Doc and Francine got into it, a good one, something about an old boyfriend she bumped into, one thing leading to another, and maybe Doc got a little crazy . . ."

"How you mean bumped into?" Dolores said, reaching for Alvin's glass.

Alvin held it away from her. Kate had warned him, expectant mothers shouldn't drink, or the kids turn out more tippler than toddler. Told her to go warm some milk, then said to Fred, "Francine on the game?"

Fred shrugged, and Alvin turned to Dolores.

"What're you looking at me for?"

"You girls talk," Alvin said.

"Not about that . . . God, I hardly know her," she said.

"Anyway, he slaps her, and she slaps him," Fred said. "Cursing him got her hit again, so she split." Fred sat in a chair, the weight of the night on him. "Paula goes after her, trying to cool her down, you know. And they end up at the Flat Iron, and Francine starts on the double rums, telling Paula and the whole bar how old Doc treats her like shit, saying, 'That's right, Doc Barker, the most wanted son of a bitch in the country,' ready to give up what she knows. Paula telling her to shut up, the bartender warning them to settle down. Next thing Francine's mixing it with this booze-fueled bimbo at the bar, the two of them cat-calling. The painted bimbo tells Francine to shut her mug and sop up her drink, tired of her whining. Francine shakes loose of Paula and knocks the bimbo off her stool, the bartender getting in the middle of the clawing and hair-pulling, tossing all three out, saying he don't want their kind in his place.

"And out they go, Francine and the bimbo picking up where they left off, going Sixto Escobar in the gravel lot, side of the place, Paula trying to break it up, getting between them. Anyway, punches fly, and Paula gets dusted by one of them. Next thing, she's in it, her and Francine tearing up the bimbo till the uniforms show up, their howlers going. All three too crazy to run out of there. Top it off, dumb-ass Francine swings at one of the cops, all three getting cuffed and dragged in, drunk and disorderly and disturbing the peace."

Alvin couldn't believe it, looking to Dolores. "What the fuck?"

"What? Our sex, our fault? God."

He shook his head, put a hand to it like it might explode.

"Oh, I know, get packed." She went to the closet for her bag.

Watching her go, Alvin said, "How about Doc?"

"Halfway to Chicago by now," Fred said.

Nodding, Alvin said he'd make a call to Shimmy, needing to find a phone box, get word to Cash McDonald and stop him from getting on a plane with the money. "Could be feds waiting at arrivals by the time he steps off. And who knows what Francine gave up to the cops. And if she did, the money'd get grabbed."

"I got a Tommy and a sawed-off," Fred said, heading back to his place, telling him to meet at Harry's. Bill Weaver staying at Harry Campbell's, both of them waiting on their cut. When Fred was gone, Alvin downed the rest of his shot, feeling the world pressing down. No time for a plan, they had to leave now.

Dolores set the suitcase by the door, saying, "You drink any more, I'll be doing more than eating for two."

He just looked at her.

"Meaning, I don't drive — and you know it."

Getting the case in the trunk, he drove across the sleeping town, watching his speed, obeying stop signs, parking up the block from Harry Campbell's apartment, neither of them saying much more about it. Parking behind Fred's Chevy, they watched Fred get out, coming to Alvin's car door, glancing up at Harry's window, the light on, saying, "They'll be a minute."

Headlights showed up the block, a car coming the opposite way, switching off its lights as it approached, the driver's window rolling down, both of them with their hands in their pockets, Alvin recognizing Shimmy's man Art Herbebrandt behind the wheel. Letting go of his pistol, he stepped to the driver's window, Harry's man saying, "Left word for Cash, but far as we know, the man's in the air."

"Shit," Alvin said.

"Yeah, shit. Had a guy to catch him at Miami, but, looks like he got on an earlier flight, so who knows. Shimmy's trying to work it out." Art lifted a hand, like what more could he do.

"I'll ring Shimmy later," Alvin said, seeing Harry and Bill coming from the front of the building, a rifle bag over Bill's shoulder, Harry with a Tommy gun case, putting their gear into the back of Fred's car.

"I'll let him know." Art nodded, and he drove off.

Nothing to do but get out of Ohio, leave without the money, and hope Shimmy and his people didn't get greedy or arrested. Alvin and Fred not liking it, but agreeing to meet in Chicago, hoping they could slip in without Nitti and his people knowing.

"How you holding up?" Alvin asked Dolores, getting in the car, turning on the engine, dialing up the heater and looking at her on the passenger side, Fred's taillights disappearing ahead.

"Feel like throwing up," she said, leaning against her door, staring ahead. "Chicago, what's that, five hours?"

"Six on the outside, but we're stopping in Detroit, only two and a half." Alvin put it in gear, an idea coming together.

"You say it, only two and a half, but you don't say we're going on after that," she said, looking tired and annoyed.

"Only if you're up for it."

"Treating me like I'm old wooden-head again."

"I treat you like a princess."

"Yeah, a dumb one."

"Okay, I'm getting my money, our money, and I'm doing it tonight. Not just for me, but for all of us. Then we drive on."

"See, was that so hard?"

Alvin told her he knew a guy, Harry Fleischer, one of the Purples, running the part of town where Cash McDonald lived. Guessing if word got to Cash in Miami, he'd switch his flight and head home, to Detroit. Throwing in, "You feel worse for wear, we'll check in some place en route, let you catch a nap."

She looked at him, gave him that look that said she knew him better than that.

. . . Detroit, Michigan
September 7, 1934

A lvin smiled, the door opening as far as the chain allowed, guessing Cash McDonald had a pistol in the hand hidden from view. "I wake you?"

It took the man a moment before saying, "And you'd be Karpis."

"And you got something belongs to me." Alvin waiting for the chain to be pulled back, looking at the short fat man standing in a dressing gown, paisley with a shawl collar, slippers on his feet, a small-caliber in his cupped hand.

"I think you woke the neighborhood." Cash glanced past him, out to the street, not bothering to ask how he found him.

"Thought I'd save you the trip." Brushing by him, Alvin went in, looking down the hall and into the front room, sofa and armchairs, a wall of books flanking a fireplace, taking his hand off the 9 mm in his pocket.

"I talked to Shimmy, the two of us working it out, how to get it to you." Cash set the small-caliber on the hall table, leading him past the staircase and whoever was sleeping upstairs, going under a great chandelier, padding down a wallpapered hall to the kitchen and switching on another light.

"Gonna tell me I got a nice place?" Cash turned to him, suppressing a yawn.

"Letting my eyes adjust." Alvin glanced around, satisfied they were alone.

"Guy designed it calls it French colonial."

"French, huh? How do they say crime don't pay?"

Cash gave a tight smile.

"So, where is it? Let you get back to bed." Alvin said, leaning on the counter.

"You want coffee?"

"Want my money."

Cash shrugged and told him to take a chair. "Got it upstairs." Waiting like he needed permission.

"It's your place, but so there's no mistake, you come back holding anything but a bag of money . . ."

"It's a valise."

"Everything's French."

Alvin heard him going up, the stairs creaking, Cash coming back with it, setting it on the table and unsnapping the latch, opening it and sliding it forward. "You want to count it, go ahead."

Alvin glanced in at the bundles, thinking it looked light, saying, "Ten points, expenses in."

"Shimmy wants me holding his end."

"That's coming out of the ten," Alvin said.

"News to me. And the Cuban at the bank needed extra greasing when he found out."

"Found out?"

"Being the Bremer money. Something he hadn't been told. Hot even down there."

268

"Figured it's why you took it to Cuba, no?"

"Small world, and the feds got reach." Cash shrugged. "Plus, not like I was holding any cards."

"Money's money." Alvin looked at him, deciding this guy was screwing him over.

"Not how the man saw it. Wasn't going to touch it on account of the feds, so I sweetened it, did what needed doing. You ask me, I ought to be in line for a hat tip."

"What's here?"

"Sixty-six."

Alvin swallowed and stared at him.

"Look, Ray, it's the best I could do, best anybody could do . . ."

Alvin licked his dry lips, stacking bundles on the table, counting it. "Like I said, nice place you got here — French colonial, you said, right? With the family sleeping upstairs."

"Come on, man, where you going?"

"Got a pool out back, a fancy light in the hall, bet it cost a bundle, huh? And a nice place like this, French colonial — takes a bunch of insurance, I bet." Putting the bundles back in the valise, then looking at him, waiting.

"You got no idea the shit going on down there — Havana. This dictator Machado got tossed on his ear, a full-on revolt going on, guns and bombs blasting like the Fourth of July, a different boat-rower grabbing for power every day of the week. Think they like seeing foreigners coming in, especially us *yumas* — think again. Look, I'm dog tired, and you show up, gun in hand — the guy with every fed in the country after him, leading them to my door — middle of the night, and giving me a hard time . . ."

Alvin just looked at him.

"Guess you figure I did it for my health?"

"You did it for the money."

"Look, I owed Shimmy a favor, one like he's doing you." Cash waved his palm around. "It look like I need the money?"

Taking the pistol from his pocket, Alvin held it in his hand.

"Come on, Ray, what's this?" Cash smiled, doing a bad job hiding the unease. "The silent treatment?"

"Doing the arithmetic — taking a hundred Gs, and peeling ten off the top. That leaves ninety. Shimmy's end coming out of it, plus a cut to the greedy Cuban, means there's like eighty-five left. What should be here. Now, I didn't recount it yet, but in a minute I will, and if I come up with sixty-six again, I'm taking two pennies from my pocket, and putting them over your eyes. How's my arithmetic?" Alvin lifted his sleeve, looking at his watch.

"I got kids sleeping."

"Better hurry up then. And Cash, you touch that piece by the door, I'm gonna wake up your fucking neighbors."

Getting up slow, Cash left the room, Alvin moving to the opposite wall, taking the safety off and getting next to the icebox.

Returning a minute later, Cash showed his hands and slapped down a couple of bundles of bills. "There's your arithmetic."

Looking the man over, deciding he wasn't hiding anything in the silk robe, Alvin dropped the new bundles into the valise.

"Not going to count it?"

"I trust you." Looking at Cash as he thought it through, and he sat back at the table, telling Cash to sit too, and he reached back in the valise and tossed one of the bundles on the table.

"What, a tip?" Cash looked confused.

"You know something, Cash? Maybe I came on strong, showing up in the middle of the night. You and me getting off on the wrong foot."

"Pointing a pistol, threatening my kids, wanting to burn down my place. Think nothing of it."

"Yeah, well, the wrong foot. Look, maybe your eyes are bigger 'n your stomach, but you make a point. So, go on and tuck it in your robe."

Cash not making a move, not sure where it was going.

"I'm gonna need a place, and I figure you can help me out — right out."

Cash thought a moment, frowned, then nodded, getting the picture, saying, "You're talking about a Cuban vacation?"

"A long one." Alvin nodded.

"Take some time to set it up." Cash getting that look, like the wheels of commerce were turning.

"Money I got, time I don't."

"So we're clear, you can't stay here."

"I leave here, I don't plan on coming back. So you got till I get to the next spot. Find me some place on a beach, a nice view of the ocean."

Cash McDonald nodded, saying, "Yeah, you're looking a little pale, and I can get you fixed up, get you out of the country, but it'll take a day, maybe two, and for that . . ." Looking at the stack of bills.

Alvin frowned, taking a lighter from his pocket, opening it, and getting the flint sparking.

"I guess we're square." Cash took the bundles and tapped them on the table, tucked them in his robe pocket, and asked, "How's your Spanish?"

. . . Chicago, Illinois
September 7, 1934

K ate held her arms wide, beaming with tears welling at the same time, overjoyed seeing them after the long months.

"Looking good, Kate." Setting the valise down, Alvin hugged her like he'd never let go. No more words passing between them.

Letting him go, she reached the suitcase in Dolores's hand and handed it to Alvin, gave her a hug too, ushering them in, Alvin closing the door behind him.

Fred came down the hall, his hair a mess, barefoot and smiling, a cigarette in the corner of his mouth. "Now if I was a worrying man . . ."

"Took a detour," Alvin said, lifting the valise.

"Thought you got chased the wrong way." Fred grinned.

"Made a stop in Motor City." Handing him the valise.

"You mean Money City." Fred hefted it, grinned and ran a hand through his hair, putting it together, dragging on the cigarette and shaking his head. "You're an old dog, Ray, you know it? Always a step ahead."

"Coffee or you want to pull a cork?" Kate said.

"Coffee's a start," Alvin said, needing sleep more than anything.

Going to the kitchen, Kate offered to scratch up breakfast, careful moving a jigsaw from the table.

Dolores offering to give her a hand.

"I ain't feeble, girl," Kate said, then looking at Alvin. "You keep her on her feet she's gonna get veins like worms, along with a pair of bloated feet. How you gonna like that? You sit on down, darling." Moving the board with the puzzle to the coffee table, looking back at Alvin, saying, "Now, you want pancakes or no?"

"You keep reading my mind, Kate, we won't need to talk at all." Alvin looked at Dolores, told her she better go and sit.

"Could do with a short stack, Ma, long as we got syrup," Fred said. "But you serve these two up first. They look set to drop." Rubbing his hands together, he winked at Dolores, saying, "Fair warning, first round's more blowout patches than flapjacks, till Ma gets the heat right."

"That's not so," Kate said. "But if there's any, Fred gets the blowouts, acting all king of the house."

The sound of her in the kitchen, getting a bowl and whisk, the flour sack from a cupboard, Dolores got the milk and butter from the icebox. Kate mixing batter, explaining to her it's the baking powder that bubbles and fluffs them the way the boys like. Dolores put the pan on the burner, getting a medium heat, tilting it to melt the pad of butter without burning it. Kate thanked her, getting the batter ready, insisting Dolores take a load off while she fixed the coffee. "No joke what happens to a young mama's feet when she's on them all day, get ankles like mine, like big old boloneys. Let that no-good tend to you once in a while. They're just dogs on two legs, all of 'em in need of training."

"I can hear you, Ma," Fred said.

"Well, being up the pole's any girl's best chance to balance the scales," Kate saying it loud enough for them to hear. "You set them right, and you reap it the rest of your days. Take my word, honey."

"So I got to get knocked up anytime I want something my way?" Dolores said.

"Set it right from the get-go. It's something to do with the genes, their wiring's pretty simple. Maybe you noticed, but don't be hard on him, I don't think he can help it." Kate winked at her.

"Guess I got some learning to do," Dolores said.

"And best thing to learn straight off, don't cook worth a dang. I mean it, girl. You burn the toast, dry out the meat, and you'll be going out to supper most nights. And with his kind of dough, let him get you a char-girl, do the cooking and cleaning while you put them legs up."

"You're twisting her poor head around, Ma," Fred called, settling in the armchair by the front window.

Alvin stretched out on the sofa, feeling he could sleep for a day, saying to Fred, "Any word on Paula?"

"Cops piled up the charges, assault and disorderly," Fred said. "Once they found out who they were, they tried to cut a deal, threatening them with aiding and abetting."

"How'd Doc take it?"

"About the way you'd figure." Fred looked at the valise, saying, "Bag looks kinda slim."

"Just shy of seventy-five."

Fred was quiet before saying, "The sharks been circling, taking some bites."

"Yeah, a hungry bunch, but it's done."

"Maybe Doc Moran went missing too soon."

"Cash worked it so we can duck to Havana, hide out long as we want, part of the deal."

"With all the shit going on down there?"

"Won't be no feds hunting us."

"And you trust him?"

"Like I got a choice."

Fred shook his head, saying, "Know Doc won't go. He's heading to Chicago — think he's still got it in for Nitti." Then he grinned. "And me, I promised Ma the Sunshine State. Think I better make good this time. I dash her hopes again, she's gonna crown me with that skillet. Her words."

Alvin yawned, fighting sleep.

"When're you going?"

"After some blowout patches, I could use a nap. We divvy up, and I'm gone. You get George's share to his widow?"

"Sure."

"You want to get in touch, Cash says to leave word with Joe at the El Commodore."

Fred nodded, knowing the hotel in Miami, and Joe the manager, a friend to anybody in the rackets.

"So, this'll be it a while?" Fred said.

"Looks like."

Kate calling them to the table.

. . . *Havana, Cuba*
December 3, 1934

"Cleveland raids turned up nothing," Shimmy read to him on the line, using the phone at Sugar's a block from the casino, the article in the *Plain Dealer*. Explaining the feds mounted the raid on the rented house, found where the money had been stashed. "And came up empty on Ma's South Shore place, still dusting the coffee pot for prints." Working on dead-end leads and coming in after the gang had gone. "Understand a list with phone numbers and addresses got turned up, fallen behind a chest of drawers, numbers for the Lantern, the casino, the station house, the address of Ma's Chicago apartment, leading them to it." Telling him Fred got her out days before agents showed up with the warrant and battering ram.

"You fellas got horseshoes, I'll give you that," Shimmy said. "But, I'm wondering if somebody leaked it."

"Like who?"

"Like maybe Ziegler's widow. The woman not right since old George passed." Shimmy making it sound like taking a double shotgun load to the face was dying of natural causes.

"Nobody knew about the Cleveland place." Alvin not saying more on the phone, guessing the feds had Ziegler's place staked out, Fred getting the man's cut to his widow. Could be he'd been tailed back to Chi-town, not spotting them and leading them to Kate's.

"Oh, another thing, a Dade County patrol turned up a Ford south of Miami."

"Lot of Fords in Miami."

"One registered to Raymond Hadley, bought in Ohio."

The one Joe Adams, the hotel manager, was supposed to have ditched in the Everglades, Alvin paying a hundred bucks to get the serial number filed off and the car torched. Alvin eyed a pale-skinned couple walking through the lobby of the Parkview. The couple speaking English, something that caught his ear down here. Watching them go to the desk, the man setting down their luggage, letting bags off his shoulders, giving their names, and Mendo behind the desk happy to check them in.

Living low-key in the suite on the second floor — Alvin ordering up room service, not going out much, using the lobby phone anytime he needed to call stateside. Dolores making it clear she hated staying in this place with the lagartijas crawling up the walls, cucarachas lurking under the bed, the creatures waiting for dark, and her pregnant. Telling him the Hotel Nacional beat this place hands down, nicer rooms and better food, an Olympic pool, and they fumigated the rooms once in a while — Alvin had taken her there for dinner — Dolores finding out it had daily maid service along with a house doctor, a place knowing how to treat an expectant mother. Loving the decor, explaining to him it was art deco. And if they had to hole up in this so-called Paris of the West Indies, why not in a place with some class?

No arguing about the decor, but the Parkview was owned by Nate Heller, a one-time racketeer pal of Shimmy's, with Chicago ties on the side. Had the place run by Joe Adams, a second cousin to organized crime. Meaning they were safe with Nate's man Mendo on the desk, watching out for them, and that beat art deco any day. Dolores saying Nate Heller had no taste and could be colorblind, and if he had an ounce of class he'd paint the place and have his people take sulfur and wage war on the crawling things in the shadows and cracks.

"I lose you?" Shimmy asked on the line.

"I'm here."

"So, this patrol cop pulls over some hotel gofer, a beaner kid getting by on tips, driving this Ford way past his pay-grade around Miami, talking to the chicas out the window like he's a roller, cruising Ocean Drive. You get the picture. Anyway, the cop runs a check and tosses this culo flaco in a cell, sweated him while he did a trace. Took about a minute, and the kid gives up some guest who left it months back. The feds come in the picture and they question Joe Adams, and he tells them they get lots of guests. When they show him your mugshot, he tells them you look like a million others, and when pressed, he looks again and says yeah, maybe he remembers you, checks his ledger, gives him the name you were using and sends them looking in Cancún."

"Good man."

But the feds would come sniffing around Havana, only a hundred miles from Key West, Alvin knew that, not enough ocean to slow the G-men down for long. Saying, "That the good news?"

"Good news is Doc got hitched."

"To what?"

"Got himself a wife."

"This the same Doc?"

"Way I understand it, she's a sweet girl."

"Francine?"

"Mildred I think, yeah, Mildred. The other one, Francine, she's awaiting trial."

Alvin shook his head — Doc marrying the next woman he met. Trying to picture the older Barker brother married, couldn't imagine him doing it sober, then wondering if Kate baked a cake.

When he hung up, he nodded to Mendo, the night man behind the desk, then took the stairs to the second floor. Dolores curled asleep on the bed, lightly snoring, her breasts full, her belly like a basketball under the sheet — something that scared Alvin, that life in her belly — the French doors open to the balcony, the warm sea breeze puffing in. It wasn't just the Paris of the West Indies. All that Alvin had promised her it would be.

It wasn't just the cucarachas, she'd been uneasy with the unrest down here. Not exactly the rumba music and artists in the street, bohemian cafes and promenades, the flower-lined streets with palms called feather dusters of the gods swaying and leading to white sand beaches, ex-pat hangouts like Sloppy Joe's serving up dishes of pescado and mojo criollo, el ron and mojitos — these exchanges of gunfire like fireworks as soon as the sun set, once right out in the street out front, revolucionarios shooting it out with el militar, the sounds of mortar fire rolling in from the hills, the sharp crack of rifles and low rumble of explosions, shaking the walls. Cuba like a cracked egg in the wake of Batista's coup the year before. Armed soldados looking serious, carrying rifles and patrolling the streets. Alvin comforted her, patting her hand, thinking a fellow could get rich coming down here with a boatload of Tommy guns, selling them to the guerillas for twice what they were worth.

Dolores nattered there was more gunfire here than back home, except the two of them weren't sticking their necks out anymore, talking like she was part of the gang.

Alvin told her she'd be fine as long as she didn't talk politics in the cafes. Just a couple of yumas without the sentido común to head back home. The unrest sending most of the turistas packing, leaving the casinos and nightspots deserted.

On top of the bugs and the shelling, she was unhappy about the nativity of this place, the baby ending up a Cuban, likely to be branded a cubano back home. Alvin promising he'd get the kid the right papers, and that they wouldn't stay for long, steering for Spain, where the kid would be welcome, this place giving them a chance to learn the lingo. Dolores finding out cubano was different from Castilian.

Alvin saying, "Yeah, but it's a good start." And another thing in the affirmative, he had plenty of cash to live in either place, the exchange being in their favor.

Still, the call to Shimmy left him uneasy, meaning he had to look for a new place before long — thinking he could charter a cruise ship at the Golfo de Batabanó, take them to the Caymans or the Dominican. He'd go out the back door and over to Donovan's later, this ex-pat hangout, and ask Jonesy the manager if any yumas in suits had come around showing photos and asking questions. Better to be wary than in some Cuban lock-up, waiting on deportation. Nobody but Shimmy, Cash, Nate and Joe knew they were here, not even the Barkers knew where he was. Alvin getting Cash to lay a false trail for the extra ten grand, making it look like he fled to Cancún, throwing the feds off long enough till he figured how to get to Spain without leaving a trace.

The bureau had been a long step behind, bumbling agents like Purvis and Hanni looking dumb in the papers, but Hoover was a relentless son of a bitch, and he was building something, whipping up the media to help him do it. And Alvin was feeling those steps in between getting shorter. Charlie Floyd had been gunned down by Purvis and his goon squad in an Ohio cornfield last October. And George Nelson bought it in a shootout near Chicago a month after that, Baby Face taking a couple of feds with him to the Pearly Gates.

Letting Dolores sleep, he slipped on the sandals, taking a pack of Luckys and a strapped pack of American bills from the case under the bed, wanting to exchange it at the Royal Bank as soon as it opened. Thinking he'd get some pan tostado and café con leche while he waited.

"Where you going?" Her eyes were sleepy, opening to slits.

"Got the fidgets, going for breakfast, and maybe a walk."

"You were just out."

"I made a call, Mother. Everything's fine, now get some sleep." He leaned across and kissed her forehead, brushing a strand of hair from her cheek.

Her eyes opened more, and she looked at him, sensing something was up.

"I called Shimmy, seeing what's happening. Everything's fine, really, nothing to worry about. Now get some sleep, the baby can use it." He kissed her again, promised to take her to the Hotel Nacional for lunch, holding back the news that Doc got married, knowing it would get her up, and she'd just start up about how they should get hitched too, leading to more talk about why he hadn't got the divorce papers from Dot yet, then she'd be back to questioning his love, her hormones going all Fourth of July lately.

"Get me juice, okay? Grapefruit if they got it."

"Sure."

Leaning against the stone wall outside George's American Bar, he lit a cigarette, feeling the morning sun, letting the eggs of breakfast settle, waiting on the bank to open, drinking the coffee that was too strong, thinking of his next move, watching the same couple he saw in the lobby of the Parkview coming this way hand in hand, the man asking directions in English, a Midwest accent, looking for Prado's.

Putting up his hands like he didn't understand much, flashing his teeth with the cigarette in the corner of his mouth, smiling and saying, "Leider spreche Ich kein Englisch." Alvin pointed them diagonally up the block. Watching the pair cross the street, Alvin not wanting to talk to anybody on the street, especially Americans. Lifting the cup, watching the woman's sway in the falda cubana, remembering when Dolores moved like that. Before her feet looked like they'd been inflated, Alvin remembering what Kate told him about the blue veins. Dolores always getting him to rub them now, complaining they were sore. Alvin sipped the coffee that was too strong and bitter, the reason it needed so much sugar.

The explosion knocked his head into the plastered wall, coffee splashing across his shirt, the cup shattering on the stone walk, felt like somebody clapped both his ears. Staggering to gain his balance, the cigarette falling from his mouth, he was looking at thick smoke billowing from the blown-out storefront that had been Prado's, gray boiling into the clear blue. Rubble and broken glass scattered in the street, the couple down on the cobblestone street out front, the woman propping herself on a bloody elbow, pushing up, looking at her bloodied hands and wobbling to her feet, standing there looking at the hole in the building and the smoke and flames crackling and licking up the stucco front. She staggered but stayed on her feet, trying to make sense of what happened, then looked down at the unmoving man, her mouth open long before the animal cry, the woman dropping to her knees next to him, trying to shake him awake.

People were rushing from the bar and up the street. Turning the other way, Alvin felt the bump rising on back of his head, stepping on a shard from the broken cup, feeling it cut through his sandal, cursing and hobbling back to the hotel. People passing him the other way, curious eyes, nobody asking this bleeding yuma about it, a squad of soldados coming on the double, rifles at port arms, Alvin leaving a bloody track up the front steps of the Parkview. Closing the double doors behind him, he hobbled to the desk.

"Hola, señor Lohman." Mendo was just finishing his shift, taking off the jacket, realizing something was wrong, asking him, "Qué bolá?"

"You not hear that?"

"Perdón?" Mendo looked confused.

"The politics in your streets, man. The explosion? Never mind, look, you got a bandage?" Alvin tugged off the sandal and showed his bleeding foot, blood dripping on the tiled floor.

"From la bomba?"

"Yeah, la bomba, got a shrapnel souvenir."

"Sí." Mendo shook his head, looking at the bloody foot, said he was sad about what was happening to his country.

"Look Mendo, I don't wanna mess up your terrazzo . . ."

Snapping out of it, Mendo said, "Lo siento."

"There some place I can rent up the coast, a cottage, you know, a cabaña, some place with no bombs?"

"Déjame pensar." Mendo went to the office behind the front desk, hung up his jacket, banged around before coming back with an adhesive roll, a bottle with a stopper and scissors.

"You know I got a baby coming, right?" Alvin held onto the counter and lifted the foot up onto the mahogany top, balancing with his hands. Wondering about the American couple in the street, now having doubts the man had been a fed agent.

"Sí, I know." Mendo swabbed on iodine, snipping a length from the roll and pressed it down.

"How'd you like your baby born in this?" Alvin showed the blood on his fingers, his ears still ringing, a rushing sound like his head was stuck in a conch.

"I have cinco." Showing the fingers of his hand, Mendo crossed himself, then reached in a drawer for a folded hand-kerchief, holding it out to him.

Wiping at the drying blood, Alvin offered it back.

"You keep it, señor. Maybe you need it." A glimmer of resentment in the man's eyes.

Reaching in his pocket, Alvin took his roll of cash, the American way of saying "lo siento," and always good persua-sion down here. Peeling off a ten, he noticed the stain on the bill, looking at it, then at the next bill, then another, the stains from when they buried the bags under the back of the Toledo house. Looking dumbfounded — the money Cash McDonald was supposed to launder. Alvin thinking Jesus Christ, looking at more of the bills, taking one and handing it to Mendo.

Giving him a curious look, Mendo said, "Estás bien, señor Lohman? The choque maybe?"

"Yeah, the shock, that's it, but not like you think." Alvin feeling it in his gut, the numbers on the bills he'd been spending were leading the feds right to him, to Fred and Doc too. "So, this place to rent . . ."

"Maybe there is a place, sí, a cabaña, one I know . . ." Mendo, holding the bill in his hand, glancing at it, hesitating long enough for Alvin to catch up.

Alvin slid another ten across the counter, more money likely to leave a trail right to him, but it was all he had.

"Por la costa, in Matanzas, you know Veradero."

"Yeah, the place nice?"

"Safe, sí, with no explosiones."

"Okay, how about you set it up?"

Mendo saying he'd make the arrangements and get him a conductor, meaning driver, the roads up there tricky for americanos.

Favoring the cut foot up the stairs, Alvin played it out, knowing it would be temporary, the feds would come looking for him. They had to leave Cuba, his altered features and missing fingerprints wouldn't be enough. Thinking how to run when every dollar spent left a trail? Before turning from the desk, he said, "That couple, ones booked a room when I was on the phone?"

"Sí."

"They won't be back." Telling him what happened.

Back in the room, he turned the key in the lock behind him, pulling the suitcase from under the bed, opening it on the rug, taking the straps off the stacks of bills, having a closer look. More than a dozen of the stained bills in the first pack. Alvin cursing.

"What's going on? Jesus." Dolores said, propping herself up, her voice groggy. "That noise, what — more shooting?"

"A truck backfiring."

"Thought you went to the bank." Looking at the money on the floor.

"Not open today."

"It's Monday."

"Yeah, they're closed, some holiday. Virgen de Cobre, something like that."

"That's in September."

"What can I tell you?"

"The truth would be nice. A truck backfiring, give me a break." Looking at him like she did every time she caught him lying.

"Don't want you worrying, is all." Taking off the sandal, seeing her looking at his bandaged foot, he told her, "Okay, somebody blew out Prado's. I pulled this couple from the street and must've stepped on something."

She looked at him, then at the bandaged foot. Frowning, saying, "You get my juice?"

He shook his head, smiling, saying, "I got something better than juice."

She looked around, but didn't see anything.

"Got us a place down the coast, Mendo fixing us up with a nice quiet one — this town down in Varadero."

"With no trucks backfiring?"

"Nothing like that. A quiet spot on the beach with lots of palms."

"I guess you're gonna tell me to get packed." Dolores never happy having to pack and go, but, if it got her out of here . . .

"Oh, and guess who got hitched?"

He told her about Doc as he packed up the money and gathered his things, going back down the stairs when he was done, tilting the straw hat low as he approached the desk. Aleja, the assistant manager, sat smoking her usual cigarro, telling him Mendo was off shift now, but he'd be back later, sometime tonight, asked if there was anything she could do. Alvin asked her to send up a couple of cubanos and bottles of Hatuey. Nothing to do but wait in the room.

A restless afternoon, Alvin pacing and ordering up glasses of Cuba libre, looking past the shutters till the heat of the day gave way to evening, Dolores snoring on the bed when he went back down just before midnight. The pain in his foot was gone, the half bottle of Bacardi helping.

"How's the foot, señor Lohman?" Mendo stood behind the desk, nodding for him to follow into the office in back, said the cabaña was all set. But, he had no luck finding a driver, nobody wanting to negotiate the roads on account of ruts and rebels, not at any price. Alvin saying he'd drive himself. Mendo saying he was having trouble finding a carro too. "But, there is an autobús. Take you close to there."

"Okay, get us on it."

Mendo said it left at ten in the morning, pointing him past the church spire, to the square where to catch it, Alvin guessing ten meant eleven. Mendo hesitating.

"What's wrong?"

"Was a man came in."

"When?"

"Was before."

"American?"

"Sí . . ." Going to the ledger, Mendo read a name. "Kingman, a man with the insignia, wanting a room, then asking after americanos, and showing Aleja pictures, looking for somebody."

Alvin realized he stopped breathing.

"Maybe it was you, but not calling you señor Lohman. Thinking it was you and a woman in the explosion."

"He alone?"

"Maybe no."

"And he's staying here?"

"Comes from Miami, so he wants to rest, sí. Aleja put him on cuarto piso." Showing the room number 402 with his fingers. "That's his coche." Nodding to the rental car out front, parked past the stone steps.

Slipping him another of the tainted bills, Alvin thanked him.

"Sorry you are leaving us, señor Lohman."

"But not if this Kingman asks, you understand?" It took another bill for Mendo to nod his understanding.

"Matter of fact, when he figures it out, tell him you heard me say Canada, but hold back a couple of days, okay?" Alvin slid a final bill across the counter.

"Sí." Mendo nodded like he understood, got them a couple of warm bottles of Tropical, Alvin checking out and paying the bill, leaving more evidence for Kingman, not needing Mendo to tell him to take the back way out.

Going up the rear staircase, nearly up the first flight when he heard somebody coming down, Alvin tugged the straw hat lower, not looking up, weaving and humming like he was having trouble handling the local rum, a man passing him on the stairs, saying, "Hey, you an American?"

Shaking his head, Alvin muttered the same line in German, staggered past his room to the far end of the hall before chancing a glance back, making sure the fed Kingman didn't turn and follow him. Going to the room, he snapped his fingers, telling Dolores they had to go now. Not sure if Kingman made him, wishing he had a pistol.

"How about the bus?"

"Can't risk it." Alvin grabbed the suitcase with his clothes and money, slinging her bag over his shoulder, then had a look out into the hall, taking the back staircase, leading her out behind the hotel, going along the side, the alley between the neighboring building, a big rat scurrying under some stacked boards, stopping and sniffing at them, Alvin hissing at it, stomping his good foot to get it to dash off. At the corner of the street, he set the cases down and handed her the bag, waiting in the shadows, a couple of soldados with rifles walking past.

Looking at the fed's rented car out front of the Parkview, a Model A Ford, Alvin told her to wait. Going past the columns by the entrance, seeing the back of the man he'd passed in the open doors, another man next to him at the front desk, both firing questions at Mendo. Guessing Mendo saw him slip past the entrance, Alvin went to the driver's door, finding it locked, the window rolled down a couple of inches. Squeezing his arm in, bending his elbow and reaching the knob, fumbling and pulling it up, hoping the soldados wouldn't come back. Getting in, he left the door hanging open, yanking the ignition wires from under the column, a trick from his misspent youth. Looking into the front of the hotel, he hoped he paid Mendo enough to keep the two feds engaged. Touching the wires, he fired it up, worked the shift and rolled to the mouth of the alley. Getting the bags in back and Dolores in front, he drove them out of there.

"Not exactly a bus." Dolores looked at him.

"Made a new friend, lent me his ride." Alvin looked in the rearview, nobody behind him.

"You made a friend, huh?"

"Why, you think I can't?"

"This friend got a badge?"

"Didn't hang around to ask."

"You're so full of it, Ray, or whoever you are today." She eased back on the seat, happy not to be waiting on a bus, and pleased to be getting out of Havana. "So this place we're going, what'd you call it?"

"The airport."

She looked at him, started to object, then stopped herself, realizing there was no point, understanding they were on the run again. "You mind if I ask where to?"

"Not we, just you. You're catching the red-eye to Miami."

"You forgetting this?" Her hand on her belly.

"Hard to forget with you reminding me. Look, it's a short hop, be there before you know it."

"What about you?"

"I'm catching a steamer to Key West, then a train from there."

"Carsick, seasick, airsick — sure can show a girl a good time."

"They'll be looking for a man and a woman."

"Think they know I'm expecting?"

"They stop you, then you'll know."

"So what, I just sit on my big old butt and wait at some crummy airport?"

"You get a cab to take you to the El Commodore, ask for Joe Adams, he'll take care of you. You just sit tight and wait."

He checked the bills when they stopped, gave her a dozen tens that looked clean and put her on the plane. Then he drove to the Havana docks, found a phone and called Joe Adams in Miami, told him Dolores was on the way, asked him to try and get word to Fred and Doc.

. . . Miami, Florida
December 15, 1934

"I want to have it here." Dolores thinking she was giving birth any minute, the baby kicking inside, the issue of *American Girl* open and face down on her belly. No doctor, no granny midwife and no Kate, but they got out of Cuba. Getting no reaction from him, she said, "Or at the side of the road if that works better for you."

Alvin looked out the top floor window, this room Joe Adams booked at the Anchor, third floor overlooking the main drag. Calling it temporary digs till Joe found them a house to rent, the hotel man trying to make up for the car jockey getting caught joyriding in Alvin's Ford, the one Joe was supposed to torch and dump.

Using the name Elmer Wagner, Alvin kept the FBI guessing. Handed Joe enough of the dirty cash for a Buick, a roadster or Series 90 coupe this time.

"The baby. Hello?"

He turned to her. "You want to name it Ray, fine by me."

"I'm talking about having it here." Wrestling with her patience, something she was having trouble with since coming back stateside. Running a hand over her forehead. "At least the baby'll be American."

"You okay with this heat? Can get a fan if you want."

"No different than Havana, maybe cooler at night. Main thing, nobody's shooting up the place — well, not so far." Rolling her eyes at him.

"Not the kind of heat I meant." Alvin said, liking the way she was going from girl to woman. Still of two minds about fathering a kid and sticking with the same woman the rest of his life, but then again it felt right, and he was thinking it could work.

Dolores propped herself up, looked awkward doing it. When she walked, she leaned back with her legs apart, Alvin thinking she moved like a duck. Wondering if she'd get that tight body back, be a shame if she didn't. Telling her, "Told Joe to see about a doctor."

"Not another quack?" Dolores looked at him, drawing her legs together. "Like the one that did your face."

"That guy's gone."

"I want the kind with a diploma and the little bag, and that thing around his neck. A guy who can spell *obstetrics*."

He didn't answer.

"A place like St. Francis . . ."

"Too risky."

"A place with a medical ward, nurses, the right instruments, no flies or dust motes."

"Instruments?" Alvin playing flute in dumbshow.

"Forceps and anesthesia, genius." She stuck out her tongue at him, but couldn't help smiling.

"Hum some of it, 'Forceps and Anesthesia.'" Alvin liked when they were playing, trading shots.

"And how about 'Twilight Sleep,' you know that one?" she said. "Or how about 'Dilating the Cervix,' you'd love it, comes with a peep show."

"The reason they keep men clear of the birthing room — see something like that, sex life goes out the window."

"Poor baby."

"Need some of that Kama what you call it . . ."

"Sutra."

"What were some of them? That one we did . . . Cowgirl's Helper. Think it's my favorite. And . . ." He mimicked a pose, pumping his hips.

"Good God!" She laughed and tossed a cushion at him.

"Magic Mountain, remember?" Alvin bent his knees and thrust his pelvis.

"You keep it up, you'll be doing the missionary on your own." She crossed her arms over her breasts. "Now, about the name?"

"What name?"

"The baby's name. Ray's the perfect name, don't you think? 'Less you want something different."

"Ought to be good at it, coming up with them, all the names I come up with, but you're right, Ray's perfect."

"You mind if he's not a Karpis?"

"And deny him his rich heritage?" He smiled.

"My daddy's the most wanted man in the country. What's your daddy do?" Her smile didn't hide the sadness behind it.

"Yeah, you're right — wouldn't wish Karpis on him."

"What if it's a girl?"

"You can tell by the shape, you're carrying low." Alvin motioned with his hands.

"Where'd you get that?"

"Second, you're more mellow than moody."

She shook her head, looking at him, checking if he was serious, saying, "It was Kate wasn't it? Spinning those old wives' tales. And you bought it."

"It's how it was for her, all four times. Carried low and felt mellow every time, and out popped four boys."

"But say it's a girl . . ."

"Then you'd carry high, and you'd be in a mood right now."

"Well, I won't go against what Ma says, being four-and-oh. Now, back to the name . . ."

"Ray's good."

"How about we add a little of me — Ray Delaney."

"Ray Delaney?" He twisted his mouth and nodded, taking another glance out the window, saying, "Yeah, Ray Delaney. It's got a ring."

"Well, a ring's more than I got, but then, this whole life's not been how it's supposed to be."

"But not boring?"

"No, nothing about you is that," she said.

"I told Kate about it . . ."

"The name?"

"About the Kama Sutra, all the things you got me doing."

"You did not!" Looking at him shocked, hoping he was kidding, knowing the way he and Kate liked to talk over her jigsaw puzzles. And when they got into the sauce, it was no holds barred.

"The Chairman, Reverse Cowgirl, Stand and Deliver, the whole bit."

"You really did?" Dolores felt her cheeks flushing.

"Knew what I was talking about too, just didn't know all the names."

"Can't even picture her understanding Stand and Deliver." She covered her mouth, shaking her head. "Can you imagine . . ."

"Said she wants to try it."

"Oh, my God. On who?"

"Whoever — just hope he's got a strong ticker."

"Which one you think she'll go for?"

"I'd put her down for Sleigh Ride."

"Oh, my God." Rolling to her side, Dolores shook from laughing, finally putting up a hand like she wanted him to stop, propping herself back on the pillows. "Let's get back to if it's a girl."

"Can't call a girl Raymond."

"Rayleen."

Alvin repeated it and nodded, liking it, then saying, "But it's a boy."

"Not saying it's not, but a girl be so bad?" Looking at him hopeful.

"Boys are easy, coming up."

"Till they're what . . . two? And you have any doubts on that, just go ask Kate, I dare you."

"You two talk about the baby?"

"Talk about all kind of things."

"But not the Kama Sutra."

"No, not that."

He was grinning, remembering the times Kate said she had no girls, looking into space like she wished she had.

"We get settled, I want a dog too, a little one in the yard," she said.

He was quiet again. This girl going domestic, still in her teens.

"And a porch swing, a big one."

"You, me and Little Ray on a swing — that's good, a moving target's harder to hit for Old Hoover and his feds."

"Why we're moving to Spain, where they got no jurisdiction."

"Listen to you, knowing about the law."

"Be nice, see you not looking out the window every two minutes."

"Likely got to grease the civil guard, their idea of local cops over there."

"You'll teach the little dog to bark in Spanish, let the maid know if the guards are coming."

"A maid, huh?"

"Heard what Ma said, plus I'm gonna have my hands full with baby Ray."

"How about when the dog craps in the yard?"

"Everything that breathes does that, Ray."

"But not in my yard."

"So you go clean it up."

"But it's your dog."

"Okay, you clean up little Ray, and I'll go pick up after the dog."

"How about I get you a cute little shovel at Christmas, tie a bow on it. You finish cleaning up Ray, you go in the yard and get some fresh air?"

"Hoping to get my shape back, the one you like. Means I'll need to rest, you doing the nappies, getting up middle of the night, take your cute little shovel in the yard. You want I'll watch out the window, keep an eye out for the civil guard."

"Not a natural thing for a man, cleaning up that kind of mess."

"Sight of a little poop bother you?"

"Not so much, so long as you don't go blabbing about it to Fred and Doc, especially Doc."

"You got my word." Dolores was smiling.

"What's funny now?"

"Thinking about this hard man putting his gun on the floor and changing the baby, going *shh shh*."

"I've seen worse, believe me."

"Nothing to worry about then."

"Maybe I'll surprise you."

"Ray, you never stop doing that."

"Fred and Doc hear about it, they're gonna lose all respect." He was looking past the curtains again, back to wondering what was taking Joe Adams, should have shown up by now with his new car. Alvin Karpis doing his bit for the failed economy, helping Franklin D. with his three Rs: relief, recovery and reform, preventing a repeat of those times of economic hell, buying one car, stealing another, renting houses all over the country.

"Big bank robber changing his kid," she said — the magazine starting to slide off. Dolores catching it, not wanting to lose her place, re-tenting the *American Girl* on her belly.

"Changing the kid — you hold it up by the ankles, put the hose to it, that right?"

She tossed the magazine at him and missed, its pages fluttering like wings. Then she was thoughtful, saying, "At first, I was thinking of Margaret for a name, if it's a girl, I mean. It's got a ring too, don't you think?"

"Except she'd get tagged Maggie or Madge." He shook out a match, puffing a cigarette to life, remembering the smoke had been bothering her lately, holding it away. "Told you it's a boy. And Ray's a name nobody can change."

"Sometimes I think you'd go along 'cause it don't matter so much. I mean, let's say I said Desdemona, or . . . Jezebel . . . or how about Aereola?"

"That even a name, Aereola?" Alvin stubbed out the cigarette and sat next to her, taking her hand, saying, "Margaret, Ray or Rayleen, I'm good with any of it, boy or girl. Because you're having it, my baby. The only thing that matters."

"Oh, my God, Ray . . ." Looking in his eyes, speechless.

"But, I'm telling you, it's a boy."

Then came the tap at the door. Alvin letting go her hand, reaching to the bedside table, for the pistol that wasn't there — something else he asked Joe to get him, along with a pump shotgun. Putting his finger to his lips, he went and put his ear to the door.

A voice saying, "I see you fixed the screen."

It took him a second — goddamn — it was Kate's voice, and he flipped the door bolt, and eased it a crack, looked out, then took off the safety chain, pulling the door back.

"You ought to see your face," Fred said, standing in the hall with his arm around Kate, coming in and clapping him on the arm, delighted to see him. "Worth coming down just to see that look. Hey, Lolli girl, how you doing?"

Alvin's heart slapped against his ribs. "The hell you doing here?" He swept an arm around Fred, the other around Kate, holding them close, saying, "Goddamn . . ."

"Goddamn right," Fred said, clapping him on the back. "Gonna make us stand in the hall . . . holy smokes, Loll, I think you got the bustle the wrong way round." Going to her, watching her get up, and taking in her swollen belly, reaching in for an awkward hug.

"Think I just about dropped it," Dolores said, putting her arms around his neck.

Holding Alvin at arm's length, Kate said, "Boy, you're all skin and bone, and brown as a bean, I could pass you on the street." Turning to Dolores and putting a hand on the baby, delight on her face, putting her arms around her, whispering something in her ear.

Alvin nudged the door with his foot, Joe Adams coming up the stairs with the suitcases, smiling and hip-bumping the door back open, coming in and setting the luggage down, closing the door behind him, saying to Alvin, "You wondering where I been?"

"You do this?" Alvin looked to Joe, couldn't believe it, taking his hand and pumping it, saying, "Lolli, you believe this guy?" Then looked back to Fred. "You knew how to get in touch, you could'a wrote." Remembering Fred couldn't write.

"Expect me to send a postcard from Cleveland?" Fred said. "With you not letting me know where to send it. Me, I figured you were in Havana."

"They even got postcards in Cleveland?" Alvin said.

"Bet they do."

"Like of what?"

And the two of them were grinning, Alvin slinging his arm around Fred again. Kate hugging Dolores, telling her she was glowing, and looking ripe. Her hand still on her belly, saying she could feel it, calling it her little miracle boy. A grandson. Putting an ear down and listening for its heartbeat, saying it was strong, talking to it, saying, "It's Grandma." Then telling the room, "Gonna be another two weeks, three days on the outside — just miss being a Christmas baby."

"Don't want its birthday and Christmas the same day anyhow," Dolores said.

"Dutch Sawyer helped me find them, this place, Lake Weir," Joe said to Alvin. "These two going by the Blackburns."

"I promised Ma Florida, right?" Fred said. "So I made good, got down a couple weeks back, after we beat out some fed raid."

"I heard about that," Alvin said. "That old Barker horse-shoe's holding up fine."

"Sure I didn't leave a trail, but Joe gets hold of Dutch at the Lantern, and between them and a couple of Chicago connections they tracked me. This one drives up and stands in the front yard, calling out, 'Hey, Fred don't shoot.' And when I didn't blast him, he comes in and tells me you're down here, not three hundred miles off. So, next day, I get Ma in the car, and, well, here we are."

Kate told Dolores, "The weather's dandy, and the only thing looking like snow's in the icebox." Sitting next to her on the bed, Ma looked happier than Alvin had ever seen her, telling Dolores, "Ought to come up and have the baby where I can do you some good."

"I'd love that." Dolores said, forgetting about bugs crawling or flying, and doctors in white coats. Turning to Alvin, looking hopeful.

"Well, why not?" Alvin said. "They got you doing puzzles in the sun, Kate? You got color yourself."

"Been bobber fishing for cats," she said. "You come up, I'll take you out in the rowboat, catch you some, and we'll pan-fry a mess, cats or perch, fresh from the lake. Do 'em in butter, alongside some collards, like nothing you ever had."

"Not sure I can handle fish right now," Dolores said, making a face, her hand on her belly.

Joe saying, "You want fish, I got a guy with a charter boat, thirty-footer called the *Lucky Strike*. Ties up at the river. Goes for tarpon, wahoo and bills. Got to see the beasts they pull on board." Showing how long with his hands. "I mean, perch are fine for the pan, no offense, Kate, but these are the ones you put up on the wall, fish with a fight you never forget. Speaking of which . . ." Reaching in his suit pocket, he handed Alvin a Colt .45.

"Can go for billfish with this." Alvin feigned hauling up on a fishing rod, then blasting the imaginary fish, tucking away the pistol.

"And nobody'll tell you different," Joe said, holding up a set of house keys.

"How about it?" Alvin said, taking the keys from Joe and wagging them for all to see, looking at Fred and Kate. "How about you stay for the holidays? We'll do up Christmas, get in some deep-sea fishing. And after New Year's, we'll head to your place . . ." Looking at Dolores, seeing how she felt about it. "I mean if you can hold out that long."

"Oh, I can hold, and I can travel too." Dolores loving the idea.

Kate saying again she'd make it past Christmas.

"Well, we sure didn't drive all this way just to turn around," Fred said. "And Lolli's got Ma, in time for the blessed event."

Kate and Dolores were nodding and smiling.

"Only thing, no way I'm getting on a boat," Dolores said.

"Gonna strap you in that fighting chair, Loll," Alvin said, his arm still around Fred.

Joe went down and checked them out of the room, Fred helping Alvin take the bags and put them in the trunk of the new Buick Special 8, all of them getting in, three in the front, three in the back. Alvin driving, Joe pointing the way to the rented house. The men getting the bags in the door of the new place, having a look around while Kate got Dolores settled in the bedroom in the back, fussing about her in this place with running water, a gas range, light fixtures in every room. Even an electric fan in the bedroom.

After a supper of sandwiches, the men stood drinking Canadian whiskey on the front porch, secluded from the street, the oaks with dripping Spanish moss, the fine-trimmed Bermuda grass, the sound of winter warblers.

"We're back to not spending dirty money," Fred said, talking about the cash that never got laundered, saying he wouldn't mind running into Shimmy Patton and Cash MacDonald sometime, and ask, "What the fuck?" Saying, "Meantime, I'm thinking of a bank down here, maybe an armored car. Someplace they don't know us."

"Think we're too hot, even down here," Alvin said.

"Well then, Alabama or Georgia. You want in, Joe, just say so."

"I do better on the sidelines," Joe said, the man never firing a handgun in his life.

Changing the subject, Alvin said, "How's the newlywed?" Smiling and shaking his head, saying he couldn't believe Doc got hitched.

"Don't hear much these days." Fred frowned. "Took the bride to Mud City — in winter."

"His idea of a honeymoon? Chicago in winter."

"Heard through Dutch, he's been drinking hard enough to thaw the whole place."

"You get word to him, maybe he'll want to come down," Alvin said, in spite of the misgivings, he missed Doc.

"Got himself mixed with another crew, a bunch of hams according to Dutch," Fred said, not happy about it.

"Well, then it's left to us — let's do Christmas," Alvin said, his heart not in pulling another job, maybe it was on account of the baby. "Ma can cook up a big old bird, all the trimmings. And sure good knowing she'll be around when it's Lolli's time. Gonna make you boys uncles." Alvin raised his drink, the three men clinking glasses. Trying to remember what happened to those cigars he lifted from Shimmy.

"Ma'd love it," Fred said. "And you just ducked talking about doing a bank."

"Yeah, guess I did. And there's no point kidding myself — running thin on the cash on hand." It was rob another place, or try and get money from one of the accounts he had under false names. Not sure the feds hadn't found out and were waiting for him to try it.

Fred nodded, leaving it at that, saying, "Florida's a place a guy can get used to." Looking at his empty glass, adding, "Come on, let's get a fill-up — it's Christmas for Christ's sake."

...*Miami, Florida*
January 9, 1935

"She's not an egg, Mr. Wagner. If she's up to it, she can travel. Though with leg cramps, piles and fatigue, I wouldn't recommend a long trip," Doctor Greenshaw told him, finishing his examination, Joe Adams asking the hotel doctor to come and take a look, promising Alvin he was a man of discretion.

Alvin was set to drive to Lake Weir, Kate wanting to be part of it, helping with the birth. Changing plans when Joe got wind that feds were in town, looking into more of the ransom bills turning up after he bought Alvin's Buick. Deciding to travel north in two cars, Fred left a couple of days ago, taking his ma. Kate promising to be ready for Dolores.

Coughing into his fist, Greenshaw got Alvin's attention, saying, "The main thing's to keep her off her feet."

The Braxton Hicks contractions had them fooled soon after Fred and Kate left. Sure it was coming then, Dolores short of breath and suffering fatigue.

"This Braxton thing change how long she's got?" Alvin looked at her, her face pale and covered in sweat, the skin

303

on her belly like a balloon about to pop, worried about the long drive to Lake Weir, seeing her giving birth by the side of the road.

"Her body's way of getting ready for the big moment," Greenshaw said. "And it's hard to say, but she could go full term. No reason she won't." Saying, "I'd like to book her into St. Joseph's, where she'll get the best of care."

"I got no doubt, doc, only thing . . . I guess you got an idea about who we are."

"My concern's with my patient, Mr. Wagner. You want, I can put Jane Doe on the intake form."

Alvin knew the feds would have an eye on every hospital and clinic, likely knew she was expecting, a fake name wouldn't hold up long.

"Or, there's St. Francis, or Christian Hospital, 'though they do treat Blacks."

"How about if she has it here?"

"Here?"

"Well, here or a place by a lake."

A look of surprise, Greenshaw glanced around the house, saying, "Surely, she'll be more comfortable in a maternity ward. Where she'll get the best of care and a first-rate nursery."

"She's been talking about a natural birth, what she calls it. With the food she likes, music and everything familiar."

"I understand that, but, forgoing anesthesia, antisepsis and asepsis . . . How about cesarean, you thought about those outcomes?"

"Hoping to keep it simple, doc."

"Well . . ." Greenshaw ran a hand over his forehead, holding on to the professional demeanor, saying, "I suppose I could arrange for a midwife." Explaining to Alvin what that meant.

When he was gone, Dolores looked at him, saying, "How about warm milk. That be too much to ask?"

Pouring a cup's worth in a pan, he set it on the burner, hearing another car pulling up, wheels crunching on the crushed shells up front. Taking the automatic, he went to the front and looked out, letting out a breath, seeing Joe Adams step from his Caddy. Opening the door, Alvin looked around and stepped onto the porch, tucking the pistol behind his belt. Started to say he was about to have a heart attack, seeing something was wrong.

"Got bad news," Joe came to the steps like he was carrying a weight.

Alvin stepped down and walked him several feet from the open front door.

"They got Doc . . ."

"How you mean?"

"Up in Chicago."

"Didn't ask where . . ." Grabbing his arm, Alvin faced him.

"Staked out the place of one of his crew, a guy named Red Bolton. Agents waited till Doc stepped out, and they were on them. Doc nearly broke away, and might've except for the ice, slipped and fell, and they piled on him."

Alvin kept staring.

"Cuffed him, and he tells them they're lucky he left his gun inside."

"Yeah, that's Doc." Alvin tried to smile.

"Raided a couple other places the gang used. Killed one, and got the rest."

"Fred know?"

"Dutch's trying to get him word."

Alvin nodded, looking at his bare feet.

Joe said, "Don't need to tell you, you gotta clear out — now."

Alvin just stared at him.

"A chance one of Doc's crew takes a deal."

"They don't know shit, and Doc? Hell, he won't talk." Alvin thinking of putting Dolores in the Buick with her piles and cramps, set to give birth.

"Red Bolton. How about him?" Joe said.

"Get me another place then, someplace close," Alvin said, starting to think Dolores wouldn't make the three-hour drive to Lake Weir.

Joe let out a breath, and nodded. "Got a cabin I use, shoot some ducks. But it's no place for her: no water, electricity, nothing like that."

"Draw a map. Let's go."

The morning sun was gaining, Alvin feeling the sweat under his arms, not sure how long Red Bolton would last before clawing at a deal, the man in on the Hamm kidnapping and the payroll robbery, killing the cop in the middle of the street in front of eye witnesses. Not sure what Doc might have let slip to Red when they were on the sauce.

"Ray, the milk!" Dolores called from the house.

And he jumped up the steps and into the door, hearing the hissing on the stove, the smell of burning milk spilling from the pot.

. . . Miami, Florida
January 16, 1935

Same day they moved into the cabin, Harry Campbell came with Joe Adams, faces like grim reapers, neither saying anything, stepping up on the porch.

"As a welcome committee, you two are the shits," Alvin said, looking from man to man, getting a sinking feeling.

Joe held out the *Daily News*, looking away. Harry stood on the porch, something about his shoes causing him interest.

The headline froze him: *Outlaw and Mother Shot to Death — Bloody Wednesday at Lake Weir*. Alvin felt his knees go weak, looking at the photo of Fred and Kate laid out on slabs, the image below of the house, its walls shot up, the windows blown out, handguns, clips, a pair of Tommy guns and drums laid on the steps out front of the ripped-up screened porch, a pair of rifles, a shotgun leaning by the door.

He read the words and wanted to call past the screen door for Dolores to get packed, his throat too dry to do it. The piece told how agents surrounded the house at dawn, calling for Fred to come out and surrender himself, the feds thinking he had the rest of his gang with him, all armed to the teeth.

Agents lying in ambush by his car in the garage, more across the street, and all around the house, cutting off any escape.

Fred's words rang around Alvin's head, how he was never going back inside. Catching images of him fixing a drum on his Thompson, putting Kate in an upstairs room in the back, going to the front and taking them all on, shooting and moving from window to window. The article telling how Ocklawaha residents woke to the rattle of gunfire, stepping from their screen doors, witnessing flashes from every window in the house, the agents sure they had the last of the gang pinned down, misfiring tear-gas canisters, bouncing them off the boards of the house. Agents with rifles and shotguns blasting up the screened porch, tearing holes through plaster walls and boards.

By the time they were done, every window had been shot out, every wall and every stick of furniture on the main floor shot to kindling. One panicked agent shooting at a woman and her daughter as they fled from their house two doors down after a bullet tore through their parlor, the lead thumping into their china cabinet, the agent mistaking her for Ma Barker and a gun moll making a break, his aim as bad as his judgment, taking a potshot at them.

The firing at the house stayed steady for four hours, Fred holding them off, the agents missing with more tear gas, unloading thousands of rounds, none of them daring to rush the doors.

Quick as it all began, a quiet descended. Agent in charge, Earl Connelly, got hold of Willy, the caretaker of the rented house, and in spite of the drifting tear gas, he sent the coughing Willy to force the door and call inside. The fed chancing the Barkers wouldn't shoot a man they knew. Willy opened the door, calling for Fred not to kill him, and two minutes later he showed at the shot-out upstairs window, calling for the agents not to fire on him. Connelly wanting to know if they were in there, fearing they got away.

"Yuh, they's here."

Connelly calling back, "What are they doing?"

"They's crossing over," Willy called.

Ma Barker caught a single round, Fred lying next to her, shot multiple times.

"Time to go," Alvin said, swallowing something bitter, looking from Joe to Harry, calling into the house, telling Dolores they had to get a move on, thinking he should have been there.

"I can get you passports, put you on a plane." Joe saying he was taking his wife and kids on a sudden holiday, not sure where yet.

Alvin held on to the porch rail, knowing the feds would be watching the airports, saying his best bet was to drive out of state. "How about you?" He looked at Harry.

"Can't hang around here." Meaning his suite at the El Commodore. Harry knowing the feds connected him to both kidnappings, linking him to Alvin and the Barkers, coming for him too. Saying, "I know a guy in Atlantic City owes me a favor."

"Then that's the spot," Alvin said, glad Harry was with him.

"How about Dolores?" Joe said.

"She'll have to make it." Alvin taking it one step at a time. His mind fighting thoughts that if it wasn't for her wanting this kid, he would've been at the lake, him and Fred taking on the feds, getting out of there.

"I'll bring Winona, can be a help with the baby," Harry said.

"She done it before?"

"She's a woman." Harry shrugged, saying, "And better than me or you."

Alvin nodded.

"You're gonna need some clothes," Harry said, looking at Alvin's sandals, the print shirt and short pants. "Cold as a miner's belt up there."

The two of them agreeing to meet at the Standard Oil up the highway by Boca, next to the Cabana Club.

Alvin shook Joe's hand, getting the feeling he wouldn't be seeing him again, thanking him for all he'd done. Harry getting in Joe's car, and the two of them driving off.

Throwing belongings in a suitcase, Alvin told Dolores to hustle, grabbing papers, extra cartridges, looking for anything he could leave that would send the feds on a false trail. Putting the .45 under the seat of the new Buick, the Thompson and shotgun, suitcases, and the valise with the remaining ransom money in the trunk. The rushing around kept him from thinking of Kate and Fred. Calling again for Dolores to get a move on.

"Duck waddle's my top gear, you asshole. Hello, I'm pregnant, or you forget?"

"Can't forget when you keep reminding me." Alvin helped her with the last bag, Dolores having to pee one more time, leaving him pacing the porch planks, picking up the paper Harry left, reading a statement from Hoover, the top cop at a Washington press conference, stating how a dozen of his crack agents brought down a grandmother with no criminal record, painting Kate as Mad Ma, Arizona Barker, the mastermind behind the Barker outfit, spitting out four sons dedicated to a life of crime and evil. Taking on the FBI with a Tommy gun. Found dead on the floor by the front window, clutching the weapon in her cold, dead hands. Alvin knew she likely caught a round intended for Fred, left bleeding over one of her jigsaw puzzles in a back room.

Hoover droning on to the press how crime wasn't a result of poverty or economic disparity, but a deterioration of family values as in the Barker case, boasting his war on crime was nearly at an end. There was only one more of the gang to track down, promising his men were closing in on Old Creepy, ready to show him the same kind of mercy.

Alvin wanting that man dead, vowing to kill him personally. Betting old Speedy wouldn't see that coming, the number one most hunted man in the country getting past his agents, coming for payback, the hunted getting the hunter.

Dragging the suitcase, Dolores banged it through the door, seeing him standing there staring at the paper, saying, "Oh, what a gent. And you keep yelling, guess what?"

"Who's yelling?"

"You. Something about wanting some guy dead."

Alvin folded the paper under his arm, wasn't aware he had yelled it out, taking the suitcase from her and cramming it in the trunk, Dolores getting herself in the car, shutting the door and crossing her arms, sitting in silence. Alvin driving north to meet Harry, swiping the back of his hand over his eyes, heading up the Dixie Highway — couldn't be more than seventy miles east of Lake Weir.

"Hope she's not gonna make those fish, what'd she call them, cats?" Dolores looked at him.

"Not where we're going."

"Oh, sweet Jesus, I should've know. What the fuck now, Ray?"

"Atlantic City, you ever been?" Making it sound like they were on vacation, Alvin arranging travel plans, telling her it was a nice place, always wanted to see it.

"Yeah, and how far's that?"

"Hope it's far enough."

"How about Fred and Kate? They meeting us?"

He didn't answer, didn't know how.

"And how about when my water breaks?" She was getting steamed.

And he looked at her, that hangdog look.

"Oh, what? Not a time to be expecting a kid?"

He gave her a look, that feeling of blaming her for not being at the lake with Fred and Kate.

"What's with you?" she said.

An idea coming to him through the pain. "Dropping you at the train station, you're going north with Winona."

"Treating me like the luggage again. Come on, what the hell, Ray?"

"You wanna know, well, I can't be on the dodge, with any minute your water bursting —"

"Breaking, and I'm sorry to be such a —"

"Fred's dead!"

She looked at him like he hit her.

"Kate too."

Her hand went to her open mouth, stifling the moan coming from her core. Tears filling her eyes as she stared at him.

Alvin put a hand on hers, reaching to the floor, showing her the paper.

"You had to tell me like that?" She buried her face in her hands, sobbing.

"There a good way to tell it, I'd sure like to know." If he had a hankie, he would've handed it to her, Alvin saying she'd be safer away from him, on the train. Alvin betting they had somebody with medical training on board. Saying Harry was booking them a couple of rooms. Harry going by John Walcott, the two of them as the Bradfords.

"Why up north?"

"Atlantic City, you kidding? It's the playground for millions. Got a beach, a five-mile boardwalk, hotels built on the surf, seashore rickshaws, clubs like you wouldn't believe, finest restaurants, you name it." Repeating what Harry told him about the place. "You're gonna love it."

"How am I gonna do that?"

"It'll give us time."

"Same shit you sold me about Havana," she said, wiping at her eye with the back of her wrist, adding, "And you know it's winter, right?" Pointing at his shorts and sandals. Taking the paper from his lap, wanting to read it for herself, tears spotting the newsprint.

... *Atlantic City, New Jersey*
January 19, 1935

It stayed on his mind, killing Hoover, the lying, spying son of a bitch.

"I'm never going back inside." Fred seeing himself slipping into the shadows, or going down shooting. Accepting that end. But he never would have put Kate in the line of fire — maybe called to the agents to get her out of there. But they just opened up on the house and killed her too, a woman who did nothing but case a bank one time, something Hoover likely found out from his wiretaps and his spies in the bushes. The man spinning the story any way he wanted, making up Murdering Ma Barker, and getting his press pals to twist the words, using her like that. Alvin feeling the guilt for getting her involved.

Playing it out in his mind, walking into the Bureau of Investigation, their new digs in the Department of Justice Building at 9th and Pennsylvania Avenue. Dressed like a serviceman, an Otis elevator mechanic or Otto Orkin the Rat Man, a tool case or bag with a disassembled Tommy gun, Hoover sending his crack agents out to beat the bushes. Asking directions, he'd walk up to the man's personal secretary, one Helen Wilburforce Gandy — take his .45 from his overalls, shove her into the office ahead of him, jam a chair under the doorknob, get the director blubbering on his knees by the window, make him plead for his life, open the window and call down, let the press gather and get some honest shots, make the son of a bitch confess his lies. He'd take his pistol and put one in the man's ear, the way his men had done to Kate. Shoot him cold, the way Fred did the night marshal, back in that small town in Arkansas. Then he'd assemble the Tommy gun as agents pounded on the door, and he'd take Helen Wilburforce Gandy by her turkey neck, hold her in front as the door splintered, and he'd take down as many of them as he could. His own standoff — and end it there. With any luck the man's sidekick, Clyde Tolson, another miserable pervert, would catch a stray round. And he'd meet Fred at purgatory's gate. Fred holding out a drink, saying, "Now that was one hell of a show, Ray."

Hoover twisted this five-foot-tall child of the Ozarks into a stone killer, the woman who made Alvin feel part of the family, loved him like one of her own, more than his own folks had ever done. Remembering his own folks fighting over whose fault it was that he turned out the way he was back when he was ten. His mother, Ona, blaming it on coming to America, and for not taking a switch to him often enough, or letting him go without supper, making him kneel on rice in the corner. His father, Jonas, grabbing him by the throat, eyes burning into him, telling him he was a bad seed after a local copper nabbed him for selling dirty pictures on a Topeka street corner, dragging young Alvin home and banging on their door, holding him by an ear, asking his folks what they wanted in this country anyway.

The feds had located the Ocklawaha house from a post-card Fred had someone write and mail to Doc, telling about a three-legged gator the locals dubbed Old Joe, inviting Doc to come down with the new wife, wanting to go hunting Old Joe, the two of them using Tommy guns. On that lead, the feds searched across the panhandle, zeroing in on Marion County, asking about this lame gator, and finding their way to the Lake Weir house Fred rented under an alias.

The two rooms Joe Campbell booked for them were down the hall from each other, the Danmor being a quiet four-story hotel, middle of Monopoly City. Alvin guessing he was no more than three hundred and fifty miles from FBI head-quarters, thinking of renting a house on the Jersey Shore: Cape May, Wildwood or Ocean City, betting any of them would be nice after the thaw of an Atlantic winter. From there, he'd lay out his plan to kill Hoover, working out the details, same way he planned the kidnappings.

Otto "Abba Dabba" Berman, accountant to Dutch Schultz, might help him out, a guy he met at the Lantern when Otto blew into town to lie low for a while.

He and Harry spelled each other, driving non-stop through the Carolinas, Virginia and into Maryland, getting caught in a blizzard, having to pull over and wait it out, not making New Jersey until the middle of the night, leaving Alvin's Buick Special 8 in the carpark across Kentucky Avenue, having to wake Mrs. Bradford, the night manager. Signing the register as Bradford and Walcott, their wives arriving on the train hours ahead, already up in the rooms.

Crawling in bed next to the sleeping Mrs. Bradford, Alvin got under the blanket and curled against her, sliding his hand across her belly, feeling for baby Ray's kick.

She stirred, warm from sleeping, smiling and kissing him, saying, "Nice you made it. Now, get that cold mitt off me." Curling against him, the two of them making love and falling asleep like that.

In the morning, he eased his arm from under her head, letting her sleep, getting dressed and tapping on Harry's door, the two of them going for coffee, both wanting to find a men's wear shop, needing heavier clothing for the biting weather. Asking at the front desk, getting directions to Sloteroff's on Arctic. Walking the frozen sidewalk, Alvin wearing two shirts under his thin jacket, twin pairs of socks inside his sandals, trying not to slip and slide on the slick pavement. So cold, he felt he might lose a toe.

Getting into a pair of long johns, Alvin picked a pinstriped wool suit from a rack, a navy overcoat, a beaver-trimmed hat, a long coat with a faux-fur collar for Dolores. Wearing new leather Oxfords and the overcoat, carrying his bags out. Looking to Harry in his new ulster, they turned on the sidewalk, Alvin smiling and saying, "You see 'em?"

"Can't miss them," Harry said, not looking over at the two men across the street, both turned to the gift shop's window, watching them in the glass reflection. "Think it was the sandals."

"You bring a piece?" Alvin said.

"For shopping?"

Walking the block past Babette's Supper Club, they turned into an Irish pub on the north side, a place called Toots, the place dark and empty, smelling of last night's good time. A bartender of middle age, slicked-back hair turning gray and a paunch, glanced up from wiping his glasses, looking at these tourists with their shopping bags. The man saying, "A little early, gents. We're not open yet."

"You got a back way out, pal?"

"Back way's for customers." The bartender eyed them and kept polishing.

"Except you're not open yet." Alvin looked to Harry, saying, "You believe this guy?" Setting the bags down, he reached in his pocket, slapping a five on the bar.

Looking at it, the bartender nodded to the exit, leading into an alley. "Could be rats, big ones on account it's garbage day."

"Cousins of the ones coming in and asking about us." Not having more cash on him, Alvin took off the fur hat and set it on the bar, sliding it across.

"That muskrat?" The bartender eyed it.

"Beaver. Tell the rats we're in the can."

"Both of you, like queers?"

"Bet you get plenty in here, right?" Alvin's eyes went to the front door.

The bartender shrugged and lifted the hat, patting it like a pet, then slid it back, looked at him and said, "What's in the bags?"

"This guy," Alvin said to Harry, frowning, then he laid the one with the suit on the bar. "They don't seize it, it's yours."

"What color?"

"Navy."

"I'm good with navy." Pointing his thumb to the back exit.

Taking the beaver hat, Alvin went around the bar, took a bottle of whiskey, told the guy to lock the can door, and he followed Harry out, moving down the alley leading to a side street, hurrying along another frozen alley, making their way back to the Danmor, ducking in the rear door. Waiting and watching, each taking a pull from the bottle. Then up the back stairs to the top floor, Harry thinking they should wait for night before driving out of there, not wanting the Florida plate spotted. Alvin agreeing, and fumbled for his room key, needing more sleep before running again.

Setting the bottle and the remaining bag with Dolores's coat down, he went peeking through the curtains, looking onto the avenue. His Buick in the carpark across the street, the Thompson and shotgun in the trunk.

"Something wrong?" Dolores stirred in the bed.

"Just being careful."

She glanced at the bag. "You get me something?

"I got you a coat, me a hat. Anything else you need, we get it later."

"How about the truth?"

Alvin ignored that, and kept looking out, Dolores taking the coat from the bed, sitting up, with the pillows propping her up, wrapping it around her, saying he had pretty good taste for a crook, then, "Come to bed. You were flipping all night."

"Yeah, I could use it." The long drive north taking it out of him. Alvin not able to sleep most of the night, knowing they'd be driving out of there again before long. Setting his .45 in the drawer with the Bible, he took another belt from the bottle, set it down and got in next to her, saying, "Missed you on the road."

"You had Harry."

"Harry's not you."

"Keep talking, smoothie." She reached across him, her hand sliding down his leg, knowing how to get him relaxed.

Smiling, he said, "You're something, you know it? Even like this."

"Like this? Like one of them big snakes that swallows stuff whole, looking like I just ate a cow?"

"Kate called it glowing."

"Nice try." She smiled, fighting tears again. Turning her hip enough, she fake-punched his jaw, slipping her free hand around his neck and kissing him. "Not going to forget what you said."

"Promising you a good time?"

"About taking me shopping. Though it'll be a raincheck, I know, I can feel it on account of that look you get."

"That what you're feeling?"

"That's not what I'm feeling, but you know, better if we go shopping when I'm not fat."

"Radiating, I heard Kate call it that."

"Why Ray, I believe you're losing the backward." Running one hand through his hair, the other stroking him, getting him there.

So worn down, he curled against her after and felt himself sinking into the mattress, and he drifted with her arms around him. And he slept a fitful sleep, dreaming of Fred and Kate in that house on the lake.

Sometime later the rap at the door startled him awake, disoriented, the room in late-afternoon light with shadows stretching across the ceiling.

He'd slept through the day. Reaching the .45. Dolores sawing logs, on her side and curled away from him. Getting up in his new long johns, he tugged on his pants and went to the door, thinking maybe it was part of a dream. That, or it was Harry.

Flat against the wall by the door, he listened, then it came again, the light tap on the door.

"What is it?"

It was Mrs. Morley, the manager's wife, saying there were men downstairs asking questions.

Alvin cracked the door, his arm up along the doorframe, the pistol along his leg, keeping it out of view. "What men?"

"They got badges, one of them anyway, and they're asking for you, not by name, but they got a picture looks like you." She glanced at him standing barefoot.

"Well, they got the wrong guy."

"That's what my husband told them, but look, mister, we don't want no trouble."

"You did the right thing, Mrs. Morley," he said, looking out into the hall. "How many of them, you say?"

"The one asking questions and two by the door, acting like it's Buckingham Palace."

Alvin looked to the exit at the end of the hall, the back way out, guessing they'd have a man down there. Closing his door behind him, leaving Dolores sleeping, he moved along the hall, Mrs. Morley trailing him, seeing the pistol in his hand, saying this was a quiet place, and reminding him they had a dress code, looking at him in his bare feet.

"Go tell them we didn't come back, out drinking, or gambling, or whatever you got in this town."

Nodding, she turned and went down the stairs, heading back to the lobby.

Standing to the side of 403, Alvin raised his hand, the door opening before he knocked.

"We got company," Alvin said, stepping in.

"Yeah, I heard," Harry said, already dressed, Winona behind him, packing a bag. And they heard commotion on the stairs, Mrs. Morley protesting about her guests being disturbed.

"You want to get yourself arrested, lady?"

Harry closed and latched the door, the two of them listening on either side of it.

Winona, with the suitcase open on the bed, kept tossing clothes and belongings into it, whispering, "Jesus Christ."

The knock was loud, a voice saying, "Police, open it."

Harry motioned for Winona to speak.

"I'm alone," she called.

"We'll see about it. Now open up."

"I'm not decent."

"Open up!"

"What are you, a sicko?"

"I told you, police. Now, get decent, you got ten seconds."

"How about I put on my undies while you show me your tin." Winona put her hands on her hips, getting into it. "Go on, slide it under. Let's see it."

"You'll see it when you open." The man pounded on the thin door, another voice telling him to shoulder it, Mrs. Morley protesting about the cost.

"You're acting more pervert than police — this town's full of you," Winona said. "Not doing anything till I see some tin."

Mrs. Morley was doing her part in the hall, raising a fuss, complaining they were waking the whole building, complaining her paying guests had rights.

"Put a sock in it, lady." The cop demanded a passkey. "That, or I raise my boot — your choice. And I mean now."

Alvin nodded, and Harry waved for Winona to get down next to the bed. Slapping the suitcase closed, she knelt behind the bed.

The key scraped the lock, and Alvin and Harry aimed above the knob and each put a round through the door, the wood splintering apart.

Hearing a yelp past the ringing in his ears, Alvin ripped back the door, a detective looking shocked, holding his bleeding wrist, a uniformed cop retreating for the stairs, his arm outstretched behind him, and he fired blind over the detective, knocking into a screaming Mrs. Morley, sending her down the stairs ahead of him, the woman practically tumbling.

Flat against the wall, Alvin and Harry traded shots with the detective in the hall, the lawman diving against the wall, then backing down the stairs, him and the cop on the landing getting off a couple more rounds, the bullets splintering the banister, tearing into the wall, another cop down there with a rifle, all of them firing, holes pocking the walls, chunks and dust falling from the ceiling. They were yelling downstairs, more cops coming up the stairs.

More shooting, rounds tearing through the floorboards by the window. Alvin and Harry returned fire, knowing more cops would be on the way.

A scream from down the hall — Dolores — and Alvin was out the door and sprinting past the open staircase, firing down, bullets tearing into the wall, zipping past his ear, a ceiling light shattering, shards of glass and plaster raining in his hair. Running into his room while Harry covered him, keeping the cops from rushing up the stairs.

Dolores lay on the bed crying out, clutching her right thigh. Tearing the bloodied sheet, Alvin wrapped it around her leg, yelling down the hall for Winona.

"Woman coming out," Harry yelled. More shots as Winona ran past the stairs and along the hall, going to Dolores and wrapping the bloodied bedsheet tight around the leg, doing what she could to stop the bleeding, crying for him to get some towels.

"Ray, let's go!" Harry yelled from down the hall.

Getting an armload of towels, he dropped them on the bed, wanting to help.

"I got this," Winona said.

Ripping open the suitcase, he took a spare clip, reloading and telling Winona he was going for the car, leaving everything, saying, "Hang on, baby." Telling Winona to get her down the back stairs.

Winona tried to help Dolores sit up, her hands clamping the bleeding leg.

And he ran back down the hall, drawing the cops' fire. Rifle rounds tearing through the floorboards, slivers of oak sticking up like spears. More cops on the landing firing up — Alvin charged after Harry down the back stairs. Plunging with his suitcase, Harry waving the pistol in his other hand. More rifle fire from above them. At the bottom, they stood to either side of the back door, hearing the cops rushing after them, coming down the stairs. Alvin firing back blindly.

"I'm out." Harry said.

Throwing open the door, Alvin stepped into the cold, the two of them slipping on the icy ground, making their way to the end of the block. Had to get to the car.

"There they are!" a voice shouted, and men were running and shouting at them, a couple more shots fired.

Alvin returned fire, scattering the running officers, maybe a half dozen of them behind them. One of them slipping on the ice and going down. Alvin ran, right behind Harry, trying to keep from falling, making their way around the building, running across the street past a parked patrol car, to the parking garage.

Grabbing the Thompson from the trunk, Alvin passed it to him and got behind the wheel, Harry cranking down his window, the Thompson at the ready, the shotgun on the backseat. Praying the engine to start, Alvin turned the key, the engine straining and cranking, turning over, the two of them roaring out of there, banging into a patrol car parked in the street, steering away from the running cops. Harry leaned out with the Tommy and fired a burst, the cops diving for the frozen ground. Sliding along Kentucky, sideswiping another car, Alvin turned down the alley, tires sliding around the back of the Danmor, looking for the women.

"Come on, come on." Thumping the steering wheel.

More shouting behind them, then a rifle report, the round tearing into the trunk, another shot taking out the side mirror, the car shuddering. No sign of the women.

"Go, go, go!" Harry was yelling, leaning out and blasting behind them.

Alvin looked to the back door, willing her to come out.

Another bullet tore into tail end, the rear glass shattering.

"Go!"

Alvin stomped the pedal and drove, no idea where he was going, no map, no plan, and no Dolores — that sinking feeling that the cops already had her. Crossing into Wilmington before he realized he was barefoot, his feet on the pedals, and he was shaking from the cold coming through the shot-out window.

... Warren, Ohio
April 24, 1935

They fled across Pennsylvania, skirting Cleveland, stealing a Ford and switching cars, Alvin tempted to stop and see Shimmy about money that stayed dirty, but by now the feds had to have eyes on the casino.

Laying low in the back room of a Toledo cathouse, drinking down the anger and emptiness, the worst time of his life. Playing cards with a small-time operator named Clayton, a guy Harry knew from Youngstown wanting in on a score. The cash on hand wouldn't last, Alvin thinking of the suitcase left behind in the room in Atlantic City, along with the love of his life. He couldn't risk accessing the accounts he kept under different aliases, needing to find someone to do it for him.

Not daring to go out, they sent Clayton for dailies from the newsstand out front of the Rexall, the corner of Bancroft and Swayne Field, finding out Dolores gave birth to a son in a Philadelphia hospital — handcuffed to a bed with a guard at the door — named the baby Raymond. "Told you it was a boy." Alvin smiled, talking to nobody. A judge sent his namesake to be raised by his parents, the old couple agreeing to it, not something Alvin would wish on any kid, but nothing he could do about it for now.

Dolores drew a nickel in Milan, Michigan, meaning Raymond would be five before he got to know his mother. His parents' house would be under the watchful eye of the feds, his son used like bait.

Volney Davis had been nabbed in St. Louis, and escaped while being transported to Chi-town. A couple of bounty hunters caught up with Dutch Sawyer in Mississippi and took him easy. And, working on a tip, feds pinched Bill Weaver hiding out in a backwoods place in the Everglades. Dutch and Bill being held over for trial.

His people were disappearing, and his world was shrinking, the FBI gaining muscle since the passing of the Lindbergh Law. St. Paul shutting its doors to the lawless, shaking off the Lowertown image, crooked politicians and corrupt cops under investigation, the Green Lantern shut down and padlocked, the Chicago mob doing its own house-cleaning, sweeping out the last of the independents there.

Needing cash, Alvin and Harry laid plans for a payroll job in Warren. Harry trying to get word to Volney Davis, and Alvin thinking of Freddie Hunter, a blackjack dealer he knew from Shimmy's casino. Davis was in hiding, and Hunter felt it was too hot, Alvin's mug on every front page, wanted dodgers on post office walls, with every lawman in the country hunting him. Clayton backed out too, so they settled on Joe Rich, a two-bit hustler and stick-up man with a needle habit, set to pull the job with just three men.

Soon as it got light that Tuesday morning, Alvin drove the Ford east, Harry riding shotgun, Joe sleeping off a junkie high in back, pulling in sight of the Warren train station, a single-story on South and Main, middle of the main strip.

Drinking coffee and smoking, Alvin listened to Harry talk about Winona, thinking his own thoughts on Dolores and the baby, Joe Rich snoring in back. When the mail truck pulled to the depot, he started the engine, moving the car, not wanting to draw attention from the guards, parking along a side street till the train whistle sounded. Harry roused Joe as the locomotive chugged in, hissing steam.

Moving the car to the original spot, Alvin watched armed couriers loading payroll bags from the train's mail car into the back of the truck. One of them standing guard with a rifle. When the truck rolled out, Alvin followed to the first railway crossing, the gate down for the same freight leaving on schedule.

The only vehicle waiting on the signal light, Harry and Joe got out and walked up either side of the mail truck with pistols drawn and held low, Joe forcing the guard out, taking him behind a row of cedars, tying the man hand and foot. Harry banging his pistol on the driver's window, getting him to slide over, taking the man hostage, waiting till the caboose passed. Harry driving the mail truck, Alvin following in the Ford, to an abandoned garage Harry had scoped out, pulling inside behind the mail truck. Harry looking out, making sure they weren't followed, then shutting the garage doors.

"Easiest one yet," he said, clapping his hands.

Alvin gave a nod, thinking of the Fairbury job, Earl Christman bleeding and dying slow on that backseat, Alvin finding the man's vein and pumping in the morphine.

Joe was gagging the driver. In spite of the junk, Joe was all business, helping Harry dump out the payroll bags, the two of them counting out seventy-two grand, packing it back into Alvin's trunk, leaving the driver on the floor of the shed. Then they drove the two and a half hours back to Toledo, up twenty-four grand a man.

Joe went looking for a fix, and Harry set his sights on some "French" at Mary Testa's. Not wanting the company of his own dark thoughts about Dolores locked in some cell with her breasts leaking milk, their baby put in the hands of his own forbears, Alvin stopped in at the Studio Club, Unholy Toledo being the gambling jewel in the crown of the Midwest.

Going by Ed King, he stood at the craps table, nursing a drink and playing on his renewed luck, up a couple hundred when he bumped into Yonnie Licavoli, an outlaw from his bootlegging days. The two of them finding space at the bar and talking old times, running the hard stuff for the Gennas. Yonnie had stepped up, head of the Sugar House Gang now, branching from bootlegging to keeping union members in line, his outfit acting as leg-breakers, staging the odd accident and keeping order among the ranks. Yonnie saying, "You got to keep with the times, brother."

Out of habit, Alvin kept an eye to the entrance, watching past the bouncer for men in suits looking like they didn't fit in anywhere, the .45 tucked under his jacket.

Yonnie picked up on it, saying, "You got no worries here, Ray." Spelling out anytime somebody looking like the law came in that door, Trev the bouncer signaled Louie the band leader, and the man waved his baton, and the band struck up "(I'll Be Glad When You're Dead) You Rascal You." A signal to everyone in the joint.

"The reason we charge more for drinks." Yonnie smiled a gold tooth.

The two of them drinking Old Hermit and recounting tales of when they made runs from the alky cookers, the Genna brothers supplying the corn sugar, yeast and know-how, Alvin and Yonnie delivering the goods across the Canadian border. They always got along, Alvin hailing from Quebec, and Yonnie doing time in the Great White North on a concealed

329

weapons charge, trying to hook up a shipment on the Windsor side, saying, "Them mounties are mean fuckers, dressed like bellhops, and they got no humor."

"Worse than the feds?" Alvin said.

"Strip 'em down, they're all the same, a bunch of savages. The reason we got a place like this, where you lie low as long as you want." Yonnie's way of looking out for his chums.

"My kind of place." Alvin looked around, already in love with Toledo.

Booze flowed like water, the live jazz, the high rollers, the women in tight outfits and smelling nice. A blonde cigarette girl walked past their table, the hat, the corset and frilly skirt in matching red. Alvin looking her up from the floor, stopping at her tray, asking for a pack of Chesterfields.

"Ought to try my Luckys," she said, the smile saying the rest.

Dropping a fat tip on her tray, Alvin smiled back, opening the pack and watching her move past the tables.

"Thought you were gonna eat that girl alive." Smiling, Yonnie laid a key on the table, a room number stamped on it, saying, "Like I said, I look out for old chums."

Alvin glanced across the room, the cigarette girl taking off the tray, setting it down and walking for the exit without a glance back, the same exit he'd been watching all night. Saying, "Don't think I caught her name."

"It's Yvette." Yonnie flashed the gold tooth again, watching him get up, saying, "I'll catch you later, brother."

. . . *Hot Springs, Arkansas*
August 5, 1935

Harry Campbell stayed juiced, and when they stumbled into each other at the Studio Club, he told Alvin he'd been struck by love, the woman was Alice, Harry thinking he found the new love of his life, picked her up at Mary Testa's. Known her two months since leaving Winona in Atlantic City, awaiting trial, and he was already set on getting hitched, and stepping out of his past life.

Alvin wished him luck, not saying more about it.

"Saved by Cupid's arrow. That or some fed's gonna lie for me with a Tommy gun," Harry said. "Think this way I got a chance." Saying he had enough money stashed to live out his days.

"You got a problem with that?" Looking at Alvin.

"No, I got no problem." Calling him a lucky dog and extending a hand.

The same day, Freddie Hunter came looking him up, done with dealing cards at Shimmy's tables in Ohio. Finding Alvin through a one-time bartender at the Lantern, Freddie walked into Studio Club, told him he had a change of heart. "You plan something else, Ray, I wouldn't mind."

"Why the switch?" Alvin asked, remembering Freddie thought working with him was too hot. Alvin wondering if the feds set this up.

"Had time to think on it." Freddie sat at his table, wanting to talk.

Alvin said he was starting to think he'd run through his luck, happy to spend a few nights with Yvette the cigarette girl. Knowing his money was running low, and with everybody else gone, he told Freddie he'd think about it.

Next day, he asked Freddie to take a drive, the two of them making their way to Hot Springs, another haven where the local law held a hand out, willing to look the other way. Through Yonnie, he rented a cottage on Lake Hamilton, a little place with a wooden runabout tied at the dock. Cruising around the lake, jigging for bass and drinking cold ones and getting sun-baked, Freddie asked about some of the scores he made with the Barkers, the ones he read about, and the kidnapping of the beer barons. Alvin told him some of it, enjoying his time on the water, taking in Bathhouse Row after sunset, the two of them dropping in at the Arlington and Southern Club. Alvin going through money like he had holes in his pockets.

Yonnie fronted him some more, and set him up with a couple of elected officials, Alvin glad-handing with Leo McLaughlin, the mayor handing him the key to Spa City. Weighing Freddie's turn of heart, wanting to throw in with the most wanted guy in the country, Yonnie finding out gambling debts haunted Freddie, down for ten grand in Shimmy Patton's book, a two-point vig added to it every week.

Volney Davis had been arrested again, this time in Chicago. Doc, Dutch Sawyer and Bill Weaver drew life sentences, all of them sent to the Rock. Most of Alvin's former gang members were in prison or in the ground, the real reason he was sizing up Freddie Hunter. Measuring if he could count on him if the chips fell.

Saying to him in the boat, "A while back, you told me I was too hot, and I'm wondering why the change?" Seeing if he'd tell the truth.

"Well, you got me thinking I been sticking my head in the sand, working nine to five, easy money drifting past my eyes, and I'm making chump change, guys like you living it up, no offense."

"Easy money can get you killed."

"Yeah, but who lives forever?" Freddie looked at him, showing he was ready, saying, "Meantime, what've I got to show?"

"Tell me about what you owe."

"Yeah, there's that." Freddie hesitated, like he was embarrassed, not asking how Alvin found out.

"Think you got a bite." Nodding at his bobber twitching in the water, Alvin watched him reel up his line. Then he eased back in the bow, letting the beer, the sun and the gentle lap at the hull rock him. Pictured the two of them walking in a place armed, thinking how Freddie would handle it.

Getting snapshots of the time he and Fred Barker got their release back in '31. Walking that rail line before it really got started, coming up on that dirt-floor shack in Tulsa, the first time he set eyes on Kate, the woman trying to fix her screen door, with nothing to show for her life. He and Fred hit that bank in Fort Scott, walking in with a crew. Same ones that took the Cloud County in Concordia, making off with a quarter million. The Second National in Benoit gave up fifty grand more. And when Doc got turned loose, they walked into the Third National, then the First National in Fairbury. Gang members coming and going, working like freelancers with Dillinger, Floyd and the Touhys. There was the taking of Willian A. Hamm, and the Stockyards payroll, hijacking the bank messengers in Chicago. All of them getting rich. After they took Edward Bremer, the heat cranked up, and they fell under Hoover's spotlight. Sending his mind back to killing Hoover, Alvin still thinking on it.

Nearly dusk when they docked and walked up to the Hatterie, Alvin getting to know the madam, Grace Goldstein, being invited to her table, first time he ever drank champagne. Alvin taken in by her laughing eyes, dark curls and throaty laugh. The woman with a knack for taking life easy, a decade older than Dolores or Yvette the cigarette girl, but she got his attention. And with Dolores doing time, he pined more company, and Grace promised all the company he could handle. Costing him two hundred a week, the madam proved worthy of every nickel, helped him get some of his own funds from a Chicago account he had under the name of Gant, not charging him a cent for taking the risk.

The pair going by Mr. and Mrs. Parker, traveling to Dallas, taking in a performance at the Majestic on Elm, catching *Annapolis Farewell* at the Capitol. Changing their names to Wood when they headed on to Austin, then on to Little Rock and Memphis. Freddie taking up with Connie Morris, a curly blonde working at Grace's pillow house. The couple tagging along, all of them having a good time.

Grace did the legwork and switched Alvin's cottage at Lake Harrison for one at Lake Catherine, helping him hide, Alvin signing the lease as Lyman Burns. Scanning the dailies, a long-time habit, he had Grace bring him the *Trib*, the *Gazette*, the *Times*, the *Daily Eagle*, calling herself his high-ticket papergirl. Alvin catching up on the war on crime, and the rising troubles in Europe, moving to Spain always in back of his mind.

Dining with Mayor Leo and the local movers, along with the Costellos, Morans and Lucianos, when that crowd breezed into town. Grace introducing him to Dutch Akers, chief of detectives, and police chief Joe Wakelin, getting together with their wives for dinner and drinks and the live shows, Alvin picking up tabs and greasing palms, the lawmen promising to tip him off anytime federal men came looking.

Finding out J. Edgar intended to be ringside — along with his shadow, Clyde Tolson — catching the Joe Louis / Max Baer fight at Yankee Stadium in New York, scheduled for September. The perfect time to do the world a favor. Saying it over dinner with Freddie, Dutch, Joe and their women, how he was booking a flight and a ringside seat, planning to walk up in the first round, whisper to Hoover this was for Fred and Kate, and put one in his ear, giving the top fed some payback.

In bed that night, Grace said he was getting too much sun in that boat, asking if Alvin was forgetting Joe and Dutch were cops, telling him it was crazy even thinking about killing Hoover, middle of a crowded arena — but, talking about it in front of cops . . .

"Thinking of giving my ticket away," he said.

She looked at him a while before saying, "As in get somebody else to do it?"

"I wouldn't mind." He smiled, telling her he already sent the ticket to Kid Cann up in New York. "Kid's gonna get one of his guys to sit in the seat, using my alias, see if he gets picked up. A sure way to find out if somebody's talking." In back of his mind, Alvin wasn't sure he could trust Freddie, or any of his new lawmen pals.

"Can't tell if you're nuts or just plain crazy." Either way, she said it was hard to keep up with him.

"What keeps me out of prison."

"So, you got no interest in the fights?"

"Sure I do. Fact, I'm laying a grand on the Bomber. Anybody knowing the game can see the man's gonna plant

Madcap Maxie on his ass, likely in the first round. Just got to stay away from Baer's right."

"It's what I like about you, Mr. Burns. You sure keep me guessing."

"That's what you like?"

"Hard to keep up, but, yeah, it's one of the things." Grace slid closer, sliding her hand down, saying, "I can think of other things."

He was a meal ticket, no pretending it was anything more. Thing was, she kept him from that sinking feeling he had about Dolores and the baby. Swinging his arm around her, the soft skin of her arm, remembering he hadn't paid her for the week, staying most nights in her top-floor suite, what she called her hot-pillow house. Thinking he'd take care of it after.

. . . Youngstown, Ohio
September 6, 1935

"W e're hitting a train." Alvin looked at the faces around the table of Clayton Hall's three-room place. An out-of-work steelworker, Clayton needed the money to keep from losing the house. Harry Campbell had grown tired of what he called being yoked, done with married life in less than a month, writing it off as "the mistake of matrimony." Sam Coker, another prison pal of Doc's from his McAlester days, came looking him up through whatever grapevine was left. Ben Grayson was an old running buddy of Ed Bentz's, a guy long in the tooth, but one who knew his stuff. Milton Lett tossed down his broom and quit sweeping floors at the Harvard Club, an ex-fighter who spent his life in trouble with the law, and had the hunger in his eyes, another guy Alvin got to know working at the casino. Then there was Freddie Hunter, who could now be trusted. It wasn't the gang Alvin once had, not even close, but if they stuck to his plan, and with some luck, they could pull it off.

"A train? You mean, riding in like the Daltons, with horses and six shooters?" Sam Coker grinned, looking at Clayton, then Milton.

"Like the Barker-Karpis Gang," Harry said, not smiling. "With Tommy guns and an airplane."

Alvin told them to have one more drink for nerves, but there'd be no more booze.

"I want to hear about this plane, and rather you didn't talk like my old lady," Sam said, glancing at the others for support, reaching the bottle, splashing some in his glass, half filling it.

Reaching across matter of fact, Alvin swiped it from his hand, the glass smashing against the wall, did it like he was swishing off a bug, saying, "We're flying out 'cause they won't expect it." Pointing a finger at Sam as the bigger man started to rise. "And it's one drink on account you make a mistake, and we all pay."

"Mistake like you're making now," Harry said to Sam, his hand going under the table.

"You make rules like that for Fred and Doc? Not the way I heard it," Sam said, half out of his chair, looking at Alvin, then at Harry.

Putting a hand on Sam's shoulder, Milton kept him from getting out of his chair, clapping him like he was being good-natured.

"You couldn't shine their shoes," Alvin said, waiting for him to sit.

Sam let himself be pushed back down.

"So again, how come an airplane?" Milton said, wanting to get on with it.

"Like I said, on account they won't expect it," Alvin said. Nobody had ever flown from a robbery — not even Dillinger. Telling them he had a pilot lined up, John Zetzer, a guy who used to fly moonshine down from Canada, set to wing them out of state the day after they made the score. In spite of this gang being tossed together, Alvin was sure of it, counting on the payoff. Harry coming to him with this one, getting a tip through a mob connection on the coast. Harry stood and spelled out how the payroll got delivered by train.

"How much dough we talking about?" Ben Grayson asked, leaning back in the chair, sipping his one drink.

"Seven hundred grand," Harry said, waiting for their reactions.

Looking poleaxed, Clayton Hall's lips were moving, the man figuring his share.

"We stick to the plan, every man holding his end, and we're in and out." Alvin looked around the table, couldn't help but think, except for Harry Campbell, either of the Barkers was worth more than this whole bunch.

"Bringing train robbing to modern times," Harry said, nodding at them.

"With all the cop eyes on you," Sam said, looking at Alvin, hate in his eyes, swiping at the whiskey staining his shirt. "Could be they'll be waiting for all of us."

Making a show of glancing at his wristwatch, Alvin said, "Chief of detectives in Hot Springs is notifying the feds how he stumbled on my place at Lake Hamilton." Thinking of Dutch Akers, calling in the feds, pointing to the evidence.

"A cop rat, yeah, that's some pal," Sam said.

"The kind of evidence that gets them looking the wrong way," Alvin looked at him, felt like he was talking to a kid. Kept his eyes on him, wondering if he had to make a show of dealing with this guy.

Sam looked around the table, like he wasn't convinced, but averting his eyes from Alvin.

"You got it figured solid, Ray," Freddie Hunter said, clapping Alvin on the shoulder, wringing his hands like he was set to go. "Sounds like a piece of cake."

"Do like the man says, and we cut up a big pie," Harry said, looking around the table.

... *Garrettsville, Ohio*
November 7, 1935

The back-room sawbones called it gonorrheal arthritis, Sam Coker having to back out. Alvin knowing Coker wasn't past having his drink slapped away, but he was glad the man was gone. Getting John Brock to fill in, another guy who knew Doc from the mechanic shop at the Joplin pen.

John Zetzer couldn't get the plane he wanted, something about engine trouble, Alvin having to lay out a couple grand for a four-seat Stinson, Zetzer taking care of the rest. The smaller plane had him sending Milton Lett and Clayton Hall to a Ford dealer over in Akron, told them to buy a getaway car with a V8, handing them enough cash from the Bremer kidnapping, knowing it would leave a trail, but it couldn't be helped.

The two of them walked in the dealership, raising the salesman's suspicion, suspecting he was about to be robbed. Lett and Hall walked through the sales lot, kicking tires, when the cops showed up. Taken to the station house, they were separated, questioned and later released, the cops handing them their personal belongings, letting them walk with the tainted money.

In spite of the signs, Alvin stuck to plan, believing in one last big score, the one that would have him sipping sangria on the Costa del Sol.

Behind the wheel of the Pontiac Harry stole, Alvin drove the crew within blocks of the depot lot, keeping Freddie Hunter next to him, a sunny morning with a crowd milling on the platform, departure and arrival lines blending together. Giving the outfit time to get in position around the crowd.

The Erie 626 pulled in on time, chugging and whistling, steam rising from its stack. Stepping from the Pontiac, Alvin draped an overcoat over the Tommy gun, two sticks of dynamite in his pocket. Leaving Freddie behind the wheel, telling him to breathe deep and think of what he'd spend it on. Walking past the crowd, the caboose, the Jim Crow car, the passenger cars, Alvin walked around the milling people, making his way to the mail car. Catching sight of Harry and Clayton among the crowd, looking like they were waiting to board. Passing John Brock and giving him a nod.

Climbing the mail car's steps at the same time Ben Grayson stepped up in the cab, the man leveling his pistol on the engineer and fireman, letting them know there was going to be a delay.

Looking through the barred slot at the two postal employees inside the mail car, Alvin tapped on the locked door.

"Official business only, pal," the older man said, peering out.

"It's official."

"Yeah, show me something then?" the old man said.

"I got a winning smile," Alvin said.

"Less you got a badge or something, scram."

"The company give you a decent pension, granddad?"

"You calling me granddad?" The old man squinted through the barred window, looking him up and down, saying, "Beat it, or I'll give you a taste of old man."

"Want me to show you something?"

"I want you to get lost."

Alvin shrugged and tossed an unlit stick of dynamite through the bars.

"Hey! What the hell, you crazy?" The old man stomped a boot like he was trying to put it out.

Alvin waited till he was done, the old man glaring through the bars, out of breath.

"Son of a bitch. I ought to come out, except you'd —"

"Next one'll be lit." Alvin held up the second stick, taking the lighter from his pocket, flicking it and saying, "I'll count five while you decide how crazy." He touched the flame to the wick, letting it catch and fizzle. "One . . ."

"Jesus, the fuck!" The old man threw up his hands, spreading his fingers across the bars, trying to keep Alvin from tossing it in.

"Two . . .

"Three . . ."

The bolt was thrown back, and Alvin shouldered the door, tossing the hollowed stick to the old-timer, its wick fizzling down. The old man stared at it in his hands, tossed it to the other postal man. The wick going out, nothing happening.

Raising the Tommy gun, Alvin forced both men against the wall, getting their hands up.

"Bet it ain't loaded either," the old man said, ready to jump.

"A hell of a bet." Alvin aimed at his chest.

The other man took hold of the old man's arm, saying, "You know who that is? Old Creepy."

In spite of hating the nickname, Alvin grinned as Milton, Clayton and Harry hurried along the platform, past the Jim Crow car, stepping in.

"Show me the payroll." Alvin kept the muzzle on the old man.

"Can't do it."

Alvin gave the line about the company giving the old man a pension, nodding to Harry.

Harry struck the younger man with his pistol, chopping him behind the ear, blood splashing as he dropped to the floor, arms over his head.

"Okay, lay off," the old man said, pointing to the payroll bag for Warren.

"Where's the rest, the bags for Youngstown?" Harry said, grabbing the bag, looking inside, holding the muzzle on the fallen man.

"There's nothing for Youngstown, not this run," the older man said.

Harry kicked the man on the floor, catching mostly arms as the man covered his bleeding head.

"You got it, that's all of it," the old man said. "Leave him be."

"There's supposed to be better'n seven hundred grand." Harry looked around, kneeling down, sticking his pistol against the younger man's jaw. "I'm gonna shoot out his teeth, mess up all this mail."

The younger one groaned and tried to pull away.

"Shoot me too," the old man said. "Either way, that's all that's on board."

"You know any prayers, old man?" Alvin said.

"Know plenty, probably more'n you, and fairy tales too, on account I got grandkids." The old man pointed to a ledger hanging on a nail, easing over to it and tapping a finger at an entry. "You got it wrong, ain't nothing for Youngstown. Go on, see for yourself. Just for Warren."

Checking the ledger entries, Alvin nodded. Harry snatched the Warren bag and stepped off the car, Clayton and Milton following him out.

Alvin reached the unlit dynamite stick from the floor, holding it up and saying, "A lot of folks on the platform in case you feel like yelling."

The old man looked at it like he doubted it was real, but he nodded, going and bending to the younger man curled on the floor.

Shutting the mail car's door, Alvin stepped down and moved across the platform, keeping an eye out for uniforms, the Tommy gun in plain view now. People parting, the conductor holding his arms out to the crowd, not wanting anyone hurt.

The three sacks were tossed in the trunk, and Freddie Hunter drove them out of there.

... *Port Clinton, Ohio*
November 8, 1935

The kind of thing that never happened when the Barkers got hole-and-corner intel through Big Tom Brown or Dutch Sawyer over at the Green Lantern, filtered down from politicians and officials, some through mob contacts. Alvin looking at the count, thirty-four grand on the floor of pilot John Zetzer's garage, a long way from the seven hundred grand Harry Campbell was promised by a bribed clerk at the Erie line. After what he laid out for the plane, the guns and ammo, it left thirty-six hundred a man.

Leaving the others to drink, a couple of them talking about the next heist, he went and flopped on a cot in a back room, pulled a bedroll over his shoulder and slept.

Zetzer drove to the airstrip just past first light, checking his controls, flying to Memphis. Alvin, Harry and Freddie on board. Harry telling Alvin he was going to give married life another shot.

Milton Lett and Clayton Hall driving the hot Pontiac back to Ohio; Ben Grayson heading home to Chicago, giving John Brock a lift, both of them done with the rackets.

The twin-engine swooped off the runway, Alvin looking out as it climbed, the Ohio countryside shrinking beneath them, the patchwork fields, motorways like lines, cars and trucks looking like toys. Playing with the notion of taking Grace to the Gulf before heading back to Hot Springs, get her to withdraw more of his money from one of his accounts. The cash from the train heist wouldn't last, meaning he'd be looking for another score before long. Grace arranging to rent the same house on Lake Harrison, the one the FBI men had tossed, looking for clues, leaving town as empty-handed as he was feeling now, going off and hunting for him someplace else. Alvin counting on the feds not returning to the same house they already searched.

"Next time," Freddie Hunter said over the roar of engine, holding up a thumb, looking like he was hoping there would be a next time.

John Zetzer turned, saying, "Can't believe it, this fucking gauge." Pointing to a dial.

Alvin asking what that meant.

"Means it read full, now it's at half."

"Meaning?"

"Meaning we've got to land," Zetzer shook his head, complaining the ground crew filled the tank, had to be the gauge acting up.

"Something you should'a checked?" Alvin shouting to be heard, not wanting to touch down, suspecting it could be a set-up.

"Same way you planned the train job." John Zetzer looked at him, adjusting his flaps, saying there was an airfield at Culperville, pointing ahead.

Feeling the pistol under his jacket, Alvin let Zetzer talk to him like that five thousand feet in the air, flying at a hundred miles an hour, but if he saw anybody in a suit when they touched down, Zetzer would get it first.

. . . *Beaumont, Texas*
November 17, 1935

"You gonna pout all day, sugar?" Getting tired of his mood, Grace Goldstein spread the Absorbine Jr. on her shoulders, leaning back in her deck chair, soaking up sun at the ranch house her brother owned, Grace telling him it wasn't exactly the King Ranch, but it was a nice place: corals and rolling acres, the stalls and quarter horses, some roaming the pasture lands. Freddie Hunter and Connie Morris going for a walk, hand in hand, across the open ground.

"Look at them lovebirds," she said, smiling and turning to him. "Now, I'm looking at you."

"What?"

"All this pouting."

"Who's pouting? I'm thinking, got the old wheels turning."

"Well, maybe you ought to go have a look at your face, Mr. Wheels."

"Then don't fuckin' look." Alvin tipped the straw boater down, kicked off his shoes, letting them fall, saying, "You know I can't help the face, doll." Not letting her into his thoughts — thinking of Dolores again, figuring how old his namesake was now, wondering if the boy had teeth yet, if he took his first step, saying his first word.

"It ain't the face, Ray darling, it's the bug up your shorts." She'd been talking about the house at Lake Harrison, the owner refusing to rent to her again, telling her no more gangsters, not after the feds used a ram on the front door, stomping in with their warrant and tossing the place like a salad, tearing holes in the walls and slashing mattresses, busting up the furniture. Then leaving it like that, the front door hanging busted, the sash and jamb like jagged teeth. Grace renting him the new place outside of town, saying it was just as good.

"That's no bug, darlin'," Alvin said, making a face, understanding he was getting on her nerves.

"How d'you think it made me feel, that man not liking the color of my money? Talking like I was Jew trash."

"You a Jew?"

"You're a son of a bitch, you know it, Ray." Play-slapping at his arm.

"The first time you felt like that?"

"Jewish or trash?"

"Don't matter to me, I think you're a doll, Mrs. King." He grinned, the two of them traveling west as Mr. and Mrs. Ed King.

"Anyway, this spot I got you, it's sweet, and all you do is pout — and on a fine day like this."

Fanning himself with the boater, he looked at her, saying, "Guess the heat's making me screwy. Think we need a cool one, or you want, how about we go walk hand in hand, look all cute." Alvin glanced at Freddie and Connie off a distance now, walking among the pastured horses.

"Think you're changing the subject." Frowning at him.

"Okay, this house that ain't on the lake, why's it so good?" Not sure why he was annoyed with her.

"South of town on a hill, with shade trees hiding it, flower gardens, a romantic spot, not that you'd notice, and a guy willing to rent it to you." Grace looked at him. "And you can see a badge from a mile off." Then mimicked him, "Why thank you, Mrs. King, that does sound real nice."

"Okay, Mrs. King, you got it done, and I thank you." Alvin raised the boater, gave a mock bow. "Now how about we head in, and you can fix us that drink."

"You just had breakfast."

"Yeah, and now I want to wash it down." Showing a pinched forefinger and thumb, meaning a short one, Alvin needing to stay sharp since finding out postal inspectors were working the mail train robbery, along with the fed agents. Every lawman in the country gunning for the number one most wanted guy left in the country. The inspectors identifying two of the men involved in the train robbery, tracing the car to the dealer in Akron, meaning they likely nabbed Clayton Hall and Milton Lett. These postal inspectors getting more done in two weeks than Hoover's feds carried out in the past six months. Alvin knowing Hall and Lett wouldn't hold up to interrogation. Turning and looking as Freddie and Connie strolled back across the grazing land, Alvin wondered how long Freddie would last, handcuffed to a table, agents staring at him deadpan, firing off questions, threatening him with life in prison, 'less he went for a deal.

And like that, he made up his mind, there was no going back to Hot Springs. He'd send the women back, and if Freddie wanted, he could go too, or he could come along, Alvin thinking of taking a drive along the Gulf Coast, where he hadn't committed any crimes, redneck law enforcement not knowing him. Maybe he'd get on a plane in Miami and fly back to Havana, then make his way to Spain.

. . . New Orleans, Louisiana
April 14, 1936

The *Arkansas Gazette* told the story: Acting on leads coming through the grapevine, federal agents stormed the farmhouse outside Hot Springs, rented to Karpis under an alias, identified him as being behind the Garrettsville train robbery. Surrounding the house, they aimed Tommy guns and rifles, lobbed in tear gas, expecting to pin down the last of the Barker-Karpis gang and having to blast the hell out of the place like they did at Lake Weir, firing thousands of rounds and making a turkey shoot of it.

In a WBNO broadcast, Alvin heard more about the man he vowed to kill. J. Edgar taking backlash in Washington, his methods under question, criticized for maneuvering the press, not sharing information with local law enforcement, his shoot-first bureau not being held in a favorable light.

In a senate hearing room, Hoover had gone seeking to double the bureau's budget, demanding better arms for his men, bringing along his charts and statistics and doing his song-and-dance. The subcommittee chairman, McKellar, the senator from Tennessee, stopped him mid-sales pitch, wanting to know where the director studied criminology. Hoover saying he wrote the book on the subject. McKellar calling it a book of folk tales, demanding to know if the director knew truth from fiction, then asked if he ever personally made an arrest. Turning red-faced, Hoover asked if the senator forgot who brought down Dillinger, Nelson, Kelly, Floyd and the Barkers, and the rest of the filth serving time, all at the hands of his bureau, all under his direct orders. Saying it was funny, a senator talking about the difference between truth and lies. Hoover not backing down to this soft-handed politician.

Tugging at his double chin, McKellar called Hoover a master of stretching the facts, pointing out four G-men had been slain bringing down eight desperados, making it two-to-one odds by his count, and not good enough in his book. The senator swinging the conversation to misappropriated funds, claiming Hoover was a ham-fisted spinner of tales the press was feeding on. McKellar asking, in light of such incompetence, why the subcommittee should approve putting even one more firearm in the hands of such a department, asking again if the director ever personally arrested anybody.

Rising from his seat, Hoover blurted, "I'm the chief, the one who hands down the orders."

"Shall I take that as a no, chief?" The senator leered.

Rising out of his seat, Hoover turned to the assembly, gathered himself with a smile, saying, "Gentlemen, it's so cold this day, I witnessed the good senator here outside having to put his hands in his own pockets for a change." Waiting on laughs that didn't come, Hoover wanted to know how the good senator could keep a straight face in light of his own dirty deals, feigning to take the higher moral ground. Told the assembled to stand back — lightning was about to strike —

then he snatched up his papers, called them a bunch of stiffs and stormed from the hearing room.

Alvin smiled, old Hoover going for humor, not telling the joke right, losing his cool, and not coming away with any more guns.

Not staying in any place more than a night or two, Alvin left a pair of Tommy guns and a suitcase of clothes in the loft above Grace's brother's stalls, taking Freddie Hunter along, winding through the port of Corpus Christi and into Galveston, changing cars and driving the Louisiana coast, going parish by parish, living on gumbo and crawfish, and on into Mississippi, visiting a cathouse in Gulfport, spending a night in a roadside joint outside Biloxi, meeting good-time women at a tourist camp outside of Pensacola, flopping in a shotgun house at a beach town on the panhandle, dining on conch and gator tail.

Getting a good fill of sun and sand, they headed back to New Orleans, Alvin renting an apartment on Charles, Freddie taking a room on Canal. In spite of Alvin's rule on it, Freddie sent for Connie Morris, wanting to get her out of Hot Springs, asking her to quit working Grace's cathouse, finding out she needed syphilis treatment and wanting to take care of her. Freddie promising he wouldn't allow her contact with anyone back in Hot Springs: no letters, no phone calls to Grace Goldstein or her own family back east. Nothing that would have the feds looking. Alvin telling him he ought to start looking out for number one.

Daring one call himself, Alvin called Grace, telling her he couldn't chance her coming along, sure the feds were keeping watch since the raid on the rented Hot Springs house, bugging her pillow house, tapping her phone, could be listening in on this call.

"You losing your trust, Ray honey? Or you find somebody new?"

"You're solid gold, Grace, think you know that. Fact, as far as trust goes, you're more'n gold. Now, I got another favor — need you to make another withdrawal, send me some green."

"You trust me with your savings, or there's no one else?"

"You know it's trust." Alvin hating to do it, but giving the number to one of his accounts back in Chicago. Throwing in he'd like to get her something nice.

"Something, like what?"

"Something measuring up to your heart's desire. Show you the kind of trust I got."

"Well now, Ray, I believe you got me gushing."

"I guess that's good."

"And, speaking of trust, I don't want to spoil the moment, but suppose I need to . . ."

"Need to what?"

"Dutch and the chief came by the house."

"No surprise."

"Not for that."

"This something you want to say on the line?"

"Wanted to split the reward."

"The twelve hundred?"

"Told me all I got to do is point. How you like them apples?"

He grinned, liked that Grace just gave up the crooked cops, the woman knowing her phone line was tapped, and giving fair warning to him at the same time.

Grace asking, "You still on the line, sugar?"

"Guess there's no surprise in it." Telling Grace he was heading to H-town, slipping below the border for a while. Promised to call her from there.

Hanging up, he thought of the dough he stuffed in the pockets of politicians and law dogs like Dutch Aker and

Chief Wakelin over the last five years, more than any twelve-hundred-buck reward. Loyalty that lasted till the last of the hush money was gone. Leaving him wondering how long before Grace Goldstein felt the squeeze, forced to give him up. It wouldn't be right away, and it wasn't on account of treachery or money. She was a tough old bird, but when the feds came pounding on her door, they'd take her in and try to sweat her, threaten to shut her down, charge her with running a place of ill repute, harboring and abetting known criminals, something like that. And she'd laugh at them, every politician and cop in the city in her black book, but she'd stop laughing when they threatened to send up her brother in Texas, charge him with aiding and abetting, raiding his Beaumont ranch and finding the Tommy guns and personal effects Alvin left above the stalls. Maybe she wouldn't drop the dime like Anna Sage did on Dillinger, rumored to be standing next to the Jackrabbit when some fed put a round behind his ear, but Grace would give him up in the end, the reason he didn't give her his address on Charles Street, getting her to withdraw ten grand from his St. Paul account, asking her to send it to Freddie.

As far as Dillinger went, Alvin didn't buy the story the papers told. The Jackrabbit too sharp to get set up and ambushed like that, having just undergone surgery to alter his looks. Rumors floated in the shadows how he set up a lookalike to go to the Biograph with the ladies that night, catching his last picture show, *Manhattan Melodrama* with Clark Gable and Myrna Loy. Anna Sage setting up the dupe for the feds lying in wait. The feds stepping from the shadows and plugging the wrong man. Dillinger smart enough to know the feds would cover up killing the wrong man, throwing the sheet over his face, the coroner whisking the body out of there, agents telling the press they got their man. Alvin betting the old Jackrabbit set it up, catching a ride west, coloring his hair and growing a beard, trying his hand at ranching, maybe farming, buying a spread with some of what he had stashed around the country, taking off and living out his own days.

Still had enough of the payroll money, but Freddie was talking about hitting a bank in the French Quarter. Alvin telling him he'd think on it, being careful since Freddie picked Connie up at the train station. Alvin driving north on his own, up to Iuka, Mississippi, looking into a payroll heist on a construction project he read about, paying for some inside intel from an assistant in Governor Bilbo's office, a gal he met at the Buckhorn in Lafayette. The woman finding out the workmen's wages came in cash, and by mail car — taking Alvin's money, more marked bills from the Bremer kidnapping.

Planning it out for a couple of days, Alvin checked out of the Sunrise Motel, had a late supper of Cajun fried chicken — nothing as good as what Ma Barker cooked up — and he drove the six hours back to New Orleans, arriving ahead of daybreak, catching a couple hours of sleep. Then calling on Freddie since there was nobody else, needing a second man.

. . . New Orleans, Louisiana
May 2, 1936

D ropping the towel-wrapped pistols in the trunk of Freddie's Essex, Alvin told him his red Terraplane was a beacon, Freddie showing off his ill-gotten gains, a lesson Alvin learned back in West Plains. They drove both cars, Alvin leaving his penny-plain Pontiac at Weaver's garage, a couple miles from his place, just opening for business. The Creole mechanic came out wiping his hands on a rag, Alvin telling him the front end was pulling to the right, slipping him an extra five if he got to it sooner than later, passing the queue of waiting cars. Pocketing the money, the mechanic got behind the wheel, rolling it into the dirt-floor garage, putting her on the SkyHi and got to work. Alvin thinking back four years, that time in West Plains, after robbing McCallon's, getting a tire fixed, Bill Weaver telling jokes to the mechanic, Fred Barker shooting Sheriff Roy Kelly.

Freddie Hunter drove them to Lyle's Cajun and Creole, a storefront cafe with an open sign, the two of them ordering Cajun scramble, shrimp and grits, and southern coffee.

"Gonna tell me where you been?" Freddie said. "Called on you twice."

"I answer to you now?" Alvin said, looking at him, catching a look of worry.

"Maybe I'm getting jumpy, but I seen this DeSoto, dark and kinda blue-green, coming off the parkway, slowing outside my place, a guy in a fedora behind the wheel. Got the chills when he looked over," Freddie said. "Sure I seen the same car later, a different guy behind the wheel."

"What'd I tell you?"

Freddie looked at him, not sure what he meant.

"Forget it." Alvin sipped coffee, holding back what he had on his mind: Freddie bringing Connie and her syphilis down here, renting a place on a main drag, driving around in a beacon-red car. Even down here, something like that begged for attention.

"Kept an eye out the window, looking for the car . . ." Freddie said. "Thought I saw a light, top window of the vacant place across the street. Why'd somebody be in there?"

Alvin kept looking at him, Freddie not meeting his eyes, glancing out the window at a couple passing, saying, "Guess my mind's playing tricks."

"Told you not to bring the twist." Alvin kept his voice steady, holding back his anger, this guy crippled by this Jane who'd go with anybody, the poor fool thinking he was in love.

"Connie's good people, you just got her wrong," Freddie said, angry, but turning his gaze. "Could be somebody made you from the papers. The reason everybody stays clear of you."

Alvin knew the truth of it, saying, "You don't want to do it, I'll get somebody else." He shrugged like he believed it, knowing there was nobody else, but one thing was sure, this was the last job with Freddie Hunter.

"Guess I need the dough, same as you," Freddie said. "Then I'm taking Connie west soon as she's good to travel."

"How about we head out now, do the job, and you call her after, tell her to get on a bus, pick her up someplace. Give you a chance, make sure she ain't grown a tail."

"Told you, you got her wrong." Freddie turned to him, balled his fingers around his fork. "You know, I feel sorry for you, Ray. I bet you never trusted nobody in your life."

"Not exactly a trusting life."

"I guess not."

"Can phone her from here," Alvin said. "Tell her you'll pick her up when you get back." Alvin nodded to the pay box on the opposite corner.

"Girl's gone through a lot. Now trusting me and coming down here, and like I said, you got her wrong." Freddie gazed back out the window, letting his grits go cold.

Alvin wasn't wrong, he was sure of that. Connie was clinging to her looks, getting treated on account her garden gate swung open anytime some guy came calling. She'd sell him out in a minute. Wiping up his own grits, saying, "I'm walking to the garage, then catching some sleep. You want to do it, then be ready when I show up."

"When's that?"

"When I show up." Leaving a tip, Alvin got up and walked back to the garage — passing a nitery, its sign inviting him in for some Old Union lager, next door to The Mecca, a swank supper club that Grace liked, its stucco painted pink, touching the bricks of the nitery. Isham's Theater next to that, boasting burlesque entertainment and good times. Sam T's Open Hall promised a dance with the hostess, a crude painting on the glass, a voluptuous woman straddling a dancing chair, her legs apart, breasts set to pop from a cinched corset. A statue of Evangeline looking over from outside the Baptist church on the opposite corner. Nodding to an old Black man on the walk pushing a broom, Alvin loving this town, a place you could eat, drink and screw, then go and confess it all on the sobering morning, all within a short walk.

A feeling telling him to forget the job and drive out of here, head back to Key West, get on a boat to Havana, check into the Park View till he could stow on a steamer to Spain.

He had more money stashed around the Midwest, bank accounts under different aliases, some in business fronts. But getting to any more of it was risky now. What he had left from the train heist, the ten grand Grace sent, and what he figured to make on this payroll job would get him out of the country — last him for a few years.

Pulling this job needed a wheel man, and Freddie was the only guy around. Recalling again what George Nelson said about setting your sights at ten, getting twenty, but always needing more.

Alvin pushed the worry aside, counting on Lady Luck one more time. The Pontiac was running fine, no shimmy from its front end now, Alvin driving to his dive on Canal, nothing like the usual haunts he rented. Always making a habit of lodging first-class, not what lawmen expected from crooks on the dodge, most of them opting for roach-holes like this place. His shoe crunching down on a roach when he walked in, he got undressed, lay on the bed and had a fitful sleep through the daylight sounds around him — voices down the hall, cars and trucks going by the window — at one point dreaming of Dolores on the backyard swing she used to talk about. Saw her pushing a fair-haired boy, full of laugh and life. The boy egging her to push him higher. Alvin standing in front of them with his arms raised, telling the boy to jump, wanting to catch him from the air. Then the dream faded and was gone.

Slept longer than he wanted, waking to the orange glow and heat of late afternoon. Slapping a mosquito against his arm, he hurried into his clothes and drove to Canal and Jefferson Davis, keeping watch for a dark DeSoto, a man in a panama hat behind the wheel. Putting eyes on the vacant place across from Freddie's apartment, no sign of life about the place, the windows dark. Driving past Freddie's Essex, he parked around back, slipped his .45 under his belt and stepped out with his boater tipped low, lighting a smoke and looking up and down the lane. Dragging on it, he smoked it halfway, grinding it under his heel, then he pushed open the back door. Going down the hall and tapping on Freddie's apartment door, he waited while the sap said so long, Connie hanging on his neck, seeing her man off like he was going to war.

"I'll meet you out front." Alvin giving them another minute. Getting to the Pontiac, using a toothpick on the breakfast still between his teeth, slipping his piece under the seat, rolling down his window in the hot afternoon, swinging around the front of the building and letting it idle by the curb. Turning his head, watching for Freddie to come out. The man walking to the Pontiac, a bag in his hand, reaching for the passenger handle.

A car swerved across the Pontiac's front end, its tires screeching, Alvin catching the dark DeSoto as he reached under his seat. Two men jumped from the front, pistols drawn, two more stepping from the back, rifles coming up. "I wouldn't do it!" came the shout.

Alvin about to throw it in reverse, a second car pulling up behind, blocking him in. More men jumping out. His hand was halfway under the seat, his fingers touching the grip. Pounding feet as men rushed from the vacant building across the street, more rifles and shotguns aimed.

"Hands on the wheel!" the driver of the first car yelled, stepping past Alvin's hood, aiming through the windshield. *"Now!"*

Nothing to do but edge his hands up. Ten men, by his guess, leaving no chance to shoot and ram his way out.

"Think you parked me in," he said to the fed coming to the window, wrapping his fingers around the steering wheel, keeping them in plain sight.

More faces stared in, all of them aiming and looking serious.

The one next to the window turned and called across the street, "Okay, we got him, chief."

Past the agent, Alvin saw a man rising from behind a parked car diagonally across the street, brushing at the knees of his suit pants, straightening his tie as he crossed the parkway. Another man gripped a camera, coming with him.

And Alvin was staring at the director himself, saying, "You're Hoover."

"And you're under arrest, you son of a bitch. Go on and flinch, and see what happens." Hoover was halfway across the street, waiting on the boulevard for a passing car, turning to the newsman, saying, "This fish has been hoo—"

The newsman popped his flashbulb, the director blinking as he stepped across the lane, his men holding positions, leveling weapons at Karpis.

Alvin saying, "Looks like you got those guns you were after." Started to dip his shoulder, thinking he could reach the pistol, bring it up and get off the shot, kill Hoover, as his men opened fire from all directions.

Hoover recited, counting off his fingers, "You're wanted for the murder of Sheriff Kelly, the kidnapping of Edward Bremer, that of William Hamm, and plenty —" Still blinking, Hoover yelled, pointing over the car's roof, "Hey . . . get that one!"

Freddie Hunter had turned from the car, all the attention on Alvin, and tried to slip back into the building.

Alvin kept his hands on the wheel, weighing his chances of killing the man, Hoover ordering him to step out. Blinded by another popping flashbulb, the director blinked like he had an affliction, rhyming additional charges against Karpis, the agent in charge opening the car door, a second man sticking his arm in and rousting Alvin from behind the wheel, turning him against the car and patting him down, several of them barking orders.

The director asked for handcuffs. Some of the men patting their pockets, nobody carrying a set.

"Didn't think we'd need them, chief," the one in charge said, holding his muzzle against Alvin's spine, saying he figured it would go a different way, whispering to Alvin he wished it had.

One of the rookies holstered his pistol and tugged off his necktie, offering it to Hoover, saying, "Go on, chief, you do the honors." Making a crack about not using a Windsor knot.

Another flashbulb popped.

Back of his mind, Alvin always expected to end up like Fred Barker, and it didn't matter, it would be over in a second. Now, he was letting them take him. Too late to kill the chief, but he'd done what most of them didn't do, got himself arrested instead of being gunned down.

Thinking if Dillinger could break out of Crown Point, then so could he, guessing he'd end up at the Rock, the same place they had Doc, George Kelly, Capone and other guys he knew — be like a reunion, like that New Year's he missed out on at the Lantern. And with all those guys, how hard would it be to plan an escape?

... *Torremolinos, Spain*
August 14, 1979

"So, that was it, the end of the war on crime," the man called Graham said, looking around for the waiter, saying the service in Spain was awful, worse than Italy, nothing like what they had back home.

"You're sounding American again," his wife, Edna, said.

The old man smiled, his teeth gone yellow, his hair thin and combed back.

Graham shrugged, looking at him. "So, you were saying . . ."

"Worst part of the bust, it gave Hoover what he wanted most, ultimate power. Nobody left to hunt down, letting him lap up attention."

"Heard somewhere he was queer."

"Him and Tolson . . . maybe." The old man grinned, having heard those rumors. "One thing's sure, nabbing me gave him what he wanted most, letting him spin his way out of the deep end. It got him the funds he was after, not just for guns and his lab, but it let him go on paying the media, covering his lies and making his shady deals. No senator stopping him after that."

"Shady deals?"

"Take the Hamm kidnapping; the feds tried hanging it on the Touhys, the investigation botched at every step. Had his feds perjure testimony against Adam Richetti for his supposed part in busting Pretty Boy loose in Kansas City, what they called the Bloody Massacre. Spun his lies about Kate Barker too . . ." He would have gone on, but he was getting tired of telling the same stories over and over, drinks or no drinks.

"Not like Shelley Winters in *Bloody Mama*?"

"Nothing like that." The old man picked up his glass, looked at it, then set it down, saying, "She was a mother who loved her boys, no matter what they did."

"So, what Hoover said —"

"Every word a lie. That son of a bitch painted himself as some fearless lawman taming the Wild West, the press helping him do it, had the public swallowing it. If it's printed, it's got to be true, right?" The old man shook his head, took it down a notch and smiled at the woman. "Had me pose next to him for the camera that time in New Orleans, smiling through his teeth while he denied me a lawyer. You want more truth, it was me that gave him his fame. You think the man ever said thank you? Left me handcuffed to a radiator for five days. Sorry, I guess I'm a sour old man . . . Edna, right?"

"Yes, and oh, you don't sound that way to me . . ." she said, putting a hand on his, patting it, slow taking her hand back again. "I think you're one of the most interesting men I've met." Smiling at him.

Liked that she did it right in front of her hubby, Graham looking around again for the waiter. And the old man touched on the decades spent in prison, thirty-six men trying to escape the Rock, including the attempt that got Doc killed. Frank Morris and the Anglin brothers the only ones who might have made it, never seen or heard from again. The warden sure they drowned in the bay, but the marshals' service kept looking into it.

Then he told them how he tried to teach Charles Manson to play the six-string, an old acoustic one of the inmates had, telling them Charlie wasn't any good at it, about as bad as Dolores trying to play "Chopsticks" on the piano. Little Charlie saying he was going to be bigger than the Beatles.

He skipped talking about rotting in that cell for twenty-six years with his memories and his thoughts of getting out, often figuring he made the worse choice, giving up instead of lifting the pistol from under his seat that first day of May in New Orleans, taking Hoover with him. It would've been a quick way out. But, in that second of time, he chose to stick around long enough to meet the boy Dolores named after him. And he wanted to see her again too, with thoughts of picking up where they left off. Then he got a letter from her and found out she made a new life for herself long before his release. So he left her alone to her new life after he got out, figured it was the least he could do for her, and he never tried making contact with her, or with his son, again.

Edna was patting his hand some more, tears welling in her eyes.

Funny, Fred Barker talked about it, how he was never going back inside. Fred keeping to his word. Alvin and Doc ending up on the Rock, till Doc tried to escape in '39, gunned down by guards looking for any excuse. And Alvin stayed on the Rock, living with hopes of breaking out some day. Every year more rumors floated in that the Justice Department was talking about closing down Alcatraz, and he'd get his chance when they transferred him to another maximum place. But he just sat in that hell all that time, except for a six-month transfer to Leavenworth, finally meeting his son, Raymond, for the only time in one of the visiting rooms. The two of them talking, the young man curious about who his father was, and Alvin trying to see himself in the young man's eyes.

Released into times he no longer fit into, just an old man walking in sackcloth and ashes, deported from the U.S. to Canada before he could scratch up enough of the money he had stashed away all those years before, most of it lost to time. Finally making his way to Spain.

"Well, you got some regrets, I guess who doesn't?" Graham said. "Having to leave all that money. But, man, what a ride, am I right?"

The old man nodded, saying, "A bit late for regrets and making amends, and if I dwell on it, well, where's that get me?" The old man pushed away the three-hanky thoughts, wrapping that hard shell around him.

"What say to another round?" Graham said, snapping fingers at the passing waiter.

"No thanks," the old man said, giving a wave of his hand.

Excusing himself, Graham said he had to visit the little boys' room, whispered to Edna about having a siesta before a late dinner.

Looking into his near-empty glass, not able to drink like he did back in those days, the old man rose after Graham left, saying it was time to go to his flat.

"You need a siesta too?" she said, smiling, looking up at him.

"Gonna put on a fire." Telling Edna he was up in room 12 around the back, that he was feeling the chill of evening coming on.

Acknowledgments

It's a blessing to get up every morning and do what I love. In this, I consider how fortunate I am to have the unwavering support of long-time publisher Jack David. From early on, he encouraged me to write what lights me up, and I've followed that advice ever since. Thanks to Jack, his words of wisdom have served me well.

Every one of the dedicated team at ECW Press is great to work with. I appreciate the care and attention that they bring, making every step of the process seem effortless because they do it all so well. Many thanks to each of them.

To my brilliant editor Emily Schultz, a special thank you. Firstly for getting my work, and secondly, for her keen insight and thoughtful notes. Emily has a generous spirit and is always cheering me on. I am grateful to have worked with her again on this one.

They say it's all in the details, so thank goodness for the eagle eye of copyeditor Peter Norman, who checks and double-checks every one of those details. Exceptional, indeed.

I think the cover is a winner — a great illustration and creative use of color, light and shadow — capturing the mood of the story quite well. Thank you to the talented Ian Sullivan.

And a big thank you to my loving family, Andrea and Xander, who make my world a little brighter each day.